# ANGEL FALLS

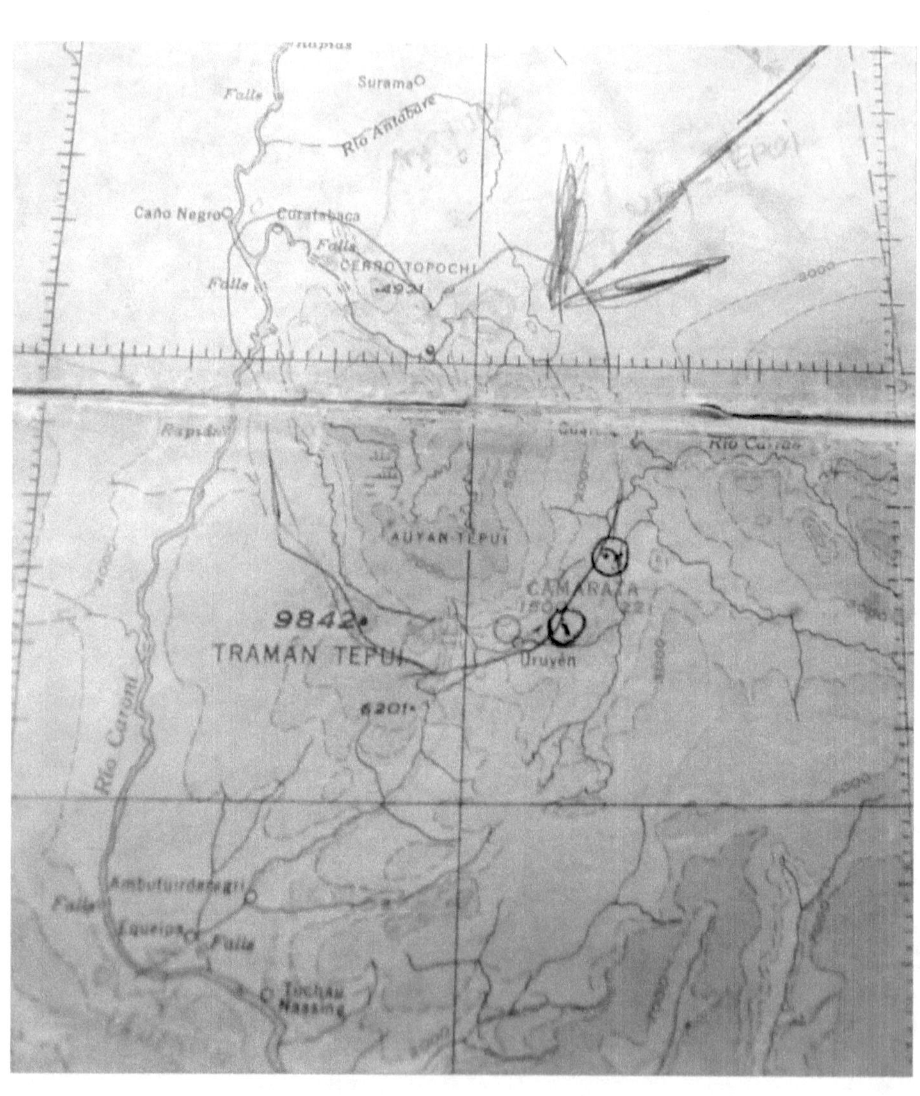

Suramo O
Falls
Río Antabare
Caño Negro O
Curatabaca
Falls
CERRO TOPOCHI
Falls
491
Rapids
Guar
Río Carrao
AUYAN TEPUI
CAMARATA
9842
1500
281
TRAMAN TEPUI
Uruyen
6201
Río Caroní
Ambutuidasegri
Falls
Iqueica
Falls
Tochau
O Nassing

# Angel Falls

A Novel

by Kathryn Casey

Ruth Robertson Marietta was born in Illinois in 1905 and died in Texas in 1998. The accounts of her life in this book are fictional but inspired by her writings, photographs, and mementos. Of the nonfictional characters, two names have been changed: John Hightower and Jim O'Brien. For clarity, Ruth's husband's name was changed from Charles to Chuck.

Although sections of the book are based on the life of a real woman, Angel Falls is a work of fiction. All characters—except for Ruth Robertson, those associated with the Angel Falls expedition, the folks at *National Geographic*, Art Neumann, Clayton Knight, Vihjalmur Stefansson, and Eric Eareckson—are products of the author's imagination and are not to be construed as real. Any resemblance of the fictional characters to anyone living or dead is purely coincidental. While some scenes throughout are based on historical records, all incidents and dialogue in the book—including those involving real people—are to be considered fictional.

NOTE: The prologue photo of the San Bernard River was taken by the author. All the other photographs scattered throughout the book are from the Ruth Robertson Collection and are printed courtesy of the Harry Ransom Center at the University of Texas at Austin. Author's photo courtesy of Lisa Billeiter.

Cover image: Shutterstock.com    Cover Design: Andrea Purdie



ISBN: 979-8-9882477-2-2

*For my Aunt Elaine, who has set an exceptional example of growing old with grace. And for everyone who pursues a dream against all odds, even when the world calls them crazy.*

# PROLOGUE

**Brazoria County, Texas**

**March 1993**

T HE POWER HAD been off for hours, and candles flickered inside Ruth's house. Through the windows, she watched a raging tropical storm dump waves of warm Gulf waters upon the saturated earth. Engorged, the San Bernard River surged beyond its banks as the Texas winds roared. A palm in her front yard bent in the gusts, leaning sidewise and flinging out fronds like surrendering arms.

As the thunderstorm threw its tantrum, Ruth thought back to the day, three decades earlier, when her husband, Chuck, had moved them to the small house on stilts, ten miles upstream from where the San Bernard spilled into the Gulf of Mexico. Since then, the river had been a mostly benevolent presence. Its brackish waters provided fish for their table, and the tall spindly pines and massive oaks along its banks supplied shade during blistering summers. On quiet nights, bubbles escaped from the San Bernard's silted bed, emitting sweet strains that mimicked invisible violins.

Through Chuck's death more than a dozen years past and the trials of her unrelenting aging, the river had been Ruth's constant companion. In her darkest hours, it gave her solace. The sun glistened on it each morning, and at night she gazed out at moonlight shimmering on its calm waters.

Yet the Gulf could be a fickle neighbor. At times it birthed hurricanes that spawned dangerous winds, tornadoes, and torrential rains.

Staring out at the dark, ominous skies, Ruth considered that she had lived through many such gales. Most eventually blew inland, traveling north and east until they dissipated and vanished. But there were those bad times when muscular currents devastated the land, sweeping away trees, boats, cars, even houses.

How long would this storm last? What damage would it leave behind?

The daggers of lightning and the pounding thunder set Ruth's nerves on edge. She clicked fresh batteries into her radio and turned the dial to a favorite station. The familiar strains of Artie Shaw playing "Begin the Beguine" on his clarinet filled the room. The music soothed her, and she thought of the old days: Chuck sitting at the kitchen table and reading the newspaper to her while she cooked dinner, gay nights laughing at clever remarks and commiserating over whispered confidences with long-dead friends. *Now I am too much alone*, she thought, *alone with my past.*

Her past?

As she had so often over the years, Ruth opened a frayed black scrapbook. Fragile, yellowed newspaper clips announced her name in banner headlines. She ran her hand gently over fading cables of congratulation signed by presidents, first ladies, celebrities, and explorers.

Once, decades earlier, she'd made history.

At the time, she'd believed her triumph to be a great legacy. She'd trusted that her accomplishment would be remembered always. How foolish. The world, of course, had quickly moved on to the next news story, and Ruth had become yet another forgotten curiosity.

Absorbed in reminiscing, she didn't notice the passing hours. Her small terrier, Ginger, raked Ruth's leg, eager for attention, but Ruth paid no heed. Although physically present, her mind had drifted off to another world, to another place.

The storm, the river, her home, and more than four decades of her life melted away. The arthritis in her back eased. Her legs felt strong and straight again. Transported back in time, Ruth once again stood on a Goliath rock, mesmerized by a glistening wall of water cascading from the heavens to the earth.

# CHAPTER ONE

**Houston, Texas**

**Hours earlier**

HER HUSBAND SNORING beside her, Gabby Jordan strained to smother an overwhelming urge to scream. When daybreak finally came, she lay dead still while Jeff showered and dressed for work. As he bent over the bed and gave her a peck on the cheek, his musky, achingly familiar aftershave enveloped her, but Gabby—fighting a sinking feeling in her chest at his touch—kept her eyes closed, her breathing steady. Only after the door slammed behind him did she finally crawl out of bed.

The effort was exhausting.

The soreness in her arms and legs, the throbbing in her head, brought back the terror of the night before. Rubbing her aching shoulder, she walked through the condo and considered the damage. Their white-pine coffee table, one leg snapped off, balanced precariously on its side, the books and candlesticks it had held scattered across the knobby gray rug, and in the shattered mirror hanging over the fireplace, her face looked as distorted as a cubist painting. At her feet, jagged fragments of off-white porcelain—the remains of what had been the base of her favorite lamp—resembled shards of broken bone.

*Why?* she wondered. *Just why?*

Yet she knew. She'd known for a very long time. Jeff needed no reason.

Hoping to ease her tension, Gabby flicked on the TV, and a local newscaster's voice blared about a tropical depression in the Gulf of Mexico. "We're okay if this storm moves fast. But folks, this one's bringing a bunch of rain, and it looks like it might stall. If it does…"

Paying scant attention, Gabby grabbed a broom and dustpan from the pantry, then swept the wreckage as she thought about all the other times—the smashed plates and knickknacks, the wrecked furniture, the painful bruises that took weeks to fade. In the past, Jeff had been careful to hit her only where long sleeves and pants covered. *Not this time. Last night was…*

Pouring the debris into a trash bag, Gabby glared at the three-legged table as if it were somehow to blame. With a deep breath to calm frayed nerves, she inspected the broken lamp's shade. A golf-ball-size dent and a four-inch tear disfigured the delicate fabric. She flipped the ragged edge back and forth and murmured, "No way to fix it."

Gone were the days when the condo had been her sanctuary. Tucked into an inner-loop neighborhood just fifteen minutes from her downtown Houston office, the place had once given her a sense of accomplishment, of pride that she'd bought it on her own. Alone in the evenings after a long day at work, gazing out at the city lights, she'd felt a sense of peace. After they'd married and Jeff had moved in, bedlam invaded and never left.

Reexamining the cracked mirror, Gabby mumbled, "Seven more years of bad luck. If I—"

The thought stopped her. Shuddering, she sank onto the couch and folded her body into a ball. It was then that the tears finally came.

An hour later she ran a trembling finger down her list of phone numbers, deciding, *No, not her* and farther down the list, *No, not him.* On her third swipe through, she stopped at the name of a childhood friend. Cynthia lived in Corpus, and they hadn't seen each other in a very long time, at least a decade before Jeff.

"Can I stay with you? Just until I figure out what to do?"

"Gabby, I"—her friend's voice held sympathy but also dread—"don't want to get involved."

Pushing aside her pride, Gabby begged. "Cyn, I know it's a lot to ask, but I don't have anywhere else to go."

After a tense pause, a reluctant sigh. "Okay. But come tomorrow. There's a storm, and—"

"No. Today." Gabby heard the urgency in her voice, the fear. She knew what would happen when Jeff walked through the door, carrying a bouquet of flowers—as he always did after one of his rages. All evening long, he would watch her, searching for any sign. The one time she'd tried to leave him before, he'd picked up on something— she didn't know what, some clue to what she'd had planned—and he'd—

Cynthia broke the silence. "Okay. But if you're running late, promise me that you'll stop somewhere and find a phone."

"I won't be late. I'll be there before dark."

"But if you are, Gabby, don't let me sit here and worry. Call me. Please."

RAIN FELL GENTLY but steadily on Gabby's short drive through Houston traffic to the bank, where she emptied her secret savings account and withdrew the maximum allowed out of the ATM. At the gas station, a persistent but gentle breeze buffeted the narrow overhead awning, and by the time her tank hit full, her jeans hung wet and limp against her legs.

It didn't take long for her to realize the magnitude of her mistake.

Staying off the Interstate, she took a lesser highway, reasoning that fewer cars meant fewer drivers to notice her. She covered ten miles, twenty, and fierce winds pummeled her silver Camry. The farther south she drove, the harder the rain fell. Gabby clenched the steering wheel until her nails embedded crescent moons into the black leather. Unfamiliar with the roads, she could barely make out the signs. Panicking, she cranked up the wiper blades to full speed and turned the defroster on full blast.

*I should have known better. A storm like this...*

For the briefest moment, she considered turning back. But no. She would never have made it home before Jeff walked through the door. Once he saw that she'd packed her clothes? That she hadn't cleaned up the mess? How long before he noticed the money she'd pulled out of the ATM? Maybe he had already.

The rain bucketed down, and the ditches on both sides of the road overflowed. Twice she pulled onto the shoulder and parked beneath an overpass to try to wait it out, once staying so long she nodded off from the exhaustion of having been up all night. A crack of thunder jerked her awake. The storm hadn't eased. Worried about the time, Gabby pressed on, missed a turn, and mistakenly veered off onto another desolate highway. All around her, pools of rainwater rose and merged, converging into rushing streams. The roadbed disappeared under a dark, wet sheen.

"Where am I?" she whispered. The dashboard clock warned that hours had passed since she'd left the condo. If she didn't pick up speed, she'd never make Corpus by dark. Gunning the engine, Gabby wondered how far she had to drive to get through the storm. If the bad weather was tracking north, there might be blue skies south.

Instead, the rain fell at a blinding rate. The right front tire hit a pothole, and a swell engulfed the hood, swamping the windshield. The wipers thrashed—left, right, left, right—helpless to keep up. Over the clatter of the storm, Gabby's heart pounded as the wheels lifted, and the Camry hovered above the road. Fighting to steer, she struggled to aim straight ahead, where the road should have been, but the car refused to obey. The front end slid left as the rear end shifted right, water exploding from beneath all four tires.

No longer in her control, the Camry skidded onto the opposite lanes.

Desperate, she slammed on the brakes. The back end whipped forward, sending the car into a spin. Although belted in, Gabby was thrown to the side as the car whirled once, then twice. The engine quit, and the Camry stopped dead, blocking both oncoming lanes.

A horn blared.

As if it had materialized out of the ether, an 18-wheeler drove directly at her. Hands trembling, Gabby cranked the key in the ignition. "Come on! Come on!" The engine ground but refused to engage. She smelled the faint odor of gas.

The truck's mammoth tires kept turning, and the distance from the Camry shrank, narrowing by half. Then by another half. The truck bore down. The horn blasted louder.

Gabby froze behind the steering wheel.

As she watched, the truck skidded on the wet road, sending out a deafening screech.

Shoulders hunched, she squeezed her eyes shut and braced for the inevitable crash. Another loud squeal from the truck's tires. And then…

Silence.

When Gabby opened her eyes, the truck had come to a stop across the highway.

Relieved, she let out a long breath, trying to calm her jagged nerves, as the door to the 18-wheeler's cab swung open. The driver sprinted toward her, bent over to keep the pounding rain out of his eyes. Trembling, her breath ragged, Gabby wanted to thank him, to apologize. But then she remembered how important it was that she not be seen.

"Please, start!" She turned the key twice before the engine fired awake.

Gabby threw the car into a sharp U-turn, and the truck driver jumped back to escape being run over. When she glanced in her rearview mirror, he was waving at her to stop, until he disappeared behind a curtain of rain.

A FEW MILES down the highway, Gabby spotted a faded red-and-white convenience-store sign. The rush of adrenaline had left her with shaking hands and a roiling empty stomach. Although the store's sign beckoned, she had a plan, one that included not stopping anywhere until she reached Cynthia's house. Yet she worried that she was headed the wrong way, and something else needled at her: the promise she'd made to Cynthia that she would call if she ran late.

Stores had pay phones. She could ask for directions and about road conditions ahead and get her bearings. Yet did she dare chance it?

Still debating, she made a sharp turn onto the gravel lot at PETE'S GRUB & SUCH. *I'll be quick*, she thought, *in and out. No one will even notice me.* She parked at the edge of the lot—far enough back that she hoped no one inside would get a glimpse of her car—grabbed the door handle and got ready to make a run through the rain. But the open sign wasn't lit, and the lights inside the building were dark. The store appeared closed.

The downpour pounded against the Camry's steel skin, and the exhaustion she'd fought rushed through her. Gabby closed her eyes, defeated, and surrendered to the roar of the wind and the hammering of the rain.

*It sounds the way my life feels. Like a war.*

Drained, she nestled her face against her hands on the steering wheel. "Ouch," she whimpered when she touched her right eye.

A boom of thunder, and she wondered what to do next. She was considering going on her way, looking for somewhere else to stop, when the store's double doors popped open and a man sauntered out, lanky, in a brown plaid shirt, jeans, and cowboy boots, carrying a blue-and-green striped golf umbrella.

Despite the dense clouds, Gabby grabbed her oversized sunglasses off the passenger seat. When he knocked on the window, she looked up through the dark lenses to find him gazing down at her. She lowered the window a few inches and managed to curl her lips into the suggestion of a smile.

"You want to come in and get out of this monsoon?" He leaned forward, his dark eyes scrutinizing her through the narrow opening. "Not much sense sitting in the car."

"Have you got a pay phone?"

"Yup. Electricity's out, but the phone oughtta work. Come on in, and you can give it a try."

The window back up, she slammed the door and then splashed through puddles beside him as they rushed toward the store. Once there, they paused under the overhang while he shook off the umbrella. All around the store, in every direction, Gabby saw nothing but trees, fields, and empty highway.

"I'm thinking it's probably going to blow through soon," he said, eyeballing the gloomy skies. As if to prove him wrong, a jagged spear of lightning cut through the clouds, followed by a thunder strike so loud the store windows shuddered. "Then again, maybe I'm overly optimistic. I've been accused of that in the past."

Out of the corner of her eye, Gabby watched the man's thin lips edge up to a slow grin.

The shelves were neat if somewhat bare, but the store stocked the essentials—bread, canned chili and vegetables, along with four-packs of toilet paper and single rolls of paper towels. Blister packs of bacon, sausage, hot dogs, and lunch meat hung in a cooler beside the milk. On a hotplate, the glass coffeepot was streaked a muddy brown, the liquid inside as thick as molasses. Craving caffeine, Gabby poured a cup anyway, only to discover it was cold. Reasoning sugar might help, she decided on a cup of ice cream, the kind with a wooden paddle tucked into a paper lid. But a strip of silver duct tape secured the freezer door.

"Sorry. Don't want all the cold to escape," the man explained. "No telling when the power'll go back on. Sometimes around here, well, it can be a day or more."

"What about a Pepsi?"

"Sure, help yourself. Nothing in the soda case will melt."

Her sodden tennis shoes squished on the linoleum floor as she walked to a refrigerated display against the wall. As she peered through the doors, the glass reflected the muted image of a slightly round woman, pale, with straight brown brows peeking over the tops of her dark glasses. Reaching to a lower shelf, Gabby claimed a can of soda. She pulled the tab and gulped a swig. Its sweet foam tickled her throat.

From behind the counter, surrounded by racks of cellophane-wrapped sweet rolls and bags of homemade beef jerky, the man asked, "Anything else?"

"Just this." Gabby grabbed a blister pack of some kind of dried sausage, far from healthy but protein, nonetheless.

"Register's not working either, but that'll be two seventy-five."

Gabby put her brown leather bag on the counter, unzipped it, and lowered her eyes to find her wallet. When she did, her sunglasses slid down her nose. She hurriedly pushed them back, but when she looked up, the man's smile had turned downward.

*He saw.*

As casually as she could manage, she handed him three one-dollar bills, and he gave her a quarter out of his pocket in return. "Thanks, Pete."

Putting the dollars beside the register, he said, "The name's Nick. Pete's buried in the church cemetery. Folks around here say it was a heart attack, but I figure the poor guy died of boredom from owning this place."

She tried to manage another weak smile, but the right side of her face ached. "You think?"

"Well, Pete was eighty-six, so no telling." He offered his hand. "Nick Foster. Glad to meet you."

"Ga..." She coughed and swallowed the rest of her name, looking up to find his eyebrows bunched together. Questioning. Taking his palm in hers, she said, "Ma-Maddie. Maddie Gregg."

"Nice to meet you…Maddie." His slight hesitation bothered her, and she felt sure that she hadn't fooled him.

The futility of it all crashed down on her. Stopping at the store had been foolhardy, she realized. She could have driven on and looked for an outdoor pay phone to call from, despite the rain, and tried to find road signs to get back on course. But then she considered that maybe it had all been ill-conceived. Why did she think she'd be able to pull it off? She'd never been good at lying, so there was no reason to think she'd be good at hiding.

The store felt uncomfortably quiet, and Nick focused intently on her. When the still air became even more awkward, he asked, "Anything else I can do for you? You're welcome to hang out here and wait for this storm to pass, but it could be a while."

Gabby took another gulp of Pepsi, then put the can on the counter and tore open the sausage pack. He knew Maddie Gregg wasn't her name. She felt certain of it. She took a bite, thinking. He appeared curious. *Why wouldn't he be? I've certainly given him reason.* But then she sensed something else, a sadness in his eyes. The guy looked concerned. Worried. For her? Maybe. At thirty-five, Gabby guessed that Nick Foster was seven or eight years older, somewhere in his midforties, but strands of silver streaked his dark brown hair, and deep cervices marked his broad forehead over his deep-set brown eyes.

Determined to play it all off as nothing of importance, she shot him a reassuring grin, fighting not to wince from the pain. *Nothing going on here,* she tried to telegraph. Holding up the sausage stick, she said, "I'm fine with just the Pepsi and this. But I could use that pay phone."

"On the side wall, near the restrooms."

Coins inserted, Gabby punched in a number. The dial tone buzzed as she twisted her straw-colored hair into a knot, anchoring it with a few bobby pins out of her pocket. "Cyn, I've run into a snag. I'll be later than I'd hoped. You were right about the storm. The weather's bad, and I got turned around on the road."

For a moment, Gabby listened while she nibbled on the stringy meat and scanned ads on a bulletin board above the phone. Teenagers offered their services for babysitting and grass cutting. A man had a shed for sale for a dollar to anyone willing to move it off his property. One note scribbled on a torn half sheet of yellow legal paper, written in a shaky hand, caught her attention: "Live-in companion needed for elderly woman."

When Gabby returned her attention to the phone, she heard worry in Cynthia's tone.

"No, please, if I'm too late, you don't need to wait up. Just leave me a key under the front mat. I'll sleep on the couch and see you in the morning."

Sensing his eyes still on her, Gabby glanced back at Nick. He stood fifteen feet away in front of the counter filling a BIC display, slipping the brightly colored plastic lighters into rows on a small turntable. When Nick swiveled the rack to stock the other side, Gabby turned her back to him and leaned against the wall next to the bulletin board.

Outside the rain beat down, but it sounded softer on the store's roof. Maybe Nick had been right; perhaps it was finally letting up. While Cynthia talked, Gabby reread the ad posted by the elderly woman searching for a companion. "Cyn, I know you don't want to get involved. I get that. But I need help. And I promise that it will be for just for a little while. A few days. At the most, a week. Just until I—"

Cynthia's tone spiraled higher. She was angry now. Upset.

Gabby's voice rose as she struggled to get her friend's attention. "Cyn, you said I could stay at your place. I can't go back. I have nowhere else to—"

A click, and the connection ended.

Her fear felt like a vise squeezing her heart. Unsure what to do, Gabby stared at the handset. When she turned toward the cash register, Nick's eyes were solidly on hers. She hung up the phone and cleared her throat. "Is there some place around here to stay? A motel or something?"

His heavy brow knotted as if he'd heard her bad news. How could he not have? "There's a hotel in Lake Jackson. Or a couple of places in Freeport. Both are usually maybe a twenty-minute drive. In this rain, no telling."

"Oh, well, I—"

"Most likely some of the roads have flooded." When Gabby said nothing more, Nick added, "But I can call Freeport for you, see about a room, if you want."

Silent, Gabby listened to the rain. It was finally letting up, but what did it matter? It felt over, and she had no way to recover. Nowhere to go. Yet, she couldn't return to the condo. The moment she'd walked out the door that had ceased being an option.

Rubbing her forehead, she felt exhaustion gnawing at her. There were so many things to think of, to be careful of, to consider. So many ways she could get caught. Jeff would track her credit cards. He'd have people looking for her car, her license plate number. A hotel was out of the question. *I have to be careful. No more mistakes.*

Gabby squinted through the windows at the highway and thought about how remote the place seemed. Then she turned back to the bulletin board.

# Chapter Two

**Brazoria County, Texas**

**March 1993**

"SHE SEEMS OKAY. Nice lady. Saw your advertisement on the community board. She says her name is Maddie Gregg."

Gabby heard doubt in Nick's voice when he uttered the phrase: "says her name is."

As she'd done with him when on the phone with Cynthia, Nick turned his back toward her. Still, Gabby could hear his every word. "Ruth, I know this is kind of odd, but I think this lady's in a bad jam. My guess is that she needs a place to lay low for a while. Maybe you two can help each other out?"

Gabby wished she could listen to the other side of the conversation. The woman would undoubtedly say no. Who would take in a stranger who pulled into a convenience store off the highway? It probably wouldn't help that Nick had told Ruth that Gabby was in trouble. But he was trying to help her; she could see that.

"Okay, I'll tell her." Nick hung up and gave Gabby a half shrug. "Well, the good news is that it wasn't a complete turndown. Ruth says you can drive over and talk to her, and she'll see."

Unsure how promising that sounded, Gabby still shot him a grateful, "Thanks."

He rattled off directions, and she made her way to the door. As she reached to open it, Nick stopped her. "Listen, Maddie, the thing is, Ruth's a great gal, good people. She needs help, but I'm sure that she can't afford much."

"Money's not important," she said, thinking that she'd happily pay for a safe place to stay.

"That's good, but the other thing is that like lots of old folks, she's a bit of a contradiction." He stopped as if considering how to explain. "You should know that Ruth gets testy sometimes. Agitated. I think it's because, off and on, she gets more than a little confused."

"I understand." Gabby tried not to sound impatient. She wanted to get going. It would be getting dark soon, and she needed a place for the night, hopefully longer. *If this doesn't work out...* But from the look on Nick's face, he had more to say. "Is there something else?"

When he grimaced, Nick's cheeks squeezed his eyes almost shut. "Listen, don't get your hopes up. I know Ruth will like you, but she sounded skittish on the phone."

With a resolute nod, Gabby grabbed the door handle, thinking about how concerned Nick seemed, how he'd gone out of his way for her. She turned back to him. "Nick, thank you."

"You're welcome, I—"

"And something else."

He looked expectantly at her, and she thought about Jeff, how he'd stop at nothing to find her. For once, Gabby decided, she needed to not worry about being sensible; instead, she needed to go with her gut. And her instincts told her that Nick Foster wanted to help her. "So that we start out being honest with each other, Maddie isn't my real name. It's Gabby."

"I thought you weren't telling me the—"

"Gabby Jordan."

Nick smiled and nodded at her. "Okay. Good to meet you, Gabby Jordan."

"And if anyone asks if you saw me, asks anything about me—"

"You were never here."

THE RAIN EASED to a steady drizzle as the sun sank lower in the sky, the storm heading northeast. From the convenience store, Gabby drove under the highway. Downhill toward the river, the road narrowed into two scruffy lanes of asphalt. On both sides, scattered woods glistened wet from the storm. She passed a cattle ranch and modest wood-sided cottages.

Minutes later, the house appeared on the left. Just as Nick had described it, the green clapboard structure stood propped up on ten-foot stilts. A deck wrapped around the front extending out toward the river. In places the  paint had peeled, exposing decaying boards, and slatted shutters flapped loosely in a stiff breeze. Lattice panels painted white enclosed the area under the house, and a rusting beige Plymouth sedan sat nearby under a tree, weeds and grass growing tall beneath it.

Sheltered under an umbrella borrowed from Nick, Gabby scanned the swollen river. Out of its banks, it stopped within a few feet of the thick beams that supported the deck.

Now that she'd arrived, Gabby debated the wisdom of walking up the rickety wooden stairs to the door. It was late in the day, the sun low in the sky. Night was coming, and Gabby wondered if the time would be better spent putting as many miles as possible between her and Jeff. *This woman will just tell me to leave. Why would she let me stay?* But then Gabby surveyed the river and the considerable distance to the neighbors' houses. She could barely make them out behind the trees. On the drive over, she hadn't encountered any other cars.

Abruptly, the door swung open at the top of the stairs, and a frail, elderly woman stared down at her. "Come on up, will you? No sense standing out in this rain!"

ONCE INSIDE THE house, they stood in the kitchen, and a blond-and-brown-haired terrier barked at Gabby's feet, sniffing her soggy tennis shoes. "That's Ginger. If anything, she's overly friendly. No doubt she'd lick a burglar to death." The old woman eyed Gabby. "And you're the woman Nick called about? Maddie?"

"Yes, and no." Gabby had thought about how to handle this wrinkle on her way to the house. "Nick did call about me. But my name is Gabby—Gabby Jordan."

"But why would Nick say…" The woman screwed her cheeks up until they pinched her eyes. "You gave him a fake name?"

Gabby bit the inside of her lower lip. This was harder than she'd thought it would be. "Yes."

"Why would you…"

Gabby drew a deep breath and held it as she wrangled over how to explain. Having to admit she hadn't been truthful wasn't a good way to win the woman over. But she knew eventually her name would come out, and then, if she'd lied to Nick and Ruth, they might never trust her. "I gave Nick a fake name to protect myself. To hide my identity."

"Huh." Ruth tilted her head slightly, curious. "But you told me your real name?"

"I told Nick, too. After he hung up the phone with you. I'm not very good at all this. It's new to me, being on the run and hiding. Nick promised that he wouldn't tell anyone that he saw me, and I believed him."

Ruth tossed her head back and let out a short huff. "Well, you've got that in your favor."

Confused, Gabby asked, "I have what in my favor?"

"That you're a good judge of character. Just met him, but you got Nick right. He's good people."

Gabby chuckled.

Perhaps wondering if Gabby had snickered at her, Ruth appeared more than a little annoyed. "What's so funny?"

"He said the same thing about you."

Ruth's eyes narrowed, but her lips curled up at the corners. "He did, did he? Guess that makes Nick a good judge of character too."

This time when Gabby laughed, a knife-blade-sharp pain radiated up the right side of her face. When her hand shot up to quell it, she jostled her sunglasses. She hurried to straighten the frames but noticed Ruth watching. To Gabby, the brief silence that followed felt heavy with unspoken questions.

"Well, okay. You're here to talk about the companion job, so let's get to know each other. I'm Ruth Marietta. I don't like being called Mrs. Marietta, so just call me Ruth. Now, let's sit down and get acquainted."

The problem was—where? The house overflowed with the possessions of a long life. In the box of a kitchen, the countertops, the battered oak table, and all four chairs disappeared under rumpled clothes and unopened mail. A cubbyhole office off to the side was in similar shape, as was the den, a narrow room that butted up to the kitchen. Three doors were closed, and Gabby assumed that they led to a bathroom and two bedrooms.

Settling the matter, Ruth picked her way toward the den, weaving between piles of newspapers and magazines. She gently eased down onto a wood-framed armchair upholstered in off-white. Behind her, books and knickknacks turned every which way on crowded, dusty shelves. Gabby followed her in and pushed aside a stack of books to claim a spot on the couch.

Outside the sun was low in the sky, and a candle burned on a glass-top coffee table. When she noticed Gabby looking at the flame, Ruth explained, "The power's out. Happens a lot on the river. We're kind of on the edge of civilization here."

"It's out at the store too." Gabby considered again how remote the area was and that it appeared the perfect hideaway. Intrigued by the stranger, Ginger pawed at her legs. The dog rolled over, and Gabby stroked its soft chest. "I bet Ginger is a lot of company."

"She's good to have around, but she's not much of a talker." Ruth let loose a raspy laugh, and the web of wrinkles radiating from her eyes deepened. Before age had taken over, Gabby decided, Ruth must have been an attractive woman. Her abundant white curls ended at her shoulders, and she had remarkable gray eyes that peered at Gabby from behind wire-rimmed glasses. Petite, with shoulders stooped from age, Ruth stood at the most five feet tall, and delicately boned, she couldn't have been much more than a hundred pounds.

Ruth smoothed her wrinkled white cotton blouse, pulling on the sleeves to straighten them, as she said, "So, you'd like to live in and work for me for a bit, Nick said. That right?"

"I would. Yes."

"You need a place to stay, I gather?"

"Yes. I do."

Assessing Gabby as she gave her a thorough once-over, Ruth cocked her head to the left. "You know, I never trust people when I can't see their eyes. That window to the soul thing, I guess. So, why not take off those sunglasses? I'm pretty sure you don't need them in here, and from the way you flinched earlier, it's unlikely that I'll be surprised by what they're hiding."

"Well, I…" Gabby hesitated, then did as asked. She cringed as the right stem brushed her face. An angry bruise encircled that eye, deep-purple veined with red.

"That's one heck of a shiner." Ruth's lips tied into a knot. "I hope you gave him one to match."

On the couch, Gabby turned away, embarrassed. "Silly thing. You know, I had a run-in with a door. In the dark and—"

Gabby stopped midsentence.

For a moment, neither woman broke the silence. Gabby considered what she'd just said and shook her head, disgusted. Her voice laced with a painful recognition, she confessed, "I've been lying for so long it's become second nature."

"You're pretty good with that story. Sounds like you've had a lot of practice." Ruth tapped her nails in a soft click, click, click against her chair's wooden arms. "I might have believed it, except for that bruise just above your wrist. That's a nasty one. Looks like someone grabbed you."

Gabby glanced down at her left arm. That morning, the discoloration had been faint, and she hadn't noticed the shape. Now that it had darkened, she saw the imprints of Jeff's long, thin fingers. There was a time when she'd loved his hands. She shuddered, remembering how he'd jerked her arm behind her and forced it up between her shoulder blades. The pain had seared through her like a jolt from an electric cattle prod.

Weary, reluctant to explain more, Gabby said, "I thought the long sleeves would cover everything."

"Not quite, dear, but it was a good try."

Gabby nodded ever so slightly and bunched the sleeve up, holding her arm out so Ruth could see. Bruises tattooed her from her wrist to just below her elbow. Many were fading, remnants of other harrowing nights.

Ruth sucked in a sharp breath and pushed it out with a loud sigh. "You're leaving this guy, right?"

"He's my husband. I…this hasn't…" Gabby swallowed, hard. How silly that she'd thought she could change Jeff. How foolish. Instead, the beatings had grown progressively worse and more frequent. In the early years, it happened rarely. Never such a brutal attack. Last night, the monster who'd come at her hadn't even looked like the man she'd married.

"I need to find a place to hide. To figure things out."

Ruth's bow-shaped lips pulled taut. "Looks to me like you don't have much to figure out. You can't stay with that man. Marriages have ups and downs, sure, but this?"

Ups and downs. Gabby considered that phrase. Lately, there hadn't been a lot of good times. Their lives, her job, everything suffered from Jeff's anger. The fear haunted her throughout the day, until she couldn't focus. An important deadline missed at the office, the condo uncared for, laundry piled up, and she'd forgotten to pick up groceries last night. After she'd promised him homemade lasagna. His favorite. That was all it had taken for him to—

"You have kids?" Ruth asked.

"No. I thought we would. Jeff wanted children, but I...I didn't want to bring them into...*this.*"

"Well, at least, that's good—not to have little ones balled up in the mess you're in, I mean."

Gabby wiped away a tear, and Ruth considered that maybe she shouldn't have been quite so blunt. But then again, it seemed that the young woman needed a healthy dose of honesty. Not that she wasn't sympathetic. Ruth had done it herself, tried to soften situations instead of labeling them what they were. "Well, I didn't have kids either. But that was my decision. I had my work. Or maybe it was more just the way my life played out."

"I try to fight back. I don't just let him..." Gabby's thin voice trailed off.

Ruth considered how frayed the young woman appeared, as if ready to unravel. "You know, I do want to help, but I'm not up to a lot of drama these days. I've got my own issues."

"Well, I wouldn't—"

"Tell you what. You staying here with me? That would be fun, I bet. I could use the help and the company." Ruth's voice turned gentle despite its hoarse, whiskey rattle. "Some days, I'm not so well, and it would be comforting to have someone to look after me. But I don't like worrying that the man who did that to you is going to show up on my doorstep."

Gabby fought to tamp down a growing sense of panic. Summoning all her courage, she insisted, "Ruth, Jeff has no way to know I'm here. Anywhere near here. He can't find me if I stay with you. And I'd do everything for you. I'd clean and cook. I'd..."

Ruth scowled, and the end of Gabby's plea died before it was spoken.

"I'm sure you believe that this husband of yours couldn't track you here, but life has taught me that things happen that we can't predict."

"No. Jeff wouldn't have any reason to ever look anywhere near here. That can't happen."

Ruth sized up the woman. Despite the bruised eye, a pretty young thing. Tall, at least by Ruth's standards. Maybe five-five, five-six or so. As much fear in her eyes as a racoon caught in a trap. "Like I said, not many things really can't happen, unless it's me being twenty-five again."

Despite the situation, Gabby chuckled, sending another shard of pain through her cheek up to her black eye.

"Stings, eh?" It was impossible to ignore the younger woman's agony. Ruth decided that perhaps there was a little something she could do for her. "Listen, with this storm, that man of yours won't be out looking for you until morning. All this rain? A bunch of the roads are under water. So, how about you stay?"

"That would be—"

"But only one night."

Gabby swallowed hard and nodded. "Okay. Thank you."

"How long's it been since you've eaten?"

"Toast this morning, and kind of a shriveled-up sausage at Nick's place."

"Oh, I love those," Ruth said. "Especially the ones with the jalapeños."

After consuming a peanut butter and jelly sandwich in six bites, Gabby retrieved her backpack and suitcase from her car. In the back bedroom lit by only a flashlight, she and Ruth stretched sheets on a twin bed with a black metal frame. Above an old mahogany dresser hung an oval mirror etched with a border of flowers that dated back a century or more. The floorboards moaned with each step, and the house smelled of old wood and the river.

As they tucked in the blanket, an olive-green wool worn thin in the wash, Ruth pondered the situation and felt the urge to do what she could to help, yet she knew that her advancing age made it difficult to solve even her own problems. Taking on someone else's… "Gabby, get some sleep. But tomorrow, like I said, you'll need to be on your way."

The desperation in the young woman's eyes was painful to see. "But really, I can help you, and—"

"Why don't you call your parents?"

"My dad died when I was a kid. A car accident."

"Your mom?"

Gabby choked on her answer: "She passed away two years ago. Breast cancer."

Ruth pursed her lips. "I'm sorry. I know that's hard."

The younger woman's problems had struck a tender spot, and Ruth considered confiding in Gabby, explaining that she understood the ache of such losses. *My mother dying and then I made a terrible bargain*, Ruth remembered, *one that changed my life*. But to open up, to tell those things? Some she'd never spoken of, not even to her closest friends. Instead, Ruth simply said, "Try not to worry. Something will work out. You'll see."

Gabby wondered if she should argue her case, push the woman, try to convince her, but then she took a long look at Ruth. The older woman looked so fragile, so vulnerable that Gabby decided pleading to stay longer might be too much to ask. "Thank you. Even just tonight, this helps. I'm so tired, I…"

Although her own bones ached, Ruth leaned forward and gently rubbed Gabby's shoulder. It was the only encouragement she could think to give her.

"Have a good rest. Things may seem clearer in the morning."

*Life streams past*, Ruth thought as she walked from the room. Her stay on earth, long by anyone's standards, was nearing an end. Days melted quickly; todays replaced by tomorrows. With dwindling time before her, Ruth tried to concentrate on good memories, but the bad ones too often refused to be buried.

Ghost-like, they hovered in the shadows.

# Chapter Three

**Taylorville, Illinois**

**1905**

"YOU PAINTED THESE?" The other folks in the town square strained not to make eye contact and hurried past, but Momma stopped. She recognized the wooden bridge outside town in one painting and the sawmill on the river in another. The man who would become my father had a cart pulled by an old mare parked near the general store. The placard beside it read: OIL PAINTINGS FOR SALE.

"Yes. I'm an artist!" Dad said, his voice softened by the hint of a Scottish burr. "I have a studio outside town. A little place. The trees are my companions."

When Ma, my grandmother, found out Momma was keeping company with the man in the wagon, she ordered Momma to stay away from Jack Robertson. "That man's a ne'er-do-well," Ma warned. "Not husband material. Not suitable company for a good girl."

At nineteen, Momma was among the youngest of Ma and Pa's twelve children. Her name was Marcella, but the family called her Pinkie. For months, Momma hid her pregnancy until her screams pierced the darkness. Carrying a candle, Ma rushed into Momma's room and found her writhing in the bed, terrified and in the throes of labor. Shouting for my grandfather, Ma sent another of the girls in search of her sewing basket. When my aunt returned, Ma cut the girdle off Momma's swollen belly and found me pushing my way into the world.

My grandparents greeted me with outrage.

At the cusp of the twentieth century, such untoward circumstances generated gossip. An unwed daughter giving birth sullied the reputation of a good family. Neighbors had eyes and ears, and they whispered rumors.

The day after my birth, a justice of the peace performed a hush-hush courthouse wedding.

Beside Dad, Momma stood in a navy blue dress, the skirt snug across her still bloated abdomen. I was left at Ma and Pa's house, cared for by an aunt, and concealed from prying eyes. The judge recited the words that bound Momma to Dad in matrimony and recorded their marriage in the county records. Those documents legalized their union but came too late to legitimize my birth.

My parents named me "Ruth," and with their marriage I became Ruth Robertson.

I would remember nothing of my father from those early years. Perhaps predictably, the marriage faltered, and my parents quickly divorced, bringing more disgrace upon my grandparents. A few years later, my mother met a widower with two young daughters, and they married.

A beautiful woman with porcelain skin and long auburn curls, Momma loved me. I was sure of that, although my memories of her were fleeting and blurred. What I recalled was her presence, the smell of her—white lilacs in the spring, the pungent aroma of fried chicken clinging to her clothes on Sundays—the softness of her hand caressing my cheek, a sense of safety and contentment within her arms.

In my earliest recollections, we huddled together on my small bed on the second floor of our farmhouse. Through the open window, a soft summer breeze carried the scent of freshly mown grass. The only light came from a single candle on my bedside table. My two stepsisters chattered softly in the next room as my mother opened a picture book. How we laughed at that rascally Peter Rabbit, who pilfered from Mr. McGregor's garden. When the farmer took chase, Momma yelled, "Stop, thief!"

Each night, Momma tucked me in and kissed me good night, and before I fell asleep, I heard her with my stepfather in their bedroom, the whispers of familiar voices, the comfort of home.

That summer, I turned six.

I chased my stepsisters through the rows of corn playing hide-and-seek while Momma shelled peas on the porch. We had big news, a baby on its way. As the leaves turned gold and red, Momma's belly grew round, and at times she placed my palms on her apron, then cupped her hands over my own. My heart quickened as the child fluttered within her. My stepfather wanted a son to help work the farm, and my stepsisters and I plotted names, hoping for another girl.

Not long after Christmas, women from the surrounding farms converged at our house. They bustled through and took charge, gathered sheets and towels, and excitement boiled like the pots of water on the kitchen stove. The midwife, a sturdy woman with a thick brown bun and a stained cotton apron, rushed in and instantly disappeared within my parents' bedroom. Momma's screams carried through the house, rising and falling in waves. Frightened, I shut my bedroom door and grabbed my book, concentrating on Peter Rabbit and his more obedient sisters, Flopsy, Mopsy, and Cotton-tail.

The next morning, I woke at daybreak and ran to my parents' bedroom, hoping for a glimpse of my mother and our new baby.

Instead, I found my stepfather weeping in the hallway, his hands covering his face. I went to him. He grabbed me, hugged me.

"Papa, why are you crying?" I asked, but he didn't answer.

Finally, my parents' bedroom door opened, and I rushed in. There I found my new sister, Phyllis, content in her bassinet. In the bed, Momma slept.

Neighbors dropped in that strangely cold January, casually brushing flakes of snow off the shoulders of their heavy wool coats. The house smelled of a crackling fire in our parlor's potbelly stove, where the adults gathered in a circle. I sensed that they waited for something important.

Then came the morning that a neighbor whisked baby Phyllis and my stepsisters off to be cared for, I didn't know where. I asked to go, too, but they said I should stay. My mother might want to see me. A few hours later, Ma arrived at the front door trailing an air of gloom, to stand by her daughter's bedside. Perhaps that was a clue that something momentous was unfolding, since Momma and Ma hadn't talked in years.

"It won't be long now," I heard one farmwife whisper. "She's lost too much blood."

"Shouldn't we send for the doc?" another asked.

"Already did, but he refused to come. He said it wouldn't do any good, that there's nothing to be done."

I wondered what they meant.

A lady said that Momma had asked for me, and I ran to my bedroom, grabbed my Peter Rabbit book, and then rushed to her, hoping she'd read to me. But when I walked through the door, Momma floated between awake and asleep, more tired than I'd ever seen her.

Someone lifted me up onto the bed next to Momma, and she

smiled at me, but puddles collected in her eyes. Others cried too. My stepdad rushed out of the room, his shoulders slumped and shaking. "My sweet Ruthie, I'll be leaving soon," Momma said, running her hand over my arm, straightening the waves in my light-brown hair. "I don't want to, but I don't have a choice."

"I want to go with you," I said, excited at the idea.

"No, not this time." She smiled but shook her head just so slightly. Disappointed and confused, I didn't understand why I couldn't go with Momma. "It's been decided that your baby sister will live with your stepdad on the farm. You can do that too. But you have a choice to make. If you want to, you can live with your grandmother in town."

"But Momma, can't I be with you?"

"No, Ruthie. Where I'm going, I can't take you." Weak, she could barely lift the corners of her lips into a smile. "My girl, you must decide. Where do you want to live? Here on the farm or in town with Ma?"

Looking over at Ma, I considered the grandmother I didn't know, one who'd played little part in my young life. My friends had grandparents, white-haired and wrinkled, who doted on them, brought presents, baked pies, and played with them with their dolls. I glanced back at Momma in bed, drifting in and out, finding it hard to stay awake. I didn't know what to do. I wanted to be with my stepfather and the other girls, but I wondered if my grandmother needed me. My grandfather was dead, and she lived alone.

Minutes passed. "Ruthie," Momma whispered, her voice so weak I could barely hear her. "You need to make a decision."

I thought about my stepfather crying in the hallway, and I looked over at Ma, her head bowed. She seemed sad too. "I'll go with Ma and keep her company, so she's not sad," I told Momma.

The decision made, I turned to Ma and grinned, thinking how happy I must have made her, but when she looked up, I saw that my decision hadn't pleased her. Instead, my grandmother glared at me with unfeeling eyes. She didn't want me. Anxious, I looked back at Momma. I'd made a mistake, a terrible mistake. I needed to tell her. I shook her shoulder. "Momma! Momma!" But her eyelids had slipped shut and one of the farmwives whooshed me away, scurried me into the hallway and pointed toward my room.

"Be a good girl, and don't give us any trouble," she said, her voice stern. "We'll come for you when your momma is gone."

In my room I cradled my baby doll and whispered the song Momma sang to me each night. "Lullaby and goodnight, with pink roses bedight…" The hours passed, and I slept, my book open on my lap. When I woke, the sky had turned dark, and the moon shone in the window. The curtains danced in a slight draft that seeped in around the frame. I pulled my quilt up to my chin and watched the flickering white lace that reminded me of ghost stories. Scared, I called out for Momma, but it was one of the neighbor ladies who opened the door.

"Now you shush! Don't be disrespectful, causing such commotion, with your sweet mother on her deathbed."

When I woke again, the sun had yet to rise, and I heard my stepfather sobbing. Afraid, I stayed in bed, prayed, and asked God to watch over me and help Momma. Then I tried to remember the words to a nursery rhyme until I fell once more to sleep.

The next morning, a woman offered to take me to my mother. This time when I walked into the bedroom, Momma lay on the bed wearing her cream silk wedding dress. "Why's Momma so dressed up?" I asked, but no one answered. "Will she wake up soon?"

In the days that followed, the local women made coffee and brought cakes and biscuits to our house, and visitors' boots clomped loud on the old wood floors. As before, they collected around the parlor stove, remarking on the weather, so cold that eggs froze in the chicken coops. When I wandered in, the adults lowered their voices and murmured, "Poor child."

They couldn't bury Momma until the ground thawed in the spring. But a few days after she died, my stepfather brought me a tattered suitcase, one of Momma's that she'd kept in the attic. A woman from a farm down the road folded my clothes and stacked them neatly inside. I put my Peter Rabbit book on top, and she closed the case. I held tight to my baby doll under my arm. The lady buttoned my red wool coat, the one Momma had made for me by cutting down an old one of her own. Ma waited for me in the parlor. I waved goodbye to my stepfather and stepsisters as a neighbor man urged his horses to pull us in his wagon onto the road.

We rumbled across the rough frozen earth on our way to Ma's house in Taylorville. Before long I snuggled against Ma, but she pulled away. In the bitter cold, I gathered the coat's scratchy collar around my neck and held my doll close. I thought about Momma and the farm and how we'd played hide-and-seek in the fields of corn.

FROM THE DAY I left the farm, I saw little of my stepdad and sisters. Inside Ma's white clapboard house, I spoke only when spoken to, and I did all I could to become invisible.

Although the sin of my beginning wasn't mine, Ma acted as if, simply by virtue of the circumstances of my birth, I was destined to bring her continuing disgrace. She had a quick temper and an even quicker hand, one that struck without warning if I violated any of her many rules. It was as if she waited for me to disappoint her. It probably didn't help that my pug nose and gray eyes reminded her of my absent father.

Years passed.

School was my refuge. I laughed and pretended to be carefree. I made friends easily. I slept over at their homes, and we played parlor games. On the street, I jumped rope, played hopscotch and four square. The world opened up to me when I learned to read. I lost myself in books and daydreams, and each afternoon I ran to the front porch and collected the newspaper.

Homework done, I lay on my stomach on the floor, the newspaper spread before me, and I read every word. On front pages, President Woodrow Wilson predicted the new Federal Reserve would bring prosperity, suffragettes marched on Washington DC and demanded that women be given the right to vote, and the Philadelphia As beat the New York Giants to win the World Series. More than the words, the photographs drew me in, the faces of men and women, movie stars and politicians, scenes of victory and disaster.

In New York, Grand Central Station reopened after a remodeling, and the paper printed a full page of photos. I ran my hand over it, stopping on each photo. I pictured myself at the ticket window, inside one of the tunnels waiting at the tracks, and standing before the four-faced brass clock, watching the crowds hum past.

In my imagination, I boarded a train and arrived anywhere else in the world, Ma and Taylorville left far behind.

"MRS. JOHNSON, THESE seeds'll grow like Jack's beanstalk!" I promised the matronly woman in her cotton housedress who leaned against her front door's frame. She looked unconvinced. "Honest, they will. Ma planted some last spring, and we had a bumper crop."

Money always tight, I worked for what I wanted. Starting in grade school, I circulated door to door selling vegetable and flower seeds. With each sale, I earned tickets I traded for rewards from a catalog. Our neighbors tucked the seeds in the dimples of paper egg cartons filled with dirt. The tender green stems leafed out in the early spring to be planted in gardens after the danger of frost passed—tomatoes and string beans, zucchini and peas. I turned my tickets in for school supplies.

Then I decided to save for something important. Two years later, the cigar box I kept in my top drawer had grown heavy with tickets. On Saturday mornings, I counted them, then paged through the prize catalog. I used a red crayon to circle a picture of my goal, what I worked so hard for.

On a bright spring day when I was twelve, Ma and I carried bags home from the grocery store. Making conversation, I brought up my stash of tickets.

"I've got nearly enough now," I told her, my voice pitched high with excitement. "I'm getting something special."

Ma eyed me, curious, and for once I had my grandmother's full attention. "What is it, girl?"

"Well, Ma, in the catalog they have a real camera with a flash on the top, one that uses real film so I can take photographs."

"Why would you want that?" she asked, her forehead a pattern of deep lines.

"I'm going to be a photographer when I grow up," I explained. It was an idea I'd had for a while, but I'd been afraid to tell anyone, wary that they might laugh or tease me or that I'd appear the fool if it never happened. But now, with so many tickets saved, it seemed only a matter of time before the camera became mine. "Once I have it, I can practice, and one day I'll get a job with a newspaper."

I thought Ma would be pleased, but instead she frowned and said nothing.

At home, Ma left me to unpack the grocery bags, put away the canned goods, and slip the milk into the icebox. When I finished, I walked into my bedroom, then stopped and stared at the bed. My cigar box topsy-turvy on the blanket, my tickets were torn into tiny pieces. As many times as I'd said nothing to the slaps and Ma's sharp tongue, this time I picked up the cigar box and ran to her.

"Why?" No answer, just a sullen look. "Tell me why!"

"You don't need a camera, girl." Ma stared at me, a dark cold in her eyes. "Now don't bring it up again."

# Chapter Four

**Peoria, Illinois**

**1919**

THE PRINCIPAL UNEXPECTEDLY appeared during math class. "Miss Robertson, I'd like to see you in my office."

As we walked past the banner hanging outside the gym hawking prom tickets, I wondered what I'd done wrong. Many of the boys and a few of the girls in my class had been summoned this way, but I never had. I hadn't skipped classes. I'd turned in all my homework. I had four years left in high school until graduation. I worried, *What if I've done something terribly bad? Ma will be mad. Really mad.*

As we passed his secretary, the principal said, "Put that phone call through for me now, please."

She nodded, and we went inside. I sat across his desk from him, trembling with fear. I thought of Ma, how mean she got when she was upset with me. "Ruth, someone would like to talk to you. We'll have him on the telephone in a minute."

"Me? Someone wants to talk to me?" No one had ever called me before. But then, we didn't have a phone in the house. No one we knew did. "Who is it?"

"Your father."

THE MORNING MY dad collected me, I was fourteen years old. Ma wasn't anywhere to be seen, and she didn't say goodbye. But Dad threw my suitcase into the trunk of a borrowed Model T and then doffed his tweed driving cap. "At your service, Miss," he cooed, and I giggled, nervous but excited. I was fascinated by a man who looked back at me through my shade of gray eyes, who had a bit of a ball at the end of his nose like mine, whose light-brown hair resembled mine except for a dusting of silver. Yet he was a stranger.

"It's good to have you with me, Ruthie," he said, a slight trill to the *R*. "I've been wanting you to come live with me for a long time, but that grandmother of yours, she's a hard one."

Hearing his soft burr reminded me of what Ma had told me about my dad, when I'd been brave enough to press for details, that he came from Scotland to the States as a young boy. Ma handed information out begrudgingly, not eager to speak of a man she wouldn't give a good riddance for. Dad, after all, had been the start of it all, the disgrace Momma brought on the family.

The car chunked along as I departed on my great adventure. Dad laughed and sang, flashed one of those smiles, the kind that crept slowly from ear to ear, and I thought that Ma would have glowered and labeled the man beside me a charmer.

"Where are we going?" I asked.

"You'll see."

An hour or so later, we pulled into a clearing off the woods outside Averyville, on the outskirts of Peoria. A campsite, it looked like, with a stone fire ring. Anchored just off the road was a trailer on wheels, a wooden box the size of a train caboose with windows. On the side, two chairs sat under a canvas awning supported by poles.

"What's this?" I glanced about as Dad grabbed my suitcase and heaved it over his shoulder.

"This is your new home, Ruth," he said, flashing that grin yet again. "Ain't she a beauty?"

I wasn't sure how to answer. "A beauty."

"She keeps me warm in the winters and cool in the summers." Dad was a rail-thin man, not much taller than I was, and he clambered awkwardly up the trailer's steps. "She may not look like much, but she's home."

Perhaps sensing my unease, Dad laughed. "Aw, Ruthie, no frowns. You'll get used to it. It's a great way to live. Fresh air and food cooked over a campfire."

Despite his admiration for his accommodations, I wondered how we'd both fit in the cramped space I found inside. Dad had a bunk on one wall, and he'd laid one out for me opposite it.

The trailer was made even smaller by a curtain that sectioned off one corner. Momma had told me that my father was an artist, that he painted beautiful pictures. When I'd colored with my stepsisters, she'd oohed and aahed at my creations, telling me that I'd inherited his talent. But Dad and I had something else in common, something I hadn't known about when I'd saved all my tickets to buy a camera.

That first day together, I learned that Dad still painted some but mostly he made his living as a photographer. That corner of the trailer behind the curtain was where he developed his film and printed his pictures. Happy for an audience, Dad pulled out a camera, showed it to me, and told me about his work, taking portraits for school yearbooks and church directories. As he talked, I thought about my tickets torn to bits on my bed, the hatred in Ma's eyes. For the first time it made sense; I realized that I had unknowingly reminded Ma that I was my father's daughter.

Despite all we had in common, Dad and I were strangers. The withering stares Ma had given me whenever I confided in her had left a mark, and I didn't tell Dad about my dreams to one day be a newspaper photographer. I wanted to, but I worried about his reaction. Instead, I listened while Dad talked. Ma would have said he had the gift of the gab, for there was hardly a pause between his sentences. I soaked it all in, stories about his life, about his family in Scotland, about how beautiful Momma looked on the day they first met out on the street.

That night Dad's snoring rattled the thin wooden walls, and I thought longingly of my small room at Ma's house. But then I remembered that she'd never wanted me there. *This'll be okay. I have a dad now.*

Days passed, and I started at my new school. It was hard to dress and stay clean in the trailer, and I showed up at times with my clothes wrinkled, my hair mussed. My new friends looked at me, questioning. Some asked where I lived. I didn't explain, just bragged about Dad. "He can do anything," I said, and I believed it. On clear crisp days, Dad took out his easel, and I watched as he painted the scenery around us, a view of the lake, and a portrait of me.

"Is that the way I look? My hair? Is it that honey brown?"

Dad nodded. Seeing myself through my father's eyes, I felt beautiful.

It turned out that living on the edge of the woods suited me. Some days, Dad went off in search of a landscape to paint, and I walked to the library. Later, I relaxed below a thick-trunked oak with gnarled branches that filtered the sun, a book on my lap—*The Time Machine, Tess of the D'Urbervilles.* I read *The Secret Garden* and imagined I was Mary Lennox in Yorkshire.

One day I was reading under my tree when a stranger ambled by carrying a wicker basket, searching for herbs and berries. With a colorful scarf wrapped as a turban, the old woman wore a flowing skirt, a black smocked top. The Gypsy sat beside me and mentioned traveling with a carnival that had set up in town. Dad and I had walked the grounds the evening before—tents and flags flapping in the wind, the smell of cotton candy and of corn roasting on the cob, colorful banners screaming, "Come inside!" A bearded lady. A child with a rounded back outfitted with a hard shell called Turtle Boy.

"Let me see your hand." The Gypsy took mine, smooth with youth, gently in hers, calloused and bent by age, her knuckles as knotted as the branches of the oak above us.

I thought of Dorothy happening upon the snake-oil salesman who became the great Oz, and I was absorbed in the Gypsy's craggy face, her every word as she asked my name and where I lived, all the while surveying my palm. "You will live a long life," she said, tracing a line that arced above my thumb. "A very long life."

"How long?" I asked.

"One day you will be old like me." Running her finger along a crease she labeled my heart line, she said, "And you will have disappointments in love. That is not where your happiness lies."

Disappointments in love. What did that mean? "What will happen to me?"

She chuckled softly, and I was embarrassed, fearing I appeared naive.

"Palm reading isn't a way of predicting future events, but what traits will rule your life," she explained, her abundant brows arching over eyes the dark of wet coffee grounds. "What will happen, I can't tell you. But see this line here?" She pointed at a crease dividing my palm in half, more vertical than horizontal. "This is your fate line."

"My fate line?"

"Providence plays a part in all our lives, but for some of us more than for others. When it is strong, it guides us."

"My fate line," I repeated in wonder.

"Many people have no such line. But for those who do, the deeper the fate line cuts the more influence destiny has in their lives. Yours is very deep."

"What does that mean?"

"That the universe has a plan in place for your life, young Ruth."

I nodded, although without truly understanding.

"Your fate line meets your life line at the very beginning, near your thumb." I sensed from the Gypsy's solemn voice that this was important. "That means that you've already chosen a path, even now as a young girl. And I see, looking at your fate line, something else."

With each word, I became more spellbound. Rarely in my life had anyone centered so intently on me. I was thrilled, if a bit ill at ease. In a whisper I asked, "What does it tell you?"

The old woman let go of my hand and sat back, looking at me with great interest, as if reassessing the girl beside her. "Your fate line tells me that your future holds much promise."

"What kind of promise? What will I do?"

Her eyes glowed with mystery. "That, child, is your decision."

The rest of that day, I found it difficult to concentrate on my book. Instead, I sat alone under the tree, thinking of the strange woman and tracing my fate line, over and over, again and again.

EVENINGS AROUND THE campfire, Dad sometimes talked about when he first arrived in the States. As a boy, he'd lived on an Oklahoma Indian reservation, where he'd learned to live off the land. We ate wild game he shot in the surrounding woods or fish he pulled out of the nearby lake. "So, what're you gonna be when you grow up, Ruthie?" he asked one night over a plate of largemouth bass and potatoes grilled over the fire. "When you move out on your own and into the world?"

I thought about the Gypsy in the woods. It was true that I had a dream, the same dream that as a child I once confessed to Ma, only to have her strike out at me. A little time had passed since we'd begun living together, and I'd grown closer to Dad, so this time I told him my secret: "A newspaper photographer." At that, I held my breath, afraid he'd laugh or ridicule me.

For a moment, Dad seemed to weigh the idea. "You can do it," he said, one eyebrow arched high, the other cinched down in thought. "Absolutely, if that's what you want, you should do it."

His words were hard to hear, perhaps because I'd never heard them before, and I wasn't sure I believed them.

After dinner, Dad disappeared inside the trailer while I washed dishes in one basin of soapy river water, a second one of clear water to rinse them. When he emerged, he carried a small case.

"For you."

I wasn't sure how to respond. I'd received few gifts in my life, and this took me by surprise. Ma didn't believe in presents, even for birthdays or Christmases, and this wasn't either. I opened the brown cardboard box, unbuttoned the rough burlap sack inside, and pulled out a small black camera similar to the one in my catalogue. Tears welled in my eyes, and Dad seemed uncertain what to do. Finally, chuckling, he shook his finger and scolded me. "We'll have none of that, girl. That camera's not new, but when it was, I paid two dollars for it. It should serve you well."

"Thank you, Dad." I wiped my eyes and rushed over to hug him. I planted a kiss on his cheek. "I'll take really good care of it."

We huddled together in front of the campfire until late that night as he taught me how the camera worked and talked to me about setting the focus. He reeled in a spool of film and cranked the first frame into place. I sized him up in the viewfinder as he stood in front of our trailer home, proud, his arms folded, grinning as the flashbulb ignited.

For the first time in my life, someone believed in me, someone loved me enough to trust that I would find my place in the world.

Perhaps that was why I said nothing a few nights later.

Dad had been drinking when he lay down beside me and slipped his hands around me, brushed his thumb over my breast. I stiffened and waited, motionless, until the snoring began. I pulled away and left him there, and I slept on his pallet instead. At first it happened rarely, only after Dad had visited the pub or poured whisky into his tin coffee cup around the campfire. I'd never had a father before to know how one acted, and I made excuses for him.

*He's just being affectionate.*

Then came a night when he slipped his hand under my nightgown, onto the bare skin of my legs, making his way up. I pushed down on my nightgown with my hands, but he was insistent, only pulling back when he heard me cry.

Nights came and went. At school, in the classroom, I barely heard the teachers' lectures as I tried to think of someone to tell. I considered confiding in Ma. She hated Dad enough that she might believe me. But I was ashamed to prove her right, that my father was a heathen, and I was only trouble. She'd have him arrested. And I loved my father. I did. I wondered if I should tell my teacher. But no one talked of such things at school. I could never have admitted it to my friends. I felt alone, and I kept my silence. Deep in my heart, I worried that it wasn't Dad's fault but mine. Somehow, I was to blame.

Then one night in the darkness, Dad refused to stop despite my sobs. The alcohol and cigarettes on his breath surrounded me as he pushed up my nightgown and claimed my innocence on the stained mattress, threads of moonlight shining through the window, surrounded by woods where no one heard my screams.

# Chapter Five

**Brazoria County, Texas**

**March 1993**

Gabby woke to the aroma of bacon frying and, for a moment, couldn't place the room. She glanced above her at the black metal frame on the bed, at the old dresser. Then she remembered the evening before and the old woman who had let her stay the night. But just the night. That realization resurrected the knot of anxiety in her chest as she worried about what the day would bring.

Light streamed in through the thin curtains, which, like so much in Ruth's home, were yellowed by age. In the darkness the night before, Gabby hadn't noticed a framed sepia portrait hanging on the wall, one of a staunch-looking elderly couple. Something about the woman in the photograph bothered Gabby. She took a closer look and decided it was the way the gray-haired woman's lips sank at the corners, her expression telegraphing a slight disdain, perhaps even contempt.

"Ah, you're up," Ruth said when she peeked in and saw Gabby inspecting the old photo. "That's Ma and Pa, my grandparents. I keep it in the spare bedroom so I don't see it so often. She's not a good memory."

"I wondered about that. She looks kind of harsh."

"Harsh, huh… Good word for her." Ruth sighed, then asked, "How's that eye?"

In the antique mirror with the etched flowers, Gabby examined her right eye. The bruising hadn't faded overnight. If anything, it looked worse. She touched it and winced.

"No better, eh? Get dressed and come out. Breakfast is ready."

THE POWER WAS back on, and the single bare bulb hanging from the kitchen ceiling glared. Ruth had cleared one side of the table. Last night's stacks of papers and clothes had been replaced with plates of bacon and scrambled eggs, each with a slice of toast. In front of one sat a sack of frozen vegetables wrapped in a thin towel.

"Put those peas on your eye," Ruth ordered as she poured orange juice.

Gabby whimpered when the bag touched her cheek, but gradually the cold seeped in, numbing the pain.

"That should bring the swelling down." Ruth walked over for a closer look. Gabby slid the bag down, and Ruth positioned her thumb below, one finger above, and gently stretched the skin, inspecting the bruise. When Gabby shivered and pulled away, Ruth scowled. "You know, it's pretty blown up, practically swollen closed."

"This feels good." Gabby replaced the peas. With the other hand, she speared a clump of eggs. "Thanks."

"I wasn't thinking. If I had been, we would have done this last night, and maybe it wouldn't be quite so bad."

Gabby noticed that Ruth limped slightly, her legs stiff, as she walked to her chair. Ginger followed, whining. Before Ruth took her first bite, she claimed a piece of bacon off her plate, fried to a gritty black char, and held it close to the floor. Ginger latched on and scurried off to the den, where she plopped down on a lumpy cushion that looked like it had once graced a chair.

For a moment, Ruth watched the dog but soon focused on Gabby. "I think you should tell me more about yourself. Maybe I can help you come up with a plan."

Gabby heard a sincere desire to help in the older woman's words. Clearly, she wanted to offer support, but Gabby understood Ruth's reluctance to become too involved, to perhaps put her own safety into jeopardy. "What kind of plan?"

"The kind that could help you get out of this mess. Maybe—if I knew more—I could help."

Unsure what to say, Gabby chewed a second forkful of eggs and took a bite of her toast, stalling. "Well, I…" she started and then stopped. For years, she'd kept the truth locked inside her, partly because of Jeff's threats but also because of her shame. If no one else knew, she could pretend it wasn't real. Now, looking into Ruth's inquisitive gray eyes, it all seemed ridiculous. Absurd, actually. Drawing up straight in the chair, she took another bite. The buttered toast tasted dry, and she gulped down half the glass of orange juice. She cleared her throat. "I don't know where to start."

"Let's try the easy stuff. Where do you live? What do you do?"

Gabby dropped her head for a moment, thought about that, then nodded. "I have a condo in Houston, a small two-bedroom, but I like it. It's in an older building, has some character. I bought it when I was single, used my Christmas bonus one year for the down payment. When we married, Jeff moved in. I work at a downtown law firm."

"Secretary? Clerk of some kind?"

Gabby finished chewing a bite of toast. "I'm a lawyer, a junior partner."

At that, Ruth put down her fork. "A lawyer?"

Gabby understood what Ruth must be thinking: that someone who knew the law should be able to get out of even the worst situations. Gabby had thought the same—before Jeff. That was the thing about hindsight, how years later you could look back and realize that what had seemed to be one way at the time was the exact opposite.

"OH, EXCUSE ME!" she'd apologized. "I'm so sorry."

In a busy Houston coffee shop, Gabby had met Jeff by literally bumping into him. Her iced latte splattered on his shirt, and she'd grabbed a handful of brown paper napkins to dab it. As she did, she felt his eyes on her. She looked up, he smiled, and it felt magnetic.

"Now that you've made me presentable, why don't we grab a table and drink our coffees together?"

With her work piled high on her office desk, she should have turned his offer down, but something about Jeff Jordan attracted her. He was handsome, sure. A tall, big guy with broad shoulders. But it was more than that—an instant connection she'd never felt before. His piercing blue eyes seemed to probe deep inside her. She sized up the ugly brown stain on his crisp blue shirt and considered that it was her fault. Under the circumstances, it felt rude to mumble an excuse and run off.

As it turned out, they lingered talking for much of that afternoon and others to come. Weeks passed, and they christened the coffee shop "our place." There were phone calls that lasted late into the night, dinners in high-end restaurants where Jeff leaned over the table and gazed at her as if he marveled at her every word. On her birthday, he appeared unexpectedly at her condo door holding a bottle of wine and a bouquet of her favorite flowers. "You mentioned you love snapdragons."

"Where did you find them this time of year?" she gasped.

"I have my ways," he said, with a playful wink.

Then came the summer evening she left a bar where she'd had a drink with her coworkers and nearly tripped over him as he walked in the door. "Isn't this a lucky coincidence?" He'd grinned and held out his hand, taking hers. "Want to go back inside and keep me company?"

Glad to see him, she thought little of it. Only later, when she knew him better, did she realize that he must have followed her and that he had probably stood outside in the heat watching her through the window for hours.

Throughout law school and the crush of working her way up in the firm, she'd had little time for dating. She had once believed she was in love, but the man had left her a voice mail, informing her that he'd fallen for someone else. When Gabby recounted that painful parting to Jeff, he held her and whispered, "That will never happen with me. I want only you."

Five months after they met, she carried more snapdragons and wore a white suit. Jeff arrived at the courthouse in a tux with a boutonniere, and Gabby took it as a good omen that he'd gone to such trouble for a fifteen-minute ceremony. But that day, minutes before they were scheduled to recite their vows, a first brief glimpse suggested that she didn't know as much as she thought she did about the man she loved. On one of the forms, Jeff had indicated that he'd been divorced twice.

"You never mentioned that you've been married before, not even once," she told him. "Why didn't you tell me?"

"I guess it didn't come up. Does it make a difference?"

Jeff flashed that grin of his, the one that made her knees weak. The justice of the peace waited in the courtroom. Gabby shook her head. "No. I guess not."

IN THE HOUSE on the river, Ruth had a glimmer of surprise in her eyes. "So, I need to make sure I have this right. What you're saying is that you're a full-fledged lawyer?"

"Yes. The firm does commercial law, real estate, and contracts."

At that Ruth sat back into the chair. "Well, that's a surprise. Tell me about your husband. Or let's just call him the jerk."

"He's not—" A look of disgust on her face, Gabby bit her lower lip. "Of course, he is. I need to stop defending Jeff. He is a jerk. He's worse than that…I mean…in the beginning, he seemed like the best guy. Kind, thoughtful, always watching over me. Protective. Maybe a little overprotective, but at the time I liked that. He made me feel safe. When the violence started, I thought it was my fault."

"Oh, please," Ruth protested.

Gabby shrugged, as if in apology. "Well, I know, but he said I provoked him and that if I acted better, he wouldn't have to—"

"Oh, dear, no!" Ruth slammed down her fork so hard that her plate rattled and a piece of toast went flying. "You've wiped that foolishness out of your head, I hope."

Maybe not, Ruth realized when Gabby didn't answer. Instead, the younger woman pushed clumps of egg around with her fork. She speared a piece of bacon and cracked the end off between her teeth. When she finally spoke again, her voice was barely a whisper. "I don't think it's my fault, but sometimes I wonder if it's both of us. If we're toxic together."

"I see." Ruth paused a moment and considered that. She picked up the errant toast and threw it to Ginger, who caught it midair and then carried it back to her cushion. "You know, it doesn't matter if you annoy each other. I mean, most married couples do. I'm assuming you don't give him black eyes?"

Gabby shook her head.

"Well, then, we've got a clear villain in this sordid tale, don't you think?"

A long sigh and Gabby stared at her unfinished plate.

"You know, I might sound like I have the wisdom of the ages, but I honestly don't have the world figured out," Ruth murmured. "No matter how old I get, some things escape me. One of the big ones is understanding why folks who are supposed to love other folks do such horrible things to them."

At that, Gabby exhaled and nodded.

Then Ruth asked the question Gabby dreaded most: "Will this jerk come looking for you?"

Contemplating how to answer, Gabby slowly stood and made her way to the sliding glass doors. Looking out over the deck, she saw that the San Bernard had crept back overnight until it was nearly within its banks. Assessing the strong ebb and flow of the current, Gabby debated if she needed to tell Ruth everything. Did she have to explain why she was so afraid? Not a soul to be seen outside, the neighbors' houses were far off in the distance. Gabby felt as if she'd traveled thousands of miles away from her condo, away from Jeff. Perhaps she could be honest without confessing it all. But she couldn't leave Ruth entirely in the dark. It wouldn't be fair to deny the danger. "Yes. Jeff will try to find me."

"And if he does?"

"He's told me dozens of times what he'll do to me if I try to leave him."

"And that is?"

Gabby's voice went flat. "If Jeff finds me, he'll kill me."

Tears she'd held back spilled onto Gabby's bruised face, and when she turned to Ruth, her hands were splayed out in a plea. "But Ruth, if I could stay here, with you, how would Jeff find me? You and I have no connection. How could that ever happen?"

At a loss for anything else to say, Gabby kept silent, waiting for a reply. But Ruth didn't respond. Instead, she put both hands on the tabletop and cautiously pushed up onto her feet. Methodically, she began clearing the plates from the table. Nervous, not knowing what to expect, Gabby returned her gaze to the river, fighting to find calm in crystals of sunlight glittering on the surface. Moments passed until she felt Ruth's eyes on her. This time when Gabby turned toward her, Ruth's eyes were dark, her face twisted in pain. She said nothing.

"I—" Gabby stopped after that one word. It felt as if Ruth's emotions were so present, so intense, Gabby could have reached out and touched them. Based on the older woman's demeanor, Gabby concluded that she had no hope of convincing her. It seemed the kindest thing to do was to let her be. "Ruth, please don't be upset. I understand. I appreciate that you let me stay the night. I won't trouble you more. I'll be on my way."

Resigned, Gabby was walking toward the bedroom to gather her things, when Ruth uttered a single word: "No!"

Turning back, Gabby found Ruth's appearance unchanged, her jaw still rigid, her eyes stern. Assuming that she'd misunderstood and didn't realize that Gabby had agreed to leave, she again tried to put her at ease. "It's okay, Ruth. Really it is. I'll go. I'll—"

"No, you won't," Ruth announced, the dry, gravelly tenor of her voice leaving no room for argument.

"But—"

Ruth shook her head and muttered, "It worries me, I can't deny it, that the jerk you're married to will search for you. But I will *not* sit here alone, in this empty house with nothing but my thoughts, and wonder where you are, if he's found you."

"Ruth, I—"

"Or worse yet, what he's done to you."

"But—"

"Gabby!" Ruth shouted, and the younger woman swallowed the words left unsaid. When Ruth spoke again, her voice was softer. "Once I needed help, and no one came. I will not let that happen to you."

Relief flooded through her, but Gabby was unsure what to say. Stunned, she assessed Ruth's demeanor, the fiery look in her eyes.

As if she understood that Gabby felt confused by her reaction, Ruth rotated her head slowly, side to side, frowning. "That I will not abide. If I sent you packing and something happened to you? That I could never live with."

As grateful as Gabby was, she felt conflicted. She thought of what Ruth had said the night before, that nothing was impossible. "But if, somehow, I don't know how, Jeff comes—"

Ruth's frown pinched downward. "We'll figure that out when…if it happens."

Tears in her eyes, Gabby shuffled toward Ruth to thank her.

"None of that," Ruth said, waving dismissively at her. "Bring the rest of your things inside. Put them in that back bedroom, the one you slept in. Feel free to use the dresser. Once the ground dries some, we can hide your car under the house."

"Ruth, I can't tell you how much—"

Ruth cut her off. "Gabby, we all need help sometimes. Every one of us. Let's just get you moved in."

"Thank you." Gabby fought the urge to hug the old woman. As fragile as Ruth appeared, Gabby worried that she might hurt her. For the first time since she'd walked out of her condo door, she felt as if she could breathe.

The last of Gabby's misgivings eased when Ruth admitted, "The truth is that it'll be good having you here. I get lonely."

"I can't begin to tell you how grateful I am, what this means to me. You're literally saving my life."

"I…well, let's just say we'll be taking care of each other for a little while."

Turning on the water in the sink, then squeezing in a blob of dish soap, Ruth said, "And I do need the help, Gabby. I know that. But I can't afford to pay you much."

"Ruth, you don't need to pay me anything. I'll do everything I can for you, and when you want me to leave, I will. If I can just hide here long enough to figure out what to do next, it will be a godsend."

"Then, that's our arrangement. You can stay here with me. How long, we'll figure out. While you're here, you'll pitch in around the house. Help me clean this mess up." Ruth wiped her hands on a dishcloth, then held the right one out to Gabby.

"Deal," she said, giving Ruth's hand a gentle shake.

HALF AN HOUR later, Gabby had finished washing the dishes and opened the top dresser drawer to put away her clothes, only to find it packed tightly with old papers, documents, and photographs.

"What should I do with all these things in the dresser?" she called out to Ruth. Gabby picked up an aged photograph of a young girl in an old-fashioned one-piece swimsuit sitting next to a man on a stone wall. She noticed a trailer of some kind in the background. Looking closer, Gabby realized that the girl resembled Ruth and then that the man shared her bow-shaped lips, her heavy eyelids. Ruth's father?

"Pile everything up in my office," Ruth shouted back.

As instructed, Gabby emptied the top drawer, taking out the paperwork and photos and stacking them together. In the next drawer, she came upon old newspaper clippings. Gabby carefully shuffled those into order as well, to make it easier to carry the stacks. The tattered edge of one crumbled in her hand, and she slowed and took more care. When she did, she skimmed snatches of the articles, all cut out of *The Peoria Star*. The bylines read, "Photography and article by Ruth Robertson."

# CHAPTER SIX

**Peoria, Illinois**

**1921**

"YOU NEED TO start working with me," Dad announced one morning. "Together the two of us can make some good money."

I didn't object, although I still had two years of high school ahead. I felt older than my girlfriends, who talked of dates and dances, giggled over boys. Instead, Dad's suggestion intrigued me. My refuge was my camera. It had become my eyes, and I was most comfortable seeing the world through its lens.

For the next five years, Dad and I traveled central Illinois, two aging, swaybacked horses saved from the glue factory pulling our trailer. Although I no longer attended classes, I spent my days in one school after another, helping my father photograph the students. Afterward, I closed the heavy curtains that sectioned off the makeshift darkroom and developed our day's work.

By then, my father's nighttime assaults had ended.

Perhaps the reason was simply that I'd grown and was no longer a powerless child. I'd never ceased crying and pushing him away, fighting him off me. In the daylight, we never spoke of it, of what he had done, and I told no one. I was too humiliated, first that my father would do such things to me and secondly that I never knew how to stop him.

Instead, Dad and I resembled actors playing parts, he the loving father, the artist and photographer. Me? The devoted daughter, the young photographer in training.

Money came in, and we rented a storefront in west Peoria on Adams Street. We turned it into a studio. I was of age, but I didn't leave. This was the only home I knew. Dad was my only family.

On the walls, we hung our photographs and Dad's oil paintings, little yellow tags announcing their prices. For the first year, we lived in the trailer parked in the dirt lot behind the building, and then we rented our first real home, a two-bedroom apartment. Dad still drank more than he should have and too often ended up sleeping it off in a jail cell. He had a part-time job as a motorcycle cop, so they all knew him at the station. More mornings than I can remember, I was called to bring him home.

Instead of my parent watching over me, I increasingly became my father's caretaker.

Although the sadness and secrets haunted me, I pushed them aside, resolute about not wallowing in what others had thought of me or done to me. To the world, I was an exuberant young woman with a big smile, sable brown hair, and gray eyes with a hint of whimsy. I looked wholesome and happy, as if I'd grown up without harm. In truth, I had survived. That was all that mattered. And that I, no one else, was in control of my future. Other girls, friends of mine, married and had children. In my twenties, I dated, listened to a few flowery proposals, but refused commitment.

Better to stay unencumbered. The one man I had loved was my father, and he had proved untrustworthy.

Then, in my early twenties, just as our lives were improving, the Great Depression hit Peoria with all the force of a war.

Our neighbors hoed up their yards to plant vegetable gardens, stores closed, and—with no jobs to report to—men idled aimlessly on porches. On the outskirts of town, camps sprang up in the woods, tent cities occupied by those whose homes and farms had been foreclosed on. The families stayed a while, but then most moved on. Some rode off in dilapidated trucks and cars, others hopped trains to California and Montana in search of work. Without money for teachers' salaries, many schools closed. Dad and I took photos at the ones that stayed open, but the children arrived on picture day wearing frayed clothes with holes.

Dad and I suffered too. We were unable to sell his paintings, and photography jobs became scarce. We had little money for food, none for any extravagance. Like most of our neighbors, we qualified for assistance. Much of the day, I spent standing in long lines to get government butter, eggs, and cheese. At home, we made every scrap count by never wasting a leftover. When our clothes wore out, I sewed patches, redid hems, darned socks.

The years wore on, but my world remained unchanged. I felt as if I still hadn't begun to live, at least not the life I'd planned. Despite everything, I held fast to my dreams.

ANOTHER COUPLE OF years passed, times still hard, and one evening the corner bar was nearly empty when I dropped in for a rare drink with a group of friends, one a reporter at the *Peoria Star*. We gabbed about the bad economy and the high school's winning baseball team. "We're doing more sports coverage, running more photos," he casually mentioned. "Looks like we're going to add another photographer to the staff."

"I might like that," I said, trying not to sound too eager.

My friend looked a bit surprised. "Well, I guess you could talk to the editor."

The next morning, I dropped my slip over my head. It glided easily over the stockings I'd bartered to get. To save the thirty-eight cents they charged at the stores in town, I took a portrait of a friend and traded for the pair. The seams straight, I wiggled into my black pumps and fastened the straps around my ankles. I'd polished my old shoes to a dull gloss. I wore my best dress, pale blue with a frilly collar I tied into a bow at the neck. With my purse on my arm, I stepped out of the door carrying a folder filled with my photos.

Walking through downtown, I passed boarded-up storefronts and families queuing up at the soup kitchen. I considered what the editor would ask and what I'd say. I pondered how I'd handle his biggest objection, the one I knew would come. I tried out different responses, mumbling as I walked. Two young boys rushed past, one bouncing a red ball, and the taller one turned back and shot me a curious look.

Apparently, I wasn't talking as quietly as I'd thought.

In the newsroom, phones rang and cigarette smoke drifted up to the overhead lights as men in white dress shirts hunched over typewriters. I opened my folder on the editor's desk and fanned out samples of my work. "I've been at this photography game a long time—portraits and candid shots. I know my way around a darkroom, and I can cover anything you need. Anything at all."

The gray-haired man behind the desk frowned. "We don't have

women photographers."

The first complete sentence he'd uttered was the protest I'd expected. But I was prepared. I wanted this job, and I'd fight for it. "How about a bargain? I'll work for free. Absolutely free. I'll show you what I can do, with the understanding that if I do a good job for you, when the next job opens up, you'll hire me."

There was a gleam in the editor's rheumy eyes. A staffer who didn't collect a paycheck appealed to him, so it surprised me when he shook his head. "Not gonna work. The guys in the newsroom won't put up with some gal taking photos to go with their stories." His voice rose at the thought of so unconventional an arrangement. "Newspapering is a man's job."

"So, give me some features to work on at first, the softer stuff. I'll develop my film at home and drop off the photos. They'll hardly even see me. You know, the out-in-the-sticks stuff no one wants to travel to. What do you have to lose?"

I expected another rebuff. The editor's frown was exaggerated to the point that I concluded he was trying to make sure I saw it. "Well...you know, we could use someone to cover farm country."

I jumped in, not giving him time to reconsider. "Now you have a photographer to do that. And you don't even need to pay me. But if I prove myself, I get a job down the line. That's the agreement."

Closing the deal, I held out my hand. He reacted as if I were offering him a spoiled fish. The guy scowled some, but he hoisted up onto his feet and looked me dead in the eye, then we shook on it.

"OKAY, SO LET'S have all of you together over here," I said, pointing at the store's front door. "Have you got the ribbon?"

The men stared at me, as if unsure. "Ribbon?"

"A ribbon to cut, to open the new store. That's what I'm here for, right? A ribbon cutting?"

Minutes later, one of their wives delivered a green satin sash. "Don't cut through, just act like you're going to. It's from my favorite dress."

The men posed proudly, one with scissors in hand, its blades poised over the sash. No call of praise from anyone at the *Star*, but the next day it was the top photo on the local section under a headline that read, "New Dry Goods Store Opens Doors."

Between newspaper assignments, I worked with Dad. We moved again, renting a dilapidated house on Rock Island Avenue, one with a yard full of fruit trees and a rose bush climbing a trellis near the front door. Before long, we had six stray dogs, including a blind German shepherd named Bonnie.

The second year, the editor assigned me events in Peoria proper. Despite the change, I still developed and printed my photographs at home, then delivered them to the front desk. But increasingly my work showed up on the newspaper's front page, above the fold. When I dropped off my assignments, I tried to catch the editor's eye. It seemed obvious that he was as busy trying to avoid me. When our paths did cross, he waved me away. "Too busy to talk," he barked. The following year, I heard that the paper was replacing a photographer who planned to retire.

It was time to take a stand.

"I kept my part of the bargain," I said after I'd finagled my way into the newsroom and shown up at his desk. "Now it's your turn."

"You know, I just don't think the boys will…" he started, but then he blurted it out. "Robertson, you know that the men will have a cow if I hire a girl photographer! You can't expect them to put up with that!"

"I can," I said, frowning back at him. "And I expect you to live up to your handshake. We made a deal."

The editor openly glared at me, a nervous tic pulling at his right eye.

My first task as a full-fledged newspaper photographer, one collecting the impressive sum of fifty dollars a month on the company payroll, was to photograph John Barrymore, in town to promote his new movie. When the editor told me, I fought back a grin that would have been the talk of the newsroom. I knew the men gathered around getting their assignments were watching. They would have loved to gossip about the girl photographer who squealed with delight over the handsome movie star.

That didn't diminish my excitement when I arrived at the theater. I was ushered hurriedly into a room, a reporter beside me with his pen poised to grab some quotes.

"Mr. Barrymore, this is such an honor," I said.

"Yes, yes, my dear girl," he said, waving me off. "Please hurry. I have commitments!"

As the reporter fired off questions and I lined up my shots, I reminded myself that this wasn't a dream. Barrymore was one of the greats, a legend, and he was posing for me, raising his head and turning ever so slightly to show off his famous profile.

I pinched myself as I left the theater.

GRADUALLY, HOME PLAYED an ever-smaller part in my life. Instead, the newspaper became my world. I arrived early each morning and left late in the evenings, dropping in on my days off, afraid something important would break just after I stepped out the door.

"Hey, Ruth, did you hear about this Amelia Earhart gal?" one of the men shouted when I walked into the newsroom one day after covering a meeting at city hall. A year earlier the big news had been Charles Lindbergh's first solo flight across the Atlantic, the skies replacing the American West as the new frontier. "Who would've thought she could do it?"

A clutch of reporters was gathered around the radio, and the entire newsroom pulsed with excitement. "Today history was made!" a disembodied voice blared. The plane Earhart left on from Newfoundland twenty hours and forty minutes earlier had touched down in South Wales, making her the first woman to fly across the Atlantic. "The lady from Kansas has become the new queen of the air!"

I sidled up beside the men and studied their faces. I saw their admiration as the radio reporter described the landing and the small band of locals who greeted the airplane, how Earhart climbed out, tore off her leather pilot's helmet, and threw her arms triumphantly into the air. "Lady Lindy," the *Star* called Earhart in a banner headline.

When she returned to the States, our paper ran front-page photos of Amelia waving at the crowds during a New York ticker-tape parade. But when she gave interviews, she admitted that she felt like baggage on the flight. Although she had a pilot's license, a man had flown the plane. Her fame spread, but I knew what she meant. I, too, felt that people judged my abilities based solely on my sex.

In the newsroom, some men were friendly, but others grumbled when the editor told them to cover assignments with me. "You think a girl can work the field?" one of the guys challenged on a day I drew a gig photographing a high school football game.

"No problem," I said, but he smirked and walked away.

One man ridiculed me under his breath. "I bet she's a ball breaker."

Another muttered, "Robertson oughtta be home raising a brood of rug rats."

Yet I had hope as the headlines covered the achievements of a growing number of women. President Franklin Roosevelt appointed Frances Perkins as the first female cabinet official. Molly Dewson, who'd helped enact the nation's first minimum wage act in Massachusetts, played a major role in his 1932 presidential campaign. Of them all? The most famous was Earhart. When she landed safely in Derry, Northern Ireland, on May 21, 1932, she became the first woman to solo nonstop across the Atlantic. Celebrations erupted around the world. The US Congress and the French government awarded her medals. Watching it unfold, I told no one. They would have judged it silly, and perhaps it was, but I couldn't shake the feeling that I was in that airplane with her, not physically but in spirit.

In the newsroom, the men toasted her success, and I felt nearly giddy.

AT TWENTY-SEVEN-YEARS-OLD, I'D been with the paper for going on seven years. One day I tracked down the editor, and as soon as I walked in his office, he gave me an eye roll worthy of Groucho Marx. "Okay, Robertson. Now what do you want?"

"I have an idea. I want to write a regular column, short pieces to run with photos I'll take of regular folks. Kind of a spotlight on the guy and gal next door."

"Why would we do that? Nah. Not gonna happen."

I thought of what Amelia Earhart would do, how she might respond, and I took the photos and did the interviews on my own.

"I told you no," the editor said, his patience clearly frayed, when I spread them out on his desk. Then he paged through sample pieces on a brick mason, a waitress, a switchboard operator and a schoolteacher, an insurance salesman and a bank president. They were the ones who intrigued me, the salt-of-the-earth folks who lived far from the front pages. No one ever asked them what they thought of their world, of their lives.

My boss reconsidered. The people in my photographs were his subscribers. They paid their bills once a month at the newspaper's front desk, and each day they picked the latest edition up off their front porches. He christened my column "Peoria and Her People."

BUSY YEARS PASSED, and I was in my early thirties. Then came that awful day—July 2, 1937.

That morning I collected Dad again from the city jail. "Ah, Ruthie, you've come for me!" he said, feigning surprise when they walked him out to meet me. "Such a good girl, I have. A father's blessing!"

The cop at the front desk grinned at our happy reunion, and I thought, *If you only knew.* But I said nothing, just led him to the car and shepherded him home.

Afterward, with the Fourth of July two days away, I headed to the cemetery. I'd decided to shoot a patriotic profile for my column, and I tracked down the maintenance man who put flags on the veterans' graves. "It's an honor," he said, and I had my pen and pad out writing down the quote. "I'd do this for free, just to make sure the men who served our country are recognized."

The man smiled proudly for my camera, and I snapped him holding a spread of three small flags. Although it was a rather generic quote, it was red, white, and blue, and readers would love it.

Afterward as I rushed into the newsroom to collect my assignments for the next day, I thought about the date, that my twelfth anniversary with the newspaper approached. I wondered if I was up for another raise. They'd been steady if small, but with Dad not working much, every dollar helped. I decided to ask for one, when I saw the editor hurrying by. "When you get a chance, I'd like to—" I started, but he went from a walk to a run.

"No time now. Didn't ya hear?"

"Hear what?"

"Earhart. That damn fool woman's missing somewhere in the Pacific!"

The reporters in the newsroom saw it only as another big story. The presses stopped rolling while they reset the front page, putting a photo of Amelia front and center, a smaller photo of her navigator, Fred Noonan, who'd disappeared with her, tucked into the text. That night, I never left the newsroom. Instead, I waited and hid my tears. When the first copies slapped down on the reception desk, I grabbed one. As a young girl, I'd run my hand over a photo of New York's Grand Central and fantasized that it had the power to transport me there. Now I did the same to the *Star*'s front page, wishing I could will Amelia Earhart safely home.

For weeks, even months, I arrived at work and headed first to the copy desk, looking for breaking news, hoping they'd found her alive and well. Search parties spread out, and theories proliferated: that Amelia was dead, that the Japanese had taken her prisoner, that she was marooned on some unknown island. Like the world, I waited and prayed. I wondered what I could learn from a woman who broke boundaries, one who ignored the rigid lines society drew in the sand.

At night, I dreamed of Amelia Earhart, fleeting images, and I woke up yearning for adventure.

A year passed, and no news came; my hero's photo and name faded from page-one headlines. I was left with an empty feeling and the realization that time was limited for us all. We had today; all else was uncertain. One afternoon, I drove to the airport to watch airplanes taking off and landing but instead followed a sign to a shack that advertised "Flying Lessons Here."

That same afternoon, I sat for the first time in the cockpit of a sweet little trainer, my instructor beside me, as the plane's propellers whipped through wisps of clouds, climbing higher and higher into the sky. My heart opened, and my mind expanded with the horizon. I gazed down at the earth below, and for the first time in my life, I felt as if the future was boundless. No one else guided the plane; no one else made the decisions. My fate was my own.

"Earns Her Wings," the headline read. Four years after Amelia's disappearance, I became a licensed pilot. "Just like that Earhart gal!" Dad said when he held the paper the next morning, a picture of his thirty-six-year-old daughter wearing a leather pilot's cap with goggles perched on the crown.

At fifty-nine, Dad could have been taken for a decade older. The drink and cigarettes had given him a loose croak of a cough; his skin had turned slightly gray, and the whites of his eyes had yellowed. "You showed them, Ruthie, didn't ya, girl?" he said proudly.

I didn't explain that I had no intention of showing anyone or of proving anything. I wanted to live my life to the fullest, and the thrill of flying an airplane above the city and the surrounding farms made me feel as if I could take on whatever the world threw at me. I soared over downtown Peoria, high above the *Star* office, and I pictured the reporters and photographers I worked with milling around in the newsroom.

I thought that it must have felt like this for Amelia. In the air she was free.

HEADLINES UNFOLDED, AND I watched them take shape in the newsroom and on the paper's front page. But the Sunday afternoon the world stopped, I was in the backyard, reading the latest Agatha Christie. Just at the point Hercule Poirot cleared his throat to solve the mystery, Dad shouted, "Ruthie, come inside. Listen to this!"

In the living room, he had the radio on, the dogs clustered around him, and he turned up the volume. "From NBC News, New York. The Japanese have bombed Pearl Harbor, Hawaii."

Half an hour later, I rushed into the newsroom as the editor shouted, "We need local angles! I want to know how this'll affect our folks at home."

Camera in hand, I headed out to knock on the door of a couple with three sons in the army. "We haven't heard from our boys, so we're not sure what this means, but we're afraid that they'll be going off to war," the father said. I made sure the angle of my shot caught his wife clutching his hand in a death grip. Back in the darkroom, once the photo was printed, I noticed tears in her eyes.

In the week that followed, I was assigned to cover a chamber of commerce meeting and a groundbreaking, while men lined up at the enlistment center, and in the newsroom a few of my male colleagues filled out applications to become war correspondents. Before long, they shipped out to the European and Pacific fronts. I submitted my application to my editor. "You want to go where?"

"To the war. To cover it."

He laughed. "You know, Robertson, at some point, you need to realize that you're a woman." He handed the form back to me unsigned, as if I had as much commonsense as a sparrow.

"I know I'm a woman. But what you're forgetting is that I'm a damn good photographer and reporter," I said, but he didn't answer.

That was that, I feared, but weeks later, I heard about the WACs, the Women's Army Corps, a force of women working as army mechanics, bakers, and office workers to free the men up to fight. "There's a good story here," I argued. "I want to interview the women and write a feature."

The editor turned me down again.

Frustrated, I took my vacation and head-ed to Iowa on my own. I interviewed the women at Camp Dodge, snapped their photographs, and wrote an article. From there, I drove to Chicago and displayed my work on the desk of the ACME Newspictures bureau chief, a mustached man with round glasses and slicked-back dark hair named Art Neumann.

"This is good. Very good," he murmured as he read it. "I'll take it."

I had a hard time not letting my grin give away just how happy he'd made me. "That's great."

Art shot me a sideways glance, "So, how about working for us?"

It didn't take much to convince me.

After fifteen years with the *Star*, I tendered my resignation. In the newsroom, the reporters gathered around and wished me well. At the house, Dad seemed uncertain as I packed my bags, but he didn't ask who would take care of him. I worried about that as I drove off. All he'd done to me, all I'd been through with him, he was still my father. I was still that little girl who'd loved him too much to tell. But as I drove away from Peoria, the clouds lifted, and I knew I'd never look back.

NO MORE SMALL-TOWN politics and store openings. In Chicago, I covered the big stories, the ones the newswires cared about. My press badge hung from a lanyard around my neck, and it became my ticket inside the Democratic National Convention. On the second day, the president and first lady sat for a photo. Gruff, Franklin Roosevelt shooed off his attendants, to get them out of the way.

"Let's make this quick!" he grumbled.

Meanwhile, his wife coached me on how to take my shot. I dropped down on a knee to shoot up, and she insisted I stand. "If you take my photo from up high, looking down on me a bit, it helps soften this," Eleanor instructed, patting the ruffle under her chin. I strained up onto my tiptoes, as she'd suggested. "Now isn't that better?"

Each morning, I stopped at the neighborhood newsstand and bought every paper with one of my photographs on its front page, from Los Angeles to Boston. In my cubbyhole office, I stacked them on top of my desk. In time, I had to move the mound of newspapers to the floor and start a second pile. My confidence built, day to day, as the towers grew.

The world traveled at warp speed like the movies, from the silent pictures, to talkies, and then Technicolor. Art Neumann gave me a nickname, one that would stick with me the rest of my life—Robbie, short for Robertson. And one day he handed me a promotion, making me chief of the St. Louis bureau. Buzzing about the possibilities, I was at the same time disappointed.

War dominated the news as we awaited details on where bombs dropped, how many died, where and how the battles unfolded. As a reporter, I itched to be a voice in the dialogue. Despite my success, it rankled that I was stuck covering the home front.

"I know you want that war correspondent's badge, but that's not what ACME needs," Art admitted late one afternoon when I drove to Chicago for a chat. "Robbie, the bosses really want you to work St. Louis."

"I know. But that's just not doing it for me. I want more."

We knocked around possibilities, talked about the higher-ups at ACME, the reporting scene, colleagues, and the war. Then Art, an awkward man with bloodshot eyes and a habit of pulling on his right earlobe when nervous, floated a possibility. "So, there is something I've been thinking about."

"What's that?"

Art looked a bit sheepish when he suggested, "How about the two of us start our own agency?"

"Our own agency?"

"If we do that, we can send you overseas. You shoot the photos, write articles to go with them, and I'll stay here in Chicago and sell them."

"Well…" As risky as it was to quit my job for what might turn out to be a pipe dream, the idea had appeal. I had a little money in the bank, not a lot but enough to tide me over for a few months, and that made me brave. "What would we call it?"

"I'm thinking Press Syndicate."

I considered it only a few minutes before I said, "You know, I like that. You've got a deal."

The rest of that evening, we talked plans, the main one to get me overseas as soon as possible as one of the first women photographers covering the war.

Within a week, Art had opened a small office, and I'd applied to the war department and asked to be accredited as a correspondent. Weeks later, my approval arrived in my mailbox. I tore it open, elated, but then noticed something odd.

"Alaska?" Art questioned when I called to tell him. "They're sending you to Alaska?"

"Yup. I'm so disappointed. Why would they—"

"Robbie, that's great!"

"You're kidding, Art, right?"

"No! The war against the Japanese is being staged there," he said. I grew hopeful as I heard the delight in his voice. "The bosses at ACME are hot to get someone on the ground, but they keep getting turned down. Now the army is inviting you to Alaska? This is big. Bigger than big. Robbie, this is giant."

# CHAPTER SEVEN

**Brazoria County, Texas**

**March 1993**

FINISHED UNPACKING, GABBY found Ruth asleep in her armchair, tossing her head and mumbling. She wondered what visions Ruth's dreams brought, perhaps of fishing off the pier, of a lost love, or of friends and family long dead.

To get busy and take her mind off Jeff, Gabby considered clearing off the couch and end tables, organizing some of Ruth's old papers, but she worried that the bustle would wake Ruth. Instead, Gabby tried to relax on the deck, but the bucolic scenery did nothing to erase her fears. Closing her eyes, she was back in the condo on that terrible night, huddled on the living room floor while Jeff stood over her brandishing the broken coffee-table leg. Opening her eyes, she shuddered.

Antsy, worried, she felt as if she might crack open if she didn't find a way to wear off her nervous energy.

Spotting a tennis ball on the floor, Gabby lured Ginger outside, easing the door soundlessly shut behind her. In the side yard, Gabby wound up and threw, and the terrier sprinted off, weaving around the fallen branches the storm had left behind. Success, and Ginger dropped the yellow ball, dripping with saliva, at Gabby's feet. Pretending to scoff at the terrier, Gabby shook it and threw again.

Time passed, but nothing seemed to be helping—not the fresh air, Ginger's companionship, or the pastoral setting. Gabby's nerves bristled. *I need to do something. Anything.*

Back inside the house, she wrote a note she left on the kitchen table: "Ruth, I'll be back soon. Gabby"

Worried about her car being spotted, she decided to walk to the convenience store to return Nick's umbrella and thank him. The thanking him part was the most important. If he hadn't urged Ruth to meet with her, Gabby might still be driving around searching for a place to stay.

Halfway down the driveway, she eyed Ruth's shed, wondering what was hidden inside. The metal door creaked as she pushed it open. Potting and yard supplies. A lawnmower. Against the wall stood a bicycle that had started out light blue, but rust and age had eaten away all but a trace of paint. The tires were flat, and she assumed they were full of holes, but she searched the grimy shelves and discovered a hand pump behind a thick veil of cobwebs. She had to oil the pump to get it to work, but to her surprise, the tires inflated. Minutes later, wearing her oversized sunglasses and a bill cap pulled down to hide her face, she peddled onto the road with Nick's umbrella tied to the seat. Weaving in and out, she dodged fallen branches, and off and on she spotted Ruth's neighbors cleaning debris. Watching them, she thought about the mess at Ruth's place, not only the twigs and branches but the dead fish the receding river had left behind. *I'll have to get to work, get it cleaned up,* she decided as she passed a massive oak the storm had pulled out of the sodden ground, its roots a tangled ball.

A mile or so ahead, Gabby swerved onto the shoulder to avoid a speeding pickup. Once the truck was out of sight, she strained to pedal up the hill. At the top, she took a sharp left onto the store parking lot and found Nick climbing into a black Chevy Blazer. When he saw her, he lowered the window and waved. "Hey! What's up?"

It had been years since she'd been on a bike, and Gabby bobbled coming to a stop. Motioning at his umbrella, she shouted, "Thought you might need this."

"I hope not. We've had enough rain for a few days, don't ya think?"

Gabby started to laugh but quickly stopped, pain radiating from her cheek to her bruised eye. "Are you closing up so early?"

"No. I called in a pal to keep the doors open. Not that he'll sell much. I'm not anticipating a run on chewing tobacco or beef jerky."

Once Gabby had leaned the old bike against a tree trunk, she untied the umbrella. "I'm glad I didn't miss you. Where are you going?"

"To the wildlife refuge down the way. Planning to do a little bird watching. Want to come?"

Minutes later, bouncing along on the rough road, Gabby thanked Nick for helping her the day before. "No worries. By the way, how's that eye?"

"I thought you saw it." At first, she hesitated, but then carefully peeled off her sunglasses.

Nick grimaced. "Ouch! That's a bad one."

"Yup. It is."

"You're not going back to that guy, are you?"

"No. Never." But Gabby hesitated. "Not if I can manage it, I'm not."

"Gabby, you can't..." Nick's eyes were full of questions.

Gabby was unsure how to respond. It struck her that even after seeing her eye, Nick didn't fully understand. "The problem is that my husband won't just let me leave. He'll come after me. That means that I've got some things to figure out, mainly how to keep him from finding me."

"Not sure why you'd care what he does." But then, Nick appeared to reconsider. "Although I guess what you're saying is that if he does find you—"

Gabby didn't want to hear the rest and cut him off. "The good news is that Ruth says I can stay with her for a while."

Nick waited for Gabby to say more. When she remained silent, he said, "As long as whatever you decide doesn't take you back to that guy, I'm in favor of it."

"Yeah, well…" Gabby struggled to decide what to say next. She settled on changing the subject. "Have you lived around here long?"

Nick shot her a glance, one that said he understood what she was doing. "Twelve years now. Bought the store and a house downriver after I inherited a little money. I'd been back from Nam for a dozen years or so, having a hard time fitting into society. In hindsight, I would have been better off financially sinking the cash into the stock market. Heck, even burying it in the backyard. But I'm happy here."

Gabby gazed at the scenery outside the car window, the small houses tucked into the woods, the ones on the river on their stilts, and a fenced-in cattle pasture in the distance. "I guess Vietnam was tough."

"Yeah. It was. I did two tours. These days I try not to think about it much."

She sounded as if she were talking about her own troubles when she said, "It's hard sometimes to let go of the bad stuff, to not let it take over your life."

Nick squinted at her. "It gets easier the more time and distance you put between it and you."

Neither one spoke for the rest of the ride, the silence between them strained. Gabby wondered if she'd said too much, and she wondered what would happen if she was wrong. What if she couldn't trust him. Nick seemed like a good guy, but so did Jeff in the beginning. Still, she felt like she didn't have a choice. She needed help. She had to trust someone.

Once out of the truck, they hiked a path through the reserve, past a sign with the park's hours: "Opens at Sunrise. Closes at Sunset." The trail led to a wooden walkway built over the marshes and into the woods. Gabby caught the scent of salt water in the air and felt a slight breeze caress her skin. The branches of the trees surrounding them bent awkwardly, some thrusting toward them like giant elbows.

"Look there," Nick said.

Gabby searched the sky for birds but then realized he was pointing down, not up. Scanning the marsh, she discovered an alligator camouflaged within a bank of tall reeds. Its dark, empty eyes stared back at her.

"Maybe we better leave."

A half smile bunched Nick's cheek. "They're well fed here, lots to eat. He won't bother us if we don't bother him."

"You sure?"

"Yeah." Then he whispered, "Up there."

This time Nick gestured toward a tree off in the distance. He handed her his binoculars, and Gabby saw a bird that resembled a bald eagle, but with a jaunty black swoop of feathers atop its head. "A crested caracara," Nick whispered. "Some folks call them Mexican eagles. Don't often see those. Gabby, I think you brought me luck today."

For the next hour, they walked together, stopping as Nick pointed out birds, trees, a snake slithering through the underbrush. His excitement every time he spotted a new species was infectious. Soon, she wasn't thinking about Jeff and what waited ahead. She asked questions, and she learned that Nick had become interested in birdwatching not long after buying the store, in a bid to push Nam out of his thoughts. "It helped me see the world as beautiful again. Although many of those nights in the Mekong Delta, it could be peaceful. In the mornings, the birds woke us up, birds you don't see here. Spectacular."

"What did you do there?"

"We were keeping an eye out for enemy troops. But mostly I spent my time hoping we didn't find any."

A slight laugh and Gabby decided that Nick Foster seemed to be an easy man to talk to. "You know, I think Ruth was a reporter and a photographer at one time."

Nick considered that for a moment. "I've known her for years, and she's never said anything about her past. I'm surprised she told you."

"She didn't tell me. I just…she suggested I clean out a dresser to put my things in. There were a lot of photographs in there, old black-and-whites, and news articles with the byline 'Ruth Robertson.'"

Nick turned his binoculars on a hawk swooping overhead. "I've always thought of Ruth as an interesting woman."

"How so?"

Nick locked his eyes onto Gabby's, as if sharing a secret. "I've just always believed there's a lot there, a lot in her past."

"Have you ever asked her about her life?"

"No. Maybe I should have, but we're not that kind of friends."

They traveled deeper into the woods, and Nick's face glowed when he talked about the wildlife he'd seen in the park. He looked lit from inside like a kid playing with his first puppy. Then suddenly, he shouted, "Gabby, up to the left! Look at that!"

A cluster of odd-looking birds flew above them, thickly built, white with gray to black necks and heads.

"What are they?"

"Mostly wood storks, some of the most primitive birds in the world. But there's one… It's different. Has an incredible wingspan. Looks like a stork but bigger."

"Which one?"

He passed the binoculars back to her. "Look for the largest, whitest bird."

A moment's search, and she landed on it: a snow-white body, a black head and neck, and what looked like a crimson Adam's apple above its shoulders. As it passed, it let loose a strange, gruff, clacking call.

STILL THINKING OF the birds, curious about Nick, Gabby rode the bike down Ruth's driveway. At the top of the stairs, she tried to open the door, but it wouldn't budge. She rang the bell. Looking disheveled, her white hair mussed, an agitated expression around tightly drawn lips, Ruth peered out through the window. "Yes?"

For a moment, Gabby couldn't understand why Ruth didn't open the door. Then she recalled what Nick had said, that Ruth would get confused off and on.

"Ruth, it's Gabby. Remember? I'm staying with you for a little while."

"Gabby? I don't know a Gabby."

Gabby took her sunglasses off, thinking that might spur a memory. Ruth frowned, and the wrinkles around her mouth deepened. "I'm sorry about your eye, but I don't know you. I think you'd better get off my porch. I've got a gun around here. I can go get it and—"

"Ruth, please. I'm staying here with you. I left you a note on the kitchen table, saying I'd gone out, that I'd be back. Go look in your spare bedroom. There's a red backpack on the floor, my suitcase in the corner."

At first, Gabby didn't think Ruth would do as she'd asked, but then Ruth shuffled off, a look of bewilderment on her tired face. Minutes later, the door opened. "Okay, so tell me again who you are. Are we related?"

The conversation didn't take long. Either the fog had cleared and Ruth truly had remembered, or she simply decided to take Gabby's word for the fact that she was staying with her. Gabby had the impression that Ruth had learned to deal with her memory lapses by not arguing with people.

"Of course, I remember you now, I do. But what did you say your name is?"

"Gabby Jordan."

"That's right. Now I remember. Gabby Jordan."

Later that afternoon, red beans simmered on the stove, and Ruth turned the burner on under a pot of rice, while Gabby worked in the yard, cleaning up the storm debris. After dinner they sat on the deck in two worn metal rockers, gazing out at the river. The San Bernard's receding waters appeared nearly opaque, a murky brown.

"Will the river get clear?" Gabby asked.

"Not completely, but once the silt that washed in during the storm settles, it'll be better."

Before long, Ruth mentioned Gabby's husband by name, and Gabby realized her memory had returned. "Did you fall in love with Jeff right off? You did love him, right?"

"Jeff was intoxicating. I adored him. The first time I saw him, I felt an attraction. My job, my life's always been pretty vanilla. Jeff was exciting. I fell completely under his spell."

Ruth moaned just slightly. "You know, I remember feeling that way about a man once a long, long time ago. So completely in love I thought about changing my life for him."

"Was that Mr. Marietta? Your husband?"

"No," Ruth said. "I loved Chuck in my own way, but I think sometimes I married him because I felt sorry for him. We were good friends. I wanted a husband, a home, and he promised me one. He said he loved me. He told me that I'd fall in love with him eventually. It was a mistake."

"I'm sorry."

"Don't be. Chuck wasn't a bad husband. We had a good life together."

Gabby reflected on Nick's belief that Ruth had an interesting past. She thought about the photographs, the drawers full of newspaper clippings. "I saw your newspaper articles and photographs. Was Ruth Robertson your maiden name?"

Ruth leaned forward and stared at Gabby suspiciously, as if the younger woman had overstepped her bounds. "Where did you see those?"

In a steady voice, Gabby explained, "When I did what you asked me to do and cleared out the dresser drawers, so I could unpack my things."

"Ah." Apparently satisfied, Ruth eased back against her chair.

"Is that where you met this man, the one you fell so madly in love with? While you were working as a reporter?"

Ruth considered that for a few minutes. It had been a long time since anyone had asked about her life. She didn't meet a lot of people, and most of those she did treated her like she'd always been an eccentric old woman living alone on the river. "There was a man I met during World War II when I worked as a reporter in Alaska. I wanted him, like I'd never…" For a moment, Ruth grew silent, and when she spoke again, her voice cracked with emotion. "Maybe it was the war. Wars do that, you know, bring people together. And sometimes tear people apart."

"And you loved him?"

"I did."

"I hope it turned out better than my great romance."

"Eric was my one true love," Ruth said. "But then again, like I said, I wonder sometimes if it may have been as much the excitement of the war."

# Chapter Eight

**Ladd Army Airfield, Fairbanks, Alaska**

**1945**

L ATE ONE AFTERNOON, an envelope waited in my mailbox. Hands shaking with excitement, I ripped it apart. Inside I found a war department letter designating me as correspondent number 2245. Barely an hour later, the phone rang, and Art informed me that he'd asked around. When I got off the plane in Alaska, I'd become the only woman reporter or photographer in that neck of the war. "I want you to write about what you see around you, be our readers' eyes and ears," he told me. "I need your best work on the whole shebang—the effort, the troops, and the local scene."

My uniform arrived next, standard military issue. Trying it on, I stood at the mirror adjusting and readjusting the side cap, looking at it from various angles. I packed and repacked the olive-green, army-issue bags. According to the handbook, I was allowed to bring only sixty-five pounds. I lined up everything on my bed: warm winter clothes, thermal underwear, all my personal items, cameras, and film.

As the time approached, friends called wishing me well. One took a photo of me in my uniform holding one of my cameras with a shiny aluminum flash attachment on top, the glass bulb in the center, and I mailed a copy to my editor back home at the *Peoria Star*. He ran the photo with a local-gal-makes-good article under the headline:

"Former Star Photographer off to Alaska Assignment."

Less than a month before I was scheduled to leave, I walked into the Chicago Press Photographer's Christmas ball in my uniform—a wool skirt and jacket with a badge embroidered with "U.S." on the arm and over the left breast pocket another that read, "War Correspondent." I'd  positioned my cap rather jauntily, I thought, just a tad to the right, my hair in loose brown curls falling to my shoulders. I stood out amid all the folks dressed to the nines, decked out in tuxes and ball gowns.

IN ALL, MY trip north took more than a week. The first flight out in early January was on a military plane to Great Falls, Montana. Once there, I boarded a transport to the Royal Canadian Air Force Station at Watson Lake in the Yukon Territory. I claimed a seat in the cockpit with the pilot, and as we flew over mountains, I saw jagged cliffs blanketed in snow. At each stop, I waited impatiently for the next plane with room to take me farther. At night, I bunked in nurses' quarters and dispensaries, slept on mail pouches in the bellies of cargo planes, and dreamed of Alaska.

On the final leg, I cajoled a seat on the "Klondike Kutey," a mammoth B-29 Superfortress, and we made a safe landing at Ladd Airfield. I glanced out windows as I hurriedly collected my possessions. Living in Peoria and Chicago, I thought I was used to winter, but my breath was taken away by Alaska's extreme cold. It was nearly forty below zero as I walked down the tarmac, a gentle snow falling around me.

One day's rest, and I was hard at work. While getting my bearings on the base, I snapped a shot of two privates in the utilidors, underground tunnels that connected the base library, movie theater, command headquarters, mess hall, and hospital. Steam pipes ran along the sides, radiating heat. As frigid as it was outside, I wiped sweat off my brow. The salty liquid stung my eyes and clouded my vision as I knelt to take my shot.

Before long, I was making early morning runs over the Kuril Islands, where the Japanese had tens of thousands of soldiers fighting allied troops. In stiff arctic winds, the planes shuddered, and I held on tight, straining to keep my balance, as navigators computed coordinates radioed in from the base. Once the crews locked onto targets, they pushed the Fire buttons. I lined up my best angles through the windows, recording the scene as the bombs fell, hit, and exploded. Watching the action, I wondered about the battles taking place beneath us. From the air, it looked innocent enough, like clouds of dust and dirt, nothing but debris. But I knew how real the war was, that below me men on both sides lay gravely hurt, some dying.

Day and night, airlifts came into Ladd field carrying the injured, men missing arms and legs, their bodies held together by paramedics' hasty stitches. In my off hours, I walked the tunnel to the hospital, leaving my camera behind in my room. I stopped at the library and picked up a few books on the way. I paused at the nurses' desk to inquire who might be well enough for a visitor. "What would you like to hear?" I asked, holding up the books so the GI could choose what I'd read.

"Could we just talk?" they often asked.

"You bet."

For an hour or more, that's what we did. The soldiers were from San Francisco or Albuquerque, Miami, or some town of less than a hundred in Iowa, and each one seemed grateful for a patient ear, someone willing to listen while they battled back the pain, reminisced about their buddies who didn't make it, or confessed their relief to be going home. When I couldn't stay any longer, I wished them all well and said that someday I hoped to see them again Stateside, after the madness of the war ended.

"Well, what shall we read today?" I asked Jimmy O'Conner from Tulsa, the patient in bed A53. "How about a little Ernest Hemingway?"

With more than half of Jimmy's body wrapped in gauze, blood seeped through and stained it a dark but watery brown. In a deep coma, he rarely moved, except for his eyes, which occasionally flicked open then shut. They were a light green with flecks of gold, and I wondered how much of his face had been spared from the fire onboard his plane. For an hour, I read my favorite chapters from *The Sun Also Rises*, those describing the running of the bulls. I wasn't sure, but off and on, I thought I saw Jimmy smile.

Then came the afternoon that Jimmy's bed was stripped, his name off the board behind the nurses' station. "He shipped home?" I asked, pointing at the bunk. The charge nurse said nothing but shook her head.

I spent the rest of the day in my room, an open book on my lap, unable to read.

Afternoon mail call, and letters arrived from home. All too often, bad news was sandwiched into my friends' accounts of who was recently wed or who had a new job or expected a baby. Reports came of the deaths of friends who'd gone off to fight in the war, men I grew up with in Peoria, others from my years in Chicago. A war correspondent friend died in France.

On Ladd field, the war never seemed as close as when we stood outside in the darkness, holding candles. The patchwork of flames glowed like fallen stars around us as we memorialized one of our own.

One such evening, icy-cold, well below zero, we traded stories about Tony Russo. Earlier that day, he stopped responding to radio messages, and his plane failed to return to the base. A search party recovered Tony's body from the wreckage. No one was sure why the plane dropped out of the sky, but so far north ice formed quickly on wings, and instruments sometimes failed in strong magnetic fields. "We're looking into it," was all I could get out of the officers on the base. "Sorry to lose him. Tony was a good guy, heck of a good pilot."

"I met him on my way here," I explained, trying to hide my tears.

With dark hair and Dean Martin eyes, Tony had flown one of the planes I hitched a ride on. We'd spent a good portion of our hours together concocting scenarios for his marriage proposal to Sally, his girl back home in Brooklyn. The one Tony liked best would have unfolded in Central Park. "I'll sit that girl of mine down on a bench and kneel in front of her," he'd said, a grin cracking his face as he anticipated *that day*. "Then I'll pull out the ring."

I flew out on my next assignment, and the pilot swung over the crash site. Below us, twisted and broken, was a silver wing torn from Tony's plane and charred chunks of the fuselage spread across the white snow. For a moment, we were silent. I thought about Sally and how Tony's proposal would never happen.

When I glanced over, the pilot had his hand up to his forehead in a salute.

AT THE END of each week, I sent my photographs and articles to DC, where army censors cleared and released them. As soon as my work reached Art in Chicago, he peddled it to newspapers and magazines. Cables arrived weekly with new assignments editors had commissioned. Sometimes the subjects had nothing to do with war. Grateful for the break, I'd head out to Eskimo villages and whale hunts.

For a magazine piece, I grabbed an airplane to shoot the northern lights. My face was covered against the extreme cold as my guide mushed the dogs through deep snow. We arrived, and the skies were velvet black, the temperatures glacial. Above me, nature put on an unimaginable show, waves of incandescent green, blue, and red swirling in a strange dance.

My camera loaded, I looked through the viewfinder, careful to make sure that the case didn't touch my face. I'd quickly learned to respect the power of the biting temperatures. If the frozen metal touched my cheek, my skin would freeze and stick. When I pulled it away, a patch of flesh could peel off with it.

My first shot lined up, I pressed the shutter. Nothing happened.

Frantic, I blew on my camera. When that failed, I wrapped it inside my parka, hoping my body heat would warm it, but the shutter was frozen shut. In the white snow, under the dark sky, the stars blazing, I was helpless to do anything but put my camera away and stare in wonder at the swirls of color shimmering above me.

LIFE ON THE base went on.

The door to my quarters was mere yards from the Russian billet. The men, mostly pilots, were part of the Soviet force on the base. Back home in DC, Congress had passed the Lend-Lease Act, agreeing to supply the USSR with equipment, even military aircraft, to be used to fight the Japanese and the Germans. War made strange bedfellows, and the once hated Joe Stalin had become our ally.

In the evenings, I sometimes joined the Russian fliers at a make-shift bar they'd cobbled together in our shared hallway. "For mother Russia!" the man at the bar toasted. He was tall, burly, with a walrus mustache and caterpillar eyebrows.

"For Russia!" I lifted my vodka and took a swig. We refilled, and I added my own toast. "For the United States of America!"

The Russians surrounding me glanced nervously at one another. I figured they weren't sure what to make of me, this short, slight woman reporter who asked them to toast her country. After an anxious pause, their commander laughed and raised his glass. "For U.S. America!" Gulping it down, he slammed his shot glass on the bar. "Another!" he shouted.

Laughing, I excused myself and headed back to my room.

Mornings in the mess hall, I combed through the news racks. Weeks-old papers arrived with headlines about the state of the war in Europe. The battles winding down, Stalin, Winston Churchill, and FDR headed to Yalta to talk peace. Perhaps an end was coming.

If so, at Ladd field little changed. A parade of US airplanes arrived weekly to be outfitted and flown off for the Soviet Union. The bombers left on their morning runs over the islands.

The war in the Pacific raged.

MY TIME IN Alaska moved swiftly, until on a cold April evening, I stood in the central gathering space surrounded by former strangers who'd quickly become my friends—pilots and mechanics, enlisted men and officers—each of us holding a candle at yet another memorial service.

That morning the radio transmission had come in: our president, Franklin Roosevelt, dead of a cerebral hemorrhage.

Around me, many seemed nervous, and I knew that they worried. For twelve years and forty-two days, through the Great Depression, then this massive global war, FDR had set the country's course. What would become of us without him? Somewhere in the crowd, a voice rose, and others joined in singing a hymn familiar from the years when Ma carted me off to church on Sundays.

"O Lord, my God! When I in awesome wonder…"

My mind drifted back to the Democratic National Convention and the day I'd photographed Franklin and Eleanor Roosevelt. I'd just begun my work with the wire services. As I'd eyed the president and first lady through my camera's lens, I thought that I'd arrived, that I'd achieved my goals. But here I was, a war correspondent in a strange place I'd never imagined seeing.

What a journey I had begun.

I was no longer that young girl who cowered in the night, vulnerable and afraid. I had changed. I'd found my voice. As I listened to the crowd singing around me, I instinctively knew that my transformation wasn't done. And I wondered what this war would make of me.

When it ended, who would I become?

# Chapter Nine

## Point Barrow, Alaska

## 1945

"OKAY, NOW LOOK out the right side of the airplane," the pilot said, pointing east. A redhead out of Missouri, somewhere in his thirties, I guessed, he had a road map of freckles over his nose and an exaggerated underbite. "Those are the Diomede Islands directly below us. Right now, we're straddling the international date line. On the right, that's North America, Alaska, and it's Thursday. On the left, you're looking at Russia, and it's Friday."

Seated beside him, I clicked the shutter on my camera. I was surprised at how narrow the Bering Strait was, at the proximity of the two continents. The islands fell smack dab in the center. I tried to conceal my excitement, but inside I was soaring. The exhilaration was intoxicating.

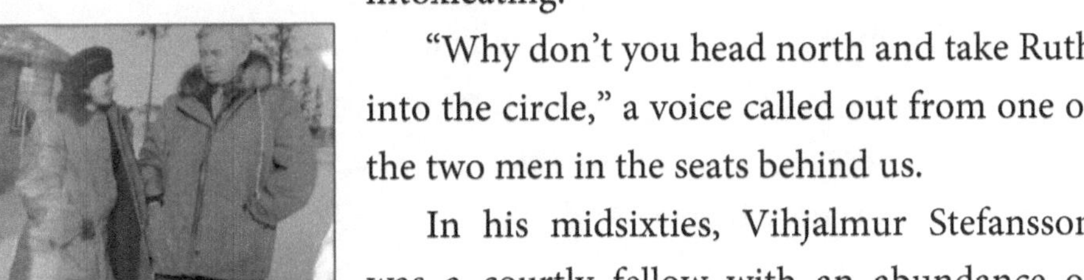

"Why don't you head north and take Ruth into the circle," a voice called out from one of the two men in the seats behind us.

In his midsixties, Vihjalmur Stefansson was a courtly fellow with an abundance of white hair that stood at attention and a prominent mole high on his right cheek. I'd flown to Point Barrow to work on an assignment, to document life at the US's northernmost base, and met Stefansson the evening before at a makeshift officers' bar in the mess hall. He'd already had the flight over the date line arranged and invited me along.

A Canadian explorer who'd spent his life traveling the Arctic, Stefansson had named mountain ranges and rivers and lived in remote Eskimo villages. Early on he'd agreed to advise the Allies on the difficulties of living and working in northern Alaska's extreme climate. "I'm on my way from the Asian front to England for meetings," he'd explained, not going into detail.

At Stefansson's suggestion, the pilot turned from the strait back toward Alaska but kept heading north. We'd flown another hour, maybe more, when he shouted, "Here we go! One, two, three. Four, five, and we're in!"

"In where?" I asked, inspecting views that, at least to me, looked little different from those I'd flown over frequently since arriving in Alaska. In every direction, I saw a carpet of white.

"Well, Miss Ruth Robertson, this is a feat," Stefansson's friend called out, shouting over the whir of the engines. A decade younger than Stefansson, Clayton Knight had flown with Eddie Rickenbacker, America's Ace of Aces, in his Hat in the Ring gang during WWI. A bespectacled man with an amused smile and a long nose, Knight had made a name for himself as a military illustrator in the years that followed. "There aren't a lot of folks who've flown into the Arctic Circle. I bet not more than a handful of women."

"You're kidding," I said.

"Not at all. You're not the first but probably one of the first," Knight insisted. "I'm pretty sure of it."

"Well, I'll be," I said, not even attempting to masquerade my glee.

Stefansson, too, seemed intrigued by his friend's observation. "Ruth, I'm thinking you should be the first, the very first, to fly over the North Pole."

"People already have. What about Admiral Byrd?" I remarked.

"My friend means no women have done it," commented Knight, busy drawing the monochromatic view out the window in his sketch pad. We were all bundled in blankets over our parkas, the cold seeping into the plane.

"Why not?" I asked.

"It's harder to cross the pole than it sounds," he explained. "The instruments aren't always reliable up here, and there's often some question if those who say they've succeeded actually have. Including Byrd, you know."

"Ruth, you should do it," Stefansson said again. "You're an adventurer. I can tell. You'd be in the history books. Young girls would read about how Ruth Robertson was the first woman to fly over the Pole."

I thought about Amelia Earhart, how she'd inspired me. Trying not to let my voice reveal my building enthusiasm, I asked, "Tell me about what you do." Stefansson looked at me, questioning, and I explained, "How you manage it. Where you get the money to mount your expeditions."

Stefansson smiled knowingly at me, and I sensed that he recognized that we had a bond, a mutual curiosity about the world. I pondered his unusual life, the thrill of exploring the unknown. His work had earned him medals and respect. As we talked, my mind swirled with a flood of possibilities, cascading ideas.

THAT EVENING, I stood at the bar in the mess hall along with Knight and Stefansson. Even indoors, I left my parka on. Tiny ice crystals floated on the edges of the glass of champagne in my hand as we talked with the pilot and crew of our plane that day. Stefansson was in a jovial mood. We all were. His pal Knight laughed and cracked silly jokes. Smiling broadly, we toasted my great adventure, my flight into the Arctic Circle. I tried to appear calm but felt nearly dizzy with the wine and the day's adventure.

"I tell you, Miss Ruth Robertson, that you *should* fly across the North Pole," Stefansson goaded. "You can do it."

"You really think so?" I asked, although I did believe him. I just wanted to hear him say it yet again.

"Yes!" Stefansson insisted. "You have the *joie de vivre*."

At that, Knight swooped into an exaggerated bow. "Everyone, meet Miss Ruth Robertson. First woman to cross the Pole."

Laughing, I began to bow at them but changed my mind and swept into a curtsy. "I should do it. I should!"

All around me, the men shouted, "Hail, Miss Ruth Robertson! The first woman to cross the North Pole! Hear, hear!"

Except for a crackling fire in the black metal stove, the room grew quiet. "Now on to more serious matters. We have something for you," Knight said, and the men drummed their palms on the bar, fast, pounding, rat-a-tat-tat, ending in a flourish, as if for a great announcement.

In the hushed room, Knight handed me a sheet of paper, a certificate stipulating that on April first, in 1945, I crossed into the Arctic Circle. By virtue of that accomplishment, I was and would forever more be a member of something called the Order of the Top of the World.

"We all have our certificates, Ruth," Knight explained. "It's an informal group and a small one. You're our first female member. And you're now an official adventurer."

There was a hearty round of con-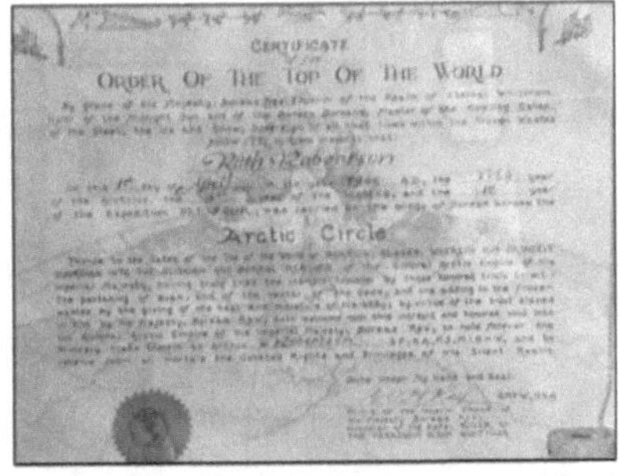gratulations, pats on the back, and soon my companions talked among themselves, while I admired the certificate in my hand. I felt special in a way I rarely had in my life. I glowed from the excitement of the day and considered how unfamiliar this moment was. In the newsroom, I had to fight for every assignment, convince the men in charge that I was capable. I looked around at the faces surrounding me, men who saw me as I was, not first as a woman but as a fellow explorer.

As we celebrated, "A Nightingale Sang in Berkeley Square" played on the phonograph, and a small cadre of officers walked in. I noticed the man in the center instantly. Something about him, the authority he exuded.

At the bar, I sipped my champagne, still chatting with Stefansson, Knight, the pilot, and the navigator. And out of the corner of my eye, I watched the newcomer.

"That's the colonel," the navigator whispered, glancing toward the man at the door. "Eric Eareckson."

"Who?" Knight asked, unimpressed.

"One of the top combat commanders in this part of the world, on Admiral Chester Nimitz's staff. A West Point grad. A hero of the battle for Attu Island," the navigator explained. "They gave him the Navy Cross and the Distinguished Service Cross."

"Yeah, but remember why he got them?" the pilot countered, accompanied by a soft puff of scorn.

Intrigued, I glanced over at the man. "What do you mean by 'how he got them'?"

The pilot had a pained expression as if this wasn't a good story. "Eareckson is an outstanding tactician. He fought in WWI, was a balloon pilot. When planes took over, he revolutionized air warfare. But he's a maverick, doesn't like red tape. Takes a lot of risks."

At that, the navigator's expression suggested he viewed what he was about to say as pure folly. "Damn fool flew so low in Attu, Japanese gunners shot at his plane and hit it. That was his plan, of course, to get them to give up their positions. Our bombers moved in and picked them off."

Again, I snuck a look at Eareckson who chatted amiably with the men around him. I wondered if what I'd just heard was true and what kind of man would do such a thing.

"Talk about gung ho! On the ground, the colonel grabbed a rifle and joined the infantry on the front lines. He was shot. Nearly died," the pilot said with a snort of indignation. "The troops love him. The brass? They don't want their best officers needlessly risking their lives. Eareckson's been up for brigadier general but never gotten it. Never will. The brass sees him as a wild card."

"The guy's his own worst enemy," the navigator agreed. "He's got multiple talents. Number one is that Eric Eareckson is damn good at sabotaging his own career."

Glancing yet again at the man standing near the door, I reflected on someone so brave (*or was it foolhardy?*) that he'd flown over enemy soldiers to draw fire. Seemingly intent on his conversation, Colonel Eareckson paid no attention to me, and although intrigued, I turned away. Instead, I listened to a conversation between Clayton Knight and a young lieutenant from Indianapolis who'd mentioned earlier that I reminded him of his first girl. The lieutenant told an amusing anecdote. It wasn't really funny, but I laughed to be polite. Just then, someone gently touched my elbow. I turned and discovered Colonel Eareckson at my side.

The military men snapped to attention and saluted.

After ordering them at ease, the colonel motioned toward my glass. "Can I buy you one of those?"

"This one's barely touched," I said.

"That's not a problem. I'll be here when you're ready." The colonel smiled at me, and I held out my hand and introduced myself.

"Well, Miss Robertson, it's unusual to encounter a woman at these remote bases. You must have quite a story."

I explained that I was a war correspondent working on an article, while I considered the man standing across from me. Slender, even wiry, he wasn't a big guy, but he was powerful, a strong personality. He looked to be in his midforties and resembled William Powell in the *Thin Man* movies, except that Eric's slicked back hair and pencil-thin mustache were prematurely silver. While others walked, he swaggered.

The hour advanced, the others trailed off, and Eric and I sat alone at a small table. I was disappointed when he mentioned that he had a wife and children back home but not surprised. Most of the men I'd encountered were married. I wondered if I should call it a night, but I was enjoying myself. I didn't want it to end. Instead, I decided not to worry. I assumed that I'd never see him again and that I wouldn't let the attraction go too far. I had no desire to begin anything with a married man. That would only be trouble. I would keep it cool, enjoy his companionship, and then say goodnight.

The phonograph filled the room with songs of dreams, love, and loss as Eric and I danced. His breath was warm against my cheek.

# Chapter Ten

**Brazoria County, Texas**

**March 1993**

THE PHONE RANG, and Gabby jumped, startled. She had drifted off and become involved in Ruth's memories. It felt good, for even a brief interlude, to forget her own troubles. When Ruth reminisced, Gabby felt as if she were there, in Alaska during World War II, when a handsome colonel named Eric Eareckson walked in a mess-hall door and entered Ruth's life.

"Hello." Ruth grabbed the handset off the kitchen wall, uttered that one word, and then listened.

Watching Ruth, Gabby wondered how often in her life she'd accepted people as they appeared without questioning. When they'd first met, Gabby assumed Ruth had always lived a simple life on the river. It hadn't occurred to her to wonder about Ruth's long past. *How much have I missed by not taking time to listen?*

"Uh, huh. Really?" Ruth's reaction drew Gabby's attention back to the phone call. "You're not pulling my leg, are you, Nick?"

Silence again.

Ruth released a long sigh. "Well, now, that is disconcerting."

Apprehensive about what Nick had to say, Gabby listened closely. "Okay, we'll see you then."

Ruth hung up and pressed her hands at the base of her spine as if it bothered her. "Too much sitting. My back's not good. And then there's the change in the weather now that the storm has passed. That always—"

"Ruth!" Gabby broke in. "I'm sorry about your back. I am. But are you going to tell me why Nick called?"

Ruth squeezed her eyes nearly shut. "Well, I don't want you to worry. Understand?"

"Understand what?"

"That worrying doesn't help."

With that, Gabby's nerves fully engaged. Whatever Nick had called about not only wasn't good news, it involved her. Most likely Jeff. It had to be him. Gabby clasped her hands together to control a slight tremor. Just the thought of Jeff had that power over her. "Ruth, I appreciate that you're trying to break this to me gently, but just spill it."

AN HOUR LATER Nick knocked on the door, and Ruth let him in. He carried two grocery bags. When he couldn't find a place to put them, he handed one to Ruth and cleared off a section of the kitchen counter. "I know you didn't call in an order. These are just some things I thought you could use. So, Ruth, did you tell Gabby about the—"

"Just that someone came in looking for me. Ruth thought you should tell me the rest," Gabby blurted out. She stood a few feet away, but no one looked directly at her. She sensed that they both understood how tenuous her hold on calm was and that they were worried about how she'd react to what he had to say. Taking a steady breath to prepare, she ordered, "Nick, I need to know what's happened."

At that, he nodded.

The brief explanation took only minutes. Yet it was followed by questions and ruminating, the restating and analyzing of each nuance. "Tell me one more time what the police chief said to you," Gabby requested.

"We've been through this," Nick protested, but when she glowered at him, he nodded again. "Like I said, Police Chief Haskell showed up at the store earlier this evening, right before closing, and asked if I'd noticed any strangers. I said no one in particular, just folks passing through like always. I made my usual complaint about how someone should have warned me before I bought the store that hardly anyone drives down that darn highway. He laughed. Then he pulled out a picture—your picture from your driver's license, Gabby—and he asked, 'Well, what I need to know is, have you seen this woman?'"

Nick paused, and Ruth ordered, "Keep going. Gabby's trying to absorb this. We both are."

"Okay," Nick said. "But this is the last time. We need to stop talking and figure some things out."

When the two women gestured in agreement, Nick continued. "So, I looked at the picture. Took it from him, studied it a bit, and then handed it back to him. 'Pretty lady,' I said. 'If she'd stopped here, you bet I'd remember. But I haven't seen her. Who is she?'"

"Go on," Gabby prodded. Although battling back panic, she noticed how Nick looked at her and smiled every time he got to the part of his story where he described her as pretty.

"So, the chief, well, he said, 'This lady's missing. Her husband's a Houston cop, homicide detective, and he's looking for her. She disappeared during the storm.'"

"Your husband's a cop?" Ruth repeated, not for the first time.

Gabby grimaced, then raised her shoulders in a reluctant shrug.

"I told him again that I haven't seen you, but I promised to call if I do," Nick continued. "The chief thanked me. He cracked a joke about how the whole time he'd been in the store, he was the only one besides me in there. Something like, 'Glad I stopped in so you'd have some company today.' Then he left."

"Not just a cop, your husband is a homicide detective?" Ruth said. "Gabby, you didn't tell me that."

Nick and Ruth both stared at her, and Gabby struggled, trying to decide what to say. Then she realized that she needed to confess everything. If Jeff had reached out to his law enforcement contacts to find her, it would all eventually come out anyway. "The chief got that wrong. Jeff Jordan isn't a detective. He's the Houston PD captain in charge of homicide investigations."

"Ohhhhhh." Nick let out a long groan.

"Well now, that's not good news." Ruth squinted at her, questioning. "Maybe that's something you should have mentioned?"

"Yes, you're right. That wasn't fair of me. I'm sorry. I just… I was desperate. I needed help."

The older woman's face crumpled into a deep frown. "Why was he looking for you around here?"

"I don't know why he would ask the chief to look for me. Jeff has no reason to believe I'd be anywhere around here."

"Whoa!" Nick held his palm up to interrupt. "I think I gave you two the wrong impression. Jeff didn't personally reach out to Chief Haskell. The chief said Gabby's husband sent an alert out across the entire state. Jeff asked all law enforcement agencies in all of Texas to keep an eye out for her, to check with gas stations, restaurants, hotels, stores, places she may have stopped. To watch for cars swept off the road in the storm."

"So, he doesn't know that she's around here?" Ruth asked.

Nick glanced at Gabby, looking as worried as she felt, before he answered Ruth. "I don't know for sure what he knows, but I don't think so. That's not what the chief said. As far as they know, Gabby could be anywhere."

"Well, that's good. But your husband does have all the resources cops can use to find someone, doesn't he?" Ruth's eyes were hard on Gabby, not looking away. "That husband of yours can use all kinds of police tricks to track you, I'd guess?"

Gabby cleared her throat but that didn't abate the tension in her voice. "Yes. But Jeff has more than that. He has the others."

Ruth's eyebrows soared, questioning.

"Ruth, I told you earlier that I didn't just let Jeff hit me. I tried to get help. I called 911 three times."

"Three times?" Ruth repeated. "What happened?"

"The police knocked on our door and questioned both of us. But Jeff flashed his departmental ID. Next thing I knew, the officers were calling him 'Captain' and patting him on his back, shaking his hand. They left me in the condo with Jeff. They smiled and waved at him as they walked down the hall to the elevator. Once we closed the door, I was alone with him. He didn't hit me again those nights, but I saw it in his eyes. He knew I had nowhere to turn. No one to help me."

"Oh, how could those officers do that?" Ruth fumed.

"Because Jeff's one of them and a powerful guy," Nick speculated. "They didn't want to rock the boat."

Gabby glanced at Nick, grateful that he understood. "When the 911 calls didn't work, I went to police headquarters on my lunch hour. But I got nowhere there either."

"What about somewhere else besides Houston PD to file charges?" Nick wondered.

Gabby rubbed the back of her neck. This was difficult to talk about. She'd hidden it for so long that confiding in anyone, even two kind people who wanted to help her, made her jumpy. "I tried that. When HPD did nothing, I went to the sheriff's office and filed an official complaint. I figured it was the county not the city. Jeff didn't have any influence there. I tried to get a restraining order and force him to move out. I thought I could get him to agree to a divorce if I promised to drop the charges."

"What happened?" Nick asked. When Gabby glanced at him, the laid-back store owner had a look on his face she hadn't seen before: anger.

Gabby's heart drummed, and her hands felt clammy. These were hard memories, ones she'd fought to bury. She sucked in a deep breath and let it out slowly, fighting to regain calm. "Jeff laughed. He told me that they'd sent a detective and a deputy to his office to talk to him. All he had to do was deny it, tell them that I'm troubled, hysterical, a crazy woman, and they were on their way. With his position at the police department, they dropped the investigation. Either they believed him, or they just didn't want to cross him. The final time I called to follow up, the detective assigned to my case said it was closed due to a lack of evidence."

"I guess we shouldn't be surprised. I've heard of that blue wall of silence thing," Nick said. "Have you ever tried to get away from him before?"

"Once, but he found me at a rundown hotel where I was hiding under an assumed name. I'd paid cash, but someone had noticed my car," Gabby remembered that day well, how smug Jeff acted. "He said if I ever left him again…the next time…"

At that, Gabby became silent. Ruth and Nick didn't press her to finish the sentence, perhaps because what she would say seemed obvious.

While the others talked, Ruth's thoughts had landed on the biggest concern. "What really matters now is if Jeff has any way of tracking you here."

Gabby considered how overwhelming her situation seemed. At Ruth's age, it must have felt even more so. Then the older woman added, "Nick said they're looking across the entire state, but think hard. Is there any reason for Jeff to believe you might have taken off in this direction? Any clues that could lead him to us?"

Gabby considered that for a few moments. "I don't think so. I found this place by mistake. I got lost on my way to Corpus Christi. And he doesn't know I was going there. He has no idea I even know anyone in that city or that I'd have any reason to head south."

"Did you charge gas on your way? Did you use an ATM machine or a credit card?" Nick asked.

"No. I filled up the tank at a gas station near our house. I used the ATM before I left the neighborhood. I haven't used a credit card since. Jeff bragged a lot about how he traced people. I know that by now he's monitoring all my accounts."

The room fell briefly silent.

"What do we do?" Ruth searched Gabby's face for an answer she didn't have. "Who has an idea?"

Resigned, Gabby whispered, "I need to leave. I can't do this to you two. I'm dragging both of you into a dangerous situation. Jeff is relentless and ruthless."

Frowning, shaking her head, Ruth said nothing. She appeared to be still digesting everything she'd learned.

Nick finally ended what had become a long silence. "Gabby, where you go and what you do is for to you and Ruth to decide, since you're hiding in her home. But in the meantime, I brought some things to help." Out of one of the grocery bags, he pulled a box of Clairol dark-brown hair dye. "We didn't have this at the store, so I ran over to Walmart for it. I figured that you need to change your appearance."

"Just like in the movies." When they both looked at her, Ruth explained, "You know, whenever anyone's trying to hide, they change their hair color, maybe put on glasses."

A curt laugh, and Nick produced a pair of reading glasses with blue plastic frames out of the other bag. "This is the lowest magnification, so I don't think they'll mess up your vision too much. And there's pancake makeup, thick stuff to cover that black eye."

"But that might help. My bruises must make me look different." At that, Gabby silently considered how bizarre her world had become that a black eye could be a good thing.

Lowering his voice to nearly a whisper, Nick gave her a sidelong glance. "Gabby, your husband has already told the cops that you have a black eye."

"He told them?"

"The chief said that Jeff wrote in the alert that you'd tripped and fallen, hit your face and knocked your head, before you wandered off in the car. He's claiming that you became confused from the injuries. He wanted to take you to a hospital, but you refused."

That news hit Gabby hard. "I don't need a crystal ball to know that this will be like all those other times. The police won't believe me. I can tell them that I didn't fall, but with Jeff saying I did—"

"He's a smart one all right," Ruth fumed.

"Jeff is claiming that you may have suffered a concussion," Nick explained. "He's issued the alert as a critical medical intervention, saying that you may be in grave danger if not found. He marked it 'highest priority.'"

Her voice had a raspy, hard edge, when Gabby murmured, "That's Jeff for you. He always has an explanation. He always thinks of every angle. Convincing guy. Pretty soon he'll have everyone persuaded that I hit him."

"You didn't mention this earlier," Ruth pointed out to Nick. "You didn't tell us what Jeff was saying about Gabby being hurt."

"Well, I was wondering if I should tell Gabby. I thought she was getting enough bad news without that too."

With all she'd heard gnawing at her, Gabby wandered into the den. While the others waited, she walked around, as if preoccupied. She stopped at Ruth's shelves where she seemed to examine the spines on the books before picking up a porcelain dog that lay on its side. After rubbing the dog against her sweatshirt to knock the dust off, she placed it back on its feet. When she finally turned back toward Nick and Ruth in the kitchen, she said, "Listen, I don't want you two to worry. It's okay. You don't have to keep anything from me. Nothing surprises me. Jeff, well, he's good at covering his tracks."

In the silence that followed, Ruth's small house felt claustrophobic. Outside the sun had begun to set, the sky gently darkening. The door to the deck stood open, and Gabby listened to the slow ebbing of the current, the river sloshing against the land. She considered how quickly life changed. Little more than an hour earlier, she was so absorbed in Ruth's stories of Alaska that she'd forgotten to be afraid. Now all she could think of was Jeff and the danger.

"Ruth, there are a few groceries in the bags too," Nick said. "It's probably best that the two of you don't go out. You and Gabby need anything, I'll bring it over, okay?"

"Thanks, Nick," Ruth said. "That's good of you."

While the others talked, Gabby grabbed a tissue out of a box on an end table and dabbed at her eyes. Her voice was resolute when she said, "No. This is kind of you, but I need to leave. I can't do this to you, Nick, and I especially can't put Ruth at risk."

"Leave?" Ruth repeated.

"Yes, leave. I can't stay here. I can't take a chance that—"

"No!" Ruth shuffled over and took Gabby's hands in hers. "Jeff is looking across all of Texas. If there's no logical reason for him to look for you here, you should be safe. In fact, this may be the only place you are safe. Only Nick and I know where you are, and we're not telling anyone. If you get back out on the road, someone will see you. Jeff will find you."

"But what if…"

"What if he comes here? Is that what you were going to ask?"

Gabby nodded.

Ruth's tone left no room for argument. "If that happens, we'll figure it out. I'm not going to be worrying about you out on the road, running, afraid, and all alone."

"But—"

"There are no buts," Ruth said. "This is decided."

Deeply touched, Gabby struggled to find the words. "Thank you, more than I can say. I appreciate you both so much. But, Ruth, are you sure? This could be dangerous. Jeff is—"

"A bully. Jeff is a bully, and we're not going to let him bully us." Gabby's chest heaved with relief when Ruth concluded, "You aren't going anywhere, not until we're sure that you're safe."

Watching the two women, Nick appeared troubled. "It's true that as far as we know Jeff has no idea you're anywhere near here, but both of you need to be very careful. If Chief Haskell, anyone else who knows about Gabby's disappearance sees you—"

"Yes, of course. We will. Thanks, Nick. Thanks for looking out for Gabby. For us."

"No problem." At that, Nick stood to leave. "I'll be back tomorrow, drop in to check on the two of you."

"I want to pay you for those groceries and the other things," Gabby said.

"Sure, but for now I'll just keep a tab for you at the store. We'll figure it out later."

Gabby wiped away another tear. "Thanks. Both of you."

"One more thing before you go, Nick," Ruth said, and he turned back toward her. "We need to hide Gabby's car."

At that, a thought occurred to Gabby. "Ruth, Jeff talked about work a lot. He bragged about how people on the run made things easy for him by leaving clues right out in the open." Nick and Ruth watched her, waiting for more. "Let's put my empty suitcase and backpack in the trunk, get those out of sight."

Minutes later, Ruth opened a hinged lattice, and Nick drove the Camry under the house. When the car was covered with an old dark brown painting tarp and the panel secured back in place, they stood outside looking in. The Camry was nearly invisible in the shadows.

When Ruth returned to the kitchen, Gabby stood at the sink mixing the hair dye.

"Nick bid you goodnight. He's headed home. You know, your hair could have waited until morning."

"No. I need to do everything I can. He's…"

Watching Gabby wipe away tears, Ruth wasn't sure how to console her. She didn't believe in making assurances that might not prove true. False hope never seemed to help anyone. "Okay, well, let's try not to be too worried. If we're careful, you should be safe here."

"I can't thank you enough," Gabby said, shaking the dye bottle with her finger over the tip. "Ruth, I—"

"You don't have to. I made my own decision." Ruth turned to walk toward her room, then glanced back at Gabby over her shoulder and smiled. "After all, you can't leave before you hear all my stories. I won't allow it."

Suspecting Ruth's words were only to make her feel better, Gabby took comfort in them anyway. "You're right. How could I even think of leaving before I hear more about Alaska?"

After Ruth disappeared behind her bedroom door, Gabby wondered what she would have done in the old woman's position. If a stranger needing help had knocked on her door.

THE CHEMICAL SMELL from the dye filled the kitchen, and Gabby piled the long strands coated with the thick brown foam on top of her head, then put on the clear plastic cap that came with the kit. On the deck, she sat once again in one of the rickety metal rockers. Timing the color on her watch, she considered the disappointing turn her life had taken. She tried to envision the future, but she feared that she had none if she failed to break free. Her thoughts turned to Ruth, frail but with an inner strength.

Distracted by a throaty clattering from somewhere in the distance, Gabby recognized the call of the strange creature from the wildlife preserve. Another loud cry, closer, and she watched the great bird emerge from above the treetops. Following the river, it flew so close, Gabby feared that it would crash into the deck. But the bird soared past her, heading downstream.

"I know that sound."

Gabby looked up and found Ruth hovering behind her. She wore a thin cotton nightgown printed with small bouquets of roses, and her cheeks were flushed with excitement. "I haven't heard one in many, many years, but I'm sure that it's a jabiru."

"A jabiru?"

"A big white stork. It has red at the base of its neck, a sack where it holds its food. Kind of like the cheeks on a squirrel."

"That's it. That's exactly what it looks like. Nick and I saw it today, when we went birdwatching. The same bird, I think, that just flew over your house. Big, white, a black head and neck, except for that band of red."

"You saw it?"

"Yes, twice today."

Suddenly, Ruth grinned. Gabby didn't understand how but the bird had broken the tension Nick's news had brought, and Ruth giggled as if she had nothing to fear.

# CHAPTER ELEVEN

**Brazoria County, Texas**

**March 1993**

MORNING ARRIVED, AND Ruth was waiting for Gabby when she walked into the kitchen. "I thought you'd never get up. We have things to do."

"What things?"

"We need to take pictures."

"Pictures?"

"Photographs. Of you. Of your bruises." In her hands, Ruth held an old Leica camera like one Gabby had once seen in an antique store, a slender silver box with a black leather facade.

"Well, I don't think that…" Gabby intended to explain that she'd tried that before, and it hadn't help. For years, she'd kept a folder in her bottom dresser drawer filled with photos of her bruises. One summer, she turned copies over to a police investigator from the domestic violence unit who said he believed her and promised to take the case. Then Jeff must have pulled rank. That was the only explanation that seemed plausible when HPD suddenly promoted the man. From that point on, the investigator had stopped taking Gabby's calls.

Not long after, Jeff went on a rampage. He smashed her camera against the fireplace, then crushed what was left into small pieces with a hammer. The camera destroyed, he'd swept through the condo, upended drawers, and searched closets. When he found the file with the photos, Jeff burned it along with the negatives in the fireplace.

While doubting that photos would make a difference, Gabby didn't want to extinguish the hope in Ruth's eyes. "Are you sure that camera works?"

"Of course. I take good care of my equipment."

At that, Ruth motioned for Gabby to sit in a kitchen chair. Once she did, Ruth wrapped a rubber band around Gabby's long hair, dyed a deep chestnut. "This color's not bad on you," Ruth announced as she looped the rubber band around a second time. The ponytail in place at the base of Gabby's neck, Ruth used her fingers to comb back the strands that refused to cooperate, pushing them behind Gabby's ears. "Matter of fact, you make a beautiful brunette."

Gabby laughed, and she noticed that when she did the bruise around her eye didn't sting quite as much. She hadn't looked in the mirror yet that morning. "Is my eye still that lovely shade of dark purple?"

"Pretty much, but it has some yellow and green to it this morning." The camera felt good in Ruth's hands. She'd missed it. Snapping the first photo, she noticed the upturn of Gabby's lips. "You need to look serious, Gabby. No smiling. Whoever looks at these needs to understand that Jeff hurt you."

Ruth clicked the shutter a few more times, making sure she had a good image, and Gabby stared straight at the lens, solemn, a lost look in her eyes.

"Now that arm."

Following instructions, Gabby pushed the long sleeve on her pajamas up, and Ruth took a few photos from different angles. "No. I don't like that."

She wandered off while Gabby waited, then returned with a white pillowcase. "Put your arm on here and turn it so I can get that handprint."

Gabby did as Ruth had instructed, and the humiliation of what had happened to her, of what Jeff had done to her, was represented in every inch of the bruise.

"That's the money shot," Ruth said. "That's the bruise he can't explain, the one that looks like his hand."

*Looks like Jeff's hand.* Gabby thought about that. "Do you have a ruler?"

Following Ruth's directions, Gabby searched the pantry and found a yardstick standing on end next to the broom. Back at the table, she laid it on the pillowcase next to her arm, which was turned to show the bruised side with the handprint.

"Take a photo like this." Ruth seemed unsure, and Gabby explained, "This way the photo will show how big the bruise is."

When Ruth finished, Gabby started to get up, but the older woman placed her hand on Gabby's shoulder and urged her back down into the chair. "We're not finished."

While Gabby watched, Ruth claimed a scissors from a mug on top of her desk, then started chopping away at Gabby's hair, cutting the ponytail off in sections and throwing the ends into the trash can. Once she had Gabby clipped to barely beneath her chin, Ruth combed the front over Gabby's forehead and fashioned thick bangs. "This'll help." Finished, she stood back and sized up her handiwork. "You know, you look a little like Audrey Hepburn with your hair like that."

"You think?"

"Hepburn around the cheekbones, not the eyes so much."

Afterward Ruth watched as Gabby stared at the unfamiliar woman she'd become in the bathroom mirror. She turned back to the kitchen, and Ruth noticed a heaviness about Gabby. "I should leave, Ruth. This isn't fair to you. I'll find a place to go."

Her chin leading, Ruth rotated her head slowly, side to side. "This was settled last evening when I told you that I want you to stay."

"But Ruth, I can't—"

"You were right to pick this place. The river…it's another world. It's set apart. No one lives year-round in most of the houses around me. They're summer cottages. The families won't show up for weeks, not until the school year ends. By then, you'll most likely be on your way. Plus, I know in my heart that we'll be okay. You're safe in this house."

"How? How do you know?"

"If I tell you, you'll think I'm the one who hit my head and went a bit crazy."

"No, never. But remember, you don't like the word *can't*. And we *can't* know that Jeff won't find me."

"No, that I don't know. But I do feel better about things." Ruth's eyes flashed with a bit of mischief. "Let's just say the jabiru told me not to worry."

GABBY WONDERED ABOUT that later, what the strange bird meant to Ruth, but instead of dwelling on it, she didn't ask, and they stayed busy. Ruth had decided after their talk about Alaska the day before that she wanted to show Gabby her mementos from the war years. Gabby suspected it was Ruth's way of distracting her, but she didn't care. It felt good to think of other places and other times. When they opened the bottom drawer in Ruth's desk, it was a mass of paperwork, newspaper clips, and photographs. Ruth riffled through and pulled out her letter from the war department assigning her to Alaska and photos of Eskimos and gold miners, airplanes and soldiers.

After they examined each, Gabby piled them lovingly, organizing the lot into correspondence, photographs, and newspaper clips and replacing them in the drawer in neat stacks. Then Ruth held up a photograph of a debonair-looking man with dark eyebrows, silver hair, and a mustache to match. He wore an army uniform, one with pilot's wings on the lapel. On the back of the photo, many decades ago, someone had stamped, "PROPERTY OF THE US ARMY."

Gazing at it in her hands, Ruth wore a melancholy smile.

"This is Eric."

# Chapter Twelve



**New York, NY**

**Fall 1945**

My homecoming wasn't what I'd hoped. Art shut down our joint venture, Press Syndicate, days before I arrived back in the lower forty-eight. "Too much competition," he informed me. As a result, I became one of more than a thousand reporters and photographers returning from the war, many of us vying for the same jobs.

"In Alaska I covered hard news, bombing runs, all types of military operations, wrote human interest features, took my own photos, and…" I went into my usual spiel for the *New York Post* editor sitting across from me, and he stifled a yawn. I knew he'd heard similar tales from dozens of former war correspondents. I wasn't surprised when he shook my hand and sent me on my way.

Luckier than most, I landed a slot on the *New York Herald Tribune*'s production desk, writing for the weekly magazine's women's section. I knew I should be grateful. A fair number of my colleagues would have celebrated. But to me a desk job tasted of failure. From the moment I returned, I yearned for the excitement of Alaska, of exploring the unknown.

Yet I settled back into life in the States and rented a small apartment, a Manhattan walk-up. My days were spent at the newspaper. Evenings and weekends, I circulated with friends to the latest restaurants and bars. I sipped my scotch and sodas, danced, and reminisced about my time as a war correspondent. We hobnobbed at supper clubs where big bands played swing and where chanteuses and tenors sang songs made popular by Frank Sinatra, Ella Fitzgerald, Bing Crosby, Doris Day, and Nat King Cole.

In many ways, I fell in love with New York. I relished working for a big-city daily, the joy of opening the building's doors and hearing the presses, smelling the ink. Yet in quiet moments at work, poring over copy needing to be edited, my mind wandered. I daydreamed about Vihjalmur Stefansson, how his eyes danced when he talked of remote places and people.

"You should be the first woman to fly over the North Pole," he'd told me. *Perhaps he wasn't kidding. Perhaps he thought I could do it.* I hoped it was true, and I wondered where my destiny lay. Fall turned to winter, and the holidays approached.

Sitting at my kitchen table, barely big enough for two, I wrote out Christmas cards, and my mind carried me back to Point Barrow, to the evening I danced in the mess hall. I remembered the way Eric held me, his touch. Yet it had gone no further. Eric had been honest, and he hadn't led me on. That evening, he'd talked of his wife, his nearly grown children. When we parted, we'd shaken hands, and I'd left convinced that I would never see him again.

Yet that hadn't stopped me from thinking of him more often than I would have ever confessed.

On a whim, I addressed a card with a jolly Santa on the front to Colonel Eric Eareckson in care of the United States Army. The next morning on my way to work, I slipped it along with my other cards into the mailbox on the corner. The rest of the day, I chastised myself for the card, for thinking of Eric, for not being able to forget him.

The holidays came and went, and no correspondence arrived in return. After a few weeks, I stopped searching for his name as I flipped through my mail. I was convinced nothing would ever come of my gambit. I wondered if my greeting had failed to reach him or if he'd decided not to respond. Either way, I told myself, this was as it should be.

Life went on.

Then one evening in February, I walked into my building, unlocked my mailbox, popped up the brass lid with the small window, and pulled out a stack of what looked like bills and ads. In a hurry to meet friends, I threw it all on my coffee table and ran back out the door. Days passed before I noticed the unopened envelopes. Shuffling through, my hands became suddenly clammy when I noticed the return address on the last item: Col. E. Eareckson. I held my breath reading the first line of Eric's letter: "Your much-traveled Christmas card reached me just this morning. I am wasting no time in answering it."

That evening, I lingered over Eric's letter, reminiscing about our encounter at the Point Barrow mess-hall bar, the night I joined the Order of the Top of the World. As I did, I understood the regret Eric wrote of, his disappointments. Following orders, he'd spent the last months of the war in London. Away from the Pacific Front, he'd missed the finale as the fighting thundered to an end. After years of living and breathing the Allied effort, he had wanted to see it through. "I resent every second of that time in England," he wrote, "because it kept me out of that fascinating phase of the war."

Rather than being personal, Eric's first letters centered on his army responsibilities and his experiences during the war. Quickly, that changed.

"Querida, Robbie," he wrote in March. By then he'd taken to calling me the nickname my closest friends used. At the end he signed, "Always, Eric."

His next letter ended, "Love, Eric."

As I reported to work at the newspaper each morning, I thought of him studying Spanish at the University of Michigan, preparing for his next assignment: an advisor in South America.

In my letters to him, I fought to keep our relationship cool. I reminded myself that he was married, that he had a family. I asked about his wife, his children, his duties, his plans for the future. Twice I wrote that perhaps we shouldn't correspond, that he had responsibilities, and that I didn't want to interfere in his life. When his next letter came, he ignored my concerns, and—although I should have cut it off, although I told myself that I must end it—I wrote back.

With each letter, our relationship grew more personal.

Eric became my confidante. I confessed my dreams, my desire to explore the world, and he commiserated with me when I admitted that my job felt suffocating. More than anyone else in my life, Eric understood that something inside me that I couldn't control stirred, that Alaska had expanded my dreams. To me, Eric became a symbol of the life I'd lost. I ached at times to see him, but I worried that there were people that could be hurt. I had never dated a married man, and I had no intention to start.

Yet I couldn't stop the feelings.

Winter melted into spring, and in Central Park the trees flowered, leaves budding out a new-born green. As the world outside the windows burst with returning life, I felt ever more trapped at the copy desk.

One afternoon, my phone rang at the *Trib*, and I heard the voice of a friend I'd met in Alaska.

"They're going where?"

"It's four guys, seasoned Arctic explorers," he said. "They're going to fly over the North Pole. I mentioned you, told them that you might be interested."

Days later at a Lower Eastside bar, I nibbled on a cheeseburger and fries while four men I'd never met before excitedly told me of their plans to fly across the Pole. They were purchasing the latest equipment, new instruments to guide them. "If you come along, Ruth, you'll be the first woman to cross the Pole, and you'll make history. We want to be part of that," one said.

My head spun with excitement.

Later back at my office, I found it hard to concentrate on photographs of the latest hairstyles and recipes for Easter ham. Was pineapple or honey a tastier glaze? I closed my eyes and pictured headlines: "Ruth Robertson, First Woman to Cross the North Pole"

In one of his letters, Eric had sent me a phone number where he could be reached, but I'd never used it. That evening, I had a long-distance operator place the call. "Eric, it's me, Robbie. Wait until you hear!"

He listened patiently, not interrupting, and even over the phone I sensed his delight. "This'll be grand, Robbie. You'll do it. I know you will."

Two weeks later, another phone call came in for me at the newspaper, this time from the man pulling together the North Pole expedition. "The funding for the equipment has dried up. Can't do it right now. Maybe in the future but definitely not this year."

When he said those words, I felt as if my last lifeline had been snatched away. I could barely breathe. After we hung up, I put my head on my desk, closed my eyes, and tried to calm my racing heart. That day, I made an excuse and left work early. In my apartment, I lay on the couch and stared at the ceiling, eyes open, for hours.

The next day, a letter from Eric waited in my mailbox. In fairness, he, of course, didn't know what had transpired. He was cheering me on, unaware that my victory had vanished. "I watch for headlines of your triumph, your trip over the Pole. I watch for your picture in the newspaper, knowing one day I'll see it, that you'll be the first woman to climb Everest or sail solo across the Atlantic! My Robbie! My grand explorer!"

For days, I didn't write. I didn't know how to tell him that the expedition had turned into a pipe dream. I felt like a failure. When he didn't hear from me, he wrote again. "You are one of the most elusive females in the world," he both complained and complimented.

A Wednesday evening after work, I was catching up on correspondence, writing letters to friends. The apartment window was open, and I sat at my typewriter pounding away. The breeze smelled of the city: exhaust and the deli down the street. Someone buzzed from the lobby.

I hit the button on the intercom. "It's me, Robbie. It's Eric."

"Eric? You're here?"

He laughed, just the way I remembered. "In the flesh."

Running my hand through my hair, I had a sinking feeling looking down at my wrinkled shirt and frayed pajama bottoms. "Can you wait?"

"I don't care what you're wearing. Let me in!"

He bounded up the stairs two at a time and grabbed me when he reached my door. In an instant, our lips pressed together, and it was the way I'd imagined, long and soft yet strong, gentle but demanding.

In the city to attend a meeting, he stayed at a hotel in my neighborhood. One evening, we shared an early dinner, sandwiched into a narrow table at Sardi's. The room bubbled with conversation as well-dressed couples chatted while waiters in white jackets delivered plates kept hot with silver warming lids.

Over salads and steaks, we reminisced about our meeting at the Point Barrow bar. Under the table, his leg brushed mine, and my heart fluttered. My body wanted him, while my brain warned me to keep a distance. I was in dangerous territory. Nothing good could come of a love affair with a married man.

Yet I hadn't felt so alive since returning from the war.

After dinner, we rushed up the block to the St. James Theatre. Waiting for the doors to open, the crowd milled around on the sidewalk in front of posters advertising Rodgers and Hammerstein's new play: *Oklahoma!* Eric lit his cigarette and lingered with the flame illuminating my face. "You are beautiful," he murmured. Then he pressed his mouth on mine in another long, slow, passionate kiss. He tasted of tobacco and wine, and I was surrounded by the leathery scent of his cologne. In a flash, it reminded me of the aftershave my father used to splash on his face. For just a moment, I was back there, in the trailer. My father…

I pulled away.

"Are you okay?" Eric appeared uncertain, concerned. "Ruth, if you don't want—"

"I-I just…" I stammered, wondering how to explain. But then I couldn't. Not even to Eric, to whom I'd confided my deepest dreams. I'd never told anyone what my father had done to me. It was…something I couldn't admit. Yet I knew the danger of keeping secrets. There'd been men in my life before, and my past had always stalked us, a presence they didn't understand that built a wall between us. As much as I'd fought to forget, my father's betrayal had haunted my life. I looked at Eric, and I saw the worry in the set of his jaw. At that moment, I knew deep inside that I needed it to be different with Eric. I needed to be free of the past. It was time. Time not to forget but to move on.

I leaned forward and whispered in his ear. "I do want."

This time I placed my lips on his, and we lingered, long and hard, a solid kiss, the type that claims the other person and draws him in. When our lips finally parted, he took my hand and kissed each fingertip, then whispered, "Oh, how I've dreamed of this."

In the theater, we sang along to "Oh What a Beautiful Morning," and Eric draped his arm around my shoulders and hummed slightly out of tune when the untamable cowboy named Curly and the girl he'd fallen for, Laurey, sang, "People Will Say We're in Love."

Later in my apartment, we shared a bottle of champagne, sitting side by side on my worn-out couch. As if I were made of the finest porcelain, he gently pushed back a strand of my brown hair, whisked it behind my ear. His hand under my chin, he held my face close to his. "That night we met in Point Barrow, I knew someday I'd see you again."

Looking long and hard into my eyes, he let his smile vanish, and I sensed a deep longing. My breath quickened at his touch, and his hands worked their way up the back of my dress.

The next morning, I awoke and felt Eric's body pressed warm against mine.

That day, we never left the apartment. I whipped up eggs from the refrigerator in midmorning as he praised my domestic skills. For dinner, I ordered delivery from the neighborhood Chinese place, and we ate with chopsticks.

"Are you in my future?" I asked, slyly looking at him as I broke open my cookie.

I didn't have to read my fortune on that small slip of paper, for Eric told me what was to come. "If you want me to be, Robbie. Just like my letters. Always."

When I talked of my plans, he commiserated with my unhappiness at being shackled to my job, and he encouraged my yearning for a great quest. "You should do it. You must do it all."

I explained that I had no real choice. "I think I will die an early death if I spend my life at a desk. I can hardly bear it."

The army had issued his orders. Now that he could speak Spanish, Eric was heading to an assignment in Peru, tasked to advise that country's armed services and try to steer them in the direction his bosses in DC wanted. I fed off his excitement and felt a connection to him greater than any other in my life, even with my closest women friends. Eric was truly the first man who understood me, the first who didn't want to change me.

Yet he wasn't free.

Since Eric's arrival on my doorstep, I'd tried to push his family out of my mind, but I couldn't any longer. I asked about his wife, his children. His eyes grew sad, and he shook his head, not really answering.

After a kiss, my hand remained at the back of his neck. His breath hot and moist, he whispered in my ear, "We're kindred spirits, you and I, Robbie. I understand you, what you're feeling. Life waits. The world is out there."

Grateful, I kissed him yet again, and we languished in our lovemaking, the feeling of his body making me tremble as I ran my hands over his chest.

"You know," he said, "I'm thinking maybe this is it. Maybe we've found what we've both been hoping for. In each other."

I gazed up at him, smiled, and put my arms around him. "How do you know?"

"Because I can't stand it when you're not with me. I go a little crazy when you're not around."

At that I laughed. Eric, always dramatic, ever passionate. He had an officer's mind, a keen intellect, and an overwhelming romanticism. At times, I feared I'd disappear in those blue eyes, lose myself and become part of him. Late that night, we made love yet again, and Eric whispered snatches of love poems in my ear.

How I wished that night would never end.

Sunday evening, he left, and the apartment gaped empty. I felt too small to fill it.

On Monday, I confided about the affair to a friend at the *Tribune*, a thirty-something reporter half the men on the staff chased. "Married men are trouble," she advised, as if I didn't know that. Yet, she certainly had good reason to judge that I needed a reminder. "Are you going to break it off?"

"I should. I know that. But I don't want to."

"What about the wife?"

I'd thought so much about his family, worried about them. "I know this is wrong. I have no business falling in love with another woman's husband, and I've told Eric that we shouldn't, that we can't." Then I repeated what Eric had said hours before he'd left for the airport, that he and his wife had grown apart, that he was always traveling and rarely saw her. "He says they live separate lives."

"They all say that," my friend scoffed. "Next, he'll claim that she just doesn't understand him."

That evening, I cried as I wrote and told Eric that we needed to end it, that we would hurt too many people if we continued.

When he called next, he ignored my letter. "I'm shooting for a ride there this weekend. I miss you."

I didn't have the strength, or perhaps the conviction, to tell him no.

Our stolen weekends raced by, the theater, socializing with my friends at hole-in-the-wall bars, quiet evenings at our favorite Italian restaurant, sharing wine over candles in Chianti bottles, wax dripping in ribbons to form a colorful skirt. Eric was handsome in his uniform, and he called me beautiful in the flame's soft glow.

After he left, I couldn't help but think of his wife and children, his life.

I wrote yet again saying that we should simply be friends, but he responded that he wanted much more. "When I was with you last, I could barely leave. I wanted to go AWOL and spend whatever time I had until they found me with you. I wanted to stay and make love one more time, and then one more time again, until I never left you. Please write. Always write. Your letters remind me of beautiful beaches and windswept shores."

Soon, when I complained that I yearned for new adventures, he no longer urged me to make grand plans but suggested I pack a picnic lunch and take a drive along the Hudson River. "Lie back under a tree and smell the cherry blossoms." I felt both flattered and disappointed. He wanted me in my New York apartment, waiting for him.

Weeks passed, and Eric's ardor intensified. After one visit, an entire week together, he wrote that he loved me, that he hoped I loved him. Nothing could ever be ordinary with Eric; he insisted his love had such depth, such passion that it exceeded any love given to any other woman in the history of the world. "Whatever you want, Robbie, no matter what, I will do it." Instead of his usual closing, that time he finished with, "Write your own ticket."

His offer hung in the air. *What do I want? What should I ask of him?*

"I don't know," I whispered in my apartment one evening, rereading his letter yet again. *Would we be happy together? Would it haunt us that we broke up his marriage? Hurt his children?*

I climbed the stairs to my apartment building's roof and stood surrounded by other rooftops, the city spread before me and the stars above me. "Look up at the night sky at eleven each night, my darling, and I'll do the same at that precise minute," he'd urged me during his most recent visit. "We'll look at the moon together, you and I. When the moon's light touches you, know that it is me making love to you. Its beams are my arms. Close your eyes, and you'll feel my kiss."

I gazed at the moon, then shut my eyes and thought of Eric. A wisp of a breeze skimmed my cheeks, my lips, and I opened my eyes wondering if Eric felt it too.

Our letters continued, my heart beating with anticipation each time I opened an envelope with his return address. His plans all in place, Eric left for Peru. Thousands of miles separated us, and my heart ached for him. Still, I ignored his suggestion that I make the decision about our relationship. I didn't know what to say or how to say it.

Perhaps it was a clue that he didn't push me for an answer.

From Lima, Eric wrote of the news in the headlines, the US government's nuclear tests on the Bikini Atoll in the Marshall Islands. "I thought you would be there, recording it all. I know you want to be."

When I read his letter at my desk at the *Tribune*, I was copyediting the fashion column, and his words cut into my heart like a dagger. Of course, Eric didn't intend it to feel that way. Although he sympathized, he couldn't fully understand how much I hated being tethered to my desk.

"I love you, Robbie, and always shall. Do you love me?" he wrote. Then he asked the question I'd considered since the early days of our affair, one that in recent weeks had never been far from my mind. "Would you marry me, if I could (without too much moral damage)? We have something that is outside my experience."

No matter what my decision, he promised he would remain stoic. But what he wanted, he said, was to have me at his side. Despite the pain it might cause, he insisted that he needed me. "Take my hand, my darling, and let's go!"

As his letter went on, he expounded on our kindred souls. "Please, be truthful and honest," he begged. Then referring to the damage our decision could do to his wife, his children, he threw out a caveat that left me wondering about his true intentions: "I'm an awful coward when it comes to tampering with a life."

For days, I didn't answer. Deep inside, I couldn't shake my doubts: Maybe his talk of not wanting to tamper with another's life, of the pain pursuing our love would cause, was his way of leaving open an escape.

In the end, I needed to know the truth.

"Come for me, my love, and I will be yours," I wrote. "Once you are free, we can be together forever."

I mailed my letter on my way to work. Would it lead to our marriage or end our affair? Saying yes had the power to change everything.

Empty weeks followed. Eric's letters stopped.

Maybe he did love me but not enough. Maybe I'd known from our start that he relished conquest. Once won, the prize had lost its allure.

Each day I checked my mailbox, and as I turned the key, I prayed I'd see a letter from him inside. Sorrow filled me when I thumbed through missives from family and friends, my monthly bills, but nothing from Eric.

Off and on during the day, into the evening, I thought of him. If I'd assumed I'd be angry, I wasn't. Instead, even as I walked the busy streets of Manhattan, worked at my desk in the crowded newsroom, I grieved for him, for the loss of us.

Finally, I wrote.

To get Eric back, I released him. "You take me too seriously," I typed, my eyes clouded with tears. "I was just kidding with you, Eric. Didn't you know? Couldn't you tell? Please, don't stop writing me." I said I shared his reluctance to hurt his wife and children. "There is somebody else to think about, no? Like you, I abhor tampering with other people's lives…I knew you weren't free. I can't say very much under the circumstances. Can I?"

Even if I had but a slice of him, I wanted him in my life. "I need you, Eric, just as surely as I need the warmth of the sun, the soothing coolness of the first splash of rain, a hand to hold as I jump from boulder to boulder. Even though I can't see you, I need to know that you are there."

I typed the last line: "You simply can't vanish like this."

Eric's response arrived quickly. He planned to travel to Washington DC on business in a few months and then spend the weekend in my apartment in New York.

I was glad for the letter and not glad. I'd meant what I'd written, that I wanted him back, but now that the bargain had been struck, now that I knew my place in his life, the spell had been broken and the fantasy laid bare.

I felt betrayed yet again by a man I dearly loved.

In the weeks that followed, I wrote less often, but Eric remained determined. When I stopped writing, he went so far as to call my boss at the *Tribune*. Worried that he hadn't heard from me, Eric asked if I had been ill. When I finally wrote him, he again professed his love, but admitted that marriage wasn't in our future. "I would rather be married to you than anyone else," he contended. Then he wrote that he'd tried to leave his wife, but the divorce "didn't take."

What I must never doubt, he insisted, was his commitment to me. "If you were on another planet, I would shuttle there just to see you, to make love to you."

His words tore at my heart. I wanted to trust him, but I did doubt.

For a brief time, our letters continued, and he promised his enduring devotion. Yet writing back became ever harder once I no longer believed in him. I'd offered him my life, my future. I wanted to share our destinies, but I now knew that would never happen. Without making a conscious decision to do so, I pulled away.

On a clear Friday afternoon, the sun shining, the sound of cabs barreling past on the street outside my apartment building, I found one last letter in my mailbox. Perhaps a letter wasn't the right description. My final communication from Eric was better called a note.

Our affair had truly ended when he professed his love and offered me anything I wanted but then pulled back when I said I wanted him committed to me. Eric saw our parting differently. He blamed me. Enclosed in the letter was a poem, one in which Eric portrayed himself as a stone cast upon my ocean. "Rebuffed, I sought my ocean home," he'd written.

In a short message, no bigger than a footnote, the one man who'd championed my ambitions blamed the death of our love on my desire for adventure. The dreams I confided in him, he used against me. Labeling them as unlikely to succeed, he wrote: "So long, Robbie. I hope things turn out as you may plan them. I have found plans to be lousy."

My tears falling on the single sheet of paper in my hands, I crumpled it up, formed it into a ball, and threw it into the round wastebasket next to my desk. I stared out the window thinking of Eric. Then I looked back over my shoulder at the basket with Eric's note inside.

I reclaimed it and pressed the note flat by running my hands over it, attempting to undo what I'd done. I put it away, pressed inside a dictionary, in the drawer that held Eric's love letters.

# Chapter Thirteen

**Brazoria County, Texas**

**March 1993**

"IS LOVE THE greatest of all gifts, the way it says in the Bible?" Ruth sat at her desk in her small office holding the final item in her Alaska drawer—Eric's last, brief missive: "I hope things turn out as you may plan them. I have found plans to be lousy."

When she handed the piece of paper to Gabby to read, the tone of Eric's words made the younger woman sad. "I don't know. Like you, I haven't been lucky in love."

Forty-seven years had passed since the night Ruth wadded up the note, then smoothed it and pressed it in a book. The creases remained. Tracing the faint lines with her finger, Gabby considered how some damage endured, while other scars faded. "What plans is Eric talking about?"

"I've always assumed he meant my dreams, that he was saying that plans like mine often don't come true," Ruth said, an emotional catch in her raspy voice. "Eric knew I craved feeling alive, the thrill of adventure. I thought he admired that in me. But in the end, maybe not, or at least not as much as I once believed."

Ruth fell quiet, and Gabby mulled that over. "The people we love have the most power to hurt us."

"How true. Looking back, I would have saved myself a lot of

heartache if I hadn't let things get so deep with Eric. There were signs, his marriage a big one, that it wasn't meant to be. Sometimes, I guess, I'm pretty good at fooling myself."

"We all are," Gabby offered.

The road past the house was usually so quiet that both women startled when tires crunched over the gravel driveway. Gabby stepped back toward her bedroom, wondering if she should hide, while Ruth investigated.

"It's Nick," she said, peeking out a window. "Nothing to worry about."

Gabby smiled. "He's a great guy."

When Ruth shot her a curious glance, Gabby hurriedly added, "I mean, as a person. He's a really good person."

"Yes, he is. He's helped me out a lot over the years. And darn good looking. If I were forty years younger…" Moments later, Ruth swung the door open and greeted Nick with a question, "You're not bringing more bad news, right?"

"Not this time," he answered, looking over at Gabby, inspecting her short, dark hair. "So, who's this lady? And where's Gabby?"

"You think it works?" she asked.

"Except for the black eye, you look like a new woman. Whoever gave you the haircut did a darn good job."

An impish grin, and Ruth curtsied. "In a previous life I must have been a hairdresser."

"Must have been," he agreed. "Gabby, I've got my helper behind the cash register, which means that I have the afternoon off. How about another walk through the nature refuge? If we stay out of the woods and go to the marsh, we can see cars in plenty of time to leave if anyone shows up."

"Are you sure that it's safe?"

"Should be. I hardly ever see another soul there."

A TEMPERATE DAY, Gabby watched as a slight breeze ruffled the tall grasses. They kept to a wooden pathway that led through the marsh, but as she eyed the landscape, the expanse of land, murky water, and sky, she suddenly felt very alone. That was what they'd wanted, not to worry about strangers seeing her, but it felt odd to be so isolated. Just then a blue heron swooped in. Knee deep in the water, the bird stood statue still. It watched, waited, then, in an instant, swung its head and long rope-like neck forward, plunging below the surface. "It looks like he got lucky."

"Probably a fish," Nick whispered.

The bird yanked his head back up and gulped down a slender silver perch.

"I love the river, the coastline, the marshes, all the beauty here," Nick confided. "People who don't live here don't understand. We have a bad flood, and I have to rebuild my little house. But I'd never leave. No storm could drive me out. I'd always come back."

She glanced at him and saw how intently he watched the bird. There was a kindness about Nick Foster, a gentleness, and she could tell that he was captivated by the beauty around them. When Gabby again focused on the heron, head cocked as it sucked in a second fish, she was struck by the bird's elegance. *There's so much in this world that I haven't taken time to appreciate,* she thought. It was almost as if she expected what Nick said next because she felt it too.

"It's the peace. When I needed it, after the war, the river healed me."

A flock of seagulls squawked overhead, and Nick pointed at one lone bird trailing them, a slash of white in the blue sky. "There it is again!"

"What?"

"That strange bird we saw the other day. The big stork with the red band around its neck."

"Ruth called it a jabiru."

# Chapter Fourteen

**Brazoria County, Texas**

**March 1993**

Early that evening, in the house on stilts nestled beside the riverbank, Gabby stirred spaghetti sauce simmering in a pot. Nick had brought fresh greens, red-tipped lettuce, and bright-red tomatoes that he tossed into a salad. Meanwhile, Ruth surveyed the river from a porch rocker and watched the sun slowly ease lower in the sky. Before long, pasta bubbled on the stove, and Nick searched for something in the cabinets.

"Ruth, do you have a strainer?"

"In the pantry. You might want to wash it. I haven't used it in years."

"Got it." he replied. He filled the sink with suds and scrubbed it clean, then spilled the cloudy pasta water through. "Dinner is served."

After clearing off the table, Gabby had set three places. As they sat down, she motioned at the piles of papers she'd relocated to the living room floor. "We should really go through those tomorrow. Now that we've organized your desk, we need a new project."

"Good idea," Ruth agreed.

Ginger slept in a ball at Ruth's feet while they twirled the long noodles in the rich red sauce. "You know back in the day, in New York, I'd have friends over, and I'd cook big pots of spaghetti. I didn't have enough plates, working girl you know, so we ate off my photography trays." The memory amused Ruth, and she giggled just a bit.

"Gabby told me that you were a reporter and a photographer. I didn't know that," Nick remarked.

"I bet there's a lot we don't know about each other, Nick. We've always been rather casual friends, don't you think?"

Nick gave her a half smile. "I guess so, now that you mention it."

"Well, it's nice having you and Gabby here. All the years I've known you, this is the first time you've come for dinner."

"I hope it won't be the last," he said, and this time Ruth's lips pinched up at both corners.

It was then that Gabby remembered. "Ruth, we saw that bird again, the big white stork, and I told Nick that you know what it is."

"The jabiru?" Ruth eyed Nick, keenly interested. "Where did you see it?"

"Flying over the marsh, in the refuge." He paused, a forkful of spaghetti halfway between his plate and his mouth. "Yesterday, it was with a flock of wood storks."

"Ah, that makes sense."

"What does?" he asked.

"That it would be with the wood storks," Ruth explained. "They're cousins, and the storks winter farther south. They're flying up this time of year for the summer. The jabiru must have traveled with the flock. That's why he's here, so far from home."

"Have you seen one before? I never have, and I've been birdwatching around here ever since I bought the store."

"Not in Texas. I saw them in South America. There were thousands. Amazing birds," Ruth said. "I had one that I thought followed me around for a while in the jungle."

"South America?" Gabby asked. "So, you went down there to see Eric after the breakup?"

"Eric?" Nick appeared lost.

"Eric's an old lover I told Gabby about," Ruth said with a nonchalant wave of the hand. "No, I never saw Eric again, not after we stopped writing. I went to South America on my own. Venezuela, actually. I lived there for years. I did my photography down there, reported on local events. Spent quite a bit of time out in the jungles."

"I never knew that you lived in South America either." Nick appeared surprised.

Once Ruth finished chewing a mouthful of pasta, she washed it down with a sip of water. "Don't feel bad, Nick. I bet that I could learn a lot about you too. The truth is that most people don't talk all that much these days. We just pass each other, say howdy, and move on."

"That's kind of sad," Gabby said.

Ruth gave her a wistful look. "Life is busy for you young folks. You're always in a rush. It's understandable that most often there isn't time for an old lady's ramblings."

"Oh, Ruth—" Gabby started.

"To get back to what we were talking about, I lived in Venezuela for a few years. I loved it there."

"And that was where you saw these birds?" Nick prodded.

"Yup. The jabirus were fascinating. Some of the males are nearly five feet tall, wing spans up to nine feet. One had a nest made of sticks, six feet across, on a rooftop across from my apartment in Caracas. I watched the birds with their eggs, teaching the fledglings to fly." Ruth stopped for a moment, her expression melancholy. "That was a very long time ago. Another life."

"Do you think—" Nick started.

But Ruth jumped in. "You know, they don't have feathers on their heads and necks. The black and red is the color of their skin."

When Ruth reached over to tear off a piece of bread, Nick asked, "Do you think this one will hang around?"

"Maybe. For the summer." She seemed to consider that. "Or as long as it's needed."

Nick and Gabby shared a confused glance but didn't ask her to explain.

AFTER DINNER, GABBY cleared the table, while Ruth again relaxed on the deck. "I'm heading home," Nick called. "Big day tomorrow. I may have a customer or two at the store."

"You think?" Gabby teased, and that made Ruth chuckle.

Then, suddenly, a knock at the door.

"Mrs. Marietta. You home?" a man bellowed. A dark figure stood outside, his silhouette visible despite the thin cotton curtain over the window.

Startled, Nick positioned himself to block any view into the house through the gap at the curtain's edge. He turned to Gabby who stood frozen, a dirty salad bowl in her hands, beside the kitchen counter. Silently, he pointed toward her bedroom. Nodding, she put the bowl down and slipped out of the kitchen into the bedroom. She began to close the door behind her but thought better of it. Whoever was at the door might hear. Instead, she pressed her back against the wall and watched through the hinge slit.

In the kitchen, Nick opened the door and called out in a friendly voice, "Chief Haskell. What're you doing here?"

"I was about to ask you the same thing. Saw your Blazer out back."

A ruddy-cheeked man, heavyset with a round belly, the police chief sauntered inside. His voice teasing, he said, "I didn't know that you and Ruth are keeping company. Has this been going on for a long time?"

"If that's what you call Nick bringing me groceries and cooking me dinner once in a blue moon, I suppose we are," Ruth said, sounding a bit annoyed. Hands on hips, she stood between the chief and the kitchen, preventing him from walking any farther inside. "Somebody's gotta look out for me. I haven't heard you volunteer, Chief."

The chief snickered as if Ruth was joking, but she scowled at him. "To what do I owe this honor?"

The man's blue uniform shirt was pressed but bunched at the waist, and his pants bagged at the knees. Gabby decided that the chief looked like he'd worked a long day.

"Personally, I think this is a waste of time," he said. "But I told Nick yesterday about a missing woman, the wife of a Houston PD captain. His office sent out another bulletin this afternoon, requesting that agencies make the search a priority. I figured I'd knock on some doors, to find out if anyone's seen her."

With the chief barely five feet away, Gabby crossed her arms over her chest to stay calm. It was then that she considered the kitchen table. The plates were soaking in the sink, but three places remained set with forks and knives.

The chief handed Ruth what looked like a photo. "Any chance either of you have any information about this lady? Saw her, maybe? Think you might have?"

Nick spoke up quickly. "I told you, not me."

"Yeah, but—"

"Like I said, Chief, I wish I had," Nick interrupted, a bit of playfulness in his voice. "Darn attractive woman."

"She is that. How about you, Ruth?"

Gabby's heart quickened as she watched the chief scan the kitchen's clutter, taking in the dirty dishes soaking in the sink. He glanced toward the table, and Gabby held her breath.

"Where do you think I would have seen her?" Ruth's voice dripped with sarcasm. "At my yoga class? The movie theater? When I went to the beauty parlor? Chief, you know what an old recluse I am. Except to sit on the deck or walk on the riverbank, I barely leave my house."

That drew the chief's attention back to her, and he looked not at all pleased. A moment's pause, and he said, "You know, this is a dead end. No reason to think that woman's anywhere near here. But, Ruth, I said I would check, so I'm doing that."

"Well, now you've asked me, and no, I haven't seen this lady," she snapped.

"Okay, well. What about your neighbors, the Wallaces and the Thibedeauxs?"

As if he'd lost his mind, Ruth smirked. "You know that they won't be here for a couple more months, Chief. And that's not a day I'm looking forward to. The kids invade the river on that darn Jet Ski. They jump from that nasty old dock, like they're pretending to be those cliff divers in Acapulco, scaring away the fish."

"You're right about that, Ruth," the chief admitted with a sigh. "Those kids are hellions."

"Hellions is a good word. Since we're talking, when are you going to do something about those kids?"

Ignoring her question, the chief peered around Nick, toward the partially open door that led to the spare bedroom, the one Gabby hid behind. She doubted that he could see her but worried that she may have left something out on the bed or the floor, anything that could tip him off to the fact that there was someone else staying at the house. Her suitcase and backpack were hidden in the car, she'd made the bed, but she wondered if he could see the dresser with her hairbrush and a few toiletries on it.

Gabby swallowed hard, but the chief turned back to Ruth. "Like you said, those houses are empty. Have you noticed any sign that anyone might be squatting inside? Hear anything strange? See any lights on at night?"

"Quiet as a morgue, Chief," Ruth assured him. "No lights, no voices, no pretty woman with a black eye wandering around."

Behind the door, Gabby cringed.

The chief stared at Ruth, his eyes hard on her face. "How did you know about the woman's black eye? I didn't mention that."

Ruth said nothing, and the room felt oddly still. Behind the door, Gabby held her breath.

"I told her, Chief," Nick said, filling the uneasy silence. "I hope that's okay. I didn't think it was a secret."

"No, but—" the chief started.

"I told Ruth all about your stop at the store and the missing woman over dinner."

The chief paused as if unsure.

Ruth shot Nick a glance, then turned to the chief and chuckled. "Made for some interesting dinner conversation. Not usually much to talk about around here. Nothing much happens." When the chief stayed quiet, Ruth added, "I hope that woman's okay. Bet her husband's frantic."

"I bet he is," Nick agreed. "Her disappearing like that. Hurt and all."

For a moment, the chief continued to look at the two of them as if still uncertain. But then the man shrugged. "Yeah, I guess he must be. He's sure pushing hard to find her." The chief turned back toward the door, but then looked at them over his shoulder. "Okay, well, Nick, thanks for spreading the word."

"I was just leaving, Chief," he said. "You done for the night? If you are, I'd be willing to pop a couple of cold beers out of the store cooler. We can sit out front, see if any traffic goes by on the highway, and solve the world's problems."

The chief appeared to consider that. "You know, the wife's waiting at home, but that sounds darn good." He eyed Ruth and said, "If you're done with Nick's services, I think I'll take him up on that beer."

"Yup. I'm not that old. I can handle the dishes. You boys run along."

"If you see that woman—" the chief said on his way out the door.

"I'll call you, lickety-split," Ruth assured him. "And I'll keep a close watch on the neighbors' houses. Promise."

"Okay, then. Thanks." With that, the two men clomped down the creaky wood stairs, while Ruth stood at the door and watched.

"All clear," she shouted when they'd driven out to the road. "They're gone."

"WOULD YOU LIKE a hot tea?" Gabby asked after she finished the dishes. Her pulse had gone back to normal, but she kept glancing at the door, fearing to find the chief's shadow. To quiet her nerves and keep busy, she'd stacked newspapers Ruth had scattered around. In the morning, she'd check with Ruth first, then, if it was okay, take them outside to the recycle bin.

"Sure," Ruth shouted back. "Tea sounds good."

Gabby poured two cups and carried them to the deck where Ruth sat but then hesitated just inside the door. "Is it okay if I come out there? Will anyone see me? Do you think the chief will be back?"

"Nah," Ruth said. "Nick's entertaining him at the store. The chief'll drink a couple of beers and then head home. He's done his duty, knocked on my door. He's looked around and didn't see anything wrong. So, let's try not to worry."

Warming their hands on the cups, they sat side by side in the rockers, looking out at the moonlight reflecting off the river. The sky had turned a deep navy pierced by stars. Eager to find a distraction, Gabby thought about their conversation at the dinner table, about Ruth's travels. "South America must have been exciting."

"I grew to love it. That's where I saw it, you know."

"You're talking about the jabiru, right?" Gabby asked, trying to pull the threads together.

"Well, that, too, but I was actually talking about the waterfall."

"Waterfall?" Gabby wondered if Ruth might be confused again.

"I'll show you." After the long day, her back ached and her knees felt untrustworthy as Ruth pushed up from the chair and made her way toward her bedroom. When Gabby didn't follow, Ruth waved her on. "Come with me. Take a look."

As she walked, Gabby realized she had never been in Ruth's room, not in the three days she'd stayed at the house. Ruth put her finger in the hole left when the knob fell out and pushed the door open, then switched on a light. From the darkness, the room emerged. Surrounding the unmade bed and a battered old dresser hung framed photographs of native women carrying children, boys in loincloths spear-fishing in a jungle river, and men at a campsite at night, their faces illuminated by a fire.

Gabby moved closer for a better look and whispered, "You took these? They're stunning."

"I did."

Gabby saw pride in the old woman's eyes and how intensely she stared at the image that hung above her bed.

"This is my waterfall," Ruth said, pointing at it. Like all the others, it was black and white, but rather than people, the subject of this photo was a landscape—the side of a mammoth flat-topped mountain. From its top a long cascade of silver tumbled into a river.

"It's—"

"Spectacular." Ruth gazed at the photo as if even now, so many decades later, she couldn't take her eyes off it.

"I saw a picture of you with a leather pilot's hat on, the one on the living room table. I meant to ask you about it. You were a pilot?"

"I was. Got my license when I worked for the newspaper in Peoria."

Gabby gestured toward the wing of a plane in the right-hand lower corner of the waterfall photo. "Were you flying the plane that day?"

Ruth stared at the photograph, seeming lost in the image. "No, a friend flew me in to take that photograph."

"But how did you end up living in Venezuela?" Gabby asked, trying to fit what she'd just learned with Ruth's earlier account of her past.

That question obviously amused Ruth, who pressed her lips into a straight line and considered how to reply. "Well, you see, it all started one evening in a New York City bar."

# Chapter Fifteen

**New York, NY**

**August 1946**

A BUSY DAY, the last before we went to press with that week's magazine, and I finally slipped the cover over my typewriter and tucked it in for the night. I'd been in better moods. I was forty-one and stuck in a job that bored me, and that morning I'd noticed gray creeping into my brown hair. After a quick ride down in the elevator, I dropped in two doors up 40th Street. The sign out front read "The Artist and Writers Restaurant," but everyone called the place Bleeck's after its owner. Like a lot of *Trib* staffers, I was something of a regular, and I claimed a stool. Nursing my usual scotch and soda, I paid no attention when the phone behind the bar rang.

"Robertson! It's for you!"

"Hey, Ruthie," a familiar voice said. "I'm in town. How about meeting me at Costello's?"

"Clayton Knight?" We'd kept in touch since we'd met in Alaska, and we sometimes got together for drinks. But this was a surprise. "When did you get to the city? What are you doing at Costello's?"

"Arrived yesterday. Meant to let you know, but I've been so busy, I forgot. I'm waiting on a bunch of flyboys. Some airline folks in from Venezuela are here with me. They're hiring. They want Americans to fill empty pilot seats."

"And you want me there because?"

"Because it would be fun to see you."

Half an hour later a train rumbled past on the Third Avenue elevated as I swung the door open at Big Tim Costello's. The place had history. Two years earlier John Steinbeck and Ernest Hemingway had met for the first time in the bar, and back in the day, John O'Hara and F. Scott Fitzgerald held court there. The James Thurber mural of his Battle of the Sexes cartoon covering one wall was, according to legend, a depression-era payment for an overdue bar tab. When I walked in, I saw the usual crowd, mostly reporters and editors, a healthy number from the *New Yorker*.

As soon as I spotted Clayton, I waved. His glasses perched low on his long nose, he was talking to two men, who I assumed were the before-mentioned Venezuelans.

The empty chairs around us quickly filled with ex-GIs. The war over, Uncle Sam no longer required their services. Once he had everyone's attention, one of the Venezuelans explained that in their country the oil industry was booming, bringing in large US corporations, and to become competitive their airline wanted to add routes to New York and a few other cities. "To do that we'll need pilots who speak English."

Laying out the pitch, a short, dark-haired guy with shaggy eyebrows threw out salaries that made American wages sound paltry. All around me, the men nodded, impressed, some grabbing applications off a stack in the center of the table.

"You should come, too," the head Venezuelan said to me when I explained that I was a photographer and a reporter. "We'll pay you to write articles about our expansion into *Los Estados Unidos*."

"What's the name of the airline?" I asked, intrigued with the idea but unsure.

"LAV. *Linea Aeropostal Venezolana.*"

"I can't work for an airline I can't even pronounce the name of." Partly, I was serious. How could a reporter function in a country without being able to speak the language? The Venezuelan, however, assumed I was joking. Without waiting for confirmation, he added my name to his growing list of recruits.

*Well, why not?* I decided.

"Venezuela, that's where that waterfall is, right?" a reporter friend asked after I turned in my resignation.

"What waterfall?" Packing my personal items from my desk in a box, I was surprised that in such a short time I'd accumulated so much. Did I really need three coffee cups?

"You know the one—Angel Falls." When I looked at her as if I'd missed something, the woman shrugged. "I thought everyone knew about it. It's supposed to be a mile high. The tallest in the world."

Not believing that any waterfall could measure a full mile, I fought the urge to challenge the woman and instead said, "Well, now, that would be something to see."

"Wouldn't it," she responded rather dreamily. "Maybe you'll get a looksee while you're there."

"I HEAR THERE'S an amazing waterfall in your country. Is that true?" Why I brought it up when I stopped at the Venezuelan consulate for my visa, I wasn't sure, but it came to mind as I filled out the paperwork.

"There are many beautiful waterfalls, but you must mean the Angel one," the clerk said. As he checked my visa application, he told the story of a man named Jimmie Angel, the bush pilot who'd found the falls. It all started when he'd flown an old prospector into the jungle looking for gold. The man directed him where to go, turn right, turn left, then finally to land on a mountaintop. Once they did, the prospector pulled gold nuggets out of a river, so many that Angel had a hard time coaxing his plane off the ground.

For years after, the clerk explained, Angel tried to retrace the route they'd taken. He'd flown across the jungle, high over the mountains, searching for that El Dorado, eager to collect his own fortune from the river. Despite dozens of attempts, Jimmie Angel couldn't find the right mountain.

"There, go look! See how thick the jungles are in my country," the clerk ordered, pointing at a large, framed photograph hanging on the wall. I leaned in close for a view of the faded image and discovered a muted landscape, a sky with billowing clouds, dense vegetation, and erupting from the earth's floor, strange mountains with flat tops. They looked as if, when they were formed many millennia ago, the gods had taken a massive axe and lopped off their peaks.

The clerk put down my paperwork and continued his story. He recounted how in 1935 Jimmie Angel set his sights on one of the largest mountains, Auyán-tepuí. "This mountain is made of black rock and has a frightening look about it," the clerk said, his eyes intent as he became engrossed in his tale. "Something about it long ago terrified the Indians, and their legends warn that those who dare to trespass on Auyán-tepuí disappear, never to return. They even gave it a name, one that warns of evil. Devil's Mountain."

For months, Angel repeatedly flew over Auyán-tepuí, convinced it was there that he would find his long-lost river of gold. On one flight, he realized that the mountain's shape resembled a heart, with an indentation formed by a canyon he hadn't before seen. Intrigued, he made a sharp turn and entered the gorge. As he flew inside, he came upon the tallest waterfall he'd ever encountered.

The gold Jimmie Angel sought remained elusive, but that day he returned to Caracas with the story of a mighty waterfall. To all who would listen, he proclaimed it a mile high, the tallest in the world. As its discoverer, he gave the waterfall his name, christening it "Angel Falls."

The clerk finished his story, and I considered what he'd just said. "How did Jimmie Angel measure it to find out that it's a mile high?"

"No one has ever measured it," the man scoffed, looking at me as if I'd lost all sense. "It is impossible to measure by air. The surveyor's tools must be set up on the ground. They measure from bottom to top. And no one has ever reached it by land. It's surrounded by the deepest jungles on earth, filled with mountain lions, jaguars, snakes, and poisonous insects. Men have tried, but all have failed. Even the Indians stay away, believing the legends of the mountain's devils."

As I left the embassy, my visa papers stamped with the clerk's official seal, I wondered about the waterfall. Could it really be a mile high? Before going back to my apartment, I took a side trip and dropped in at a library. Paging through the "W" encyclopedia, I stopped at a list of the world's tallest waterfalls. The chart ranked South Africa's Tugela Falls at 3,110 feet as the tallest.

At the bottom beside an asterisk, I saw "Angel Falls, Venezuela, height unknown."

FROM MY FIRST day in Venezuela, I found the country wildly enchanting.

A woman in a bright-red dress bordered with white lace and colored ribbons handed me a bouquet of gardenias as I stepped off the plane. "*Muchas gracias!*" I said, my Spanish phrase book in my hand.

I couldn't compare Caracas to anywhere else I'd traveled. Not New York, with its skyscrapers and cement, or Alaska, where the landscape much of the year was covered with ice and snow. In contrast, Caracas welcomed me with a riot of color: green palm trees, red tile roofs, brightly feathered parrots, and bread-plate-size hibiscus blooming in brilliant hues of pink, orange, red, white, and yellow.

Famished, I dropped my bags in my room and claimed a seat at an outdoor café near the hotel. Seasons were reversed from the northern hemisphere, and Christmas loomed, but south of the equator, it was a warm summer day. I ordered an *arepas rumberas*, a chopped pork sandwich on corn bread. Before it arrived, a boom shook my table. A frantic waiter rushed past shouting, "*Una revolucion!*"

"What's happened?"

In broken English, he explained that someone had exploded a bomb near the presidential palace. The reporter in me took over, and I ran upstairs and grabbed a notebook and pen, camera and film.

Minutes later I was rushing in the direction the waiter had pointed, on my way to the palace. Turning down one street, I crossed paths with troops searching for insurgents. On another, I was almost run over by a ragtag group of rebels hoping to hide in an alley. I wondered if I'd inadvertently landed in yet another war, but a mere two hours after it began, the revolt ended. By the following day, no one talked of the rebellion, and life went on as if it had never happened.

"I'M SORRY ABOUT this," the LAV public relations manager told me when I reported to start work. "We've decided to hold off on opening any new routes. We won't be able to use you. But we're happy to fly you back to New York."

I'd been in Caracas for one week, and suddenly I was unemployed in a foreign land where I knew few people. I was working on my Spanish, but I had a long way to go to become fluent. In the oil boom, inflation had skyrocketed, and prices for food, clothing, and rent ranked among the most expensive in the world. But nothing waited for me in New York. My job at the *Tribune* had been filled. And I didn't want to leave South America. I'd barely begun to explore Venezuela.

To bring in cash, I developed the film I'd taken of the short-lived revolution, printed the photos, and sent samples to editors at US magazines. *Life* and *Time* bought a few images and offered freelance work, assignments to write pieces on South American politics and events. Although welcome, that income would be sporadic, staggering

in when I sold an assignment. I couldn't count on it to pay my bills.

Worried about making ends meet, I lugged my portfolio with my photographs and articles to the public relations departments of a few big oil companies. To my relief, I landed a regular gig with a monthly retainer at Creole Petroleum, an American company drilling on Lake Maracaibo. Within days, I was flying to remote destinations, to makeshift towns set up to service the fields. I wore a hard hat as I snapped photos of the workers and equipment. Oil rained down on me as a gusher came in, spouting off its first barrels of black gold.

"I hear the tourist bureau is looking for photographers," a man told me one night while we listened to music in one of the clubs. I signed on and traveled the country documenting the local culture, rural farms, small towns, and bustling cities. I shot sunsets on plantations and sunrises on city streets.

I fell in love with the jungles.

"Yes," I said to the native woman. Her baby was swaddled in a scarf she had anchored around her shoulders as she tended a group of toddlers running in all directions. Friendly, she chattered happily in a language I couldn't begin to understand, so I simply kept agreeing.

Overhead a parasol of branches and leaves filtered the sun, allowing only slender shafts of light to reach the earth, giving even high noon a twilight glow. In villages, I captured images of women pounding laundry on rocks. Instead of taxis honking on Manhattan streets, parrots squawked, monkeys prattled, and raindrops smacked on thick, broad palm fronds.

At times my mind wandered deeper into the jungle, to a canyon inside Auyán-tepuí. To Angel Falls.

A good crowd milled about that night inside the American Club, which was tucked into a rickety but elegant old colonial building, a former hotel. On the palm-lined patio, expats compared stories: journalists, oilmen and their wives, and an architect out of California designing a new corporate headquarters. Thick with cigarette smoke and the smell of the alcohol-stained rug, the bar buzzed with conversation. I hung out for a while and then splintered off with a small group to a nightclub where, instead of waltzes, the patrons danced the merengue, mambos, and sambas.

Over my "*lo mismo*," my usual scotch and soda, I asked about the country, the terrain, the jungle, and Angel Falls.

"I don't believe it even exists," a woman insisted. "It's a figment of that man's imagination."

"Well, Jimmie Angel says it's a mile high, but who can say for sure?" an oil exec reasoned. He held up his hand for emphasis, tucking in the thumb and spreading out his fingers. "There've been four attempts. Four of them. None of the groups reached the falls by land, the only way to measure it. My guess is that we may never really know how tall it is."

Other nights, I pigeonholed people who'd lived in the country long enough to have followed the headlines. "What happened to the expeditions to Angel Falls? Why did they fail?"

In response, I heard tales of experienced explorers who hired local guides. Well funded, they carted heavy pallets of food and supplies for journeys that were to take little more than a week but turned into a month. The jungle fought them with every step. For each foot they moved forward, they had to cut a path through a thick wall of vegetation. Eventually, all ran out of food. Some suffered snakebites, and at least one man died. Others the jungle confused. Lost, they stumbled off never to be seen again.

"And then there are the Indians," an oil-rig worker said, raising his eyebrows for emphasis. He told stories of men who'd vanished, those who were believed to have fallen victim to tribes of cannibals. Some survivors who did make their way back to Caracas ranted about horrific conditions, swamps, and rapids.

"Even flying in that area is dangerous," a pilot friend warned.

"Most days the mountains are shrouded in clouds. Planes disappear, most likely crashed into the jungles, and their crews' remains are never recovered."

"This is the twentieth century," I said in surprise. "Surely someone has succeeded in getting to the falls by land."

"Not one," a friend insisted. "It's hopeless."

The group of friends around me laughed when I said that I would like to see the falls, and one man voiced what perhaps they all thought but were too polite to say. "The jungle is too dangerous a place, especially for a woman."

Listening politely, I didn't disregard their views, but I refused to accept that a journey to the falls was impossible. The jungle might be thick, and it was undoubtedly dangerous, but there had to be a way.

IN CARACAS, I befriended pilots who transported supplies in and rubber and gold out of the jungles. On my free days, I palmed them a little money and hopped on with their cargo, going wherever their jobs took them, shooting photos and exploring. One after another, I asked them if they'd ever seen Angel Falls. None had.

As the weeks passed, I daydreamed about the falls as one might a handsome movie idol. I closed my eyes and visualized the flat-topped mountains and a thick stream of foaming water falling white against the black rock. I'd spent my life attempting to bury my past—my grandmother's contempt, my father's betrayal. I remembered the looks of respect on the faces in the newsroom the day Amelia Earhart soloed across the Atlantic. And I mused about how someday, someone would make history by reaching the falls and measuring it.

I grew to believe that there was no reason that person couldn't be me.

Others disagreed.

"You don't know the language. The tribes have many different ones. And you'll be entering a part of the world that's unmapped, basically unknown," a friend railed one night over drinks at a local bar when I confessed my desire to find a way.

"This is insane," he concluded. "And impossible."

I heard what they were saying, but I couldn't shake my dream. I thought of those who could help me, and one man repeatedly came to mind: "Have you ever met Jimmie Angel?" I asked those I met. "I'd like to talk to him."

Some said Jimmie popped into Caracas off and on, but no one knew when he would appear or how long he would stay. "I've been living here for five years, and I've never seen him," said one oil exec. "I wouldn't be surprised to find out that the man and his waterfall are both fictional."

Another night at one of the dance clubs, music played, and women in long dresses swirled in the arms of their husbands and lovers. My friends appeared exasperated when I again steered the conversation to Angel Falls. It was evident that they were tired of hearing what they considered my folly, an ill-conceived plan to tilt at windmills. "Ruthie, you have no idea what you'd face. The dangers. If the Indians don't kill you, you'll die of a snakebite, malaria, dysentery."

Perhaps they were right. But it was a dream I couldn't shake. "You know, everything important I've ever done has been hard," I responded.

At night in my apartment overlooking the city, I considered why all the expeditions to the falls had proven unsuccessful. I wondered what the adventurers who failed should have done differently. And sometimes I mused about the irony of it all, that a waterfall named Angel cascaded off a mountain nicknamed after the devil.

Gradually, Angel Falls dominated my mind.

Off and on, I thought of the Gypsy woman's prophecy that fate would guide me. Over the years, I'd sensed its presence, the unexplained interceding in my life. Could it have been happenstance that moved my quest forward? Perhaps. But to me it felt more like providence.

I'd spent that day shooting photos of a corporate exec and that evening relaxed with friends back at the American Club. A pilot walked up to the bar and ordered a drink. We'd met before, and I asked where he was off to next. "Ciudad Bolivar, up the Rio Orinoco. Have you been there?'

"No." Ciudad Bolivar, CB to locals, lay in the general direction of Angel Falls. Considering the location, lured by the possibility of traveling closer to my goal, I mentioned, "I've wanted to see the city. I hear it's fun."

"Well, you should hitch a ride," he offered, as I'd hoped he might. "It's a swell town."

That night, I threw clothes in one bag, my camera equipment in another. The next morning from the air, I watched the Orinoco, one of South America's longest rivers, spread out beneath us. Under a tent of bright blue sky, the river sparkled, surrounded by dense, lush tropical forest.

We dropped his cargo at the airport and then drove a rented jeep into CB. A quaint city with a European flair, it had streets lined with white oleander and deep purple petunias. Standing by their carts, vendors sold palm-frond hats, rope hammocks, and leather sandals, as well as lemonade and chunks of fruit in paper cups. While we explored, I asked my pilot friend, "Have you ever seen Angel Falls?"

"I don't think so. There are thousands of waterfalls in Venezuela. I couldn't possibly know them all."

"Do you know the Gran Sabana? That's where the expeditions to the falls have kicked off from," I explained, employing the Spanish name for the Great Savannah, a rich landscape marbled by rivers and swift rapids. The vast valley was populated by an array of unusual plants and animals. "I bet that if someone flew from there, he could find his way to the falls. And wouldn't that be something to see? Some say it's the tallest waterfall in the world."

Holding my breath, I hoped that he'd offer to fly me to try to find Angel Falls, but he didn't take the bait. When I offered to pay him, he still refused. "You need to forget this. I don't even know where Angel Falls is. Trying to find it in the jungle is madness."

But the desire stalked me.

Weeks later back in Caracas, I ran into that same pilot again. This time, he was the one who mentioned Angel Falls. "Is that still your dream? To see it?"

"More than anything. I can't explain why, but it's something I have to do."

"I've asked around. I think I can find that mountain of yours."

We flew out on a delivery run to Ciudad Bolivar early the next morning, the plane ripe with the smell of its cargo of caged chickens and goats and pigs tied to walls. We unloaded in Ciudad Bolivar, stayed overnight, and then took off the next afternoon, heading toward the Gran Sabana.

When I considered that I might finally see the waterfall, my excitement built. As we flew, I scanned the scenery below. Although I'd heard much about the remote mountain jungles, the landscape spread out beneath us was more formidable than I'd imagined. As far as I could see, a thick umbrella of palms hid the earth. For the first time, I truly understood why airplanes vanished. When they crashed, the jungle swallowed them, camouflaging the wreckage from above.

Finally, in the distance, I saw the *tepuís*, the flat-topped mountains. We approached, and the surreal sight resembled nothing I'd ever encountered. It reminded me of landscapes described by Arthur Conan Doyle in  *The Lost World* and W. H. Hudson in *Green Mansions*. Every bit as dramatic, the panoramas surrounding us appeared an alien world, one where the strange black mountains erupted from a lush jungle floor. As we flew closer, we passed crystal waterfalls—some slender and tall, others so wide that they covered entire mountainsides—plummeting from rugged mesas a thousand feet or more above the earth's floor.

The plane bounced in the turbulence, and I held on as we rounded a curve, and the pilot pointed. "I think that's the mountain you want to see," he shouted over the thunder of the engines.

I'd imagined this moment for months, and my heart soared. Auyán-tepuí. At last.

As we flew closer, my perspective changed, and I could see that this particular mountain was mammoth, so tall its top disappeared inside a ring of opaque clouds.

"Where's the canyon? The one with the waterfall inside?"

"Let's take a look," he offered, and we flew closer, passed the mountain on one side, made a gentle curve in the sky, and headed back. Craning my neck to search the mountain's walls, I saw nothing, no indication of an opening and no shadows that might hide a chasm.

"I don't think we'll see anything today," he said after one more run. "No chance in that mass of clouds. Even if we find the opening, we can't fly inside. No visibility."

I knew he was right, but I begged him to try. Giving in, he made another sweep, then one more, but we saw no entrance to Auyán-tepuí's heart, no gateway to Angel Falls.

Grateful, I thanked him, and we headed back. Despite seeing Auyán-tepuí for the first time, when we landed at the airport, I felt only disappointment. The falls were waiting inside the mountain for me, but it was possible that the naysayers were right; that I would never see them.

My oil company work piled up in Caracas, but I lingered in Ciudad Bolivar.

Each day I woke early and taxied to the airport. I checked the logs and approached the pilots, asking where their jobs would take them. If they were agreeable, I offered them a little money to alter their routes to fly near Auyán-tepuí. I explained that I hoped to catch a glimpse of Angel Falls. Some refused. Others agreed.

Day after day, I hopped on planes praying for clear skies, desperate to see the chasm in the mammoth black rock that led to Angel Falls. On the flights, I kept busy, jotting down information on the jungles and rivers we flew over. I took photographs and drew maps, documenting the territory. I'd told no one, but I'd begun to consider what so many said was impossible: mounting my own expedition to reach Angel Falls by land and measure it. To my disappointment, each time we arrived at Auyán-tepuí, the mountain—shrouded in clouds—kept its secrets.

# Chapter Sixteen

## Caracas, Venezuela

## 1947

THE EVENING IT finally happened, I stood on my apartment's terrace, gazing out at the city. Always beautiful, the view was breathtaking when the streetlights cast a golden glow. Even then, Angel Falls shadowed me. I'd tried to convince myself to move on, to give up and refocus my life, but I couldn't let go of the dream. I spent every free moment with a pad of paper and a pencil, poring over my notes and photos, making drawings of the jungle surrounding Auyán-tepuí, searching for any possible way to cut down the length of the trip to the mountain.

Then my phone rang.

"Hey, Ruthie, how about having some fun?" My friend Pam lived nearby with her husband, good eggs from Indiana.

"It's a school night. I have a shoot in the morning, so I'm locked in," I explained, trying to cut off any attempt to lure me out.

"Well, I think you should get unlocked. You ought to head down to the American Club."

"I can't—"

"Ruthie, there's someone special in the bar tonight." When I started to protest again, she said, "It's someone you've been wanting to meet."

"WELL, THIS MUST be that Ruth Robertson we've been waiting for," a man shouted when I arrived. He was a stocky fellow with dark hair in his late forties, with a round pockmarked face, ample cheeks, and ribbons of wrinkles across his forehead. Tapered, penetrating deep-brown eyes sized me up and then shot me a suspicious glance. "I hear you've been looking for me."

"Who are you?" I thought I knew, now that I'd seen him. Pam wouldn't say on the phone who was at the bar, but folks had described him to me.

"Haven't you guessed yet?" he grumbled.

"Well, if I'm guessing, the name I'm coming up with is Jimmie Angel." The guy chuckled, and his belly shook. I smiled, deciding to have a bit of fun. "But that can't be true. I've been looking for him for months."

"You have?" The man before me feigned shock.

"I have. And by now I'm figuring he doesn't really exist. Maybe you're an imposter."

At first, Jimmie frowned, then his narrow lips curled into a grin, and instantly his robust cackle again filled the room. "Ruth, how about I buy you a drink?"

"My usual," I called out to the bartender. Then I turned back to the man I'd just met. I wasn't about to let him escape. "We need to find a table. I want to talk to you about your waterfall."

While we waited for our drinks, I threw out the question I most wanted answered. "Well, how tall is this waterfall?"

Jimmie snorted, as if at the ridiculousness of my query. Out of his pocket he pulled a gold nugget the size of a Brazil nut, one he toyed with and occasionally pointed at me to bolster his arguments. "Oh, my waterfall's high. The highest in the world."

"But how high? Did you measure it?"

Despite his years as a pilot in South America, I detected Cedar Valley, the small Missouri town where he'd grown up, in Jimmie's voice. "Angel Falls is a mile high. Yes, I measured it."

Jimmie sat up taller, and threw back his shoulders, as if confident, but I wasn't buying it. He rolled the gold nugget around between his thumb and forefinger. My question had made him uncomfortable. "How did you measure it? Did you fly in, or did you hike in and measure it from the ground?"

At that, Jimmie smirked. "I flew up above it. But I could see. I could tell how high." Pausing for just a minute, he leaned forward, closed one eye, opened the other wide and round, and then stared at me like a cyclops. "I eyeballed it."

I couldn't help myself. I giggled.

"That's funny?" he roared.

"Well, you can't measure it that way," I said. Then I repeated what I'd been told by every engineer I'd talked to about the falls. "The only way to measure the waterfall is from the ground. That's how the surveyor's instruments work."

Our drinks arrived, and Jimmie took a healthy swig. He slipped the nugget back into his pocket, then pushed his gray fedora back and forth on the table while he appeared to think that over. At times, he seemed ready to argue with me, but instead he bit his lip and remained silent. Watching him, I was even more certain that he was bluffing.

Puffing out his chest, he squirmed in his chair. "Have you seen the falls?" he challenged. "If you have, you know that it has to be the tallest in the world."

"No. I've flown over, but it's always too cloudy."

"The clouds? You should have gone early in the morning, Ruth, before they moved in," he said, and I wondered if it was as simple as that. Was that all I'd been doing wrong?

"Why don't you fly me in, Jimmie? We could go together. We could figure out how to get it measured. A real, honest-to-goodness accounting of its height, so there's no dispute."

"No need." Jimmie frowned at me with the look men gave women when they'd decided that we were being unreasonable. "I know how tall my waterfall is. And I'm busy. I leave tomorrow. I have jobs farther south. I'll be gone for at least a month."

I sat back and looked at him, hard. "Jimmie, if you're going to get your waterfall on the list as the tallest in the world, it needs to be officially measured. I mean, how can you be sure that it's a mile high?"

"Well," Jimmie drew up his shoulders as if warding off a blow, ready for a fight. But then he apparently had second thoughts. Instead, he sat back and waved his hand, as if at a pesky housefly. "Maybe I exaggerated a little. Who knows exactly how tall it is? It's impossible to tell."

"I bet you did exaggerate." I let out a puff of laughter. "Jimmie, I bet you did."

Jimmie shrugged, then chuckled along with me. I interpreted his demeanor as an admission that he had no idea how tall his waterfall was. Suddenly, he got serious. "This I know." He pointed at me with one of his thick fingers. "Angel Falls *is* the highest in the world. It's impossible that any other waterfall is taller."

"But if you haven't measured it? If it is the tallest, but not measured, does it matter how high it is? People won't believe it."

"I don't care what—"

"Jimmie, doesn't it bother you that Tugela Falls in South Africa is on the top of all the lists?"

"Pssssst," he hissed at me. "I tell you, I know how tall my waterfall is. It's at least a thousand feet higher than Tugela. Maybe more. There's no need to measure it."

That night, Jimmie and I sat together for hours as I peppered him with questions. On the table between us, he slid his fedora toward me, still nervously playing with it, while he reminisced about his many flights across the Gran Sabana. I listened intently, taking notes, the way I would have if I'd been interviewing him for a newspaper or magazine piece. As we talked, I realized how much I had in common with the man who sat across from me. We shared a love of flying, a fascination with adventure, a longing to explore. More than anything else, we were linked by our obsessions with Angel Falls.

In the end, we also had our differences.

As the evening wore on, I suspected that he'd picked up on my plans, and he wanted to warn me.

"You know, I almost died on that damn mountain. My wife too." On the top of a mesa covered in rock and scarred by deep fissures, Jimmie had been out looking for his river of gold. Certain he'd find what he sought on Auyán-tepuí, he'd landed his monoplane on the side opposite the only known route off the mountain. The rainy season had just passed, and the plane's wheels bogged down in the mud. When they couldn't break free, they grabbed Jimmie's stash of emergency food from the plane and took off on foot, climbing rocks, hiking across boulders worn flat by the elements, fording narrow streams—a grueling journey. They barely made it off the mountain with their lives. Once down, they happened upon a native village and help. "We were lucky, and I'll never risk that again. There are scores of ways to die in that jungle," Jimmie whispered, his eyes locked on mine. "Fall off a cliff, fall into a ravine, tumble into a river and drown, sink so far into the muck you can't pull yourself out. All the creatures that can kill you: poisonous plants, insects, snakes, jaguars. The Indians who helped us were peaceful, but not all are."

"I know, Jimmie. I do," I said. "But somebody has to go in and measure that waterfall, give it its due." Then I said it out loud, for the first time. "Why not me?"

Jimmie shook his head—speechless.

As I got ready to leave, he stood across from me. Hands on his hips, legs slightly parted, he took the universal stance of a man who wanted to make sure the woman he was talking to understood that he was unmovable.

"Listen here, Ruth Robertson. You don't know that jungle. It's damned dangerous. And my waterfall is as measured as it's ever going to get. No one can reach it by land. It's crazy to even try."

I stood firm. "You're wrong, Jimmie. Someday, if it's truly as tall as you say it is, someone is going to enter the history books by measuring your waterfall."

Jimmie Angel glared at me, as if I'd truly lost my mind. "Well, if it does get measured, it won't be by some gal newspaper photographer. Cutting through that jungle is a man's job. You'll get killed out there."

Looking at the man before me, thinking how much he resembled all those in my life who'd tried to keep me from breaking out of the box society locked women in, I tried not to be angry with Jimmie Angel. He believed he was right. I didn't doubt that he was sincerely concerned about my safety. That said, I needed to make him under-stand that I wasn't backing down. So, I dismissed his warning in five words.

"Well, we'll see about that."

# Chapter Seventeen

**Brazoria County, Texas**

**March 1993**

THE FOLLOWING MORNING, Gabby woke before sunrise with the sense that something troubling lingered just far enough away that she couldn't touch it. They'd been up late the night before, well past midnight, talking. Antsy, she listened at Ruth's bedroom door and felt reassured to hear a soft snore. Not wanting to wake Ruth, Gabby stood alone at the back window for nearly an hour, watching the road, mulling over the police chief's unexpected arrival the evening before.

Her nerves toyed with her, and she needed something to fill the time. Stacks of papers and photographs lay on the kitchen table, mementos that Ruth had pulled out of drawers to show her. Gabby paged through images of coffee plantations, oil fields, and downtown Caracas in an era long past, as well as photos taken from the air of the dense jungles. The last photo she came upon was of a man in a fedora.

"Well, Jimmie, you're quite the guy, aren't you," she whispered.

In the portrait, Jimmie Angel appeared just as Ruth described him, his round cheeks pockmarked, his eyes dark slits, and his expression one of gritty determination. As Gabby examined the man's face, so serious, she thought about how he'd spent his life searching for a river of gold.

"You up?" Ruth called out from the bedroom.

Gabby shuffled the photos, articles, and papers together, forming piles. "Yup, just cleaning up. I'm going to put these things away that you showed me last night. I was just taking a last look at that photo of Jimmie Angel."

The bedroom door popped open, and Ruth ambled out. "That man, that man! As much as I adored him, I tell you, Gabby, there were times when I found him exasperating."

The morning disappeared, and Gabby kept busy cleaning more of the clutter out of Ruth's house. In the beginning, she'd worried that Ruth might be reluctant to throw things away, but it had become apparent that she had no emotional attachment to much of what she'd collected. She simply hadn't taken the time to dispose of newspapers or magazines in the past decade or longer. As Gabby carried the third load of the day to the trash bin, she heard a car on the road. Clutching the stack of newspapers to her chest, she hid behind the shed.

Moments later, Nick's Blazer turned down the driveway. He emerged carrying another brown paper grocery bag.

"We didn't put in an order, did we?"

Nick grinned at her when she strode out from behind the shed. "No. But I've got fresh eggs from a friend who has chickens. Thought you and Ruth might like some."

Inside the house, Gabby slipped the eggs into the refrigerator and then turned to discover Nick huddling with Ruth. "So, you're not just delivering eggs this morning. There's more bad news?"

"Kind of," Nick's brow was knit into a thick twist of skin.

"What has Jeff done now?"

"Well, that husband of yours is doing his best to make you famous," he said.

"Make me famous?"

As the two women listened, Nick recounted how he'd turned on the noon news. "Hardly any customers as usual. So, I figured why not. I do that sometimes. Your picture came on right before the weather report, the same one the chief showed us. But then there were more pictures, snapshots of you with a big guy, kind of sandy hair, maybe forty years old, cement-block jawline."

"Jeff," Gabby murmured.

"They showed a wedding photo, Jeff in a tux, both of you beaming. Couldn't have looked happier."

"What did they say?" Ruth asked. "Just request folks watch for Gabby?"

"Well, pretty much."

"There was more, I bet," Gabby guessed.

At that, Nick's frown deepened. "The first part was a rundown by the reporter about Jeff reporting you missing, then the photos. But at the end, they cut to an interview in front of police headquarters. Jeff had on his full uniform, and they made a big point of explaining that he runs the homicide department, that he's one of our boys in blue, and that he needs help finding his wife."

Ruth released a long sigh. "You have to be kidding."

"Wish I was. That guy's pulling every trick he can, using his position. He even teared up, looked like he might cry, talking about how he needs help finding his wife. Said, 'I know she's out there somewhere, frightened, probably in danger. Please, help me find her.'"

Her heart racing, Gabby eased down onto one of the kitchen

chairs.

"I guess he's not worried that people will believe Gabby's side of the story?" Ruth prodded.

"Jeff's got all that covered," Nick explained.

"How did he do that?" Ruth's voice sounded strained, like she was having a hard time absorbing all Nick was saying.

"Jeff had a doctor there to talk to the press, a specialist who said that an injury like the one Jeff described could have given Gabby amnesia or caused false memories. Jeff said he plans to check Gabby in to a hospital when he finds her, a place where they can help her regain her memory."

Ruth fumed. "Oh Lord, oh Lord! That man has gall."

At the table, Gabby propped her head up in her hands and curled her fingers through her hair.

"That's not the end of it. The reporter said that he'll have more on the case at six this evening and ten tonight."

"This is hopeless," Gabby muttered. "I need to get away and start a new life. But I know Jeff. He's not going to give up. No place will ever be safe."

"Is that really what you want?" Ruth sounded indignant, angry. "To run away and hide? To give up your life? To let Jeff win?"

"Do I have a choice?"

Ruth lowered her voice and whispered, "Everyone has a choice."

Gabby considered pointing out to Ruth that she hadn't been there on the nights Jeff turned into a monster. But Ruth had a determined look, a confidence Gabby wished she felt. *Her body is old, but she hasn't given up. I used to be like that. Before Jeff.*

"We need to find help. I mean, someone who can back you up. Did you tell anyone?" Gabby looked at her questioning, and Ruth explained, "About the beatings, about Jeff? Did anyone ever see your bruises. Someone at work? A friend?"

"My mother, but she's gone now. I used to confide in her. A couple of times, early on, I left Jeff and stayed with her. Mom begged me not to go back to him, but I was in love. And he promised he'd change. In the beginning, I believed him. I *wanted* to believe him. When my mom got sick, I stopped confiding in her. I couldn't burden her with my troubles."

"Oh, Gabby," Ruth said. "She would have wanted you to—"

Gabby waved her off. "Jeff has gotten worse since she died. I guess he realized that she was the only person I could turn to, the only one I could always count on to help me."

"Think hard. Did you tell anyone else?" Nick asked. "Anyone at all?"

Gabby didn't need to take time to consider his question. She knew the answer. "No. No one. I wore turtlenecks, long sleeves, even in summer. The only ones I told, the only ones I showed my bruises to were the police officers who responded to the condo those nights I called 911. But they won't help. They've already picked a side. Jeff's side."

The mood in the creaky old house felt oppressive, like the mourning room in a funeral parlor.

Ruth slid onto the chair across from Gabby. Ginger snuggled against her leg, and the old woman picked the terrier up, put her on her lap, and stroked her. For a brief moment there was only silence, then Ruth said, "If there's one thing I've learned in life, it's that there's always a way. We're just not asking the right questions or looking in the right places."

The room remained uncomfortably quiet, everyone lost in their own thoughts. Then, something occurred to Gabby. "When you think about it, Jeff didn't live in a vacuum before we got together."

Ruth and Nick turned to her, as if waiting for more.

"He'd been married before, twice divorced."

Nick put into words what they were all thinking. "So, two other women know who Captain Jeff Jordan really is."

# Chapter Eighteen

**Houston, Texas**

**March 1993**

THAT EVENING AT seven, Gabby and Nick waited in his Blazer across the street from a midrise office building on the edge of downtown Houston. Their plan: to sneak inside her law firm's offices and access her computer. Being there made Gabby consider all she'd lost. She missed her career, her friends, her life. When she fled, she'd left work hanging, clients waiting for motions and actions to be filed, contracts that needed to be drawn up. She wondered what her coworkers thought about the way she'd disappeared. Perhaps they'd turned on the breakroom television at noon to watch Jeff beg for information on her whereabouts. Perhaps they planned to watch the late news at home and would go to bed hoping that Gabby was found.

They had no way of knowing how much she wanted to stay missing.

After the lights darkened, Gabby saw the cleaning crew drive out of the parking lot. For another ten minutes, she and Nick lingered and scanned the street, worried that someone might be concealed in the shadows. The office building wasn't far from the courthouse, but downtown Houston's streets gaped empty, commuters at home with their families. When all remained quiet, they approached a side entrance.

Gabby looked uneasy, and Nick whispered, "You okay?"

"Just nervous." Gabby inserted her key. A click and they were inside the building.

An elevator took them to the ninth floor, and they entered the firm's reception area. Gabby switched on the lights.

"Turn those off," Nick ordered. Gabby did, and the room plunged back into near darkness. From a back pocket, he retrieved a penlight. "You lead."

Down a long hallway, they stopped at a glass door stenciled with GABRIELLA JORDAN. Gabby unlocked the door, then closed the blinds and turned on her computer. Papers covered her desk, as if she'd been there that day, working. The file boxes stacked next to the desk were marked with the names of her clients. Once the opening computer screen appeared, Gabby keyed in her password.

"Will they know you've done this? Will there be a record?"

As she hit keys, Gabby shook her head. "Not unless they specifically look at the computer log, and why would they?"

Once she connected to LexisNexis, she entered "Jeff Jordan" into the search box. Hundreds of lines of citations and links filled the screen for scores of Jeff Jordans around the world. She narrowed the search by typing in "Houston, Texas," and much of the list disappeared.

"Here we go."

"Anything look good?" Nick asked.

Skimming each line of text, Gabby singled out her marriage license and registrations for cars Jeff had purchased, a few links to recent newspaper articles and television segments about her disappearance.

"Nothing here. Unless…"

In one of the documents, she noticed the address of a house Jeff had owned before they married. "He probably lived there with the second wife. If she called police…"

Gabby swiped Jeff's old address and pasted it into the search bar. No police records popped up, but she did find a link to the county tax assessor's website. According to the tax rolls, Jeff's second wife, Michelle, still lived in the house. A few more strokes on the keyboard and four more links caught her eye: divorce records from Jeff's ex-wives, another of his past addresses, and a birth certificate.

"Jeff has a kid?"

"You're married to the guy, and you didn't know that?"

"He never said a word. Not one mention."

ON THE TRIP back to the river, the inside of the Blazer stayed resolutely quiet. Although Nick hadn't brought it up, Gabby suspected that he was worried about attracting attention. Every few minutes, he glanced at the rearview mirror, perhaps checking to see if a car followed. He drove slowly, as if wary of making a mistake, to speed or glide through a stop sign. Any traffic violation could supply a reason for police, if any were around, to pull them over. If one did and recognized Gabby…

In the passenger seat, Gabby thought about her office, her empty desk chair, her coworkers and friends, the end of what she'd known as her life. Was she really willing to throw it all away and give up everything she'd worked hard for to escape Jeff? *Why should I have to do that? Why should I pay the price for his crimes?* But then she wondered, *Is there any other way?*

Once they arrived at Ruth's, Gabby laid out what she'd found on the computer search—marriage licenses, divorce records, and a birth certificate for Jeff's child, a son named Josh who should be thirteen. "So tomorrow I'm going to the houses. If Jeff's ex-wives haven't moved, I'll find them. I know it's risky, but I don't have any other options. And just maybe they'll back me up."

"Gabby, that's too dangerous. I'll go and talk to them for you," Ruth insisted.

Gabby smiled. For so long she'd felt paralyzed, and here was Ruth, willing to take on the world for her. "That's sweet of you, but no. You and Nick have done enough."

At that, Nick shot her a surprised glance. "Gabby, you're not going without me. You can't be out there alone, with half the city looking for you. I'll call in help to cover the store. We'll leave at nine sharp."

AFTER NICK LEFT, Gabby paced the small house, unable to calm down. The prospect of again leaving the safety of the river, driving in daylight into Houston, spooked her. That Nick would be with her helped, but even that didn't quiet her nerves.

"How about a scotch and soda?" Ruth offered. Gabby began to protest, mumbling about being all right, and Ruth stopped her. "The truth is that I'm thinking a stiff drink would help me as much as you."

A tense laugh caught in Gabby's throat. "Sure."

"You know, I sound like I've got nerves of steel, but I get scared sometimes, too. Don't ever believe anyone who tells you they're never afraid," Ruth said from the pantry as she grabbed the bottle of Scotch. "The important thing is not to let it paralyze you."

"Ruth, I know. Or maybe it's more accurate to say, I used to know. I've been frightened for so long, it's like…"

Ruth pulled the tab on the club-soda can as she cast Gabby a sympathetic glance. "I'm not judging, I'm—"

Gabby cut her off. "Maybe I just forgot how to fight back. Or maybe I gradually gave up."

Ruth handed Gabby the glass, the liquid bubbling on ice inside. "That's understandable. But it doesn't mean that you can't learn to fight again."

As Gabby took it, her mind turned to the coming morning. She thought again about what might happen, that when she left the security of Ruth's home, Nick would drive her into Houston, closer to Jeff. He had the whole city, law enforcement across the entire state looking for her. Was it that thought or the night breeze slipping in through the open patio doors that made her shiver?

Before long, Gabby and Ruth were sitting in the deck rockers sipping their drinks. Gabby watched the river glisten in the moonlight and listened to it lapping on the bank. The current was slow, ancient. For thousands of years, it had sounded the same.

Rocking slowly, she reflected on the past few days and how each one had brought more bad news. That thought provoked a sigh, and she resolved that she simply couldn't think about disappointments. She couldn't change what had happened. She had to look at the future. When Nick picked her up in the morning, there would finally be something she could do to try to reclaim her life.

# Chapter Nineteen

**Caracas, Venezuela**

**October 1947**

A FEW WEEKS after my encounter with Jimmie, I ran into Charlie Baughan, a big guy with a Fu Manchu mustache that drooped past his chin and a breezy, carefree manner. "Hey, Charlie!" I shouted when I spotted him on the street. We'd met a few times, introduced by mutual friends, but never had a real talk. "Where are you off to next?"

We spent the next half hour sitting on a sidewalk bench enjoying the good weather and chatting about his travels, ferrying in supplies to the oil camps. I was almost afraid to bring it up, assuming I'd hear another warning about my foolishness, but I asked, "You know, I've been trying to get a look at Angel Falls from the air. I want to take some photos. Any chance you know how to find it?"

Instead of a turndown, to my amazement he said, "Sure, I know where Angel Falls is. I've flown over it a few times, just to see it for myself. Beautiful sight. I don't know that it's as high as Jimmie says, but it's tall, that's for sure. If you want, I can fly you there."

"You will?" My pulse picked up speed, and I couldn't believe my good luck. "Jimmie told me that the only way to see it is to go early in the morning, to get there before the clouds collect."

"He's right. That's when I've seen it."

"You're okay with me bringing my camera, shooting some photos? Spending a little time there?"

"You bet, Ruth. That's no problem."

That settled, I thought about what I'd been considering for months, the best way to set up a shot that would show the falls in all its glory. "Charlie, for me to get what I need on film, we'll have to fly in low and look up at the falls, really swoop down, so I can shoot up at it. Otherwise, folks won't be able to get a sense of the height. You okay with that?"

I waited while Charlie mulled it over. When he finally started talking, he described the gorge the falls were in, the way the mountain loomed in the distance on both sides, and how the crevice culminated in a steep cliff. "Going in low? It's dangerous. The waterfall is near the end of the canyon. Once we pass it, we might not have enough time to climb out."

"Show me," I said, and I gave him a notebook and pencil out of my bag. As I watched, Charlie sketched the canyon. He put an X for the falls and another marking the steep cliff.

"There's not much room there. Not much at all." Charlie shook his head as if for emphasis.

That didn't sound good. I looked at the sketch and had to admit that, based on what he'd drawn, it did look tight. I couldn't ask Charlie to risk his life. If it was impossible, that was it. But then again, I couldn't help thinking that there was almost always a way. "I know what you're saying, Charlie, I really do, but the best way is to shoot up at the falls from as far down as possible. Otherwise, they'll look stunted. Isn't there some way you can do it?"

Charlie hesitated, apparently thinking it through. "Ruth, I'll fly you there, but I'm not comfortable going low into that canyon. I'm sorry."

As a trained pilot, I understood his fears. With so little room to maneuver, any mistake could be deadly. "That's okay, Charlie. Thanks. Just let me know when you're heading back. I do still want to tag along and see the falls. That would mean more than I can explain."

We shook on it and went our separate ways.

In the days that followed, between assignments, alone in my apartment at night, I again mulled it over, pondering how the photo had to be framed to get any sense of the height of the falls. I couldn't think of anything that didn't include flying in low. How could I do that without Charlie agreeing to give it a try? Before long, I settled on a strategy and called Charlie. "Have you made any plans to go to CB soon?"

"I was going to call you. I've got a delivery there late next week. Want to come along?"

"Absolutely."

As soon as I hung up, I called another pilot, Art Jones. A great flyer, he had a daredevil reputation. Most folks wouldn't think that when they first met him. A round, bulky guy, he was a friendly sort, kind of looked like a favorite uncle. But if anyone took the time to notice, Art had a mischievous glint in his eyes. Of all the fliers I knew in Venezuela, he had the most guts. "So, Art. I've got an idea. I want to hire you to fly me into the jungle."

"Where are we off to?"

"Angel Falls."

"Whoa! You know how to find it?" He sounded genuinely shocked and maybe a bit intrigued.

"Charlie Baughan is going to lead us there in his plane."

Art sounded confused. "Why don't you just fly into the jungle with Charlie then?"

"Because I have a plan."

"What kind of plan?"

Art stayed quiet while I described the layout, the river, the falls, and the canyon that dead-ended in a rock wall. "It's dicey, I know, but I need to fly in low. That's the only way to get a good photo of the falls. Charlie's uncomfortable with that. I'm hoping you'll do it?"

"Oh, gee. Don't know, Ruth. It does sound risky." Silence while I assumed he was digesting the idea. When he started talking, I heard the doubt. "Flying low toward a wall of solid rock? Is there time to climb out before we crash?"

"I think so. Based on what Charlie's told me, it sounds like there should be. But I'm honestly not sure."

I held my breath, wondering what he'd say.

"Well, if I agree to give this a shot, I reserve the right to change my mind once I see the setup. If it's too dangerous, I'm backing out. You okay with that?"

"Absolutely," I agreed, grateful it wasn't a solid turndown.

"Okay, then. Under those terms, I'm willing to give it a try."

I gave him the date, and Art agreed to fly to CB and meet Charlie and me at the airport. There was a chance this wouldn't work, that all my planning would be for naught, but I had to try.

Once I had Art lined up, I called Charlie back and explained that Art would meet us in Ciudad Bolivar. "He's going to fly me in low to take the photos."

"Well, I can draw you a map. Doesn't sound like you need me, then."

"No. I do need you. I've got something else in mind." Charlie started to balk, but I told him that I'd be at the airport on Friday to fly to CB. "I'll explain everything when we get there."

For days after, I had a hard time hiding my excitement. At a shoot, one of the oil company execs I was photographing for an annual report asked me if I'd won at the racetrack. "Maybe in a way, I did," I answered.

ONCE WE REACHED Ciudad Bolivar, Art joined Charlie and me in my hotel room to hear my plan. On the table between us, I laid out a map I'd drawn of Auyán-tepuí, based on my notes and photographs and Charlie's drawing. I'd filled in the position of the Churún River, the canyon it cut into the mountain, and Angel Falls.

Then I explained my proposal: I wanted Charlie to lead us to the waterfall and then to stick around and make a few runs inside the canyon with us. First, I wanted a second plane in case of an emergency. I worried that, flying in low, Art might not make a successful climb out of the canyon. If we were forced to land in the river or the jungle, I wanted someone who knew our location. I'd heard too many accounts of planes crashing in the jungle, their crews and passengers never found.

Charlie seemed all right with that. I figured he would be, but I wasn't sure how he'd respond to my second request.

"Okay, so picture this," I said to the two pilots. "I'm in Art's plane, and he and I fly in low through the canyon to the left. I'm shooting up at the waterfall on the right." I mimicked what I'd be doing, my camera in my hand, acting like I was aiming at the ceiling. Then I pointed at Charlie. "You fly higher, close to the falls between Art's plane and the waterfall. When I take my pictures, if we do this right, your plane will be in the photos."

"What'll that accomplish?" Art wanted to know.

"Charlie's plane will give the photo perspective. Folks will have something they know the size of to compare to the falls. It'll help them appreciate how wide and high Angel Falls is. Without that, it's hard for people to really get a sense of what they're looking at."

Charlie tied his mouth in a knot that looked decidedly doubtful. "How low do I have to fly inside that canyon? Those mountain walls are steep, and—"

"Maybe halfway down into the canyon. That should leave you plenty of room to fly out." I'd thought that would convince him, but he was still frowning.

Although Charlie was the one looking dubious, it was Art who would be taking the bigger risk, flying in low. Of course, I'd be in his plane, so I wasn't asking Art to do anything I wasn't planning to do myself. Still, neither one of the pilots looked particularly pleased.

For nearly an hour we dissected my strategy, debating the likelihood of success. As we talked, Art became less and less convinced that it would work. Like Charlie, he worried about the length of the canyon, the sharp climb out, and that wall of rock at the end. I argued that while it was admittedly precarious, it was doable. But neither one seemed convinced that it was even possible, much less probable, that we'd succeed.

In the end, I managed to eke out a reluctant agreement.

"We'll fly out and look at it, do a dry run over the canyon, but if either one of us wants out, we're both out," Art stipulated. "Understood?"

"Yup," I agreed. "But you'll see. Once we get there, this'll work. I'm sure of it."

Art nodded, but without any real conviction. As they walked through the door, I heard Charlie mumble, "Can't argue with a determined woman."

BEFORE SUNRISE THE next morning, we met at Ciudad Bolivar's small airport determined to reach Auyán-tepuí early, before the afternoon clouds collected around the mountaintop. I knew what I was asking Art and Charlie to do was dangerous, and I wouldn't have blamed them if they pulled out, but I had my fingers crossed.

What I didn't admit was that I was worried, too. When I'd organized my backpack that morning, I'd added a supply of Vienna sausages and apricot nectar, in case we had to force a landing and needed to try to walk out of the jungle. I didn't want to think about that alternative, but the food could be lifesaving if anything went wrong.

Then, the sky still dark, we were off with Charlie in the lead, Art and I following in his small plane.

Finally, I was on my way to Angel Falls. I could barely believe it.

So much of my life over the past year or more had been focused on that one goal. As Art flew the plane, I checked my equipment and loaded my cameras. Not long after the sun rose, I cinched a thick belt around my waist, one with a heavy metal loop next to the buckle. I pulled on it and yanked it to make sure it was secure. Satisfied, I grabbed a strap with a locking hook on one end and attached it to a tie-down welded into the plane. That done, I clipped the strap's other end onto my belt loop. To get the shot I envisioned, I would have to lean out of the plane. That meant the strap would be the only thing keeping me from falling out.

"Let's give this a test drive," I mumbled as I pulled the plane's cargo door open. The wind hit me like a boxer's punch, so hard that I lost my footing and tumbled back. The tether jolted me to a stop, and I landed flat on my duff, sprawled on the plane's floor.

"You okay?" Art shouted. He must have heard me cry out when I fell. When I didn't answer right away, he yelled, "Ruth?"

"Yeah, yeah. I'm fine."

Back on my feet, I was unsteady, but I crept forward, working my way to the door. Once there, I grabbed a metal rod near the cargo door that was part of the plane's frame. The wind pushed, but I held on.

"Looks like we're getting close," I shouted. I'd flown over this part of the jungle so often that I recognized the terrain.

"Guess so," Art hollered. "Isn't that your mountain up ahead?"

I stuck my head out of the door, the wind thrashing so hard my eyelids fluttered, and I saw Auyán-tepuí. I could barely believe it. The top was clear. The clouds hadn't moved in yet.

"Yup. That's it," I shouted back.

In the stark morning sun, I truly appreciated why the natives called it Devil Mountain. Its rugged black surface jutted up from the jungle below, regal yet threatening, impressive yet somber. The grooves on the mountain's side shimmered, the shadows taking on shapes. One moment, I thought I saw a face—alien, angry dark eyes— and then, seconds later, it transformed into an owl with pointed ears.

"That's why the Indians fear it," I said.

"What?" Art shouted.

No time to explain, so I changed the subject: "Do you see Charlie?"

"Yeah. He's ahead of us, off to our right."

"Great."

Art was careful to remind me of our agreement. "We need to

scope this out before we drop down into the canyon."

My anxiety built while Art talked to Charlie in his DC-3 over the radio, coordinating our approach. When they finished, he turned to me. "Okay. We're going to try a dry run."

By then my heart pounded like a drum in my chest. But there was nothing I could do to change anything. It was all in their hands. I held on as the two pilots lined up, flying parallel into position, Charlie on the side with the falls. Mimicking the moves I'd planned for inside the canyon, the planes tracked side by side above the gorge toward the falls. The closer we got, the faster my heart raced. My camera ready, I was determined to get what I could. If we didn't fly into the gorge, a photo from above might be my only option.

As we swerved to the right, it came into view. My first glimpse of Angel Falls. Adrenaline surged through me. I'd waited so long for this, worked so hard to get here. But it was all worth it.

The falls were stunning.

For a moment, everything stopped. Time stalled, and the earth felt as if it reversed direction. Nothing existed beyond me and that incredible sight. I could barely breathe.

We were flying fast, but I tried to slow down time to take it all in. The source started at the mountaintop. A second stream erupted underneath it directly out of the mountainside, joining the first. The two became one, forming an incredible sheer stream of glistening silver. At the base, just above the river, Angel Falls fractured into clouds of rainbows.

A dozen lightning clicks of my camera's shutter, and we'd passed the waterfall. Immediately, Art and Charlie pulled up and turned in opposite directions, practicing what they would have to do inside the canyon. Once we were clear, Art radioed Charlie. "What do you think?"

"Well, it's tight," Charlie answered, his voice blaring through the cabin. "But I can do it on my end. You're the one who'll be down low. Are you okay with it?"

For a moment, Art hesitated, and I again held my breath.

"Yeah," he finally said. "Should be okay. At least, it looks like it'll work. Let's try it."

One question remained. At that moment, Art turned toward me in the back of the plane and asked, "So now, explain to me again how far down you want to go?"

"As far as you can," I answered. "Remember to hug to the left, so I can get Charlie's plane in the frame."

If it wasn't fear on Art's face, it was at least deep concern. "We'll give her a whirl." Then he radioed Charlie. "We're going in. I'll be all the way down."

"Tell Charlie to remember to stay close to the right side of the canyon," I shouted.

Art relayed my order, and Charlie answered, "Got it."

I returned to the open cargo door, the wind buffeting me, and I held on and got ready.

Art's face a study in concentration, he headed back toward the canyon's entrance and this time dropped altitude until we skimmed over the jungle just above the palm fronds. As we flew through the chasm, at first the waterfall remained hidden. Rounding a curve, I saw its base, where it terminated in the river with a fine spray of water that the sun shattered into a kaleidoscope of light and color.

Art completed the turn, and Angel Falls filled my camera lens.

I literally gasped. It was even more impressive than from above. I leaned out of the plane, the belt holding me tight, the river flowing below me, the blue sky above, and straight ahead the most spectacular sight I'd ever seen—thousands of feet of tumbling water. As fast as my shutter would open and close, I shot frame after frame.

The waterfall was as incredible as I'd visualized it in my dreams.

Yet we had little time to enjoy the view. As soon as we passed Angel Falls, Art swung up and to the left, rapidly gaining altitude, intent on escape. My heart lodged in my throat, as I was sure his did, as the airplane struggled to climb. We seemed to move in slow motion, and as the rock wall and certain death loomed straight ahead, I feared all was lost. I closed my eyes and gritted my teeth.

Silence. Then…

"Woo-hoo!" Art shouted, and I opened my eyes to see that we were soaring above the mountaintop.

We had survived.

But it wasn't all good news. As I caught my breath, I instinctively knew that I hadn't gotten my photo, not as I had imagined it. While the run past the waterfall had happened in a flash, I felt certain the other plane wasn't on my film. Rather than tracking us, I suspected that Charlie had flown faster, passing the waterfall before we were in position.

Although my hands were still shaking, I called out to Art that we needed to do it again. I was certain that he'd tell me I was crazy, but Art turned and grinned at me. He looked exhilarated.

"Tell Charlie to slow down," I said. "Ask him to stay with us. This isn't a race!"

Art nodded and relayed what I'd just told him, as I picked up my second loaded camera. The planes swung back, and we again lined up at the canyon's mouth. In position, we entered the gorge together, hugging opposite sides, taking the turns simultaneously as we flew toward the waterfall. This time, as I took my photos, I thought that I saw the shot I wanted through my lens, Angel Falls in all its glory and

Charlie's DC-3 against the black mountain just past the waterfall. But I couldn't be sure. Was I imagining it?

In all, we made four runs. Each time I hunted for the perfect shot. Doubt still gnawed at me. As the clouds rolled in early that afternoon, Art shouted, "No more photos today!"

Unsure I had what I needed, I considered pushing for one more try, but then I thought about all we'd done, what I believed—hoped—I had on my film. And instead of protesting, I said, "Let's go home."

THE NEXT DAY in Caracas, the question remained: Did I have what I needed on film? Could I have missed it? I had to have the money shot, a photo of Angel Falls in all its grandeur. If not? This had all been a waste of time.

In my apartment bathroom that doubled as a darkroom, I closed the door and turned on the safelight, casting a dark amber glow onto my work surface. Taking a bottle opener, I popped the caps off my film canisters and then spooled the slick black rolls onto reels. Soon I had them loaded into tanks filled with developer. Carefully, I screwed down the lids.

Smack! Smack! Smack! I slapped the containers on the counter beside the sink, dislodging bubbles. The stopwatch counted off the seconds until it was time for me to shake the tanks, up and down, over and again, not hard, just so, the way my father had taught me as a teenager in our makeshift trailer home. Too hard and my black-and-whites would become harsh. I needed rich blacks, sharp whites, and every shade of gray. As I worked, the room filled with a chemical smell, a strong, overwhelming odor, one that years ago I'd hated but had grown to love.

Next the stop bath. I poured out the developer and replaced it with another chemical, four times, to clear the canisters of developer. Six minutes in the fixer, then the clearing agent, and my negatives were ready, thin strips of reverse black-and-white images. Once dry, I cut them into rows of five and slipped the negatives into transparent sleeves.

The first half of the process done, I laid out a sheet of white photographic paper, shiny side up, under the enlarger, positioned my first sheet of negatives on top, covered it with a sheet of glass, set the timer for seven seconds and flipped the switch on the enlarger.

Once I had contact sheets, I turned on the overhead light. I pulled out my loupe, held the small images up to the light, and inspected each frame. With a yellow pencil, I circled those I wanted to develop.

One in particular looked promising.

Again, I repeated the printing steps, this time with the negative that had caught my attention, placing it in the enlarger, beaming light through it onto a blank, clean, shining sheet of photography paper. Coming out of the developer, the image was everything I'd hoped for, the jungle, the mountain, the waterfall, the wing of Art's plane bottom right, and little more than a speck, halfway down from the top of the mountain and near the left side of the frame, against the black wall of stone just past the waterfall, Charlie's plane.

"Bingo," I shouted.

# Chapter Twenty

**Brazoria County, Texas**

**March 1993**

THE NEXT MORNING, Gabby walked into the kitchen and found Ruth looking weary and anxious. Her hands trembled. She had a sheet of paper in front of her, writing something down, and when Gabby glanced over her shoulder, she saw that Ruth was compiling a shopping list for Nick. The cramped scribbles nearly illegible, Gabby struggled to decipher the three items: canned tuna, tomato soup, and peanut butter.

"Ruth, you have a bunch of those."

Ruth pursed her lips and narrowed her eyes. "No. I don't. I'm sure I don't."

Gabby wondered how to respond. Perhaps she'd kept Ruth up talking too late the night before. She hadn't seen her quite this agitated, not even on that first afternoon when Ruth didn't recognize her and refused to let her in the house. Trying to decide how to approach the situation, Gabby sat across the table and covered Ruth's hands with her own. The patio door leading to the deck was open, and a warm spring draft drifted through the house. Despite that, Ruth's hands felt winter cold.

Attempting to calm her, Gabby said, "It's okay. This isn't important. Let's forget it."

Pulling her hands away, Ruth shook her head. "Show me."

"What?"

"That I don't need these things."

At first, Gabby considered trying again to convince Ruth to move on rather than confront her with her forgetfulness. But Ruth appeared determined, and Gabby sensed that she needed to see that it was true.

From the pantry, Gabby produced a dozen cans of Chicken of the Sea tuna, six of the soup in red and white Campbell's cans, and three jars of Skippy crunchy peanut butter. Ruth rested her head in her palms, as if resigned. As Gabby stowed the final peanut butter jar back inside the pantry, Ruth apologized. "I'm sorry. I shouldn't have jumped on you like that."

"It's okay."

"No, it's not. It's just that lately, I can't always put things in order in my head. Some days my mind is cluttered so that I can't think right. I wish you could organize my brain the way you're fixing up the house."

At that, Gabby sat beside Ruth and slipped her arms around her.

"You know, the past is alive for me. It's becoming my present. And this world? I'm usually fine, but there are days when I just can't…"

Gabby waited, but Ruth didn't finish the sentence.

"If I had your memories, I'd want to live there too," Gabby finally said.

With a crooked half smile, Ruth squeezed Gabby's hand. "Thank you. So, what are we doing today?"

"I'm going with Nick, remember? To the city, to try to talk to Jeff's ex-wives."

"Of course, that's what you're doing. For a minute there, it just slipped my mind."

"I WONDER IF we should have brought her, not left her home alone," Gabby said as she and Nick bounced along in his Blazer, heading north toward Houston. "Ruth seemed rough this morning, almost frantic."

"I've seen her that way. Sometimes in the store, she can't remember what she's looking for. She takes things off the shelves, puts them back, and keeps circulating, looking, but she doesn't know for what. It got so bad a couple of times that I closed the place and drove her home."

"She's such an amazing woman. This is sad."

"I guess the good news is that most of the time she's fine. That'll probably change, though, and at some point, she won't pull out of it as quickly."

An hour later, they were in the city, and Gabby tracked addresses on a quiet street in the Heights, an area just north of downtown Houston, a hodgepodge of bungalows, elegant Victorians, and lots being cleared of single-family bungalows and ranch houses to build elaborate three-story townhomes. "That's it!" she shouted, and Nick parked in front of a small, wood-sided house painted a faded Windsor blue with dirty white trim. Weeds had taken over the flower beds. Either the mailbox had fallen, or someone had knocked it down.

"What's this woman's name again?"

"Rae Ann Jordan," Gabby read off a notebook, open on her lap. "Jeff's first wife. They divorced fifteen years ago."

"This one has the kid?"

"No, that's wife number two."

"I'll knock on the door. You stay here, until we see if she's even home."

"No, I—" Gabby protested, but Nick had jumped out of the car before she got the words out. She watched as he opened the wooden gate, which hung by a broken hinge from a picket fence. At the door, he knocked, waited, knocked, waited, and knocked again. No one answered. On his way back to the Blazer, he approached an elderly man at the house next door relaxing on a porch chair. Gabby watched intently as the two men talked.

The car door opened, and Nick slipped inside.

"The neighbor says Rae Ann hasn't been around in years. They've been complaining to the city about the property. Called it a rat trap and said no one will do anything about it. He thought if the taxes were in arrears, he'd buy it, sell it to someone for a tear down. But the taxes and utilities are getting paid, a company mows the lawn, so someone is doing the minimum and keeping the place going."

"This is strange." Running through the possible explanations in her head, Gabby asked, "You think she ran away like I did, to get away from Jeff? Maybe kept the house hoping to come back someday?"

Nick considered that. "Or maybe something really bad happened to her, and someone else is keeping the place going so no one suspects that she's missing."

"Jeff?"

"Could be."

Considering what that could mean, Gabby remembered the way Jeff's rages transformed him, his voice dropping to a low growl and his blue eyes darkening until nearly black as he threatened her.

"Let's hope that's not it," Nick said.

Both lost in thought, Nick stared straight ahead at the road while

Gabby tried to concentrate on the houses streaming past. The second address led them to a suburb north of the city, a subdivision with a community center and a swimming pool, flowers in the esplanades. This time they parked across the street from a neatly kept corner house with a basketball hoop over the driveway. A woman knelt in a front flower bed, digging up brittle plants that had died over the winter.

"So, how do we approach this? What do we tell her?" Nick asked, as they sat in the car staring at the house. "I'm going up first again, but let's go over what I say."

Gabby could see that he was anxious. "Just ask her if she's Michelle Jordan and if she was married to Jeff Jordan. If that's her, wave at me, and I'll walk up."

As agreed, Gabby watched as Nick approached the woman, tall with long dark-blond hair close to Gabby's usual color. Michelle appeared to be about Gabby's age, maybe a little older, in her early forties. *She looks a little like me*, Gabby decided. Standing above the woman, Nick said something, and the woman smiled up at him. He talked again, and the woman suddenly appeared upset. She turned and scanned the street, stopping at Gabby in the Blazer. Gabby's heart sank when the woman shook her head no.

Nick appeared to be appealing to Michelle, holding his hands palms up. He kept talking as she stood and turned, then rushed toward the house. He followed, still pleading with her, as Gabby jumped out of the SUV and ran toward them.

"Michelle, I'm Gabby Jordan," she shouted, as soon as she was within earshot of the woman. "Please, please, please help me."

Michelle abruptly stopped, looked at Gabby, and then scanned the neighborhood again, as if afraid someone might be watching.

Scowling at them, she opened the door. "Get inside before someone sees you."

DESPITE THE TEENAGER who lived there, the house was neat and orderly, a cheerful vase of fresh daisies on the kitchen table. Gabby glanced about but didn't see the boy. "Is Josh here?"

"He's at school. Now, what do you want?"

"You've seen Jeff on television, I'm sure, claiming that I'm missing. But you know him, and I know you must understand why I ran away." With that, Gabby removed her sunglasses exposing the angry bruise around her right eye.

Michelle flinched and quickly turned away.

"I need to get Jeff out of my life." Gabby lowered her voice to a hoarse whisper and emphasized each word. "I need help."

A sharp breath, and Michelle declared, "He never did that to me."

Gabby swallowed hard, bit her lower lip, and tried to rein in her emotions, wondering if the other woman was telling the truth. "Okay, well, maybe he didn't. Maybe he was different with you."

"Jeff never hit me." Her voice stern, Michelle sounded defiant, but Gabby noticed the woman's body language told another story: her hands shook, and the color had drained from her face. She appeared terrified.

"It's a strange thing." Gabby fought to keep her voice calm. "I look back at all the times I lied for Jeff. I covered up for him. I hid my bruises and pretended we were okay. He was the one who should have been ashamed, but I was." She paused, hoping that the other woman would respond, but Michelle cast her eyes down and stayed resolutely quiet. "I hope Jeff didn't hurt you, but if he did, it didn't stop with you. And it won't stop with me. He'll keep doing this to one woman after another, unless we put an end to it."

"I told you that he didn't. Jeff never…" A tear glistened on her right cheek.

Softly, Gabby urged, "Michelle, I'm so sorry. I know this is hard. It's hard for me, too."

"I just can't—"

"But really, you can. We both can." Gabby glanced over at Nick, standing a few feet away. "There are good people out there. People who will help us. We're not alone."

Michelle shuddered as more tears welled in her eyes, and her voice turned cold. "I tried. I called for help. No one helped."

To Gabby, it all sounded too familiar. "I did too. And the police didn't help me. But there are others who will. And we can help each other, so neither one of us is alone and afraid. Please. If you don't help me, Jeff will convince everyone I'm sick or lying. I won't be able to get away from him. He's told me what will happen. That one day—"

"He'll kill you?"

"Yes."

For a moment, Michelle didn't stir, didn't make a sound. Then she stammered, "B-but if I help you, if I back you up, he *will* come after me. I… We have a son. I can't have that."

Quiet until that moment, Nick said, "There's something I don't understand. Jeff let you go? He let you get the divorce? Why?"

"I, a… I-I…." A deep stutter ended in a sigh, and Michelle went silent. No one spoke, until she inhaled a deep breath and whispered, "Because of Josh. When I got pregnant, things changed. Jeff's enamored with Josh, adores him. Jeff agreed to go along with the divorce. He promised that, as long as I behave, I don't bring another man into

Josh's life, he won't hurt me, because the boy needs a mother."

"But he never told me about Josh. He never sees him," Gabby said, trying to understand.

Michelle appeared surprised. "Yes, he does. The third Thursday of every month. I let Josh cut school. Jeff picks him up, and they go bird hunting or fishing. To the movies. They stay out all day, into the evening. In the summers, Jeff takes Josh on a vacation for two weeks. The entire time, I worry. I so worry. But Josh loves his father. Idolizes him."

"Guard meetings," Gabby muttered. "Jeff says he's at guard meetings on those Thursdays. He has two weeks of training each summer."

Michelle scoffed. "Jeff quit the National Guard years ago, while we were still married. Because he didn't trust me to be home alone. He couldn't watch me."

Gabby closed her eyes. How little she knew about her husband.

Leaning toward Gabby, Michelle whispered, "What do you know about Rae Ann, the first wife?"

"We were just at her house," Nick explained. "She's not there. The neighbor says she hasn't been seen in years."

"Jeff said something once, a long time ago." Michelle paused, as if debating whether to continue. When she spoke again, her eyes burned into Gabby's. "What he said made me wonder if…he did something to her."

Gabby didn't respond. Despite all she'd confessed, she couldn't put her deepest fears into words. Jeff had threatened her, but suggesting that he might have murdered another woman made it real.

"You mean you think he—" Nick started, but Michelle cut him off.

"I have a son to consider. I'd like to help you, Gabby, but I can't. What I'd suggest you two do is figure out what happened to Rae Ann.

If I were you, that's what I would do."

"Michelle, I—"

"That's all."

"But, please, if only—"

"You need to leave. Now. Before someone sees you here. I have neighbors who like Jeff, who talk to him when he picks up and drops off Josh. If they recognize you, we'll both be in danger."

WHEN NICK AND Gabby arrived back at the house a little after noon, Ruth listened quietly while Gabby filled in the details about Rae Ann's empty house, about Michelle and her son, Josh. "Michelle suspects that Rae Ann didn't willingly disappear. She suggested we look for her. But I wouldn't know where to start."

"Well, we need to figure out what to do," Ruth said. "There must be some way to—"

"We've been trying to come up with some kind of a plan, but we're not cops." Nick paced the kitchen, his shoulders sagging and his hands clasped behind his back. He stopped and stared at Ruth. "How are we supposed to find this woman? Figure out what happened to her?"

"I know, Nick, but—"

The older woman looked exhausted, and Gabby thought about that morning and how confused and tired she'd seemed. She considered how frustrated Nick sounded. "You two have done so much for me. You've been so kind. Please, don't feel that you need to…" As if something had just occurred to her, Gabby paused, the melancholy she'd worn since they'd left Michelle's house fading. Her voice tentative, she said, "You know. Thinking about this, there may be a…"

Nick stopped patrolling the kitchen and rolled his hand toward his chest, urging her to go on.

A wary smile, and Gabby speculated, "There *may* be a way to find her."

He raised one eyebrow and asked, "How?"

Gabby talked slowly, as if still thinking it through. "We could find out who's paying the taxes on her house. That could give us some answers. I did that at the firm when we needed to track property owners. Maybe we can find Rae Ann that way."

"How do we do that?" Ruth asked.

"Well, I'll go down to the tax assessor's office, talk to the folks down there, request copies of the paperwork," Gabby explained. "I'll tell them I'm working for the neighborhood association, and we want the house cleaned up. That we're getting ready to file suit. We need to know who to serve the papers on."

The worry lines across Ruth's forehead softened but didn't go away. "That could work. But won't someone recognize you? If not from having seen you around the courthouse, from your picture on television?"

"Well, maybe not now that I look so—"

"I'm going," Nick announced, his voice leaving no room for argument. "It's foolhardy for you to go. Too risky, for all of us."

The last few words hit home. If Jeff found her, she would not only endanger her own safety but perhaps Ruth's and Nick's well-being. Jeff could be vengeful. A moment's silence, and Gabby agreed. "I'll give you cash to pay for any records you find. We don't want them to have your address, so no check or credit card. Make sure you tell the clerk that…"

Gabby prepared Nick by going over each point with him and writing out instructions. She gave him the address for the tax assessor's office and explained what department to go to. As he pulled out of the driveway, she and Ruth watched him from the back window.

"He'll be all right," Ruth said. "You'll see."

Gabby tried to stuff her worries deep inside but couldn't. Her voice cracked when she said, "I won't forgive myself if something happens to you or Nick because you helped me."

"You know, no one's forcing either one of us."

"But…" Gabby drifted off, her mind troubled, back to Jeff and wondering what happened to Rae Ann. "I can't have you two hurt. I can't."

"Let's sit out on the deck." Ruth's voice was gentle. "Nick will be back soon enough. For now, let's think of other things. Instead of worrying about events we can't control, let's keep each other company."

Gabby smiled, but she couldn't hide her fears. Ruth edged over and hugged her, and Gabby whispered, "If this doesn't work, I don't know what I'll do."

"I understand," Ruth murmured back. "But it's in Nick's hands now. And fate's."

# Chapter Twenty-One

**Caracas, Venezuela**

**1948**

ALL I REALLY wanted to do was figure out a way to get to Angel Falls, but I couldn't turn any work down. If I was going to mount an expedition, I needed money. A lot of it.

Shell Oil hired me to shoot images for a calendar their public relations department was pulling together. I traveled to a coffee plantation and took photos of beans drying in the sun. I stayed in a monastery with the Capuchin monks, just outside a native village. While there, I documented the clashing cultures—the bare-breasted women wearing rough wooden crosses on leather straps and the children singing hymns, their faces beaming angelic, although none could pronounce the words. The native people I met were amiable, and I returned to Caracas with stories to tell.

"The Indians aren't all that way," I heard from a friend one evening in the American Club. "Some tribes don't roll out a red carpet." He mentioned the Motilónes. A reclusive people, they didn't take kindly to strangers. Oil was discovered on their land, and corporations moved in to drill. "But workers kept disappearing. When bodies were found, they'd been mutilated, dismembered. Maybe I don't blame them, since we bring in diseases they have no resistance to, cut down the trees, and take their land, but it wasn't a pretty sight."

Not long after, my monk friends planned a trip to deliver gifts to the Motilónes, hoping to make contact, but they, too, had heard the rumors. Instead of approaching by land, they decided to fly over and drop baskets and boxes filled with mirrors, blankets, and pamphlets about God. I tagged along, and the tribesmen shot at us with six-foot bows.

On my next night out at the American Club, I told my friends about the trip and the arrows that soared high enough to bounce off the plane's metal skin. A woman friend warned, "More folks than we know have disappeared in that jungle." By then, word had spread that I'd talked about mounting an expedition to Angel Falls. I knew she was cautioning me once again about the dangers.

"OKAY, SO THIS is what I've put together," I said to the helicopter pilot seated across from me in my apartment. I'd been looking forward to this meeting for days.

A hearty fellow with a full beard, he made his money delivering supplies to oil rigs. In Caracas between jobs, he was eager for a meeting, hoping I had work for him that would yield some extra cash.

"The other expeditions to the falls failed for multiple reasons, but the two big ones were that they had to travel too far and carried too many supplies." I'd studied these problems for months, working in my apartment on my days off until late into the night. I'd pored over the few maps I was able to find of the area around Auyán-tepuí and compared the maps to my notes and hand-drawn diagrams. Now, on the table between us, I'd spread out my photos of the area around the falls. An idea had taken shape, one I was explaining to my helicopter friend. "Food made up eighty-five percent of the weight."

"How can you change that? So many people times so many days, you need X amount of food and supplies," he said.

"From what I've heard, the expeditions in the past brought in luxuries. We won't do that. We'll go in lean, only the necessities. And I have another idea. I want to shorten the route."

At that point, I explained that all the other expeditions had flown into Uruyén, a remote airstrip in the Gran Sabana. From there, they took dugouts up a series of rivers. At the end, they attempted to cut through the jungle and travel on land to the falls. I had something else in mind. My plan: to fly into Uruyén, like they did, but then break the provisions down into smaller batches. "That's where you and your helicopter come in. I want you to shuttle us and our supplies to a spot closer to the falls. That'll make the trip shorter. We'll need fewer supplies."

On my maps, I showed him what I'd discovered during my flights over the jungle. I'd marked Ciudad Bolivar, smaller cities and towns, the Uruyén landing strip, the mountain, and the falls. I'd also plotted a handful of openings in the jungle where it might have been possible to land a helicopter. Based on my work, the pilot put a pencil to the task, calculating the distances. After fifteen minutes or so, he shook his head. "Not gonna happen."

"What do you mean, 'Not—'"

"I mean, this won't work," he said, his voice firm. "Listen, I'd like the paycheck. I could use the cash. But the distances are too far. I can't carry enough fuel to get in and back out."

THE PROBLEMS NEVER left me. I chewed on them morning and night: distance and weight of supplies. How could I cut both down? How could I give myself the edge I needed to mount a successful expedition? At first, I found no answers. But I kept trying.

"So, what do you do in Canada?" I asked the man across from me as I sipped my drink and nibbled a beef empanada. A night out at a friend's house, a small party, and I talked to her uncle, a round, short guy barely an inch or two taller than I was, five-four at the most.

"I'm a food processor," he explained. "We have a good-size plant outside Toronto."

"Canning?"

"Nah, that's old school."

He sipped his wine, swirled the glass in his hand to coat the sides, and then held it up to the light to watch the translucent burgundy liquid slowly streak down. I enjoyed seeing the way he seemed to relish the wine. I'd always appreciated people who cherished the small things in life. After taking another sip, he smiled at me. "Not bad."

"Then what *do* you do?" When the man shot me an inquisitive glance, I explained, "If not canning, what does your company do?"

"Oh. Well, it's kind of newfangled. Hasn't caught on yet, but we think it's going to be huge. The next food frontier. Lots of use for it shipping staples around the world to developing countries and for military use." He paused just a moment, and I spun my hand around like a wheel, as if to urge him forward. "Dehydration."

"Dehydration?"

The guy lowered his voice as if he were confiding a corporate secret. "We suck all the moisture out. Makes the food last practically forever. When it's needed, just add water, and it plumps back up. Voilà! Mashed potatoes, veggies, soups. Most of it even tastes darn good. The chicken soup is my favorite."

I was quiet for a few moments. "I guess that makes it easier to transport?”

"It's a fraction of the weight."

"Can I buy some?"

When I left the party that evening, I had an order in place for cases of dehydrated potatoes, onions, cabbages, carrots, and four types of powdered soups. Instant coffee. To round out the menu, I figured I'd add canned meats. That, I was betting, would give me adequate supplies for four people for a week, the longest time frame I envisioned the trip taking.

The second revelation came a few weeks later, during dinner with Jimmie Angel at the American Club. He cut into a thick steak and talked of his latest mountain adventure in search of gold. He'd tried a new section of a mountain he'd explored before. At first, he thought he had something, but he came away empty-handed again, and in the process nearly ran out of fuel flying home. "You'd think I'd be able to find the right damn mountain." Then he chuckled, as if at himself. That was one of the things I'd come to appreciate about Jimmie. He never took himself too seriously, even in the context of a river of gold.

"It'll come to you. Eventually."

"You think so, Ruthie?" By then we'd become pretty good friends. "I hope that's true, but heck, maybe not. Kind of like you trying to figure out how to measure my waterfall. What did that poet say? 'The best laid plans…'"

"Robert Burns. The best laid plans of mice and men often go awry."

"That's it," he agreed, chewing on what appeared to be a particularly problematic piece of meat. "Me and my gold. You and Angel Falls. We're dreamers for sure."

"Maybe, but I hope you find your gold. And I'm still trying to figure out how to make Angel Falls work." I told him about my disappointing conversation with the helicopter pilot and that I'd decided I'd need a small plane to ferry us into the jungle. A plane would have enough range to fly farther on a tank of fuel. The downside was that it would need a runway to land on.

"I haven't found any stretch of jungle long and flat enough to build one yet."

To my amazement, Jimmie matter-of-factly said, "You should use my airstrip."

"Your airstrip?"

"Yeah. I bet flying in there will take days off the trip to the falls."

On a paper cocktail napkin, Jimmie then drew me a new map; this time he placed an X north of the falls, at a location where decades earlier he'd cleared a strip of jungle straight and flat enough to land his airplane. The only problem: Jimmie seemed a bit hazy on the *exact* location. "It's right around there somewhere. I used it off and on for a few years, but I haven't in a long time. It probably needs clearing. The jungle takes over fast when things are let go. But it's level and high enough not to be too mucky most of the year. You ought a be able to fly a small plane in without a hitch."

"Jimmie, you are just the best—"

He frowned at me. "Yeah, well, remember when you measure that waterfall of mine that it better be a mile high. I've staked my reputation on it."

# Chapter Twenty-Two

**Washington DC**

**July 1948**

WHILE JIMMIE'S AIRSTRIP potentially solved one problem, I still had to figure out a way to fund the expedition. No matter how frugally I lived, it would be another year, or maybe two, before I'd saved enough by working.

When I searched for other options, my mind returned to Point Barrow and the celebration of my entry into the Top of the World Club. At the bar that night, when I asked Vihjalmur Stefansson how he paid for his adventures, he explained that most of his funding had come from the National Geographic Society, the foundation behind the magazine. Now, with my plans coming together, I wondered if I might be able to convince them to finance my dream.

My initial attempts weren't promising. When I wrote the magazine's editor asking for a meeting, he respectfully declined. Another letter went unanswered. As a last resort, I decided to show up uninvited at the magazine's DC offices and try to talk my way into the editorial department. If I told them my plan in person, showed the editors my photographs, I hoped, maybe, I had a chance.

I landed in New York City during a crushing heat wave. At the airport, I grabbed a cab into Manhattan. My strategy was to take care of some business in the city, drop in to see my doctor about a recurring low-grade fever I'd been unable to shake, and then head to Washington DC.

"You're not going anywhere for a while," my doc informed me after he removed the thermometer from my mouth. "A temperature of one hundred point four isn't awful, but since it keeps coming back, we have to figure out what's causing it."

Perhaps I'd caught a bug playing Tarzan with a group of native children in Icabarú? I swam in a river that entire day, swinging from vines and dropping into the water. The physician said I could have gotten the illness anywhere—from contaminated food, bad water, or an insect bite. One expert in tropical diseases diagnosed  dengue fever and then told me he wasn't sure because he'd never actually seen a case.

Ten days in a hospital bed, and I felt nearly defeated. Then Clayton Knight arrived carrying a bouquet of tropical flowers. "Something to remind you of the jungle," he said, his ever-present twinkle in his eyes.

"They're lovely, Clayton. Been feeling pretty down. This'll help." I gave him a friendly peck on the cheek and then chuckled. "Don't worry. They tell me I'm not contagious."

"Better not be. You've got to get out of that bed, Ruthie," he insisted, as somber as Clayton ever got. "If you don't, you'll mess up all my plans."

"Plans?"

"You have a meeting at the *Geographic* in two days."

"You got me a meeting?" For a moment, I didn't believe it.

"Yup, with J. R. Hildebrand, one of the mag's editors. Great guy. He's been with the magazine since the thirties. We go way back."

"Clayton, you're a doll!" I screamed, jumping out of the bed.

"I know," Clayton said with a shrug, playing at being modest. I figured he was as impressed with his success as I was. "By the way, I told him he couldn't miss seeing your shot of Angel Falls. Told him it is spectacular."

"Woo-hoo!" I ran around the room, dancing, hugging Clayton, all the while attempting to hold together the back of my hospital gown.

I ARRIVED IN Washington DC still running a slight fever but too excited to care. I'd dressed professionally—a gray business suit, heels—and my Venezuela photos were tucked into a leather portfolio. In the taxi from the train station to the *Geographic*'s headquarters on M Street, I silently rehearsed my presentation, deciding what I'd tell Hildebrand. I thought about how I'd frame my proposal and how I'd handle all his possible objections. I needed to win him over. But I also knew that if he smelled desperation on me, I'd walk out disappointed.

Nothing soured a deal faster than appearing anxious.

A bespectacled man in a brown suit, J. R. Hildebrand, or Hildee as coworkers called him, had a bald crown framed by a monk's fringe of graying hair. He greeted me in the reception area and then walked me through the editorial department. All around us, desks disappeared under piles of past issues, the covers bordered in their iconic yellow frames. Not unlike Alaska during the war, the magazine was a decidedly male world. Rows of guys in white shirts and dark slacks, most with bow ties, hunched over manuscripts and pounded on typewriters. I wasn't surprised. On the train, I'd combed through the latest issue and studied the masthead. *National Geographic* had only one woman, a research assistant, listed on staff. The two dozen board members were all men.

As Hildebrand paged through my portfolio, he asked me questions about the images—the Indian villages, the oil wells, colorful Kodachromes of the jungles and cities. The last one was the shot of Angel Falls I'd taken from Art Jones's plane.

"These are good. Very good. I can see why Clayton suggested we take a look. The one of the falls is impressive." Hildebrand sounded a bit surprised. For a moment, I hoped. Then he slammed my book shut. "I'm sorry, Miss Robertson, but this won't work for us. We need more than a flyby photo of a waterfall. We need a good story with photos. A lot of photos."

At that, I launched into my proposal. I'd practiced long and hard for this meeting, and I barely took a breath between words as I stressed what a coup it would be for the magazine if a *Geographic*-sponsored expedition measured the tallest waterfall in the world.

Hildebrand listened patiently, didn't interrupt, until I finished. Then he screwed up his mouth in disbelief and said, "My understanding is that people have tried. I hear that jungle's impenetrable."

"Yes, but they made mistakes," I told him, insisting that, as forbidding as the jungle was, it could be conquered. "I've been flying over that area for more than a year, working out ways to get it done. I've studied why the previous attempts failed, and I have a new approach. With the *Geographic*'s financial backing, the expedition will succeed."

When I paused, he said in a calm, reasoned voice, "Four expeditions by men all failed. What makes you think one led by a woman can get in?"

There it was—the question I'd had thrown in my face so many times in my life. I swallowed my frustration. "Because I'm the woman, and I'm determined to see this through. Whether or not you sponsor this expedition, Mr. Hildebrand, I'm going into that jungle, and I'm going to measure Angel Falls."

In response, he looked over his glasses and across his desk at me, and he chuckled. "Well, not with the *Geographic's* money you're not. It's too pie-in-the-sky for us."

It seemed hopeless. Truly hopeless. And I suddenly felt too sick and tired to fight. I shuffled my photos into a pile and slipped them back into my portfolio, straightened my skirt, and smiled. "Well, thank you, Mr. Hildebrand, for the meeting."

I held out my hand to shake his, and he took it.

"Of course, we are interested if you do measure the falls," he said, a hefty dose of skepticism in his voice. "If you do go into the jungle and succeed—two big ifs there I know—the *Geographic* would, of course, like a first look at your photos. But if we buy them, we would require an exclusive on not only the images but an article."

My fatigue instantly vanished. "Mr. Hildebrand, I'll take that as a promise, then, that when I pull this off, when I lead in an expedition and measure Angel Falls, you will look at my photographs. If they're up to snuff, you'll buy them and assign me an article?"

At that, Hildebrand nodded. "Well, sure we would. Of course, we would. Listen, Miss Robertson, we're not willing to put any money into this on spec, but we're pulling for you. You get it done, and we'll look at what you have."

Once safely outside the building, tears came, tears of disappointment and relief. My hands empty except for my portfolio, I held no bank check or signed contract. But I had a promise, perhaps begrudging but still a promise, that if I succeeded, if I somehow found the money and pulled it off, I had a shot at a spread in *National Geographic*. Not only would that be great for my career, but the fee they'd pay for my photos and story might be enough to keep the expedition from wiping me out.

As I hailed a cab to the airport, I didn't have what I wanted, but maybe I had what I needed.

# CHAPTER TWENTY-THREE

**Brazoria County, Texas**

**March 1993**

THE AFTERNOON HAD evaporated in the recounting of memories, and Gabby was standing behind Ruth, massaging a sore spot on the older woman's neck, when Nick pulled his Blazer onto the gravel driveway. Excited to hear what he had to say, they shepherded him in, and Gabby poured three tall glasses of sweet tea.

"You know, I'm pretty good at this. I bet I could be a private detective." In his hand, he held a manila envelope from the county tax assessor's office. "Once I got into it, the story just rolled out, no problem at all. Turns out I may be a better liar than I thought. Just like you said to, Gabby, I told the clerk that I work for the neighborhood association and we need to find the house's owner to file suit."

"I knew it would work. These types of records are public information," she said, relieved that all had gone well.

"Yup. The clerk accepted everything I told her, never questioned, didn't ask me for details or any identification. I handed her the address and Rae Ann's name and waited. She left, came back a little while later, and asked if I needed the copies certified."

"What did you tell her?" Gabby wondered if that might have caused a momentary glitch. Attorneys would want the information with a seal on it, so they could eventually submit it as evidence in court.

"Gotta say that I wasn't sure, but I just went ahead and said yes. She took off again, then brought me this stuff in the folder, even stapled the documents together for me."

"Well, we're proud of you, Nick," Ruth said. "But instead of bragging about your investigative skills, how about showing us what you've got."

"You bet." Nick opened the envelope and pulled out a folder, then turned to the third page of the second document, a copy of the most recent check mailed in to pay Rae Ann's property taxes. The bank account was in the name of Rebecca Tinsley, and the address belonged to a small law office not far from Rae Ann's abandoned house. The form filed with the payment identified Tinsley as Rae Ann's power of attorney.

"So, we have all the information we need on this Rebecca Tinsley," Ruth said. "Now we just need to find a way to use her to get to Rae Ann Jordan."

"That could be hard," Gabby admitted. "Attorneys don't give out information on clients."

"Well, there's a way, I bet," Ruth said.

Glancing over at Ruth, Gabby considered how she'd refused to let anyone or anything stop her. She imagined what Ruth was like at forty-three, on the day she emerged from the *National Geographic* meeting and cried on a Washington DC street. The odds were against her, but Ruth had walked out with the promise she needed above all else.

"We need to remember that we don't know who this attorney is really representing," Gabby explained. "It could be Rae Ann, but we have no proof of that. It could as easily be Jeff. I need to call Miss

Tinsley, not go through you or Nick. I don't want her to have your names or your phone numbers."

"If you call her, you might have to give her a phone number to get back in touch. Or maybe there's a way that Jeff could trace the call," Nick pointed out. "Now if I go see her, maybe that would be better?"

The rickety kitchen chair beneath her groaned as Gabby leaned back. "I don't know how I'm going to get in touch with Ms. Tinsley. But you can't do this for me. I don't want anyone to know that I have someone helping me."

"Well, I don't think that's a good idea, Gabby. I mean if you call—" Nick argued, but Ruth raised her hand to stop him.

"Gabby's right, Nick. This woman could be paid by Jeff, could call him right after you visit her. And he has all the tools to find you using your car license plate, and Lord only knows what else. He finds you, and he eventually finds Gabby."

Reluctantly, Nick agreed. "So, what do we do?"

As THE SUN set, Nick drove Gabby to a Walmart in south Houston. He waited in the Blazer, while she went inside, hoping that since it was past office hours the law firm's calls would be automatically forwarded to Rebecca Tinsley's home phone.

Working her way through the store, Gabby pushed a cart holding a few groceries, some canned goods, and a couple of T-shirts. Although it was nearly dark outside, she wore her sunglasses. A few people looked at her a bit oddly, but most, lost in their own thoughts, didn't appear to notice. The pay phone hung on a front wall near the customer service desk. After watching to see if anyone was showing any unusual interest in her, Gabby dropped in a coin and dialed. It rang, and an answering machine clicked on.

"Miss Tinsley, this is Gabby Jordan. My husband is Jeff Jordan. I have reason to believe that you represent Jeff's first wife, Rae Ann Jordan. I need to find Rae Ann. I need to talk to her. I believe it will benefit both of us. I'll wait at this number for five minutes. If I don't hear back from you, I'll call again tomorrow about this same time from a different phone. Thank you. The number here is 713—"

Someone picked up. "Mrs. Jordan, this is Rebecca Tinsley."

Gabby moved in closer to the wall. "Thank you for taking my call. I'm trying to find Rae Ann. I need to talk to her."

"As you said in your message. What do you need from her?"

"I'd like to explain that to her personally. I believe we may be able to help each other."

"Again, you said that. My question is how?"

Gabby inhaled a long breath and looked around to make sure no one stood close enough to hear. A clerk checked out a young couple with a baby, and a guy in a Walmart vest filled a shelf with candy bars, but no one was within earshot. "I suspect that she's been in hiding for a long time, trying to stay safe from Jeff. I'm doing that now."

"If that is true, and I am not confirming that it is, how would talking with you benefit Rae Ann?"

Gabby sighed. "Ms. Tinsley, I'm a lawyer, so I understand that you're simply protecting your client. But if Rae Ann has been in hiding as long as I think she has, that can't be a good situation. My guess is that she kept the house because she wants to move home someday, when it's safe."

When Gabby stopped talking, she heard only silence on the phone until the lawyer said, "I can't comment on any of your speculations. As a lawyer, you understand client confidentiality."

"I do. But I need to talk to Rae Ann. How do I arrange that?"

"You don't."

Gabby had expected that answer, but that didn't make it any less disappointing. "Why don't you check with her? Maybe she'll agree to talk to me. Isn't it her decision?"

Silence, then, "If you have a proposal, write a letter and mail it to my office. If I have a way to get in touch, and I'm not saying I do, I'll pass it along. Now, good evening. I need to go."

BACK AT THE house on the river, Ruth considered Gabby's news. "Actually, this isn't bad, is it?"

"It's not good," Nick explained. "Gabby really wanted to have the opportunity to plead her case in person."

"Can't you do that in a letter? Lay it all out. Tell this woman why it's good for both of you."

"I can, Ruth, sure," Gabby conceded. "But I won't be able to respond to any objections she might have. If she says no, I will have hit a dead end."

At that, Ruth understood Gabby's disappointment.

They sat together, quiet. "I'm going to head home. It's been a long day," Nick said giving Gabby a sympathetic glance. "You okay?"

"Sure, no problem." Her voice flat, she had a vacant look in her eyes. A sadness.

"Are you going to write the letter tonight?" he asked.

"No, I don't think I should. It may turn out that I have only this one chance with her. I need to think about how to convince her."

"Okay, well, let me know if I can help." With that, Nick turned and walked out the door.

Afterward, Ruth and Gabby sat together at the kitchen table in silence. There was a sense of finality, as if this complication wasn't a roadblock they could maneuver around but a dead end. "I'm sorry, Gabby. I really am."

"I know, Ruth. It's just that you're right. I don't want to go into hiding. I want my life back. And I don't want to be frightened anymore."

Ginger sidled up to Gabby, and she bent down, put her hand under the terrier's chin and looked into her dark eyes.

Ruth's lips crinkled in the corners. "Even Ginger is worried about you. I wish we could help you."

"You've already done so much. This, well, this I need to figure out on my own. I'm just…worried."

# CHAPTER TWENTY-FOUR

**Caracas, Venezuela**

**Late 1948**

"I'VE BEEN PULLING all the information I need together," I explained to the man seated across from me in my apartment. His skin golden brown and weathered from decades in the South American sun, he had a solid, calm manner and intelligent hazel eyes. I sensed that he was analyzing my every word, judging me and everything I said.

A friend had arranged our meeting.

An immigrant from Latvia, Aleksandrs Laime had near-legendary status in Venezuela, not unlike Vilhjalmur Stefansson's reputation in the Arctic. For more than a year, I'd heard tales of Laime's adventures exploring the jungles and living with reclusive Indian tribes.

Our get-together had a clear goal: Laime made his living working as a guide, and I wanted to hire him to go on our expedition.

Compact but muscular with thick dark hair, he wasn't the kind who found reasons why things couldn't be done. He had already accomplished feats that others judged impossible. We talked, and I laid out my plan to reach Angel Falls. From that first evening, I trusted him.

"So many expeditions have failed. Is it possible for a group to travel through the jungle to reach the falls?"

Laime considered my question, seeming reluctant to commit.

He stared at me, his eyes boring into mine. In the months since my trip to DC, I'd begun walking three miles a day to get ready, but I was sure I didn't strike him as particularly strong. Perhaps he sensed my determination but wondered if I could withstand the heat, the insects, the jungle with its treacherous terrain and wild animals. "It won't be easy," he warned. "Every step is a challenge. Swamps, fallen rocks, and dangerous rapids. The porters will have to cut a way in with machetes. Hard work, and even with the path, it will be difficult. The reeds are tough and razor sharp, and if you get caught in the muck, it can bury you."

"But it is possible."

"Of course, it is possible. But is success probable?" he countered. Another pause while it appeared that he again weighed the trials such a venture would present. "The most difficult part—maybe others have told you this—is to carry enough food. You can't find enough to survive in the jungle. Meat, yes, if you are a good hunter. Fish. But then your time is spent hunting and fishing, not making progress toward the falls."

"I'm working on that," I said, without going into detail. "The way I have it planned, in addition to the Indian porters, we'll have four expedition members to feed: myself, you if you agree to guide us, and two engineers to measure the waterfall. For our calculations to be accepted as official, two trained engineers must sign off on the measurements."

"You don't have to bring food for the Indians," Laime explained. "The natives in that area, the Kamaracotos, eat cassava, a dense bread made from yucca. They'll pack their own. And they are expert fishermen. They'll take care of themselves, but you can't count on them to feed you or the rest of the party."

"Of course. But that's good."

"Also, you will need only one surveyor if I go with you." When I started to object, he put up his hand to stop me. "I have a degree in engineering from a university in Latvia."

Pleased, I couldn't believe my luck. "Then we'll only need to feed three, the two of us and the additional surveyor. That's less to carry."

We agreed on nearly everything until I fleshed out my plan: to fly in a DC-3 to Uruyén, then use a smaller plane to ferry us and our supplies closer to the falls.

"The problem is that I can't find Jimmie's airstrip," I told Laime. Jimmie's best guess put it inside a triangle made up of Auyán-tepuí and two other mountains, Cerro Topochi and Uei-tepuí. For weeks, every chance I'd had, I'd hitched a ride and flown over that area searching for any sizable break in the jungle. So far, no luck. "It's probably overgrown, but Jimmie says it's there, and it's long enough to land a small plane. Once we set a date, I want you to hire some native workers and go into the jungle early, find the airstrip, and clear it."

I handed Laime the map Jimmie had drawn with the X marking the airstrip, and he scanned it and immediately shook his head.

"I don't know of this place where there was once an airstrip. I'm not saying it doesn't exist. But even if it does, it won't help us. The vegetation there is too thick to cut through. The few times I tried to enter that part of the jungle, I had to turn back."

Instead of my route, Laime insisted the only option was the one the other expeditions used, flying into Uruyén and taking dugouts on the chain of rivers, then, when the rapids became too swift inside the canyon, cutting through the jungle to the waterfall.

"But that's a days-longer trip," I protested. "We'll need more supplies, more food, and more bearers to carry the supplies."

"It is the only way."

I sensed that Laime was trying to be patient. He knew the jungle; I didn't. That had to be what he was thinking, and he was right. Still, it was my expedition. I was bankrolling it. And I'd been thinking and rethinking every wrinkle for more than a year. I took a breath to calm down and said, "The other route is too difficult. No one has succeeded going that way."

"But it is the only way," he insisted again.

No resolution, we moved on. I asked Laime about supplies and hiring the porters. He explained how it would be handled, that he would work through the chiefs of the tribes, all of whom he'd known for a very long time. I nodded, impressed by his depth of experience. I wanted this man with me in the jungle. I needed him.

Although he'd talked as if he planned to join the expedition, he hadn't yet made a firm commitment. "When we do this, will you guide us?" This was the most important question I'd asked Laime. If he agreed, I believed I had a good chance of making the expedition work. If not…

He narrowed his eyes. "We will get a lot of publicity if we accomplish this, in the newspapers and such?"

"When we announce that we've measured the tallest waterfall in the world, we will make headlines."

I didn't bring up what would happen if it turned out that Jimmie Angel was wrong. The waterfall didn't need to be a mile high to rank first, but it had to be taller than 3,110 feet, the height of Tugela Falls. If Angel Falls measured even a foot shorter, our entire trip would be in vain. Would *National Geographic* or anyone else care if we measured a waterfall that didn't make the top of the list?

That I couldn't consider.

"It would be good for my guide business to get my name in the newspapers," Laime mused. He paused a moment. "Yes, I will go with you."

# CHAPTER TWENTY-FIVE

## Caracas, Venezuela

## Early 1949

IN THE FOLLOWING months, Laime flew to Caracas off and on, and we met to firm up our plans. He still pushed to land at Uruyén and take the route the other expeditions had. I talked up the wisdom of shuttling to the clearing Jimmie used. Determined, I continued riding out of Caracas with my pilot friends when I had downtime and convincing them to fly over Auyán-tepuí, then north where I searched the treetops. But as many times as I peered out of airplanes and scanned the thick jungle below, I found no evidence of Jimmie's airstrip.

"It has to be there," I pleaded with Laime. I knew he was losing patience, but I kept needling away at him. "Compare the distances. It would save so much time."

As hesitant as Laime was, he gradually seemed to be considering the proposition. "It makes sense, I know. But it worries me."

The particulars under debate, Laime gave me a list of supplies he wanted for the expedition: machetes to chop back the jungle, large flashlights, waterproof matches, ropes, a snakebite kit. We needed a rifle or a handgun for protection and to hunt game, in case we suffered our predecessors' fates and ran out of food. We would be paying the porters, but to entice them to work hard for us, Laime had included rewards to give them: brightly colored fabrics covered in red flowers, string sandals, mirrors, combs, fishhooks and line, and an item that sent me reeling: four hundred pounds of salt.

"Surely not four hundred pounds?"

"All of that," he insisted. "The natives prize salt above all else. They use it to cure fish and meat. It's your best lure to get them to work for you."

"About the tribes we'll be traveling with…" I'd thought often of the oilmen who'd disappeared, the dismembered bodies found in the jungle. "Are they friendly?"

Laime laughed. "I wondered when you'd ask that. People have visions of native tribes that are all the same, when there are many differences. Even those that shun white men do so for a reason, no? They've been stolen from, manhandled, made sick by the foreigners' diseases."

"Yes, I'm sure that's right, but what about the tribes in the Gran Sabana?"

"The Kamaracoto are peaceful, good people, hard workers. There is one problem, though." When I raised my eyebrows, questioning, he explained, "Auyán-tepuí's reputation. They won't want to go inside Churún Canyon. That mountain and especially the canyon are greatly feared."

"I've heard they call it Devil's Mountain." I then asked the question I'd posed to others. "Why are they so afraid?"

"The Indians have many legends about that mountain. One is that a panther lives inside the canyon, a giant black cat that once terrorized an Indian village and killed all the inhabitants."

"But why that particular mountain? Why Auyán-tepuí of all the flat-topped mountains?"

What Laime said next reminded me of my own experiences with the mountain, the strange images that shimmered across it. "I believe that it's the shadows on the mountain wall, the way the light hits the rock." Laime picked up one of my photos of Auyán-tepuí and traced his finger vertically down the mountain, following the ridges that time and weather had worn into the sides. "In the right light, the shadows look like demons."

"So, the Indians believe the canyon is haunted?"

"Yes, by the spirits of their unlucky ancestors. The Indians believe that inside that canyon unfortunate spirits are trapped, held captive, and tortured by the devil."

# Chapter Twenty-Six

**Caracas, Venezuela**

**1949**

"DELIVERY FOR YOU, Miss Robertson." The truck driver held out a clipboard with a form for me to sign. My shipment of dehydrated vegetables and soups had arrived. I picked up one of the boxes, and it was light, a tenth of the weight of canned food. Later that afternoon, I mixed flakes from the boxes with boiling water and served tomato soup and mashed potatoes to a friend.

"Not bad," she said. "Not bad at all."

The next morning, I tried out another of the weight-saving options, a newfangled innovation: instant coffee.

"I'D HAVE TO charge you by the hour," Oley Olsen, a pilot friend, said when I brought up transporting the party and supplies from Uruyén to Jimmie's airstrip and then flying us out after we returned from the falls. "I can't afford to do this for free."

Olsen was among the best pilots I'd met in Venezuela. He wouldn't come cheap, but I trusted him. If anyone could land on an airfield the size of a postage stamp in the middle of a jungle, Oley could. We agreed on a price. As to when we'd go, that remained undecided. I was receiving checks for my photography, and I saved everything I could. But I was still worried about having enough to cover all the expenses.

Then April arrived and brought the unexpected.

One evening, I sat on my terrace overlooking Caracas pondering changed circumstances, worried enough that the scotch in my hand was straight. That day my main client, Creole Petroleum, had called me in for a powwow. For the more than two years I'd been in Venezuela, they'd paid me a monthly retainer. But oil prices had plummeted, pink slips proliferating in the industry, and Creole no longer required my services. *What to do? What to do?* Perhaps, as much as I hated to admit it, my best option might be to return to New York, where I could find a regular gig. Closing in on forty-four, I had to consider my future.

But what about Angel Falls?

I reflected on my bank balance and listed all the expedition's expenses. It would be tight. Very tight. But if I was careful…? I might have enough to finance the expedition. It wasn't what I'd wanted. I'd hoped for a cushion, enough so that at the end I wouldn't be penniless. This way, there would be nothing left.

My only potential savior could be the *National Geographic, if* I was successful and *if* they bought my article and photos at the end.

Those were two big *if*s. But I didn't really have a choice. This was my only chance.

I pulled out a calendar and considered a start date. I settled on the end of May. That gave me seven weeks to coordinate the details and for Laime to find and clear Jimmie's airstrip. That schedule also put the expedition well within the rainy season. With the rivers high, navigating the dugouts over the rocks and rapids would be easier. As important, engorged by the rains, Angel Falls would be flowing at its max, increasing the odds that it would be at its full height.

Satisfied that the timing stacked the odds in my favor, I contacted a friend with a shortwave radio and asked him to get a message to Laime in the jungle: "Expedition is a go. Find and clear Jimmie's airstrip ASAP. Journey to Angel Falls begins on May 25."

Once that was done, I booked a big DC-3 cargo plane to transport us to Uruyén and contacted Oley Olsen with the dates I'd need him to shuttle us from Uruyén to Jimmie's airstrip and back again.

Then, with everything in place, life did what life does: it changed yet again.

# CHAPTER TWENTY-SEVEN

**Brazoria County, Texas**

**March 1993**

"GABBY, GET UP. Come see." Ruth shook her gently by the shoulder. When she didn't immediately stir, Ruth nudged harder and shouted, "Hurry!"

Wiping sleep from her eyes, Gabby blinked at Ruth, who leered down at her. Her white hair stood straight up on the back of her head.

"Are you okay? What time is it? What's wrong?"

"You're on television. The national news."

"That's ridiculous."

"Come quick, or we'll miss it."

Minutes later, they were in the den. "I thought I'd let you sleep in. I tuned into the news to pass the time, and they had a mention of a segment on you coming up on *The Today Show*."

"Oh no." Gabby released a heavy sigh. "How can that be?"

Just then, another teaser aired before the show cut to commercials. "After the break, a missing Texas woman whose police officer husband is searching for her. He says he fears she's injured, confused, and potentially a danger to herself."

"How is it possible that people are buying into this?" Gabby marveled.

"Just wait. Let's see what they have." Ruth sat directly across from the television, as if afraid to take her eyes away.

"You were a reporter. Shouldn't they check their facts? I mean before they go off and report all of this?"

"With whom?" Ruth asked, eyeing Gabby.

"Well, I—"

"Shush, now. It's coming on."

"In Texas, the wife of a high-level law enforcement officer tripped, fell, and suffered what her husband believes may have been a concussion. Not long after, she drove off in the middle of a tropical storm and vanished. Reporting from NBC's Houston affiliate, Patrick Bush."

At that, the program cut to the dark-haired reporter in a gray suit standing outside HPD's downtown headquarters. Curious bystanders walked behind him on the street, pointing and waving at the cameras. "Houston law enforcement agencies are reaching out to the public for help in finding a local attorney. Gabriella Jordan is the wife of HPD Captain Jeff Jordan, the head of the homicide department. Six days ago, she fell in their home and hit her head. Afterward, her husband says, she sounded confused. He wanted to take her to the hospital, but she refused. The next morning, while he was at work in the building behind me, Gabby Jordan drove off in the middle of a fierce storm and disappeared without a trace. Her husband fears the worst."

With that, a montage of photographs rolled, many with Jeff, including their wedding picture. In all, Gabby appeared happy. No one watching those images would have imagined what she'd so carefully hidden, the face of a battered spouse, the bruises, the tears spilled late into the night followed by Jeff's professions of undying love and empty promises that he'd never hurt her again.

On the screen, the image shifted to video of the press conference that had taken place the day before: Jeff in his uniform with a bank of microphones before him.

"Oh, come on," Gabby whispered. "This is insane."

"Please, if anyone has seen my wife, Gabby, please call your local law enforcement or HPD. We need to find her. I love her dearly, miss her, and want her home. Your help could save her life."

At that, the program returned to the reporter on the street. "So far, there are no sightings of Gabby Jordan or her silver Camry. Many fear that in her compromised mental condition, she may be lost, hurt, or worse. Reporting from Houston, Patrick Bush."

A voice-over: "Thank you, Patrick. Next up, summer's coming. Are you swimsuit ready?"

In the house on the river, Gabby glared at the television as the scene shifted to the crowd outside Rockefeller Center, where models lined up in beachwear, shivering on what in New York was a brisk spring day. Ruth clicked the remote, and the TV screen turned black.

"How can they report that without making sure it's true?" Gabby demanded. "Really, Ruth. How irresponsible to—"

"Who are they supposed to check this with?"

"Well, someone who…" then Gabby stopped.

"Who would you talk to, if you were a reporter covering this story?" Gabby was silent, and Ruth wrinkled her brow. "They've got a bigshot cop getting up in front of the world and swearing his wife's hurt, mentally unhinged, and missing. Why would they question what Jeff says when you've done such a great job covering up for him?"

"But—"

"No buts, Gabby. You did Jeff's work for him, hiding the bruises, making excuses, explaining everything away. Why wouldn't the world believe him?"

The anger drained from Gabby's face, as she ambled over to the open door to the deck and stared out at the river. For a moment, the room grew silent. In the quiet, a memory floated out of Ruth's own past, the years in the small trailer when her father sexually abused her. *I never told anyone either. So many decades have gone by, my father long dead, and I'm still keeping his secret.*

"Gabby…" Ruth started.

The younger woman turned toward her, her voice weary. "Yes?"

"I, well, I…" As much as she struggled to, Ruth couldn't form the words, to finally disclose her darkest secret. Instead, she said only, "I'm not blaming you. I'm really not. I'm just trying to give you some perspective on what the reporters are facing."

"Yes. Of course." Gabby's chin sunk to her chest, and she cupped her palms over her eyes.

"But it would help if you *had* told someone, confided in a friend so that there was someone to back you up." When Gabby didn't look up, Ruth hesitated for a moment. She whispered, "What about your friend in Corpus? The one you were planning to stay with? You told her, right?"

Gabby shook her head. "Not until the day I called and asked to stay with her. That doesn't help. She's afraid. She's not going to go up against Jeff. She won't be calling the *Today Show* to contradict him. And what she knows came secondhand from me, after my alleged concussion." A heavy pause. "I kept all this to myself, so now it's my fault that I have no one to support me."

At that, Ruth put her arm around Gabby's waist and gave her a tender squeeze. "You're not to blame. And you're not alone. You have me, and you have Nick, and we believe you."

A wave of emotion coursed through her, and Gabby's voice cracked when she murmured, "Thank you."

At that moment, Ruth's eyes flashed, as if something had just occurred to her.

"We could call the police. Nick and I could explain—"

Again, Gabby shook her head. "It's the same issue as having Cyn call. All you and Nick know is what I've told the two of you, and Jeff will say it's my injured brain talking. Plus, then he'll find me. If they don't believe me, us, what do I do? Let Jeff check me into some clinic somewhere? Then take me home? What happens when the attention dies down, the next time he comes home angry and we're alone?"

Her shoulders slumped, Ruth released a short groan. "You're right. That won't work. But we have to think of something. There's a way. There is *always* a way."

The morning wore on, and Gabby struggled over her letter to Rae Ann. She wadded up failed attempts and threw them in the wastebasket. Ruth felt on edge and decided to take a walk along the riverbank. When she returned home, she found Gabby at the kitchen table, head down, eyes closed.

"You sleeping?"

Gabby shook her head. "But maybe I will take a nap. I can't seem to think clearly, so trying to reason through this isn't working. My mind keeps circling back to what will happen when Jeff finds me. I keep having flashbacks to that last night with Jeff. When he—"

Gabby abruptly stopped talking, when she noticed Ruth's slight smile.

The older woman shrugged. "Well, I had a thought on my walk. I don't know if it will work, but perhaps if you…"

THE OFFICES HOUSING Houston's NBC affiliate bordered the South-west Freeway. Cars and trucks rumbled by when Nick dropped Gabby a block away, her newly dyed hair concealed beneath a turban fashioned out of one of Ruth's brightly flowered scarves. Sunglasses covered her eyes, the bruise still a riot of color. Head down, worried that someone might see her, she hurried across the parking lot to the building.

Inside the lobby, six-foot headshots of the station's anchors stared down at her. Gabby stopped at the reception desk. "Please call Patrick Bush. Tell him I need to talk to him."

A woman with curly brown hair tucked behind her ears glanced up at her. "You are?"

"If you get him on the phone, I'll tell Mr. Bush."

That part was Ruth's instruction, for Gabby not to give anyone except the reporter her name. She worried that might lead to a refusal, but the unruffled receptionist acted as if such circumstances happened every day. She picked up a phone, said something, and then handed it to Gabby.

"This is Patrick Bush. Can I help you?"

"Can you be trusted to protect a source that's walked in your front door?"

"What? Who is this?"

"You can't tell anyone that I'm in the building. I have to be assured that we can talk, and that I can leave safely before you breathe a word of this to anyone. Once I've been gone for an hour, you can tell the world, if you like."

"I can do that, if I agree to talk to you. Who are you?"

"Gabriella Jordan. Jeff Jordan's missing wife. I'm in your reception area. You have thirty minutes before I walk out the front door. I want you to put me on camera. I have something to say."

Moments later, Bush had a security guard escort Gabby to a studio, and a cameraman rushed in, set up two lights, and started recording.

"Mrs. Jordan, can you tell us where you've been?"

The reporter flinched when Gabby took off her sunglasses. "I'm in hiding. My husband, Jeff Jordan, is a violent man, as you can see from my eye." Pushing up her T-shirt sleeve, she displayed the patchwork of bruises on her arm. "Jeff has been physically violent with me for years. He's threatened to kill me. This time, I ran."

"Those are terrible injuries."

Although he seemed genuinely concerned, Bush had a touch of a smile on his lips. Gabby assumed he was thinking ahead, gauging how well the interview would play on the evening broadcast. "But Mrs. Jordan, your husband is a high-ranking, well-respected police officer. He says you sustained those injuries in a fall at your home and that afterward you appeared confused. Is it possible that your memory is flawed?"

"No. Jeff did this to me." Gabby's pulse pounded. "As I said, this isn't the first time. He's beaten me before. And if he has the opportunity, he'll do it again."

"So, you're in hiding?"

"I am."

"Why did you come here?"

With that, Gabby looked directly into the camera. "There's a woman, one who knows my husband, who can help me. If she tells her story, it will be clear to everyone that I'm telling the truth. I came here today to plead with her to do that. She knows who she is. I am here begging her to please help me."

"And what do you want our viewers to know?"

"Please. Don't help my husband find me. If you do see me, tell no one. You'll only put my life in grave danger. And to the police officers who responded to my 911 calls over the years, the ones who refused to follow through when I attempted to file charges because of my husband's position, I ask: What must happen before you tell the truth? I'm hoping it won't be my funeral."

With that, Gabby stood, unclipped the microphone from her shirt, and walked toward the studio door. Patrick Bush motioned for the cameraman to follow. They shadowed her down the hall. "I have more questions!" the reporter shouted, but Gabby kept walking, through the lobby, and out the front door.

A ten-minute walk later, Nick waited in the black Blazer exactly where they'd agreed.

"How did it go?"

"Okay, I guess." She sounded uncertain. "Now we need to make the phone call."

"So, you called the attorney, Rebecca Tinsley, and asked her to let Rae Ann know you'll be on the news tonight?"

"Yes, Ruth, just like we planned." Gabby's hand fluttered up to her bruised right eye. She had a slight tick in the lid, a muscle spasm. It had been bothering her ever since she'd left the TV studio. She walked to the kitchen sink and put cool water on a dish towel, then pressed it against the eye.

"This interview really might help," Ruth speculated. "At least, we have a chance that Rae Ann will be moved by your plea. This is better than a letter. She'll be able to see you and hear your voice."

Gabby sighed. "I hope so. I need this to be over. I don't want to have to walk away from my life, but if this doesn't work, I don't see an alternative."

"Maybe not," Ruth admitted. "But let's not make this easy for Jeff. Let's go at him guns blazing."

# Chapter Twenty-Eight

**Caracas, Venezuela**

**Early April 1949**

"Hey, Ruth," John Hightower, the public relations exec I'd worked under at Creole, said when he called early one Monday morning. I hadn't heard from him since he'd told me the oil company no longer needed my services, so I was a bit surprised. I hoped he wanted me back on the payroll, but it turned out that he had something else to discuss. "I hear you're really doing it, going in to measure Angel Falls."

Knee-deep in boxes, I was cataloging the dehydrated and canned food I'd collected, figuring out what I still needed to buy. "Yup. We're leaving in late May."

"Well, I've got a proposition I know you'll find interesting." I was still thinking he had a paying job for me, a trip to cover the capping of an oil rig, a portrait of some muckety-muck in the main office, or shots of an installation going up in the jungle. I could use the money, so he had my full attention. But as Hightower laid it out, he had even better news: Creole wanted to pay half the cost of the expedition. I couldn't believe my good luck.

I should have assumed there would be a catch.

"The only way the company will donate funds is if I go with you and if you agree to take one of my friends, Jim O'Brien. He's an attaché at the US embassy."

The way my bank account was dwindling daily made the offer tempting. But instead of feeding three, I'd have to bring supplies for five. "Well, I don't know, John. I have things pretty well planned. Let me think about it."

"Ruth, I know you're a single working gal and that the money would help," he said, as if this was only for my benefit. "We can make this work. You just tell me what you need."

A FEW NIGHTS later, I walked into the American Club, and Hightower, a big gruff guy in his thirties with dark blond hair, was waiting for me along with a shorter guy with a thick mustache. They were seated at a back table, and I noticed right away that Jim O'Brien's eyes darted around the room, watching who came and went. It made sense that he'd be jumpy. I'd asked around and heard that the guy was CIA. I'd met a few spooks in Alaska, and they were always jittery, even eating lunch in the mess hall.

"Okay, so I've been thinking about this," I said after Hightower again made his pitch. "The money is appealing, for sure, but there are ground rules."

"Like what?" O'Brien asked.

"Like this is my expedition, and I'm in charge. I've been planning it for a long time, and I have everything in place. We can't have multiple leaders."

Hightower and O'Brien murmured things like, "Well, okay."

"Second ground rule. Also, not negotiable. When we get home, I write my article, sell my pictures. No one else on the expedition publishes a single word or a single photograph until my article and pictures run. It's important to me. I have a potential deal with *National Geographic*, and they require an exclusive. If either point isn't okay with the two of you, I thank you but decline Creole's kind offer."

I sat back and waited for an answer. O'Brien shrugged. He obviously didn't care.

Hightower? Point number two bothered him, and I understood why. While his current job was managing the oil company's public relations department, back in the day he'd worked as a reporter for a couple of big newspapers. I suspected that his motive for joining the expedition was to sell articles about it and get his byline back out there. But if he waited for me to publish, the newspapers probably wouldn't be as interested.

"That's it, John," I said, and I noticed him squirm a bit in his chair. I didn't care. I wasn't backing down. "I'm the one in charge, and I'm the one who writes the first article. It's great that Creole wants to step up, but I need the *Geographic* sale."

At first, my speech was met with silence. Then Hightower begrudgingly agreed. "Okay. It's your story to sell first. I'll wait until after you publish to submit anything."

We shook hands, cementing the deal. "That's great. Welcome to the Angel Falls expedition. We leave at the end of May. I suggest you both use the time to get in shape. That's what I'm doing. We'll be hiking through the jungle, so this won't be easy. When it gets closer, I'll give you a list of what you need to bring."

I stood to leave, but Hightower motioned me back into my seat. He smiled, as if he enjoyed what he was about to say. There was nothing retiring about this guy. Now that he had agreed to my terms, he had one of his own. "Well, here's the thing. That date's a problem,

Ruth. Jim and I both have vacation coming up. We really need to go during those two weeks."

At first, I wasn't too concerned. I thought, *Well, okay. Maybe June then?* "When do you have in mind?"

"The last week of April. On the twenty-third," Hightower said.

I was shocked. "In eighteen days? That's impossible!"

"Surely not impossible," O'Brien said, giving me a smug smile.

"It is impossible," I repeated. "Laime hasn't even gone out looking for Jimmie's airstrip yet, much less cleared it. We're not ready."

Hightower sat back and sized me up, as arrogant as his pal. "Ruth, I'm offering you enough money to make a big dent in your bills. This is expensive. A single woman, working freelance—it must be wiping you out. Our only requirement: we have to leave on the twenty-third of this month."

It took me little time to come up with an answer. It was the only one that made sense. The money would have been nice, but… "No. That won't work."

A few friends of mine glanced in our direction, and I realized my voice must have carried. I forced myself to get control of my emotions. "Listen, John. I'm not sure I can even get in touch with Laime. He's in the jungle with the Kamaracotos. It'll be hard to get all the supplies that quickly. And I'm still looking for a licensed surveyor to measure the falls."

"Tell me what you need, and I'll get it," Hightower offered, as if my concerns were meaningless. "Like the surveyor. That's easy. We have a bunch of engineers at Creole who are trained in surveying. They do it all the time. I'll get one of them to go with us."

"Are you absolutely certain?" I asked. Something inside me whispered a warning. This wasn't a task I felt comfortable entrusting to anyone else. The surveyor was essential. Without him, we had no reason to make the trip. Then again, Hightower did work for a big oil company. They must have had dozens of engineers. "We need to be dead sure about this, John. Without the surveyor, none of it works. We can't measure the falls, which is the only reason we're going into the jungle."

"Absolutely no problem. I even have a guy in mind." Hightower grinned at me, confident.

I thought that through. The truth was that I was coming up dry on my own. I'd asked around without finding anyone willing to go with us. If Hightower had connections, maybe I needed to find a way to work with him. "That's good, but there are other considerations. The end of April is just the beginning of the rainy season. Until the rain builds, the rapids will be more dangerous, and Angel Falls might not be flowing at full force. It may not measure at its full height."

As I listed the issues, I came to a decision. I wasn't willing to rush in and fail. "No. I can't do it. I'm only going to have the opportunity to do this once. I'm not going to risk botching the whole thing up."

At that, Hightower frowned. He wasn't happy, but I wasn't yielding.

"Well, let me think about it," he said. "We'll see what we can do."

By the next day, however, I suspected that Hightower wasn't working to readjust his schedule but pushing to bend my calendar to fit his. Out of the blue, Oley Olsen called and said he could fly us into the jungle on April twenty-third, the date Hightower wanted. I told him not to worry about it. We were still scheduled for the end of May.

Then a top executive at another company got in touch, someone I'd photographed for brochures. He asked for a personal favor. He wanted me to take along a cameraman to make a film of the expedition. "Our company wants it for promotional events, to show at stockholder meetings. We'll contribute to the expedition if you do."

As much as I hated to agree to yet another mouth to feed, the money he offered was enough to cover the expense of the airplanes, the food, and more.

Still, I had to be careful. I detailed my conditions, the same ones I'd laid down for Hightower and O'Brien: I was in charge, and no one published anything on the expedition until I did, including his cameraman. He agreed.

"One last thing, your guy can only bring essentials. We need to stay lean if this is going to work."

"You bet. Absolutely."

I hung up the phone and thought about what I'd just agreed to. Instead of three people, I was now coordinating food and supplies for six: me, Laime, the surveyor, Hightower, O'Brien, and the new guy, the cameraman. It turned out his name was Ernest Knee, a lanky fellow with slicked-back dark hair, a five-o'clock shadow, and round wire-rimmed glasses. To pound out the details, I scheduled another sit down at the American Club. Hightower and O'Brien were there when I walked in. Ernie Knee showed up a few minutes later.

All started out well, Hightower bringing welcome news. "I talked to one of Creole's engineers, and he's agreed to be your surveyor." He sat back and folded his arms across his belly, looking self-satisfied.

"That's great," I replied. "Thank you."

The discussion continued, and it seemed that he'd delivered the good news first to soften me up before they all pounced on me.

"So, Ruth, I've got my calendar cleared for leaving on April twenty-third," Knee said.

"That's when the surveyor is available, too," Hightower said, accompanied by a Cheshire Cat smile.

I shook my head. "No. We need to go at the end of May."

The squabble continued, not just Hightower and O'Brien but also Knee arguing that the April date worked better for them. "You know, Ruth," Hightower said, "everything is really in place. There's no problem other than that you're being inflexible."

Then he dropped another bomb. "I've tried but I can't do the end of May. I have too much scheduled for those weeks. Ruth, if we can't do April twenty-third, O'Brien and I will have to drop out. And of course, that means the surveyor I promised won't be coming and the Creole money is gone."

All three men stared at me. I was outnumbered. Maybe they were right. Maybe I was just being stubborn, pigheaded like Ma used to say. Maybe I needed to be more practical. What if we didn't make it to the waterfall? What if we got there but it wasn't the world's tallest? Then the *Geographic* sale would evaporate, and I'd be left penniless.

Hightower had played his aces, and I folded.

"I'm not trying to be difficult. The main problem is that I don't know if I can get in touch with Laime. If I can and he can make it work, we'll leave when you want to. But if I can't, you'll have to adapt your schedules or drop out of the expedition."

That seemed to satisfy them, and I walked out thinking I was off the hook. Laime would never be able to get that airstrip cleared that quickly.

To fulfill my part of the bargain, on the way home I stopped to talk to my friend with the shortwave. "Can you get this message to Laime for me? Last I heard, he was heading off into the jungle, but he could still be in the Gran Sabana."

The man read my note: "Considering leaving earlier, April twenty-third. Can you find and have airstrip cleared and be waiting for us there on that day?"

Two days later, the radio operator called me. "Ruth, Laime says it's a go. He's sure he can find the strip by then. Once it's cleared, you should be able to see it by flying over. Laime and the porters will meet you there on the twenty-third."

I hung up the phone, not happy with the situation but convinced I had no alternative but to forge ahead.

"John, we're on," I told Hightower when I called him at his office. "Just keep your fingers crossed that the rainy season has the waterfall at full force. And whatever else you do, make sure you have that surveyor lined up. We need him."

"It'll be fine, Ruth. You worry too much," he replied, and I could picture him grinning. "I told you this would work."

IF I'D THOUGHT caving in on the date would satisfy John Hightower, I was wrong. We planned another meeting, and all three men showed up. We'd barely sat down, when he took over the discussion, acting as if he was in charge, laying out how he wanted things done. Much of what he planned mimicked what the other expeditions had tried, including his assurance that he was bringing what he considered a vital supply—a case of top-shelf whiskey.

"No!" I interrupted. The men looked at me, startled. "That's how the people who tried this before us failed, and why some lost their lives."

Hightower started to argue, but I shut him down. "Don't fool yourselves. This won't be a walk in the park. We're going into one of the densest jungles in the world. Every ounce of weight matters. We're only bringing essentials. We're going in as fast as we can, measuring the falls, and getting out as fast as we can. As much as I love a good scotch and soda, I'm not willing to die for one."

"Isn't that a bit dramatic?" Hightower mocked, eyebrows arched.

"No, it's not," I answered. "Every pound we add slows us down. The longer the trip, the more likelihood something will go wrong. The danger increases."

Hightower huffed. "Well, if you say—"

"I do, and I'm in charge, John. We agreed to that on day one."

At that point, I pulled three copies of a list out of the folder I'd brought. "This is what each person needs to bring. We need to prepare as if we were going into battle. It's important to take care of your feet. So, there's a second pair of shoes and additional socks on the list. One change of clothes, a personal mess kit, dried fruit and chocolate for your backpacks to tide you over in case you become separated from the group. That way you'll have something to eat until we find you. But no luxuries. Nothing frivolous. No liquor."

I focused on Hightower. Begrudgingly, he said, "We'll be ready."

"Does anyone have a gun?" I asked. "Laime thinks we should bring one, and I would prefer not to have to buy one."

Still looking at me as if I'd just rained on his parade, Hightower said he had a pistol. "I'll pack it."

We shook hands, and I left. On the way home, I stopped at the cablegram office and sent a wire to *National Geographic*, announcing our departure. Despite the disagreements, the arguing about details, I was excited.

# Chapter Twenty-Nine

**Caracas Venezuela**

**April 13, 1949**

"THIS IS FOOLHARDY, Ruthie. Absolutely insane," a friend railed at me. "You'll die out there."

The gang of pals I ran with in Caracas invited me out to what I thought was an early bon voyage party. I wore a flowered sundress and red heels, and I was ready to play. Instead, it felt like a wake. Mine.

They warned of boa constrictors, rattlers, and bushmasters. One friend repeated the tale of an anaconda that measured a full forty feet and weighed upward of two-hundred pounds; it was discovered with a wild pig in its gullet. For the first time I heard about Brazilian wandering spiders whose venom was a powerful neurotoxin that paralyzed humans and made it difficult to breathe.

My friends begged me to cancel the expedition.

I listened politely and laughed it off, determined to conceal the fact that I was worried too. I knew this wasn't going to be easy and that a lot could go wrong. "You're all going to feel foolish for trying to scare me like this. My Lord, you'd think I was doing something dangerous and not just hiking to see a waterfall."

But they wouldn't let up until I felt compelled to admit that I was taking their concerns seriously. "I'll be careful. I will. Please, don't worry. I'll be fine. You'll see."

From that point on, the nightmares began in earnest. At first, I dreamed of being lost while an army of tarantulas the size of a man's fist marched toward me. I knew they were coming, but I couldn't see them until they crawled up my legs. In the most vivid dreams, boa constrictors and anacondas curled around my hammock. I woke up gasping.

For the next two days, I scoured stores for jungle hammocks I'd feel safe in. I finally happened upon one shaped like a large banana, with a canvas skin that zipped up, a mesh panel at the top, and hard ribs to prevent anything from squeezing me to death as I slept.

"I need to borrow a radio to take into the jungle," I told the minister of communications in the main government office in downtown Caracas. "Something not too difficult for a novice to handle. But it must have enough range to communicate from Auyán-tepuí."

"Oh, I see," the man said, sucking in a long breath.

A short fellow with cheeks as round as tennis balls, he drummed with his fingers while he considered my request. In my experience, Venezuelan bureaucrats weren't much different from the ones in the States. Anything under their domain ended up more complicated than it started. "This could be difficult. You'll need something dependable, so it works if you need help. But few will transmit that far. I have one in mind, however."

He disappeared from the room and returned half an hour later with a young man carrying a metal box the size of a large suitcase, with a door on the front that opened to display a panel of gauges, buttons, and switches. In his other hand, he held a smaller metal case. It turned out that the large one was the radio, the other a generator to power it. "It has to be cranked by hand. It's tiresome, but this way you're sure you will have power."

"But it's so big."

"But you'll have porters. They can carry it for you."

"It's so big, and it has so many dials," I said. The thing was covered in a thick layer of grime and dust, looking as if it hadn't been used in years. I also noticed a bit of rust. "It's too complicated for us to run."

"For that, you have Enrique Gomez," he said pointing proudly at the young man who'd carried the contraption in the door. "He will go with you."

"No. We don't need—"

"*Si*, Enrique will go into the jungle with you. You need someone to operate the radio. He will do it."

"Don't you have a simpler one?" I asked, praying for the right answer. "Really, I think something smaller, something we can manage without bringing an operator."

The minister paused as if considering options, but it was hopeless. All the while, he gazed at the radio like a proud parent. Gomez appeared to be an amiable young man, but not someone I wanted to have to feed in the jungle.

"No," the minister pronounced. "This is the best radio for you. And you need Enrique to operate it. I am a representative of my government, and I tell you to take the radio, and Enrique will go with you."

The bureaucrat looked at me bug-eyed, and I wondered if refusing could get me kicked out of the country.

At that the discussion ended, and our formerly small party of three had grown to seven, plus the porters. "I'd better go," I said to the minister. "It appears I need to buy more supplies."

As I stood to leave, he asked, "Are you bringing a gun?"

"Yes. A Luger."

"Good. If you run out of food like all the other foolish people who've chased that waterfall and failed, kill a tapir. That'll get you a hundred pounds of meat."

That same day I contacted the radio operator at the airport closest to Angel Falls and arranged to check in with him mornings and evenings once we began our journey. I gave him all our names, the route we were planning to take, and a list of my newspaper friends in the States, people he could forward my press releases to.

Still, I was worried—enough to buy three rolls of yellow toilet paper to lay on the ground and spell *HELP*. If we had to use it, the problem would be finding a clearing in the jungle large enough to be seen by a plane. At night, when I crawled into bed, exhausted from another day of planning, I blocked out thoughts of spiders and snakes by memorizing Morse Code and practicing the universal signal for distress: three short, three long, three short, over and over until I finally fell asleep.

# Chapter Thirty

**Uruyén**

**April 23, 1949**

"WE WISH YOU liked to play bridge rather than explore jungles," the note read. It waited outside my apartment door at four o'clock in the morning. Gladys and George Archibald, a sweet couple, lived downstairs. Despite their fears, they were pulling for me and praying for me. I appreciated it. Although excited, I was nervous.

Minutes later, a big red truck picked me up, and at the airport I found the others waiting—except for the all-important engineer. When I asked where he was, Hightower shrugged nonchalantly.

"He's not coming."

I swallowed hard. "Well, we need him, remember?"

Sounding less than convincing, he said, "Creole will fly one in to join us at Uruyén. If he's not there today, it'll be in the morning."

The planes were booked. The pilots paid. Our equipment and supplies were loaded. Basically, I had no option but to trust Hightower and board the DC-3 with the others. On the cargo plane, we sat surrounded by so many boxes and bags that I wondered what it would have been like if I hadn't fought to bring only essentials.

As planned, we set a course for the airstrip at Uruyén, where Oley Olsen would be waiting with his Cub Cruiser. Once we unloaded, Oley would begin ferrying us and our supplies in, a plane full at a time, to Jimmie's airstrip.

The DC-3 pilot had agreed to one detour, to fly over the section of jungle north of Sun Mountain where Jimmie said we'd find his airstrip. Now that it had been cleared, we should have been able to see it from the air. I needed to lock in the coordinates for Oley and to verify that Laime and his men were there waiting for us to begin our trek into the jungle.

Despite my nervousness, I dozed off at times over the next couple of hours, until the pilot called out, "We're approaching Sun Mountain!"

I yawned, rubbed my eyes, then claimed a window. As we flew, I watched, as did the men, expecting to see an opening in the jungle over Jimmie's airstrip. I waited. I prayed. I waited. Moments passed, a long silence.

"Come on, now. It's down there. It has to be," I mumbled.

But as hard as I searched, squinting through sunlight streaming in the plane's windows, I saw no break in the palm trees and thick vegetation below that would be large enough to land even Oley's small aircraft.

"Circle back," I called out to the cargo pilot. Understanding why, he swung into a turn, then flew the same route once more, this time skimming just above the treetops.

Nothing. No evidence of the airstrip or Laime and his crew. "Maybe we're a little off on the location," I whispered, and I looked over to see Gomez, the radio operator shaking his head.

"We should see it, Miss Ruth," he said. "Should we not?"

I didn't answer quickly enough, and Hightower shouted out over the roar of the engines, "If there's an airstrip down there, you bet we should see it!"

I would have liked to say something reassuring, but I saw no reason to try to delude anyone. It made no sense to deny that this was a potential problem. A big problem. At the same time, Hightower seemed to relish riling everyone up. We were already restless. Why make things worse?

Sadly, that wasn't all. Something else bothered me.

At first, I wasn't sure what it was, but then I realized that, as we flew over the rivers, rocks jutted out from beneath the water. The rivers were low. The rainy season hadn't yet delivered sufficient rain to replenish them. Our trip downstream would be rough. And what did that mean for Angel Falls? Would the falls be flowing at full capacity?

*This isn't good*, I worried. *We should have waited.*

Before long, the pilot made his approach at Uruyén, pulling back on the throttle as he eased down onto the flat plain. Ahead I saw a makeshift airstrip, bordered by two rows of old, battered oilcans impaled on sticks. The wheels hit hard, bounding onto ruts worn through the valley's high grasses. As the plane skipped on the rough earth and rolled to a stop, I sighed in relief to see Oley's Cub Cruiser waiting in the distance.

So much had already gone wrong. At least he had come through.

Few planes landed on the remote field, and our arrival brought natives rushing from their nearby village. The Kamaracoto children came first, the boys in red loincloths, followed by men in tattered, loose-fitting cotton slacks and shirts. The women appeared last, most dressed in red cotton underdresses covered by flowered sheaths, like the fabric we'd brought to give them.

I'd gazed down at Uruyén from above, but I'd never landed there before. A vast clearing, much larger than I'd envisioned, it was surrounded by dense brush and the encroaching jungle. On the perimeter, the Kamaracoto lived in scattered huts topped by thick thatched roofs. Far, far in the distance, deep in the jungle, behind a bank of hills, stood Auyán-tepuí, its black rock a sharp contrast to the lush vegetation, its flat top obscured by a shelf of gray clouds.

As I jumped out of the DC-3, Oley lumbered toward me.

"Have you heard from Laime?" I called out. "We didn't find the airstrip."

A sense of dread washed over me when he said, "Not a word."

Moments later one of the natives approached. A tall guy wearing western clothes and a cowboy hat, he introduced himself in Spanish as the tribe's chief and said that he was worried about Laime and his party, which included men from his village. After being in the jungle for more than a week, they were supposed to return for supplies before going back out to the airstrip to meet us. No one had seen any sign of them.

"They've been gone too long," he said, his voice a low growl. "This is not good. They are out of food."

As worried as I was, I tried to reassure the chief, but he'd have none of it. Shaking his head, he was clearly convinced something had gone terribly wrong.

Just hours into our journey, and we already had serious setbacks.

Our little band of explorers huddled around me. Oley joined us, and I explained the situation. "I'll go look for them," Oley offered. "I can fly lower than the DC-3, so maybe I'll spot that clearing."

O'Brien offered to ride along, and as my watch clicked toward noon, the two men took off in Oley's Cruiser, along with a few boxes of food for Laime and his crew.

Hoping the men would be back in an hour or two bearing good news, I helped unload supplies. After months of planning, we'd arrived, but I had no surveyor, no Laime, no porters, and no airstrip. I tried to convince myself that these were minor setbacks, quickly remedied. Instead of flying out on that same day, perhaps we'd spend one night in Uruyén. But from the ball of acid in my stomach, I wasn't quite buying it.

Once we finished unloading, the DC-3 took off and flew above us on its way back to Ciudad Bolivar. As I watched it disappear on the horizon, I hoped that when it landed, the pilot would find Hightower's surveyor eager to be ferried out to join us.

As we awaited Oley and O'Brien's return, the natives circulated around us, apparently finding us as fascinating as I found them. With deep olive skin and long, soft, dark hair, the Kamaracoto men and women were striking. From the youngest to the oldest, they wore tight bands of beads on their wrists and ankles. I pointed at their bracelets and said, "Beads," and they laughed as if I'd just told the funniest joke. "Beads," one of the women echoed, and then she giggled.

We kept busy. Ernie Knee took his movie camera to the Kamaracoto village, then returned and put up a tent. Hightower retired to his hammock for a nap while I grabbed the first of the notebooks I'd brought. Throughout my career these small pads with leather covers had been my constant companions. In Peoria I'd written quotes in them for my first newspaper articles. In Alaska, I'd scratched observations about daily life on the base. Now, in Uruyén, I wrote, "April 23,

1949. We leave on the expedition…" then described the flight in and the day as it had unfolded, including the mounting difficulties. Off and on, I searched the sky, wondering why Oley and O'Brien hadn't yet returned.

The afternoon passed, and Uruyén remained quiet. Eventually the Kamaracotos lost interest and returned to their village. The only sounds I heard were the wind ruffling through the sawgrass and children playing in the distance.

Finally, hours after I expected them, I heard a plane and looked up to see the Cub Cruiser approaching in the distance.

Our party swarmed the landing strip, eager for information. "Did you find them?" I shouted. The two men scrambled out of the plane, and to my disappointment, no one followed.

"If they'd found him, Laime would be with them," Hightower said, with a gruff laugh. "You don't see him, do you?"

"You know…" I started and then choked back what I was thinking. Turning to Oley, I concentrated on what mattered. "What happened? Why were you gone so long?"

Excited to tell his story, his words came so fast one stumbled over the other. Flying low over the jungle, Oley had spotted Jimmie's abandoned airstrip not far from where we'd searched for it. Lining up his plane, he'd angled in for a hard landing. No one was there, and there was no sign of anyone's having been there in years. The sawgrass and brush had grown thigh high in places, small palms with stiff trunks spiked up around them. Despite that, Oley and O'Brien waited for hours, hoping Laime and his men would arrive. No one did. Finally, they unloaded two boxes of food to leave in case anyone showed up and then they took off. They had to get back to Uruyén before dark because the airfield had no landing lights.

Then, over the Carráo River, O'Brien spotted Laime and his native helpers in a squad of dugouts. He grabbed a scrap of paper and quickly wrote: "Go to the airstrip… We left food there. We'll wait for you, but we must leave for Uruyén by 5 p.m." O'Brien slipped it into one of the waterproof bamboo tubes Oley carried on board for just such emergencies and dropped it from the plane.

After Laime fished it out of the river and read the note, he waved in what O'Brien and Oley assumed was agreement, so they flew back to the airstrip they'd landed at earlier. But Laime and the Indians never arrived.

"We finally had to leave," O'Brien explained. "We flew back over the river, but we didn't see Laime or the Indians. They'd disappeared."

"What about the airstrip?" I asked. "Can we use it?"

"No. I had a hard time landing and taking off. The brush is too high. Filled with cargo, the plane wouldn't make it."

In the jungle, the sun set quickly; a flash of twilight dissolved into night. Disappointed by the missteps, worried, I cooked dinner by the light of our campfire while the men tied up our hammocks in a grove of trees. By seven that evening, we were in bed. Despite everything that had gone wrong, I was glad to be in the savannah. I was happy that my adventure had finally begun. In my exhaustion, I blocked out thoughts of our missing surveyor and boas sliding down from the trees.

I drifted off to a lullaby sung by frogs, lizards, and mating insects.

"SCREECH! SCREEEEEEEECH!" RED howler monkeys woke us the next morning. One hung from a branch right above my head, upside down and staring at me inside my hammock. I held back a giggle and brushed my fingernails over the mesh making a scraping sound. The curious monkey edged closer, listening to the whirring as I opened the zipper. But when I emerged, it ran off terrified, as spooked as if I'd risen from the dead.

After breakfast, dark clouds collected in the distance as Oley and O'Brien climbed back onboard the Cub Cruiser and flew out to again look for Laime.

"Let's check on that surveyor Creole's sending," I suggested to Gomez midmorning.

He turned on his radio to call Ciudad Bolivar while I cranked the generator, which was harder work than I'd anticipated.

Soon a group of natives gathered around to watch, and one of the old men came in close for a better look at the odd contraption. In Spanish, Gomez asked for help. The man shouted in a language I couldn't understand, and a boy, maybe thirteen or so, rushed over. The man barked orders, and the boy took over for me. Gomez flipped a switch, and the machine caused a stir as it powered up, the men murmuring in appreciation as the lights blinked on.

For the rest of the morning, the boys took turns as Gomez tried to rouse the CB radio operator. But all we heard was static. "Our radio's not transmitting," Gomez finally said, looking over at me with a wary frown. Then he shrugged as if it wasn't a big deal. "I'll keep trying."

Another problem we didn't need.

The waiting, the increasing missteps. It all seemed to be escalating. Too worried to watch, I needed to stay busy. I grabbed my clean clothes and a bar of soap, then wandered down to a creek that ran through the jungle not far from the camp, its banks clear of brush for a few yards on both sides. The air smelled of moss and the thick vegetation. On the opposite side, a spray of flowers hung from a bush, blooms the size of baseballs made up of brilliant-red bell-shaped flowers with yellow centers twisted together like the yarn strands that had formed the pompoms on my knit cap when I was a girl.

I undressed on the water's edge, placed my clean clothes on a nearby rock, then eased in and swam. Dog-paddling in the center of the river, I heard a throaty cry, a rough, primitive, clacking sound. On the edge of the water stood a jabiru, more than four feet tall, with a long head and neck that shone pure black and a bright red band above its shoulders. It reminded me of one I'd watched since arriving in Venezuela, one that had a bushy nest of sticks on the roof of the apartment building next to mine in Caracas.

Its spindly legs knee-deep on the river's edge, the bird poked its head into the water, then raised its head and let the liquid drain out of its beak. As it swallowed an unlucky fish, it stared back at me. I eased my way back to the bank, hoping I wouldn't scare it off. Once there, I sat on a rock and soaped up my arms, my legs, my body, watching the jabiru plunge its head into the water time and again.

Back in camp, I found the small band of native men and boys still gathered around Gomez and his radio.

"What's the verdict?" I asked.

"Not working yet, but I'll get it." Gomez flipped switches and turned dials. Fascinated by the show, the native men milled around, and the boys lined up to man the crank. Gomez picked up the microphone and pushed the button, talking into it, but we still heard only crackling.

As he worked, Gomez clicked the radio on to receive, and a man's voice suddenly boomed through the camp. Startled, the boy manning the crank tumbled off the stool. He and the rest of the natives turned and ran.

Watching, I chuckled and thought about the tribes, how they knew so little of the outside world. Yet in the jungle, we were the uneducated ones. They understood how things worked, the order of life and the dangers. Then my mind wandered to Laime. If we didn't find him, what would we do?

The day ground on, and none of the news was good. Early afternoon, Gomez sought me out. "The radio must be damaged. I can't transmit."

"Oh no. How do we fix it?" I asked, and he admitted that he didn't know.

That wasn't the only problem I couldn't solve. Oley and O'Brien were still out looking for Laime. Once we found him, I told myself, the rest would fall in place. Maybe Oley would agree to fly back to pick up a new radio and the surveyor, if Hightower's company had actually sent one. If not, we would have to find another—and quickly. I was sure of only two things—we couldn't go into the jungle without the surveyor, and I couldn't, under any circumstances, let the men see me panic.

The wait seemed interminable.

When Oley and O'Brien finally returned that evening, they'd seen no signs of Laime and his crew. The food they'd left at the airstrip the day before had remained untouched.

"What now?" Ernie asked me.

Before I had an opportunity to respond, Hightower jumped in. "We can't fix all this. It's over. Time for us to pack up and go home."

Stunned, I turned to him. "We've barely started. We can't give up."

A big man, Hightower peered down from above me, pontificating, arguing that we had no choice but to return to Caracas.

"We can and we will work through this," I insisted. "We're not at the point we should even consider giving up."

"So, what do you suggest?" he challenged.

"Give it some time. We'll find Laime, or he'll find us."

"We're using up our food," O'Brien grumbled. "This is hopeless."

"We'll send for more," I countered. "Oley can fly out and pick up what we need." I glanced over at the pilot and felt a surge of relief when he gave me a thumbs up. At least that problem was easy to solve. "John, you can go with him, and make sure you come back with that engineer you promised your company would supply."

Glowering at me, he didn't respond.

In the end, we reached an agreement. The next morning, our third day at the campsite, Oley took the Cub Cruiser up with Gomez and Hightower onboard. If all went well, in Ciudad Bolivar, our pilot would pick up supplies, Gomez would get us a radio that worked, and Hightower would find us an engineer. Meanwhile, the rest of us would wait for Laime and his team of porters. As I watched the plane fly off, I whispered a prayer that they'd return the next day with everything we needed.

That afternoon, giggling children surrounded me, jumping from boulder to boulder in the river, while their mothers pounded *barbasco* roots against the rocks, spreading a milky substance that stunned the fish. The older boys speared the larger fish, while the younger children ran about scooping up the small ones. The women wrapped the fish in banana leaves and boiled them in a heavy clay pot. I traded salt for enough for our dinner, and we ate it with roasted pineapple.

Two more days passed. I filled the time taking photos of the natives and staring at the empty sky. On our sixth day in the Gran Sabana, a pilot friend flew in. He'd heard of our setbacks at the airport in CB. "Ruth, you need to forget this. It's just not working," he said bluntly.

"No, they'll be back soon with what we need." Then I confided the decision I'd made just that morning. "One way or another, we're going on. With or without Laime."

"Ruth, no."

"I have to. I've sunk every penny I have in this expedition. I'll never have the funds to do it again."

My friend scowled at me, troubled. "It's folly to go into the jungle without a skilled guide. No expedition is worth losing your life."

He was right. I knew that. But I couldn't give up hope. "I can't walk away before I even try. I can't."

I sensed that on one level he understood, but he didn't give up. "I'll be back in a couple of days. If you've come to your senses by then, I'll fly you home."

I shook my head. "Don't make the trip for me. I won't be going with you."

He scanned the savannah, the jungle in the distance. "Two more days here, maybe you'll realize that your life is worth more than a pipe dream."

That evening, the sunset turned the sky bright orange and pink over the jungle. A beautiful sight, but it wasn't enough to distract me from the reality we faced.

The next morning, the DC-3 that transported us to Uruyén returned with Gomez and Hightower. The pilot unloaded supplies, and Gomez showed off his new radio. But Hightower stalked off the plane without the promised engineer to act as our surveyor. Instead of apologizing, he attacked. "Have you found Laime?"

"No," I admitted. "Not yet."

"Then there's no sense continuing this charade. It's time to admit failure and go home."

"No!" My voice rose in indignation. "I'm not giving up."

Hightower brushed past me and motioned for his pal, O'Brien. As I watched, they stood off by themselves whispering, then headed over to the campsite and packed their gear. Fuming, I stood back, arms folded and watched. "You'd better come back with us," Hightower shouted as he and O'Brien prepared to board the plane. "You can't go into the jungle without Laime."

"I'm finishing what I started," I snapped back at him. "John, this is your fault. Rushing us to go. Not bringing the surveyor you promised. If you'd brought one, we could have gone in with a second group of porters."

"The natives wouldn't go without Laime. If you're smart, you won't either. You need to leave with us," he said, seething. Then he let out a rueful laugh. "You know, Ruth, I knew you never stood a chance of pulling together an expedition like this. You're in way over your head."

His words sliced through me and lodged in the self-doubt I'd fought my entire life. I wasn't giving up, but I felt wounded. "What about the funding your oil company promised?" I asked, making my voice firm. I couldn't let him hear how much he'd hurt me. "I'm counting on that to help pay for all this."

"I'm sure that now they won't be interested," he said with another terse laugh as the plane's door slammed shut behind them.

Fighting back my anger, my fears, flooded with emotion, I walked to the river for privacy. I sat on a rock, staring out at the water, disappointed in myself for allowing Hightower to bully me into making bad decisions. I should never have let him talk me into going early or trusted him to bring the engineer.

That evening, Gomez powered up the new radio—it worked with the first crank—and we put a call through to the operator at the Ciudad Bolivar airport. I took over the microphone and asked him to relay a message to a friend, an exec with one of the oil companies, someone who had come through for me in the past. "Tell him we need an engineer trained in surveying to go into the jungle with us. And tell him that whomever he sends needs to bring all his own equipment and come quickly, as soon as he can."

I held out little hope, but I didn't know what else to try.

Afterward, the three of us who were left—Gomez, Ernie, and I— sat around our campfire and listened to music on the radio. While the men relaxed, I wrote in my notebook, describing the disappointing turn of events, wondering if our expedition was doomed. The night turned cold, and I shivered in my hammock until I fell asleep.

I woke the next day in a dark mood, wondering if we all should have left on the plane with Hightower and O'Brien. In the past, I'd been the first one up, but that morning, I lay in my hammock and listened to monkeys screeching in the trees while Gomez made coffee and Ernie searched the campsite for the fork from his grub kit.

"It was here last night," he insisted.

"I bet some critter carried it off. I think I can see it over near the bushes," Gomez shouted. "There's something on the ground that looks like metal."

Ernie walked over, bent down and picked up his fork. "Well, look at that."

"What?" Gomez asked.

"A stork. The biggest I've ever seen."

"The jabiru?" I murmured, and I unzipped my hammock and climbed out. Soon all three of us were gazing at it across the field.

# CHAPTER THIRTY-ONE

**Brazoria County, Texas**

**March 1993**

THE AFTERNOON LINGERED. While Ruth sat at the kitchen table and talked of times long past, Gabby cleaned the kitchen cabinets and organized the pantry. Then, just before six, Ruth rubbed her neck, weary, and glanced at the wall clock. "The local news will be on in a few minutes. Let's see what that Bush fella turned up."

"I guess," Gabby said, with a short, nervous huff. "If you say we have to."

"Maybe there will be good news."

"Of course, it's just…what if…"

The two women locked eyes, and Ruth scowled at her. "Those are two sad words—*what if.*"

Gabby nodded, and they walked to the den and turned on the TV. They didn't have to wait long. A big story, the station ran her interview first up. They ended with her plea for Rae Ann and the police who responded to her 911 calls to come forward.

"Did you get a response from Captain Jordan?" the anchor asked Patrick Bush.

"We contacted him, told him what his wife said, and he issued a written statement. Let me read it to you. 'This interview with my wife increases my concern about her current condition. It's evidence of the confusion I saw after her fall. Again, I ask the people of Texas, every law enforcement agency across the state, to please help me find Gabby and bring her home, so I can get her the medical attention she needs.'"

"That man—" Ruth exclaimed.

"Have you talked to any sources? Has anyone confirmed or disputed Mrs. Jordan's charges?" the anchor asked.

"We attempted to talk to her neighbors, but no one claimed to know the Jordans well. Said they kept to themselves. We called Mrs. Jordan's place of work, but they refused comment. One thing: I ran a records check covering the past five years at the Jordans' condominium building."

"What did you find."

"There are no records indicating Gabby Jordan ever called 911."

"This is a strange one. Thank you for the report, Patrick. Next up, how's the weather looking for the coming week? We'll tell you after the break."

A car dealer's grating commercial boomed, doing nothing to relieve the palpable tension in the house on the river. As Ruth turned off the television, Gabby muttered, "No police records documenting my 911 calls? Of course, there aren't any. Jeff is a powerful guy, and he had it all erased from the records. Absolutely predictable."

Ruth shrugged. "Gabby, remember why we did this? You weren't thinking the police would come forward and back you up. You went on TV to reach Rae Ann. If she's heard you, it was just now when this interview aired. We don't know yet if this will work."

"Yes, of course, but..." Gabby buried her mouth in her hand, paused as if to catch her breath. "Ruth, this is too much. I can't do this. I'm not as brave as you are. Putting myself out there puts me in danger. If Jeff found me, he would..."

Troubled, Ruth sank into her favorite armchair. Ginger tried to jump up to join her but missed. The dog stared up at Ruth, eyes blinking like a baby bird who'd fallen out of a nest. It was then that Ruth broke the silence. "Gabby, if you run, you'll always be hiding. That's the last option, the one you don't want to take."

Brooding, Gabby paced. She stopped a few feet from Ruth and crossed her arms across her chest. The women locked eyes. "I know you're right. But this whole thing boils down to my word against Jeff's. He said versus she said. And he has the advantage. And what you said earlier is true."

"What did I say?"

"That I gave it to him by not confiding in anyone. Sure, I told my mom. I called 911, I reached out to people in law enforcement, but I shouldn't have stopped there. I realize that now. I should have asked for help from people at work, maybe friends, and revealed what was going on inside our condo. I should have stood up to Jeff, hired a lawyer or something." At that, Gabby grimaced, as if disgusted. "I'm a fool."

Ruth's voice turned shrill. "No, you're not. And I wasn't blaming you. I was explaining the reality of the situation, the hurdles the reporters covering the story face."

"But I should have—"

"Gabby, it's not your fault," Ruth interrupted. "You did what a lot of women do. What I did."

At that, an uncomfortable silence filled the room as Gabby shot Ruth a curious glance.

Ruth hesitated. She inhaled a long, slow breath, and when she spoke again her voice was so low that she could barely be heard. For the first time in her long life, she uttered the words: "When I was a teenager, my father sexually abused me. I lived with him. It was just the two of us, and he treated me like a wife, not a daughter. It went on for a long time."

Now Gabby was the one who searched for the right words to say. "Oh, no. Ruth, I—"

"My point is that, like you, I didn't tell anyone. Not until this day, this very moment. You're the first one I've ever confessed this to. So, I do understand why you kept Jeff's secret."

Ruth's voice sounded haggard, and her gray eyes clouded dark. Gabby rushed over, bent down, and slipped her arms around her. "You weren't to blame. You were a child."

"Yes. I was a child. And no, it wasn't my fault," Ruth said. Gabby wiped tears from her eyes, and Ruth did the same. "You're not responsible either. Gabby, this was always Jeff's sin. Never yours."

"But I'm an adult. I'm—"

"It wasn't my fault, and it's not yours." Where Ruth had been hesitant before, the words now poured out, as if she had to release them all or become silent again. "And in many ways, it is the same. I could have told my teacher, someone, but I didn't. Because I loved my father. Because I didn't want bad things to happen to him. Because I was afraid."

"But—"

"Gabby, for much of my life, I blamed myself for what *he* did. I thought that somehow it was my fault. But now, going through this with you..." Ruth paused, overcome with emotion. "I realize for the first time that I shoulder none of the responsibility. My father abused me, and it was *his* sin, not mine. Jeff beat you. It was *his* sin, not yours."

"Oh, Ruth, but I should have done—"

"No!" Ruth shuddered. "It wasn't me. And it's not you. The blame belongs to them. All of it. And I understand why you didn't tell anyone. I didn't tell anyone either."

Gabby mulled over what Ruth had just told her and realized how hard those words must have been to say. "I know that you're right. And I understand that you were trying to explain why the reporters are listening to him, believing him, why they might not believe me. But what do I do now?"

Ruth exhaled a long breath. "Beyond praying, I'm not sure there's much we can do until we find out if the one person you needed to reach is going to respond."

"Rae Ann? What if she doesn't come out of hiding? Or what if she's not in hiding. What if Jeff killed her? Maybe Rebecca Tinsley works for Jeff. Maybe he knows all about my phone call to her. If that's true, then there's no one to help me."

"You're doing that what-if thing again."

"But—"

"We can't think about that right now." The sadness and pain were gone from Ruth's voice, replaced by a controlled patience. "Right now, we need to hold tight. You've planted the seeds, and all we can do is wait to see what grows. This time tomorrow, maybe we'll have answers."

"Give it time," Gabby repeated.

"Yes. Give it time."

# Chapter Thirty-Two

**Uruyén, Venezuela**

**1949**

THE SAME MORNING Hightower and O'Brien left, maybe an hour after the jabiru flew away, a man emerged from the jungle and shuffled toward our camp as casually as if he'd just arrived home from a swim in the creek. He was stooped and wrinkled but probably not more than forty or so, and his shirt and slacks were ragged and stained. "This is one of Laime's men," the chief explained, delivering the first good news I'd had in more than a week. "He's been traveling for days to get here, and he comes with a message."

The chief translated as the man explained that Laime had cleared an airstrip, but not Jimmie Angel's. Instead, he'd made a new one farther east. He described how to find it, and he said that we could fly out at any time, that the rest of the porters and Laime were there waiting. Finally! I shouted at Ernie and Gomez to tell them, repeating each beautiful word.

Then, a couple of hours later, more good luck.

The *brrrrr* of a plane's engine, and I recognized Oley's Cub Cruiser in the sky pointed at the landing strip. The door opened and the first one out was my friend, the oil executive I'd reached out to the night before. Behind him trailed another man, someone I didn't recognize.

"Ruth, this is Perry Lowrey, one of our engineers. He's agreed to act as your surveyor," my friend explained. "Treat him well, and bring him home safely."

Lowrey resembled other oil-field engineers I'd known. Tall, with just the hint of a potbelly, he wore what looked like a brand-spanking-new khaki safari outfit and a hat to match. His eyes keenly intelligent, he glanced around at all of us as if silently computing the odds of our success. He reminded me of a kid I'd known in grade school who worked math problems in ink for fun. Thrilled, I fought off the urge to hug the man, afraid it would spook him and he'd get back on the plane.

"I brought extra supplies," Oley said. "Thought I'd stock you up. Canned meat, rice, beans, and oatmeal."

"Thanks," I said, grateful. "You arrived at the perfect time. We just got news about the location of Laime's airstrip. Can you stay and shuttle us over tomorrow morning?"

"You bet!" Oley sounded nearly as happy as I felt.

For the first time since we'd arrived at the Caracas airport, I believed that we had a shot at pulling it off. It seemed that nothing else could go wrong—until early that evening, when someone else walked out of the jungle, a white man followed by a group of the most bedraggled natives I'd ever encountered. They all looked like they'd been to the wars—or spent weeks in the jungle. At first, I wondered if it could really be him. But it had to be.

"Laime? What are you doing here?"

"I DON'T UNDERSTAND why you came here," I said, still shocked that he wasn't at the airstrip. "We were flying out to join you in the morning." I poured him a cup of instant coffee. He took a sip and made a disgusted face, scrunching up his mouth. I gathered he was indicating that it didn't quite measure up to the real thing, which, if he'd asked, I would have admitted.

As I listened, Laime described all he'd been through in the previous weeks. He'd found Jimmie's airstrip without any trouble, but he judged the ground too soft to land a plane. I disagreed, reporting that Oley had landed his Cub Cruiser there twice, but Laime pointed out that Oley's plane hadn't been loaded with cargo and said he feared that if heavier, it would have sunk into the earth.

"We're entering the rainy season, Ruth, and that field will get mucky. By the time we want to fly out after we measure the falls, we won't be able to. You must trust me on this. I know the jungle."

"Your man says you found another site."

"I did."

Greedily shoving oatmeal into his mouth, then holding his bowl up for more, Laime described how he'd discovered another clearing closer to the falls that was long and solid enough to accommodate Oley's plane. He hadn't worried about getting the news to me, because he assumed that we'd spot it from the air. Sadly, we'd never flown over that section of jungle.

When O'Brien dropped our note, Laime thought that we'd found his new airstrip. But when he arrived back there, he found none of the promised food. Two days later, he concluded something must have gone wrong and that we had given up and returned to Caracas.

At that point, out of food, living off fish they pulled from the river, Laime saw no alternative but to return to Uruyén.

"I'm sorry, Laime. I'm so sorry you've been through so much."

"It's okay, Ruth." He appeared tired but not angry. "We're here now, so it's all okay."

So far, this wasn't terrible news. Laime had returned, and he and his crew had all survived. Knowing that everyone was safe was a great relief. And this turn of events didn't necessarily present a problem. Now that we knew where the new airstrip was and that it was ready, Oley could simply fly us there with the porters, our supplies, and equipment.

Then I realized there was one thing Oley couldn't fly in, something essential to our journey. "Where are the dugouts?"

My heart sank when Laime answered, "We used them to get here. They're a day's walk away on the river."

That news hit me with all the force of a physical blow. The dugouts were too big and heavy to carry on Oley's airplane. And no matter what course we took, we couldn't travel to the falls without them. All the possible routes ended with a boat trip up the Churún River into the canyon.

We had no other choices. We had to take the long route to the falls, the one all the other expeditions had attempted and failed.

"Oh, no. Laime, this isn't—"

"We waited for you!" For the first time, Laime became indignant. "We ran out of food. We didn't know what was going on. What did you expect me to do?"

"I know. But couldn't you have—"

"Have done what?" Laime shouted. "I did what I thought wisest. We came to Uruyén."

As disappointed as I was, I knew he was right. In his circumstances, I would have done the same.

In the days that followed, we prepared for what would be a more arduous journey than we'd planned. The natives Laime had traveled with were exhausted and refused to accompany us, so we paid them for the work they'd done, and they went home to their families. In a neighboring village, Laime secured other porters and helpers, the only catch was that along with the fabric and salt we'd brought, they wanted twice the money we'd promised the first group. Reluctantly, I agreed, realizing I had no other option.

The day before we left, a bright, sunny Monday, the tenth day I'd spent at the Uruyén campsite, Laime and I organized the supplies. With the extra food Oley had flown in and without Hightower and O'Brien to feed, if all went as planned, we thought we would have ample provisions to take us to the falls and out.

The others also repacked their gear. One heavy box held Perry Lowrey's surveying equipment. Ernie's movie camera, film, and equipment took up two boxes. Then there was Gomez's bulky radio and its generator to contend with. In addition to the personal items in my backpack, I had three cameras, film, and flashbulbs.

As Laime and I worked together, rearranging things to reduce the number of boxes, I worried that two things were missing. The snakebite kit and the gun, the Luger, were gone. Hightower must have taken them with him.

When I told Laime, he paused briefly, tilted his head to the side with a look of deep disappointment, and said, "Ruth, don't tell the others. All we can do is hope we don't need them."

After dinner, I wrote a press release, and Gomez sent it out to my newspaper contacts, to tell them we were starting our trek to Angel Falls.

Then, just before bed, we gathered around the campfire, and Laime warned us of the trials ahead. "Be careful where you put your hands. If you get up at night, turn on your flashlight before you put your feet on the earth. There are scorpions, spiders, and snakes in the jungle. Watch out for ant mounds. The stinging ants are hard to see, and they swarm."

"I've been in jungles before," Ernie boasted.

"Not like this one," Laime cautioned. "There are no others like this. This is the densest I have ever encountered."

When it came to the porters, he reminded us to be respectful of their ways. Unknowingly, we'd already upset them. Throughout our stay in the savannah, we'd washed our dishes in the river. "Don't do that. Bring water to the campsite and, when you're done, spill the soapy water on the ground. The Indians believe you're making the water dirty and angering the river gods. They don't want the spirits mad at them."

Then he lowered his voice and explained that under the best of circumstances, the porters would be skittish going into Churún Canyon. I'd heard this before, but he laid it out for the others. "We must be mindful of their beliefs, in particular when we reach Auyán-tepuí. The tribes have many terrifying legends about that mountain, the worst is that there are spirits living on top of it who look for opportunities to hurt them. These wicked ghosts threaten them each time thunder shakes the jungle."

# CHAPTER THIRTY-THREE

**The Rivers**

**May 3, 1949**

W E HAD FIVE in our party, and Laime hired ten porters to help us.

Old Reya, one of the tribe's elders, had a worn face, a serene demeanor. Despite his age, he was strong, and the others considered him their leader. The only woman in the group, Juanita, solidly built with long dark hair, I estimated to be in her twenties. She knew the river better than most of the men and had names for many of the waterfalls and creeks. Of the six younger men, one was Juanita's husband, who was an excellent shot fishing with a bow and arrow. Most of the men sported various versions of western clothes, ragged pants and shirts, but Juanita's husband wore only a red loincloth.

To my surprise, Laime had also signed on two children: Manuel, a shy twelve-year-old with big brown eyes. And Jacinto. From that first day, I fell in love with Jacinto, nine-years-old, overflowing with energy, a wide white smile, and an impish sparkle in his eyes.

Our journey began with a hike through the Gran Sabana, to an

Indian village that missionaries long ago had named San Rafael, where our dugouts waited. While not far, ten miles to the east, it was a grueling journey. I carried a heavy backpack, and each step required raising my legs high above the sharp grasses. The men struggled, too, except for Laime and the Indians, whose pace resembled a trot more than a walk.

Trying to ignore the pain radiating up my calves to my thighs, I focused on the valley's beauty. At our feet, a carpet of flowers wove through the sawgrass, blue and purple blooms, pink orchids, and a white blossom that reminded me of the lilies Ma planted in Illinois when I was a girl. We'd hiked for only an hour or so when I spotted a strange creature stalking parallel to us, barely visible, a long, sleek black cat. One of the Indians called it an "*onza*," and I wondered if it was actually the mythical animal I'd heard whispered about or if the camouflaging vegetation disguised a common jaguarondi or an exceptionally dark lynx.

As the day wore on, the sun beat down, and with shorter, less muscular legs, I needed to work harder than the men to keep up. At times, Laime waited for me, and I worried about that. If I fell behind in the meadow, what would it be like in the jungle, in much worse conditions? Still, no one complained, at least not within my earshot. I reminded myself that in San Rafael we'd board the dugouts and begin the trip on the river.

Our party arrived at the village in early afternoon, but we'd been unable to carry everything in one trip, so the bearers and Laime had to return to Uruyén for a second load. The following morning, the local tribe threw a fiesta to wish us well on our journey. A pig roasted in a pit, and I traded salt for the loin to feed my group.

On the second day, the tribesmen built a ceremonial fire in the center of the village and handed out drinking vessels fashioned from gourds filled with a version of moonshine. As foul as it tasted, I sipped and grinned. The tribe's chief watched me as he beat the ground with bamboo rattles, and members of the tribe danced around the flames. Putting down the drink, I grabbed my camera and snapped photos while Laime, Knee, and the other men ate *chicharrones*, fried pork rinds dipped in *aji*, a type of chili sauce.

Our third morning in San Rafael, the good weather ended, the skies turned gray, and the rains finally began.

In a slow drizzle, Laime and Reya directed the packing of the four dugouts. I doubted all the gear, supplies, and men would fit, but within a couple of hours they had everything secured. In my boat, Reya manned the paddles, while little Jacinto sat upfront and watched for rocks, logs, anything we might hit in the river. Boxes of food filled the center. Bows and arrows, bug repellant, shoes, and canteens were secured to the sides. Near the back of the boat, tarp protected my cameras and film bags from the rain.

As we pushed off, I draped my hand over the side, and ripples trailed from my fingers. The jungle air wasn't terribly hot but oppressively humid, and the water felt fresh and cool. The river meandered, and on the banks, narrow paths had been cut through, some perhaps centuries old, well-trodden routes connecting villages.

After one twist in the river, we saw a jabiru fishing along the bank. "Look at that!" Ernie shouted. "Maybe it followed us."

"Sure. There's only one in Venezuela, right?" I said with a laugh.

As we passed, the jabiru called out and then stood at attention, its eyes following as our boats floated away.

"Rapids!" someone shouted as we rounded a sharp curve.

The water shallow, we poled through, Reya expertly guiding our dugout. At times, the boat swirled and rocked. I held on tight.

As the day wore on, the rapids multiplied. The dugouts slipped and slid as the rushing river gushed over the tops of the barely submerged rocks. At times, I was pushed side to side, grasping the edge of the boat. If we'd hit a big enough rock or a

sharp one, the dugout, its contents, perhaps those of us inside could be lost to strong undertows.

On stretches where the river churned like a boiling pot, we pulled to the side, unpacked the boats, and made multiple trips carrying our supplies and the dugouts past the rapids. Where the river calmed, we reloaded.

Although the porters did the heavy lifting, we all pitched in. I hauled boxes, carried my own cameras and film, and helped to hoist the dugouts through tight spots in the jungle, maneuvering around the thick trunks of the palms rising above us. Slick moss covered the rocks, the earth, fallen logs. Nearly everything we touched.

Yet most of those first days evaporated on the river, riding downstream on sluggish currents. We took turns on the oars, and soon my hands stung, the skin blistered and calloused, but we made progress. At night, we camped in clearings or old shacks tucked into the jungle that Laime knew about, and I cooked our dinners over an open fire, the way my dad had taught me when we lived in the trailer in the woods.

Late one afternoon, a plane circled overhead, and I recognized it. Charlie Baughan, the pilot who'd first flown me to look for Angel Falls, buzzed us, made a wide turn, and then swooped down again. He was checking on us, I knew. Glad to see him, I stood in the boat and punched my fists into the air like a boxer in a ring, signaling that we were fighting our way to the falls. Around me all the others, even the porters, waved and called out.

Perhaps because of the language barrier, the porters tended to keep to themselves. But as the days passed, I gradually gained a better understanding of my fellow explorers.

Laime, the only professional adventurer among us, routinely took the lead. While friendly, he appeared most comfortable mingling with the porters. We had no idea what they were talking about when Laime would say something in their native tongue and the entire group would shake with laughter. I tried to imagine him in New York or Chicago and decided that sometimes we were exactly where we were meant to be.

For Laime, the jungle was his natural habitat.

Of us all, Enrique Gomez was the shyest, and much of the time his brow was furrowed in worry. Protective of his radio, he carried the boxes himself when we portaged. When the action waned and the days stretched long, Ernie Knee told silly jokes. In the beginning a few I hadn't heard, but he soon dug out well-worn one-liners, ones he'd most likely encountered in a bar or at a party a decade earlier. Like Gomez, Perry Lowrey was quiet. Our engineer was the most intellectual of the bunch.

I wondered what they all thought of me, the woman who'd brought them together.

Much of my adult life, I'd been one of few females in a man's world. Now Juanita and I were the only women on this excursion into the jungle. At times, I considered what Ma would think of all this, but then I willed those thoughts away. She was long dead, no longer above ground to criticize my every move. Dad still lived in Illinois, but I'd stopped seeing him years earlier, weary of the charade. And then Eric came to mind. It had been three years since we'd gone our separate ways. I hoped that wherever he was, he'd heard the news and that, despite our parting, he was cheering for me.

Days passed, and the rainy season took firm hold. What began as a persistent drizzle became waves of pounding rain, at times so thick that it left little room for air. Of us all, Old Reya appeared most annoyed at the bad weather and looked up wearily at the dark skies as he paddled, half blowing and half spitting toward the offending clouds, "Pah-too! Pah-too! Pah-too!"

Playfully, one day, I decided to help him. "Pah-too! Pah-too!"

At first, he looked confused, but then a smile crept over his wrinkled face until his shoulders quaked with laughter.

We grew accustomed to the constant clamminess of our saturated clothes. Before dark, we lit a campfire, dried our socks and shoes around it, and told stories while, a distance away, the Indians congregated in their own encampment, cooking fish they'd caught on the river, eating cassava they'd brought from home.

At times we watched them in astonishment, noticing how they used what they found in the jungle in ways we couldn't imagine. We struggled to light wet branches to build a campfire. The Indians shaved the bark off to make tinder. Once lit, they tossed the slender pieces back and forth in their hands, adding ever more of the brittle wood until they had a fire intense enough to start wet jungle logs burning. We copied them, but our fires dwindled and died while theirs endured throughout the night.

Our days were spent on the river, but the evenings and early mornings camped out in the jungle fascinated me.

Brightly colored parrots flew above us squawking, and monkeys scurried branch to branch. I bathed in natural pools as stunning as the Hollywood sets in an Esther Williams movie and washed my hair in gentle waterfalls. A caterpillar I happened upon resembled a crabby old man wearing a fluffy sweater, and ants paraded past as formally as any army regiment. Each carried a jagged bit of leaf to their mound— enough, I was sure, to supply a banquet.

After dark, the jungle only vaguely resembled what we saw during the day. Night-dwelling animals and insects crawled out once the sun set. Perhaps the strangest insect I encountered was a one-inch-long beetle with high beams on its head. Although dog-tired, I became so fascinated by it that I lay awake in my hammock and watched the small creature weave through the grass.

Yet the danger never seemed far away. While we were on land, we'd see venomous snakes draped over branches above us. I nearly tripped on a massive python, its body as thick as a fire hose. Laime insisted that the snake was more afraid of us than we were of him, but he moved our camp. Then there were the low growls from somewhere deep in the forest. On nights when the rumbling of stalking cats grew ever louder, closer, we took turns staying awake to keep the campfire lit.

Off and on we sought shelter in abandoned huts, places Laime or the Indians knew. Our hammocks hung off the walls, until we hastily pulled them down and rushed out in the middle of the night to sleep under the stars, when we scratched at unrelenting fleas. During nights spent in swampy areas, I worried that the mosquitos might truly eat us all alive. One morning I had so many bites on one hand, I couldn't make a fist.

My nightmares before the trip had featured boa constrictors, pythons, and ferocious cats. They were all out there. I didn't forget about them. But soon I had as much fear of insects as snakes and cougars. *Jejenes*, no-see-ums, bit me when I bathed, and tiny, nearly invisible fleas burrowed into folds and crevices in our skin, especially around our feet, where the females lay egg sacks. At night, the men sat around the campfire, cutting them out.

One night, little Jacinto offered to help me remove the eggs, but the kid ran off screaming as soon as I took off my shoes and socks.

Laime, who'd spent so much of his life in the jungle, walked over to see why, then laughed and called to the other men, "Take a look."

At that, I realized I must have terrorized the boy. He'd probably never even heard of nail polish. Before we'd left on the expedition, I'd painted my toenails a bright red.

AT FIRST THE porters willingly churned the wheel on the generator to power the radio mornings and evenings when we attempted to reach our contact in Ciudad Bolivar. But the crank was hard to turn, and they grew tired of it. Before long we all took shifts. Our only link with the outside world, the radio allowed us to contact my pilot friends. We used it to let them know they didn't have to worry and to alert them to our location. For two days, Gomez couldn't get through. Late the second afternoon, while we were setting up camp for the evening, I heard a plane. Through a break in the palm trees, I saw Charlie Baughan flying overhead in a gloomy, tented sky. He had to be looking for us. I held my breath and prayed that he wouldn't crash, until I heard his plane finally fly away.

As we made steady progress on the rivers, we passed the flat-topped mountains, some in the distance, others soaring up nearly beside us. The rapids were the most treacherous where the rivers narrowed, the water cascading over giant rocks that, over the ages, had fallen from the mountaintops. One afternoon, we cornered a bend and fierce currents took us by surprise. I was at the paddles. Until then, Reya had always navigated our dugout through dangerous waters, but this time the boat jerked so violently that he couldn't climb over the boxes to help. The dugout whirled, slapped a rock, and then spun, while I attempted to control it. I panicked as we barreled toward a massive boulder. Reya leaned out and extended his arms, and I worried that he'd break a bone trying to push away. I shoved my paddle against the great rock with every bit of my strength, until we finally wrenched free.

That night around the campfire, we all admitted that we had feared we wouldn't make it through the rapids, that one or all of us would perish in the river.

THE RAINS SEEMED like they'd never end. Then, strangely, we woke up to clear skies.

In the dugout that day, Reya looked as happy as if he'd been handed a beautiful gift. A few of the Indians spoke a bit of Spanish, and he pointed at the sun, then at the mountain we were passing, Uei-tepuí. "*Lo mismo!*" It was the phrase I used to order "my usual," my scotch and sodas at the American Club. Reya was using a different meaning: "The same." I didn't understand until I remembered Uei-tepuí's nickname, Sun Mountain.

An hour later, after we rounded the next curve, the black rock of Auyán-tepuí became visible ahead. I felt a surge of anticipation. The mountain was majestic. We were so close, just days away. I could visualize the canyon. The waterfall. My heart hastened with excitement. But I saw the Indians' reactions, which were very different from my own. Dread showed in all their anxious gestures and fear in their muffled voices.

The next morning, Laime predicted that we would merge that day onto the Churún, the river that led into Auyán-tepuí's canyon. Minutes later, I was loading my cameras with film when everyone suddenly stopped talking.

"Ruth," Laime said. "The Indians."

I looked up, and they surrounded us, Old Reya, Juanita, the two boys, and the men. Looking at them, I had a sick feeling. They'd painted their faces with some kind of red paste, jagged and straight lines, thick dots. Their expressions somber, they stared at us. I thought of the Western movies I'd seen where North American tribes put on war paint before going into battle. I knew our porters were nervous. I'd seen it in their eyes. We were getting close to Devil Mountain. But why had they done this?

I smiled at Juanita and said an English word I'd taught her by pointing at flowers: "Pretty!"

She didn't smile back.

A conference ensued. Laime asked about the paint, and the Indians pointed up at the mountain. "They think the paint will make them invisible to the evil spirits," he reported.

He talked to them again, and Juanita held out a small pot of the paint she carried in her palm. When Laime seemed to ask her something, she responded, and he turned to me. "Ruth, they want you to paint your face like theirs."

I undoubtedly looked confused because I was. But Juanita handed me the paint and pantomimed dunking her finger in it and then smearing it on her face. I held it up to my nose and smelled some kind of jungle berry.

"Why me?" I asked.

Laime shrugged. "Better not to ask and just do it."

Reya, too, motioned to show me how he wanted the paint to look, acting as if he were drawing lines with dots on my cheeks, a squiggle on my forehead. I didn't argue. While I wondered why the men weren't asked to do the same, I was touched that the Indians wanted to protect me, and I did as they instructed, dabbing a finger in the sticky, sweet-smelling paste and smearing it on my forehead and cheeks. Once I'd finished, Juanita smiled at me and said, "Pretty."

I bowed just a bit and said, "Thank you."

We walked to the river but stopped when we saw the dugouts. The Indians had painted the paddles with the same abstract designs.

"Is that to make the boats invisible?" I asked.

Laime nodded, then turned to the Indians and said something I couldn't understand. "I thanked them for protecting all of us."

While the Indians feared Auyán-tepuí, I found it incredibly beautiful. We paddled toward the mountain, and soon the dark rock surrounded by jungle towered over us. As I marveled at the sight, the Indians murmured among themselves. Twelve-year-old Manuel had a wad of twigs and herbs he'd tied into a ball. Off and on, he muttered and held it up to the sky. He shook it like a rattle, either entreating the gods for help or commanding the evil spirits to stay away.

The boy looked terrified.

To break the tension, we laughed and joked, even sang our favorite songs. At first, the Indians watched suspiciously, curious, perhaps even a bit shocked. But soon the mood lifted, and they seemed to enjoy our songs. For my turn, I sang songs from *Oklahoma!* the play I'd seen with Eric in New York. I thought about how much my world had changed since then.

Once we reached the Churún, we headed south, and now, instead of traveling downriver with the current aiding us, we crawled upriver, fighting against it. As the rapids became more frequent, we struggled to make progress. We had expected this section to be hard, but Laime wanted to stay in the boats as long as possible. When we were forced to leave the dugouts, we would have the dense jungle to contend with.

"How much farther?" Lowrey asked, at one point, rubbing his shoulder.

"I hope much farther," Laime answered. "Once we're in the jungle, this part of the journey will seem easy."

Finally, midafternoon, Laime motioned for us to stop. We'd arrived at a spot where the land rose up to form a sandbar and a rocky beach, just before yet another stretch of swift rapids.

"This is it," Laime announced, more beat than I'd ever seen him. "We're finished on the river."

# Chapter Thirty-Four

**The Jungle**

**May 10, 1949**

WE DRAGGED THE dugouts onto the shore and tied them to the trunks of trees. I didn't argue. As much as I dreaded the prospect of marching through the jungle, every muscle in my body cried out from the pain of taking my turn with the paddles.

We'd talked this through many times and had our plan in place. The final leg of our journey should take no more than six days: a two-day march to the waterfall, two days to measure its height and take photographs, then a day or two to hike back to the dugouts. From this point forward, we would carry only the barest essentials, the equipment we absolutely needed and six days' worth of rations. Everything else would remain with the dugouts to await our return.

That evening, as we reorganized our supplies, we heard monkeys overhead, creatures we couldn't see rustling through the underbrush. Gomez was hunched over his radio searching for a signal when he shushed us. "Quiet a minute."

We all heard it, the same guttural clacking we'd heard back in Uruyén.

"It's the jabiru," Gomez said. "Don't you think?"

Ernie and Laime shot him skeptical looks, while our ever-logical engineer, Lowrey, shook his head and snickered.

It couldn't possibly have been the same bird. It probably wasn't even a jabiru but some bird that sounded like one. Yet I stared up into the trees, hoping I'd spot it in the distance or hovering overhead.

No jabiru appeared, and the rest of that evening, we quietly packed our gear for our trip into the jungle the next morning.

After dinner, we hung our hammocks on the trees. Laime wandered off, I wasn't sure where, and a short time later, I heard a grating sound, like someone working with a tool. I swept my flashlight across the jungle and found Laime hauling one of the dugouts closer to camp.

"What're you doing?"

Laime glanced around, checking to see if anyone else was close enough to hear. Then he whispered. "I walked by the camp. The Indians are frightened, and I heard one of the men trying to convince the others to take the dugouts and leave us here while we sleep."

With that, he headed back to pull another of the dugouts to higher ground. I hurried to help. "You need some sleep," I pointed out. "You can't stay up all night and guard them."

"I'll sleep in one. And this way, they're closer to the camp. We should hear the Indians if they try to leave."

There was no need to discuss it further. Laime didn't have to spell out what would happen if the porters fled in the dugouts. There was a good chance that some or all of us would perish in the jungle.

The next morning, Reya and the others applied more red paint and asked me to do the same. For some reason, they still didn't seem to worry about the men. This time Juanita didn't joke with me. We didn't tell each other that we looked pretty. As she smeared the berry paint on my cheeks, her hand shook.

The sun was up, and the skies were clear, but as always, it was twilight beneath the jungle's ceiling of palms. Two of the Indians took the lead, chopping a path with their machetes. They bent and hacked, throwing the cut branches and stalks into the brush, forming a narrow trail. In the procession, I claimed the rear, not wanting to hold the others back if I lagged.

The trail wasn't like any I'd ever walked before. The vegetation wasn't completely mowed down. The Indians had left a foot of sawgrass, stumps, and branches. I understood that it was the best they could do, but as I walked, I had to lift my legs high, much as I'd done on the walk out of Uruyén. But here, the reeds were sharper. The grass pierced my khaki pants, and scratched my skin. Before long, drops of blood collected on my shoes.

Determined to forge ahead, I concentrated on keeping up with the others. In the canyon, the jungle surrounded the river. Then, perhaps a mile or more back on each side, the canyon walls towered above us.

The black rock mountain. The intense green jungle. I don't know what I'd expected, but this was so much more beautiful than I'd imagined. Wisps of sunlight filtered through the palms. Mammoth rocks had fallen off the mountaintop over the millennia, some so large we couldn't climb over them, and the porters were forced to cut a path around them. As spectacular as it was, the thick jungle rattled my nerves. It felt claustrophobic, suffocating.

I tried to follow in the others' footsteps, but I gradually fell behind. Off and on I stepped onto what looked like solid earth, only to sink into a pool covered by a dark-green mold. Slippery moss grew on nearly every surface, including the rocks and fallen logs. If I didn't step high enough or watch where my feet landed, vines caught my shoes, and I tripped. To stop my fall, I reached out and grabbed the closest palm, astonished when, at times, their trunks crumbled in my hands. The trees long dead, they'd deteriorated to mere shells. But the dense jungle propped them up, keeping these ghost trees from falling.

The farther we traveled, the more bruises, scratches, and cuts covered my arms and legs. When we crossed creeks, the water burned my open sores. Fording one fast-moving stream, I lost my footing on the mossy bottom. I plunged into the current, arms flailing, fighting to seize something, anything to keep from drowning. But everything I touched was slimy, and I couldn't hold on. I went down, gulping water.

Just as I feared the river would carry me off, a strong hand grabbed my arm, reclaiming me. When I burst through to the surface, Reya stood above me, yanking me back from death to life. I choked and hawked up creek water as I stumbled beside him onto the bank. On land, I fell to my knees, gasping for air.

"Pah-too!" Reya spit and pointed up at the mountain, glowering as if the feared Auyán-tepuí were responsible.

That night in camp, I ate cassava and chipped beef sandwiches with the others and felt as if I'd walked, as the old saying goes, to hell and back. As soon as I finished the last bite, I collapsed into my hammock and fell asleep to the splatter of rain on a tarp suspended overhead.

*This is it. The last day to the falls*, I reminded myself when I woke the next morning. I looked up at the crown of palms overhead and realized that if my pilot friends were looking for me, they'd never see us. We had truly disappeared into the jungle.

Then, not long after sunrise, we were at it again.

At times, I was awed by Laime, who, like the Indians, seemed completely at ease in our treacherous surroundings. The other men had to expend more effort, but of us all, I was clearly the weakest.

While no one complained, I noticed the others glanced back at me, and I wondered if they believed I was holding them back.

Meanwhile, the canyon gradually narrowed, and I remembered from my flights over, how it tapered a bit not far before the falls. The realization that I drew closer with each step gave me the energy to keep putting one foot in front of the other.

Hours passed, and suddenly I heard shouting ahead. Exhausted, I pushed harder, wondering if the cries meant what I hoped. Rounding a curve, I recognized a familiar rock formation. Then, twenty steps later, the path turned. The men stood a short distance ahead, their eyes turned toward the heavens.

There it was, before us, in the distance certainly, but for the first time visible: the silver waters of Angel Falls, tumbling from the sky.

BREATHING IN THE jungle's rich oxygen, my heart labored inside my chest as I gazed at the most beautiful sight I had ever seen. An outcropping hid the base, but it was unmistakable; this was the siren that had called to me for two years, and it was spilling off the mountaintop with all the force the rainy season had brought.

"We're about two miles from the falls," Laime estimated, disappointed that we were moving so slowly. Yet he didn't complain. "We need to stay here tonight. We'll start out in the morning when we're fresh and get there with enough time to settle in before nightfall."

We set up a rudimentary camp, and I wrote out a message for Gomez to transmit to our radio contact in Ciudad Bolivar announcing that we would reach Angel Falls the next day.

When the skies darkened, we gathered and contemplated the stunning sight as the top of Angel Falls turned gold in the moonlight.

# Chapter Thirty-Five

**Angel Falls**

**May 12, 1949**

WE LEFT THE campsite at daybreak. For some reason I had hoped that the last day of the journey would be easier, but our proximity to the falls made no difference. The jungle fought us as we inched forward. In fact, it seemed the angry mountain gods the natives so dreaded had done their best to foil trespassers, throwing down giant boulders that blocked our way.

Meanwhile, the closer we got, the louder the falls became, the thunderous, cascading waters pounding so hard, it was near deafening. As we pushed on, I caught another glimpse of the waterfall between the palms. My muscles ached, strained and raw, and my body begged to give up, but I had at least another mile to go.

Eventually, I fell behind and lost sight of everyone else in our party. I felt truly alone in the jungle.

All around me, I heard the buzzing of insects and saw lizards sunning themselves on the few branches where strands of light seeped through. Off and on, I heard strange noises, and I watched the shadows, wondering what might be staring back at me.

I struggled to catch up, but my shoes slipped on the mildewed earth. Climbing over a massive fallen tree, I lost my footing and slid helplessly down its moss-covered trunk.

At noon, I finally caught up and found the others standing atop a massive boulder. Laime held out his hand and helped me climb up, while, a grin etched across his face, Ernie shouted at me. I couldn't hear him above the din.

Once I stood beside him, he said it again, "Welcome to Angel Falls!"

In front of us, the falls roared, taller than any skyscraper in the world. With tears in my eyes, I watched the winds whipping through the canyon pick up the cascading water and make it dance, drenching us in its spray.

Suddenly, my weary arms forgot to ache. I pulled a camera from my backpack and peered through its lens. The falls were more beautiful than I'd ever imagined. The tribes feared the canyon and wouldn't go in, and the explorers who came before us had never reached their destination. Over and again, I considered that we might be the first humans to have seen this view.

That afternoon, I let Angel Falls reveal themselves to me as I explored the cavern at the base, a pool of crystal-clear water. I bathed where no one had before, shielded from view behind the falls. The bug bites and the cuts on my legs burned like hundreds of bee stings. Even my scalp hurt. But none of it diminished my joy.

"I can't get a response on the radio," Gomez told me as evening fell. "No answer. Like they're not there, Miss Ruth. But I'll keep trying."

I'd written a message for him to read to our contact in Ciudad Bolivar. Well after midnight, he finally succeeded. "To Ministry of Communications, AP, UP, Caracas Journal, May 12. Expedition Salto Angel today reached the falls. Weather perfect. One of party bathed under the falls. Perry Lowrey directing work to measure the height of the waterfall."

I knew that communiqué would quickly make its way around the world, carried on the very newswires where I'd once worked. I pictured the excitement in newsrooms when editors learned of the expedition's success. What I forgot was that my message would go out with the original list of our members, the one that included the names of John Hightower and Jim O'Brien. I'd neglected to inform our contact in CB that they'd left the expedition.

If I had only…

The next morning, Perry Lowery rose early and shouted, "Anyone superstitious?"

The date was May 13th, a Friday.

IMMEDIATELY AFTER BREAKFAST, Lowery and Laime gathered the surveying equipment and left to find a prime spot to set up. A few of our bearers, still wearing their red paint, went along to help. To get the most advantageous angle, the men waded across the Churún, shallow below the falls, and settled on measuring from the other side.

Despite good weather, Lowery's Friday the thirteenth wake-up call colored the day.

It started at lunch as Gomez relaxed next to the campfire holding a bowl of hot soup. "*Levántate!*" Laime yelled. "Get up!"

The radio operator jumped high, so quickly and so skillfully that he never sloshed a drop. When he looked back, he saw a huge spider, the size of a lunch plate, one of the dreaded

Brazilian wandering spiders, perhaps a foot from where he'd sat.

"Stay back!" Laime grabbed a branch, thrust it into the fire until it flamed, and then speared the giant insect. It sizzled and burned as he twisted the stick, driving it farther into the spider's body. When he was sure it was dead, Laime pitched the charred shell into the jungle. No longer hungry, Gomez threw out his soup, and the rest of the day we all monitored where we walked and especially where we sat.

Under the clear, blue afternoon sky, I took photos around the camp, of the mountain and waterfall, of Lowery and Laime with their surveyor's equipment, conducting the official measurement. Finally, I pulled our small band of explorers together, set the timer on my camera and grabbed a shot of all five of us in front of the falls. Once that was done, I returned to the camp and made a cup of tea.

Not long after, Lowery found me. "Ruth, I have some bad news."

I looked up at him and took a deep breath, dreading what he'd say. "Spill it."

But he was reluctant; he squirmed and remained quiet.

"It's not going to make it any better drawing it out," I remarked.

Our engineer put his hands in his pockets and hunched his shoulders, resembling a turtle pulling into its shell. "I've made some preliminary calculations."

"And?"

"And I don't think that waterfall is going to be as high as you think it is."

My heart slipped in my chest. I closed my eyes. I reminded myself that it didn't matter if Angel Falls wasn't a mile high, as Jimmie boasted. For it to be the tallest in the world, the falls only had to beat South Africa's Tugela Falls. If Angel Falls measured 3,111 feet or higher, it was the tallest in the world. Anything more was gravy.

"Okay. What are you estimating?"

My heart nearly stopped beating when he said, "I don't think it's much more than two-thousand feet high. I'm not done yet, but that's my guess."

I couldn't speak. I'd done so much, given up so much, for a dream that wouldn't come true. I'd spent every penny I had and hiked into one of the world's deepest jungles only to find that Angel Falls wasn't the tallest waterfall in the world. At two thousand feet it wouldn't even rank in the top ten.

Lowrey must have understood my disappointment. He slunk off and left me alone. Minutes earlier, I'd felt triumphant. The bad news brought with it a deep fatigue.

I refilled my cup with tea and walked down the trail our porters had cut until I came out close to the river. Across the way, Lowrey and Laime were taking more measurements. I sat on a rock and gazed at Angel Falls. I was alone. For some reason I couldn't explain, I searched the riverbank, wondering if I might see the jabiru. In a land of brightly colored parrots and elegant pink flamingos, I was attached to a bulky white stork with a bulging red Adam's apple. But all I saw were a few small birds flying over the river.

"You're a daydreamer, Ruth," I whispered. "Maybe this is a good lesson for you. Maybe it's time to come down to earth."

I thought of Ma, of the sad years, the sour look on her face the day she tore up the tickets I'd saved to get a camera. How she ridiculed my dreams. My father said he believed in me, but then he violated my innocence. Finally, Eric. I replayed the message on his last note: "*I hope things turn out as you may plan them. I have found plans to be lousy.*"

For an hour, perhaps longer, I sat alone looking up at the falls, such a beautiful sight, and I cried. Actually, I sobbed. I wept so hard, I wondered if I'd ever stop.

ALTHOUGH I WAS disappointed—I couldn't pretend that I wasn't—that evening brought perspective.

A full moon shone down through the trees, and for hours I sat on our giant boulder, my hands wrapped around my knees, gazing up at Angel Falls. It was a calm night, but off and on a wisp of a breeze misted me with spray.

I breathed in the jungle, the falls, the world around me, mysterious and magnificent, and I tried to embed it all, just as it was at that moment, in my memory. Above me, the top of the great falls melted into the darkness, and it seemed impossible that they measured only two thousand feet. But then, I had no instruments other than my heart with which to gauge the height of Angel Falls.

One way or the other, however, I decided that I had no regrets. No matter what anyone said, I hadn't failed. I'd succeeded where no one else had before me—I'd launched an expedition that had measured Angel Falls.

OUR FINAL DAY at the falls, I took more photos, and Ernie worked on his film, while Lowery and Laime double-checked their work and took more measurements. While I bathed in the pool under the falls one last time, I inspected my body—bruised, scratched from my scalp to my feet. Oh, how I longed for a bubble bath, a night sleeping in a bed.

"Oley will pick us up in a few days," Ernie informed me when I returned to camp.

We were heading not to Uruyén but to the airstrip Laime had cleared, which was significantly closer. Our odyssey from Uruyén to the falls had taken nine days, but since the path had already been cleared, Laime intended the walk back to the river to be done in a single day, and from there we'd be rowing downstream, so he estimated that the entire journey should take only two days—three at the most.

The only part of the plan that worried me was the one-day hike back to the dugouts. I'd barely made it in two. How could I walk out in one?

Searching through my backpack, I retrieved my last blank notebook, which had crinkled and aged during the trip, as had I. My pens were all out of ink, but I found a stub of a pencil and sharpened it with a knife. Absorbed in my task, I didn't notice when Perry Lowrey walked up beside me.

"Ruth?" The man looked embarrassed, and I wondered what that meant. "I may have made a mistake."

I closed one eye and stared at him with the other, thinking that if he was going to tell me what I hoped, what I wanted more than anything, I had the right to make him squirm for the worry he'd caused me. "What are you saying?"

"The waterfall may be taller than I estimated."

I inhaled a deep breath and paused just a moment to settle my nerves. "How tall?"

"Somewhere around three-thousand feet."

I closed my eyes, and my head fell forward. That was promising. Lowery was close to the number I needed. *Maybe with a little luck…*

"When will you know for sure?"

"Not until I get back to Caracas, and I have all my charts and equipment."

"How long will that take?"

"A few days. Maybe a week."

My heart raced so fast that all I could do was nod.

THAT NIGHT I baked corn bread by spreading the batter between two rocks I placed in the fire. All went well until one of the rocks exploded, shooting pieces out into the jungle with the force of cannon balls. No one was hurt; we laughed, and it turned out that the corn bread wasn't half bad.

The following morning, I cornered Laime as he readied the camp to leave. "I'm going to take off now, so I can get a jump on the rest of you. It'll give me a head start, help me keep up."

Laime protested, but I insisted, and half an hour later I was trudging through the jungle in a light drizzle, following the path the Indians had cut to get us to the falls. Once or twice, I became confused and wandered off a bit, but I quickly realized my mistake and got back on track. Nothing out of the ordinary happened until I reached a bend and saw what appeared to be a lair. From the size of it, it was the home of a mountain lion or a jaguar. In the center lay the half-eaten carcass of a big rodent, probably a river rat. Blood glistened in the scant light eking through the thick umbrella of palm fronds.

The kill was fresh.

I glanced warily around, searching for eyes staring back at me from the shadows. I listened for the men, hoping they were right behind me, but I heard no one. I had no gun, no machete, only my pocketknife—no match for a big cat.

I took a deep breath and tried not to panic. The best option was to get out of there as quickly as possible, before the animal returned. But I had a problem; my feet simply refused to move. Motionless, I watched as a lizard rustled through the dead leaves on the jungle floor paying scant attention to me and in the distance a bird pecked at the jungle floor. It looked like a distant cousin of the chickens I'd fed on the farm as a girl. Life was all around me, none of it panicking, while I stood like the palms, rooted and immobile.

"Okay," I murmured. "Time to go."

Still, I couldn't convince my feet to obey me.

Then I heard it.

I looked up, and something flashed overhead. I'll never be sure, but I was convinced that the large white bird that flew directly above me was my jabiru. It called out, once, twice, and then disappeared.

An hour and a half later, I'd gone farther down the path when the others caught up. Relieved to see them, I kept my secrets, never mentioning my panic or the creature whose presence had given me courage. Quickly, they pushed past me, and I found myself once more at the rear. I tried, but it was impossible to keep up. Even the men, except for Laime and the Indians, struggled, panting hard and sweating, their faces flushed with the effort.

Little more than half an hour before the sun set, I heard Gomez shout, "Camp!"

None of the posh hotel rooms I'd stayed in, not my apartment in New York or the one that waited for me in Caracas, could ever have been as welcoming as that clearing where our supplies and the dugouts waited. Laime brought me hot beef soup, after which I crawled into my damp hammock and slept the sleep of the dead.

The sun rose early, and my arms and legs ached, but at least there would be no more hiking through the jungle. The Churún gushed, buoyed by the rains, running fast downstream, urging us along. As we paddled, the rainy season's nascent waterfalls splashed into the river.

Two days later, at the airstrip, we cheered when Oley flew in. I used my timer again and took a photo of the entire party, including some of our porters. We never would have succeeded without their wisdom and courage. We'd braved a jungle, but they'd conquered centuries of tribal superstitions and fears. They'd faced down the devil to help us. Afterward I thanked them and gave each one a gift, Laime translating as I told them that I'd never forget any of them. When I bent down to thank little Jacinto, he put his arms around my neck and hugged me.

LAIME STAYED BEHIND to travel back to Uruyén with the natives in the dugouts, while the rest of us flew out in batches to Ciudad Bolivar. When I reached my apartment in Caracas, Gladys and George, the neighbors who'd left the note, rushed in to hug me.

"Ruthie, you look terrible!" Gladys proclaimed. My body covered in cuts and bug bites, I did.

They'd piled my mail on my desk, including cables of congratulation from all over the

world. I paged through quickly but didn't see the one I'd hoped for. Nothing from the editors at *National Geographic.* But then I had no reason to expect one, not yet. They were undoubtedly holding off, waiting as I was to find out if Angel Falls was truly the tallest in the world.

Reporters knocked on my door, and instead of the interviewer, I became the one interviewed. Most assumed I would have accounts of jaguar attacks and snakebites, not grueling conditions, dangerous rapids, troublesome fleas, and a poisonous tarantula.

That afternoon, I joined Ernie and Gomez at the Ministry of Communications for a news conference. By then, Perry Lowrey had returned to his job at the oil company and Laime was still making his way out of the jungle. I barely noticed when Hightower and O'Brien showed up, but I did wonder when they slipped in behind our group as the photographers took our picture. I wasn't worried. So what if they were in the photos. We had a deal. Everyone had agreed that this was my story to tell. And when I did, O'Brien and Hightower wouldn't even be a footnote.

"We'll know soon," I answered, when the reporters asked the height of Angel Falls. They pushed for estimates, but I gave none. Not until I was sure.

Luckily it wasn't too long before I heard. On May twentieth, eight days after we'd arrived at Angel Falls, three days after we flew out of the jungle, Perry Lowery called me.

"Good news, I hope?"

"Very good news," he confirmed. "The total vertical drop of Angel Falls is 3,212 feet."

"The tallest waterfall in the world," I whispered.

My heart soared just saying the words.

# Chapter Thirty-Six

**Brazoria County, Texas**

**March 1993**

WHEN RUTH SLIPPED out of her bedroom early the next morning, Gabby had already taken a cup of coffee out to the deck to watch the river. The sky was a storybook blue, and the leaves on the oak trees were darkening from a spring to a summer green. "This is a beautiful place. I can see why you live here."

Ruth joined her, the weathered wood planks rough beneath her slippers. She fleetingly wondered if the old and worn house would outlast her. Scanning the view, the river and trees, she considered that even after she and the house were long forgotten, the rest would endure. That brought a sense of peace. "It can be lonely on the river, especially in the winters, but it's home," Ruth said. "I met my husband in Caracas, and we married there. Chuck was an engineer who worked for a South American oil company. He had family who lived not far from this house, so that's how we ended up on the San Bernard. To me it's a special place. Here, life makes sense."

Gabby agreed. "You, Nick, and this place have been a godsend for me."

Ruth rubbed the younger woman's shoulder, then they ambled back into the house.

The first news of the morning aired with no mention of Gabby, not until six thirty when a local news anchor teased, "When we return, an interesting development in the ongoing saga of Houston's runaway wife. Is she delusional or fleeing domestic violence?"

"Oh, Lord, this doesn't sound good," Gabby worried. "I wish they wouldn't use the word *delusional*."

"No reason to fret. Let's see what the big breakthrough is."

Minutes later, a camera focused once again on Patrick Bush in front of HPD headquarters. After clips from his interview with Gabby the day before, the anchor asked, "Have you heard from this mysterious person, the one Gabby Jordan pleaded with for help?"

"I have," Bush said. "Late last night."

Gabby covered her eyes with her hands, as if afraid to watch the screen. Ruth put her arm around her and whispered, "Just breathe."

"What did this person say?" the news anchor asked.

"She's offered to meet with me late this afternoon at an undisclosed location. We'll air the interview on the evening news."

"Yes!" Gabby screamed. "Rae Ann is doing an interview. An interview. Ruth, she's alive. And she's going to talk."

"Now, I need to send a message to Gabby Jordan," the reporter said. "Please call me as soon as possible to arrange a time late this afternoon for a follow-up interview. You don't need to come to the station. We'll do it on the phone."

"WE'RE TRYING TO be a little cagy, trying to confuse your husband," Bush explained when Gabby called him from a pay phone a dozen miles from Ruth's house. Nick had driven her, and he stood watch to make sure no one approached. "Rae Ann Jordan has agreed to an interview, but she stipulated that you have to do it with her, in person."

"I'm not doing a telephone interview?"

"No, we need you here at the studio. And it's not late afternoon; it's this morning."

Gabby wondered if it was a trap, if the reporter, even Rae Ann, could have been working with Jeff. "I don't know. To drive into Houston again? With Jeff looking for me, knowing I'll be talking with you. This is…risky."

Bush said he understood, but he didn't back down. "It's not perfect, I know. But we think it's the best way."

Gabby glanced over at Nick, their eyes met, and she shook her head, signaling that what she was hearing didn't set right. How could she know if she was being lied to? "I can't do this. I'm not going to—"

"Mrs. Jordan…Gabby, I don't know how to convince you, but all I'm trying to do is interview the two of you and do it in a way that keeps you both safe."

Gabby remained doubtful. She knew Jeff. She knew what he was capable of and how powerful his connections were. "How can I be sure Jeff won't be waiting for me when I show up?"

"We would never do that. This plan—feeding him false information about where and when—is designed to prevent that."

"Why don't we meet somewhere else, in case Jeff has the station under surveillance?"

"We considered that. But we're worried that he'll have someone follow me. We think the safest place is here, where we have security at the gate and inside the building."

When Gabby didn't respond, the reporter said, "Listen Gabby, isn't this what you wanted? Why you came to me in the first place? To find Rae Ann and have her back you up on camera?"

"Yes, but—"

"This is your choice. But it may be your only chance. Rae Ann has made it clear that she's terrified of Jeff Jordan, so much so that she's asked us to haze out her face when we air the interview. She doesn't want anyone to know what she looks like now. As afraid as she is, she may never agree to do this again."

Gabby hesitated, thinking it through. "Okay. I don't know that I have another option. What's the plan?"

"All you need to do is get someone to drive you here in a car no one will recognize. We'll take care of the rest."

Gabby glanced at Nick, smiled, and considered how she'd come to rely on him. "I can do that."

After the reporter laid out what else she needed to know, he said, "Gabby, Rae Ann is adamant that you have to be with her or her interview is off. So do your best to get here."

AN HOUR LATER, earlier than expected, Nick arrived at Ruth's house to drive Gabby to Houston. Seeing his stooped shoulders and sour expression, Gabby sensed something was very wrong.

"Nick, you look like you've just buried your best friend. You might as well tell us the bad news." Ruth crossed her arms over her chest and stared at him, waiting.

"It can't be that bad, right?" Gabby asked.

"It is pretty bad," Nick admitted.

As the two women listened, Nick recounted how Chief Haskell had waited at the store when he'd arrived that morning and followed him in the door. The cop was bubbling with excitement at news of a major development in the Gabby Jordan case. "That woman's picture is on TVs all over the country, and she was right near here on the highway the night of the storm."

Nick had done his best to appear surprised, raising his eyebrows and his voice. "You've gotta be kidding me, Chief. She was right here?"

"Yup. That day when it was raining like crazy. She spun out on the highway. A truck nearly smashed into her. The driver pulled over to make sure she was okay, but she hightailed it down the road. Description of the car matches, and the truck driver got part of the license plate, so we're sure it was her. It happened not far from your store, Nick, maybe a mile up the road."

At that, Nick couldn't think of anything to say except, "Gee, I wish she'd stopped at the store. If she was hurt like her husband says, I might have been able to help her."

For just a moment, he'd worried that he saw a hint of doubt in the other man's expression. But then the chief said, "Wish she had, too, so you could'a got her an ambulance or something. The truck driver called HPD this morning, after he heard about the missing woman on TV."

"Well, that's something," Nick said, and the chief had put his hands on his hips and nodded in agreement.

As Gabby and Ruth listened intently, Nick concluded, "I'm pretty sure the chief believed me when I said I didn't know anything about Gabby being in the area. He pulled out of the lot, and I gave him quite a bit of time before I called my guy in to take over at the store and came here."

"So, they know Gabby was around here?" Ruth queried. "They're sure?"

"Yup."

When Gabby thought back to that day on the road, it seemed distant, like it had been ages ago. So much had happened since. "I did almost get hit by a big semi. It was terrifying. But I could have been going anywhere. They don't know that I'm *still* here."

"True. But Gabby, they're taking this dead serious," Nick said. "The chief warned me to drive carefully for the next few days. They've brought in troopers to pull over random cars to search for you."

"Can they do that? Stop folks without a reason?" Ruth sounded outraged at the prospect.

Nick shrugged. "Don't know, but they are doing it."

With news that grew progressively worse, Gabby wondered if it would ever be possible to come out of hiding. Perhaps not. Maybe, like Rae Ann, she'd have to live the rest of her life in the shadows, wondering every day if Jeff would find her. To never have to worry about him again was worth any personal danger, but she couldn't risk Nick's and Ruth's safety. "Well, that's it then. You can't drive me into Houston. It's too dangerous."

"But then Rae Ann won't give the interview," Ruth protested.

Gabby glanced over at her. "There's nothing to do about it. We can't risk getting caught."

"You're right. I know," Ruth admitted. "I just hate for it to end this way. I hate for Jeff to win at all. And mostly, I want to keep you safe. How do we do that without Rae Ann's help?"

They sat quietly for a few moments, shrouded in their collective disappointment.

"Well, maybe, there's a way," Nick ventured, his voice tentative, and the two women looked at him expectantly. "My guess is that the cops will stay around the highway. They won't be on the local roads."

"Don't we need to take the highway into the city?" Gabby asked.

"Not necessarily." He gave her an uncertain glance. "It's not easy, but we can stay on the back roads, the ones the ranchers use."

Ruth squinted at Nick, unconvinced. "It'll take a lot longer. A lot of those roads are in rough shape. And what if you're wrong? What if they pull you over and find Gabby?"

Nick shook his head. "That's the best I can do."

The women exchanged anxious glances.

"Look, you ladies are doing the right thing. Gabby needs to get her story out. She needs that other woman to back her up. And I don't see another way to do it."

"Nick, what if we're caught?" Gabby asked. "Jeff would go after you with every ounce of influence he has."

"I'm willing to take the risk." He reached for her hand, then leaned forward and whispered, "If we're going to end this, we all need to stop being afraid."

The room fell silent while Gabby considered that Nick's words rang true and that she'd come too far to let fear hobble her. "If it'll take that long, we'd better get going."

"THAT'S GOTTA BE uncomfortable. It's probably safe for you to sit up now. At least until we get to Houston." They'd been driving for nearly an hour on narrow roads that twisted and turned. At times, Nick crept along, trying to avoid the deep ruts that hot summers had melted into the faded asphalt.

Lying on the floor behind the front seats, Gabby peeled the black blanket down to uncover her face. Her back ached from the SUV's bounce and her awkward position. While sitting up appealed to her, she was worried. When they'd crossed the highway up the hill from

Ruth's, Nick had seen police lights flashing in both directions. But so far, his prediction had held true, and they hadn't encountered any searchers on the back roads.

"How much longer?"

To her disappointment, Nick estimated, "Maybe forty minutes."

*No unnecessary chances*, she decided. "I'm okay. I'll stay here. Let's just keep going."

Time passed. In Houston, Nick picked up speed, changed lanes, and took the freeway exit off Interstate 59 toward the TV station. As he veered onto the ramp, he glanced in the rearview mirror.

"We're being followed," he whispered, covering his mouth with his hand.

Gabby's breath caught in her throat. "Who?"

"A squad car. HPD."

"Drive around the block. See if it follows us."

"No. That'll look suspicious. We need to act like we have nothing to hide. Stay down. We're going in."

Concealed beneath the blanket, Gabby felt the SUV take a sharp right, then abruptly stop at the entrance to the television station's fenced employee parking lot. Nick lowered the window and Gabby heard a man's gruff voice, she assumed the attendant's, ask: "I'll need to see identification."

"I was told that wouldn't be necessary. I'm here to see Patrick Bush. He gave us a code word. Submarine."

Moments later, the gate opened. Nick started to edge forward, but a short blast from a police siren stopped him. A car door directly behind them opened and then slammed. "Stay where you are. I need to see your license."

Gabby heard the strain in Nick's voice when he called out, "Is there something wrong, officer?"

"What are you doing here?" the lot attendant shouted. "The station manager told you to stop harassing our customers. What's up with you cops today?"

From under the blanket, Gabby listened to the two men argue. The cop, his voice firm, ordered the parking lot attendant not to get involved. But the attendant was having none of it. "This is the sixth car you've stopped coming into our lot this morning. You want me to call the station's manager again? You want to be on the noon news explaining why you're searching our customers and suppliers?"

"I said, 'I want his license!'" the police officer shouted back. "That's an order. Not up for debate."

Gabby's pulse accelerated but her hands felt like blocks of ice. Then another voice, a woman shouted, coming closer. "Officer, I want to see your badge. We have a call in to headquarters to ask what's going on. Why are you harassing the station?"

"I'm following orders," the officer said, angry.

"This vehicle is on our driveway, on private property. Officer, I suggest you stay by your car. We'll have the chief on the phone in a minute," the woman ordered.

Gabby heard the parking attendant again. "You're blocking traffic. I'm going to have this guy drive farther onto the lot and wait. You can pull your car onto the driveway off the road, but you do *not* have permission to enter the lot. Is that understood?"

The officer must have agreed, because Nick edged the Blazer a short distance forward and put it in park. He again cupped his hand over his mouth and whispered, "The reporter has called out a cameraman. They're filming the cop. That reporter is really going after that guy." Seconds later, Gabby heard relief in Nick's voice.

"We're good. Going in."

Nick drove forward. A garage-type door cranked up and then closed behind them.

"We're safe."

Gabby pushed off the blanket and sat up, blinking as her eyes adjusted to the bright lights. On the loading dock, Patrick Bush stood beside a woman in her midforties with a dark-blond ponytail and bangs.

"Rae Ann?" Gabby asked as she scrambled out of the SUV, her dyed hair again covered by a scarf. She took off her sunglasses, revealing the fading bruise around her right eye.

"One and the same," the woman said. "It feels good to hear you say that. I've been in hiding so long that it's been years since anyone has called me by my real name."

Rae Ann wrapped her arms around Gabby and hugged her. "I'm sorry I didn't stop him. I tried. If I could have, he wouldn't have done what he did to Michelle and then to you. But no one would help."

Gabby considered how similar they were in appearance and perhaps in other ways. Michelle, too. Jeff had a type, and it had been her bad luck to fit it.

"How did they get you in?" Gabby asked.

"In the back of a garbage truck," Rae Ann answered with a short laugh.

A back elevator took them to the second floor. In a cavernous studio, a cameraman waited. As the interview unfolded over the course of the next hour, Gabby revealed more details about her own story, including how she'd called 911 and reported the assaults, only to have police refuse to press charges. "It doesn't surprise me that my husband was able to erase all the records. He has a powerful position.

But there are officers out there who know that what I'm saying is true."

"Your husband says—" the reporter started.

"I believe you!" Rae Ann blurted out, and Gabby saw tears in her eyes. "I believe you because that's exactly what happened to me."

From that point on, the interview focused on Rae Ann.

"Just like Gabby, I called 911, but no one ever followed up. When I called to check on the status of my complaints, I was told that they had no record of an officer ever being dispatched to my house. I knew Jeff wouldn't let me go. He'd threatened me, time and again. If I told anyone. If I tried to leave. He threatened to kill me. The year before I went into hiding, he broke my collarbone. One night, he knocked me out. When I came to, he was throwing clothes into a suitcase. He thought I was dying, and instead of calling for help, he was getting ready to run. The next day, while he was at work, I took what I could and left. I've been in hiding ever since."

"Where?" Patrick Bush asked.

"I can't tell you that. If he's not stopped, I'll have to disappear again."

"What's it been like, having to hide?"

"I haven't seen my parents in years. I wasn't able to watch my nieces and nephews grow up. I've missed Christmases, New Years, Mother's and Father's Days, just the everyday joy of being with people I love. I lost my job. I used to be a nurse. Now I clean houses for a living. But I have no choice. I am terrified of Jeff Jordan."

"Why aren't we showing your face on camera?"

"Because I don't want anyone to recognize me. I don't want Jeff to know what I look like today."

"You divorced Jeff Jordan?"

"He divorced me when he wanted to marry someone else. By then, I'd been in hiding for more than a year."

AFTER THE INTERVIEW ended, Rae Ann again embraced Gabby. "At least we now have each other. Jeff can say what he wants, but we know the truth. Stay safe."

Grateful for Rae Ann's willingness to put her own life in danger to help her, Gabby whispered, "You too."

"We need to get both of you out of here," Bush said. "Follow me."

Minutes later, Gabby crouched in the back of a red van driven by a reporter who smacked a thick wad of chewing gum. They circled around to a side exit and headed onto the feeder road.

"There they are," she said. "Reinforcements have arrived. Watch and see what happens."

Peeking through the heavily shaded rear window, Gabby saw Nick's SUV pull out of the main entrance. Two police cars, lights flashing, were waiting for him. Nick pulled over, and four uniformed officers rushed toward him.

"Will my friend be okay?"

"Without you in his car, he'll be fine."

After they rendezvoused a few miles from the station, Gabby was again under the blanket on Nick's back floor. "Those officers didn't give you a hard time?"

"They searched the Blazer. I asked them what they were looking for. One got kind of nasty, said it wasn't any of my business. I'm pretty sure they were breaking a few laws pulling me over for no reason, searching my vehicle without permission, but I didn't point that out. I was just glad when they told me to take off."

The plan called for Nick to drive Gabby directly to Ruth's house, but halfway there, she worried. "What if we're being followed?"

"I don't see anyone."

"Well, but what if we are? We'll be leading them to Ruth."

Instead, Nick drove to an open field in the nature refuge where they could easily see if anyone approached, and they sat on folding chairs he kept stashed in the back of the Blazer. An hour or so passed while they talked about what Rae Ann had said about Jeff, how at first he'd seemed like such a great guy until they married. Bruises. Broken bones. Jeff stood beside her as she lied to doctors and nurses, blaming a fall on a loose board or a bunched-up carpet.

"Did you notice how her voice quivered when she talked about him?" Nick asked. "Even all these years later?"

"This isn't the type of fear you ever get over."

For a long time, Gabby and Nick remained silent, watching birds swooping in and feeding. No cars drove up. No one interrupted their solitude. "I think we can go," he finally suggested. "I'll drop you at Ruth's house before I go to the store."

As he lifted the chairs back into the Blazer, she said, "You've taken a lot of time off since I arrived in your parking lot. I'm not sure how I can ever repay you."

"No need to. I did it because I wanted to."

"Yes, but…" Gabby felt overcome with emotion, and her voice faltered. "It was kind of you."

As Nick opened the door for her, he hesitated. "Maybe I shouldn't be saying this, Gabby, but I feel a connection with you. I don't know if you feel it. I don't want to presume."

"Nick, I…"

"I wonder if maybe, down the road, when your life is more settled, if we might…"

"It's just that—"

"I'm sorry, Gabby." Nick turned away from her and appeared upset, not with her, but with himself. "I know that you're going through a lot. I should have known better than to—"

"Shush!" she ordered.

Edging closer to him, she rested her palm on his cheek, rough with stubble. "Nick, I feel something too. But my life is in so much turmoil, I'm not sure what it is, or what it means, if anything. All I can say is that I am grateful."

At that, Nick sighed. "You're right. My timing is way off here."

"Please, don't—"

"But there's no reason to be grateful. What I've done for you, I've done because I wanted to. I don't want you to feel you owe me anything or to confuse gratitude with…other feelings."

Gabby's chin rose as she half smiled at him. "Thank you."

The uneasiness had passed. "You're welcome."

She rubbed her thumb over his cheek, they locked eyes, and Gabby considered how different he was from anyone she'd ever had in her life. "You need a shave, you know."

He puffed a short laugh. "I've been a bit busy. Maybe somewhat distracted."

Leaning forward, she gave him a gentle peck on the cheek. Resting against his chest, she felt the heat of his breath as he kissed her forehead. "Once Jeff is out of my life, we'll figure this out, see if there's anything real here."

"I look forward to it," he whispered.

A short drive later, Nick dropped Gabby at Ruth's and headed to the store. Inside the house, Gabby replayed the afternoon's events, laying it all out, until she had nothing left to tell. "Do you think this will work, Ruth?"

"I don't know, Gabby. I hope so. I think it might. But the one thing I'm certain of is that you've done your best. Now we'll just have to wait and see what happens."

# Chapter Thirty-Seven

**Caracas, Venezuela**

**June 1949**

EXPEDITION MEASURES WORLD'S TALLEST WATERFALL

Our success shouted from headlines around the world, including the *New York Times* and London's *Daily Mail*. We became celebrities, the woman photographer, the seasoned guide, the filmmaker, the radioman, and the engineer who'd conquered the jungle and made history. It felt as if I'd landed on some unknown planet where everything I'd dreamed had come true.

Even money worries didn't faze me. Once the waterfall's measurements made a new round of headlines, the call from the *Geographic* followed. I could hear the respect and excitement in Hildebrand's voice. "Well, you really did it, didn't you?"

"I did. And now you want the photographs and story?"

"You may just have a sale, Ruth Robertson. Get yourself up here to DC, and let's take a look."

"Will do!"

I made my plane reservations, and I pulled together a portfolio of my Angel Falls photos, the best work I'd ever done. I was a shoo-in; I knew it. I could envision the layout, my name in the byline.

In Caracas, Angel Falls fever had taken hold. Wherever I went, folks quizzed me about the expedition, fascinated that their country had such a hidden gem. I didn't display the new images, guarding them until they ran in the *Geographic*. But I printed copies of my aerial shot of Angel Falls and put them up for sale at a bookstore in downtown Caracas. They sold out in one day, and the store owner begged for more. I printed a bunch before heading to the States, and when I walked into the bookstore to drop them off, people stood in line waiting to buy them.

"When can we get another batch?" the owner asked.

I felt on top of the world.

On the way back to my apartment, I stopped at a newsstand to pick up a few papers. As I pulled change from my pocket to pay, I noticed a box on the front page of the *Miami Herald* announcing a three-part series, starting that coming Sunday, June fifth—an account of the expedition to Angel Falls based on Ernie Knee's diary.

"This isn't what we agreed," I whispered to myself. "We had a deal!"

If that wasn't bad enough, the articles were being syndicated to newspapers around the world. I couldn't believe it. My *Geographic* gig? Hildebrand had insisted that the magazine had to have an exclusive. This could kill it.

As soon as I got home, I called the *Herald* and got the editor on the phone. "Yes, we're running the series. We've already paid Mr. Knee's representative."

"Who is that?"

"Just a minute, I have it here." A brief pause, and he was back on the phone. "A Mr. Hightower."

"John Hightower?"

"Yes. It was our understanding that he was part of the expedition. His name was on the press releases, and he was in the group photo."

Livid, I slammed the door on my way out. I was loaded for bear, as my oil company friends liked to say.

When I reached Hightower's office, I stormed past his secretary.

"Ruth, what a nice surprise." He was sitting at his desk, and he didn't look at all surprised. He'd been expecting me, I was sure of it. His secretary had followed me in, but he waved her off. "Glad to see you. I've been wanting to call you, maybe get together for a drink. I might have some work for you, not now but down the road."

"This is wrong!" I shouted. "All of you, including Ernie, agreed not to sell anything about the expedition until after my *Geographic* piece ran. You both gave your word."

He folded his arms across his chest and grinned at me, as pompous as I'd ever seen him. "Oh, calm down, Ruth. You sound like a hysterical woman."

"You'd better get those articles pulled, you sorry piece of—"

Hightower cut me off with a hoarse laugh. "You're a newspaper woman, Ruth. You know I can't stop the presses. The contracts are signed. They're running."

I stared at him, seething. "John, you're a coward. You deserted us in the jungle and took the snakebite kit and the Luger with you. For all you cared, we could have all died in that jungle."

"It was my gun, I—" His grin was fading.

"When things got tough, you ran off like a spoiled child."

"Well, you didn't have Laime. You didn't have a surveyor. We—"

"We didn't have a surveyor because you didn't bring one." I felt disgusted just looking at him. "The bottom line is that you and your pal O'Brien chickened out."

"I-I, we—"

I leaned down and fixed my eyes onto his. "I want you to remember, John, from this day forward, every time you look in the mirror, the man staring back at you is a coward."

He babbled something. I turned and left.

Back at my apartment, I called friends in the newspaper business, and we sent cables to the *Miami Herald*. Some called the editor personally, trying to get the series killed. But it ran that Sunday with bold illustrations and a sensational headline: "Journey into a 'Green Hell' for Humans: Daring group penetrates jungle, shunned by Indians, to measure world's highest waterfall."

When I read the piece, I was furious all over again. Knee had turned the expedition into his story, treating the rest of us like bit players. Worse: he'd made our brave native guides sound like drunken heathens.

"MR. HILDEBRAND ISN'T in today," the receptionist said. "You'll be meeting with Mr. Ross."

The *Geographic* editor hadn't been encouraging on the phone, but I'd given him my schedule and flown to DC anyway. Now this? It wasn't a good sign.

Moments later I was in a conference room with Kip Ross from the magazine's photo department, who said pretty much what I expected. "Ruth, that syndicated series scooped you on your own story."

I talked fast, explaining that a member of my own expedition had betrayed me. Ross listened sympathetically but appeared doubtful. I knew what he was thinking: that this wasn't his problem. "Ruth, we were really looking for an exclusive. Now you don't have that. And—"

"But, Kip, they don't have *my* story. And they don't have *my* photos. What I'm offering you is still an exclusive."

"Well, that's true about the photos. They didn't run any with the series," he said, frowning. "Let's look at what you have."

I flipped open my portfolio and had to remind myself to keep breathing. As Ross paged through, I gripped the table edge so hard my hands hurt. They were all there—Laime, the entire party, all the Indians, including Juanita, Reya, and little Jacinto. As he considered the images, Ross appeared drawn to them.

"Who's this?" he asked, looking down at a photo of Reya weaving palm fronds into a pattern. Ross listened as I recounted what had happened that morning. While we packed our supplies at the end of the expedition, Reya sat off by himself working on his creation. Somehow, he turned the palm leaves into a beautiful bowl, which he gave me as a gift moments before I boarded the plane to leave. "We'd been through so much together, and we both knew that this was probably the last time we'd see each other. We hugged, and said our goodbyes."

For a moment Ross and I were both quiet. "The photos are wonderful," he finally said, sounding touched by my story. "First rate."

"Thank you."

At that, Ross picked up a phone and said, "Please, ask Mr. Grosvenor to join us."

After days of anguish, I relaxed.

Minutes later, Gilbert Grosvenor, the president of the National Geographic Society, popped into the conference room. A stodgy looking man with thinning gray hair, glasses, and a thick mustache, he looked at me as if I've just flown in from Saturn.

"Chief, I think we should go with this," Ross said. "The photos are good. Our readers will love them."

Again, I held my breath, this time while Grosvenor paged through my portfolio. He stopped at my portrait of Jimmie Angel, then at one of the falls, the native children fishing, Laime and Lowrey measuring the falls, all of us lined up in front of them. What he said next, I didn't expect, although perhaps I should have.

"Well, it's certainly breaking precedent."

"What is?" I asked.

"Well, a girl going in and measuring the waterfall. It's all anyone is talking about."

It was no time to protest or to get angry. "Well, I did it. No question about that."

"You sure did."

As we talked, he explained that this was an odd situation for the magazine. For the most part, the society funded the expeditions it covered in the magazine, and that presented a dilemma; he wasn't sure what to pay me.

"You know, Mr. Grosvenor, I financed the entire Angel Falls expedition myself. I put all my savings into it."

"How much did you spend?"

I told him.

For a moment, he hesitated, apparently mulling the figure over. But then, he wrote an amount down on a piece of paper. "Take this to accounting," he told Ross. "Tell them we're buying Miss Robertson's photos, and that she'll be writing an article for us. Tell them that we're paying this amount."

When I left the Geographic's office later that afternoon, I had a signed contract and the promise of a check that would cover all my expenses.

# Chapter Thirty-Eight

**Brazoria County, Texas**

**March 1993**

IN THE HOUSE on the river, Ruth rustled through stacks of papers and files. First, she showed Gabby a frayed black scrapbook. "This has my Angel Falls mementos in it."

Opening it, Ruth turned to a map she'd drawn for Laime at one of their first meetings, to show the position of Angel Falls. Next, she stopped at the note O'Brien and Oley dropped in the river from the plane. Gabby skimmed cables of congratulation and newspaper articles from around the world. As she read, her smile crept wider.

Finally, Ruth handed Gabby a November 1949 copy of *National Geographic*. The banner at the bottom advertised that a single-issue cost fifty cents, but readers could buy a year's subscription for five dollars. The fourth cover headline from the top read: "Jungle Journey to the World's Highest Waterfall."

On the article's first page, Gabby admired the byline: "By Ruth Robertson, with illustrations and photographs by the author." The piece began with a description of Angel Falls "spurting from a cliff more than half a mile high in the jungle…"

Captivated, Gabby paged through. She found photographs of nearly everyone Ruth had talked about, the natives fishing and the members of the tribe who went on the expedition, Manuel, Jacinto,

Juanita, Reya, and the others.

Aleksandrs Laime wasn't as tall as Gabby had envisioned, and in one photo Perry Lowrey relaxed inside his banana-shaped jungle hammock. Ernie Knee lined up a shot with his movie camera, and Enrique Gomez dialed in his radio. Native mothers cuddled their children and washed clothes in the river. Angel Falls in all its majesty roared from the top of Auyán-tepuí.

"And here's Jimmie Angel again." Gabby pointed at the same photo she'd admired days earlier, the one of a round-faced fellow with dark penetrating eyes.

"The man himself," Ruth exclaimed, and then she chuckled. "Full of himself? Sure. But still a good guy."

"Do you hear from him anymore?"

At that, Ruth's expression saddened. "Jimmie died a long time ago, back in the midfifties. I was living in Mexico at the time. Chuck and I hotfooted it out of Venezuela after the commies took over and were fighting to control the press. They didn't like my reporting, so they bombed my house."

"Bombed your house?"

With what struck Gabby as a surprising lack of emotion, Ruth said, "Not the whole thing. They set off a small bomb near the front courtyard. I don't think they wanted me dead, just gone. I took the hint. Packed up and left. Chuck and I headed to Mexico, and I worked there for quite a while. Then we came here."

"That's quite a story."

"Sometimes I look back and think about things I wish I'd done differently. Mistakes I made." A quick shake of the head, and Ruth shrugged. "But in the end, I think it's all unraveled as it was meant to. It was my life to spend. I did the best I knew how to with it."

Pointing at the photo of the man in the fedora, Gabby asked, "How did Jimmie Angel die?"

"Rough landing in Panama. Hit his head. Then, right after, he had some heart trouble. Poor Jimmie went downhill. Not sure what finally did him in. He was just fifty-seven. His wife and some friends flew over Auyán-tepuí and scattered his ashes over Angel Falls."

"What about the others?" When Ruth looked at her questioning, Gabby explained, "What happened to the other men on the expedition."

"Oh, I don't know about Perry Lowrey or Enrique Gomez. We lost touch. I'm pretty sure that Laime's still in the jungle. He and Charlie Baughan, that pilot friend of mine, started a business flying tourists over the falls. Although they're both old now, if Baughan is still alive. Laime's got to be closing in on eighty."

"Hightower? O'Brien? Ernie Knee?"

"Well, after what happened, I cut off communication with the three of them. I don't know about Hightower and O'Brien, but I heard that Ernie died back in the 1980s. After Venezuela, he became a fairly well-known photographer, lived in New Mexico and hung out with artists like Georgia O'Keeffe."

The room grew silent, each woman lost to her own thoughts.

"Ruth, I—" Gabby wanted to tell Ruth how remarkable her story was, but she was interrupted by the phone ringing.

"That was Nick," Ruth said, when she hung up. "He'll pick us up in twenty minutes. They want to talk to you at the district attorney's office."

# Chapter Thirty-Nine



**Downtown Houston, TX**

**March 1993**

"I CAN'T UNDERSTAND what's taking so long."

"The DA is a busy man, Ruth. Let's try to relax," Gabby urged. She was nervous, too, but trying not to show it. After Nick had dropped them off, he'd driven to a nearby coffee shop where they'd agreed to meet later.

Restless, Ruth picked wisps of thread off her navy blue sweater, and Gabby worried that it had all been too hard on the older woman. She looked exhausted. Gabby had suggested that Ruth wait at home, but she'd insisted she wanted to come along.

Time crawled while men and women wearing Houston Police Department uniforms trekked through the waiting room. Gabby recognized a sergeant, a friend of Jeff's she'd met at a department Christmas party. When she told Ruth, the older woman narrowed her eyes and glared at him, as if daring the man to talk to them. He scowled back but then tramped off in a huff.

"Let's just read the newspaper," Gabby whispered, handing Ruth a copy of that morning's *Houston Chronicle* off a table. Then she noticed the front page. A headline over Gabby's picture read: "HPD Captain's wife claims abuse."

"Oh Lord," Ruth sighed.

"Mrs. Jordan?" The woman standing above them smiled down at her, and Gabby nodded. "The district attorney will see you now."

"Well, it's about time," Ruth mumbled.

Their escort buzzed them through the secure door and led them to an office with a wall of windows that offered a view of downtown Houston's gleaming skyscrapers. District Attorney Porter Edwards, a tall man with thick-rimmed glasses and a fringe of dark hair, sat behind the desk.

"Come in, Mrs. Jordan," he said, holding out his hand. "And who is this with you?"

"A friend," Gabby said. "Just an old friend who came to support me."

Ruth chuckled. "Well, old is certainly appropriate."

Edwards' eyebrows arched up. "I assume you have a name?"

"This is someone who's been helping me," Gabby explained. "I need to keep her name private."

"I have to say this is rather a first." The man let loose a short laugh, perhaps a bit too nonchalantly, and Gabby tried to smile, but it came off as more of a grimace. "May I call you Gabby?" he asked, and she nodded. "Please, Gabby, both of you, sit down."

Once they did, he folded his hands on the desk. "This is going to be recorded. Are you okay with that?"

"Of course," Gabby said. "I actually prefer that."

"I forget. You're a lawyer, aren't you? Civil?" Gabby nodded again. He positioned the recorder between them on his desk, pressed a button, and a red light lit up. "So, Mrs. Jordan, let's talk about how you got those bruises."

For more than an hour, he peppered Gabby with questions, details about her marriage, Jeff, and the violence. At first, Gabby held up well, shooting back answers. As it wore on, however, her emotions bristled. To keep them at bay, she tried an old law-school trick, advice she'd given clients who faced emotional testimony. She tried to pretend she was reporting on something that had happened to someone else. She wasn't the victim but a witness. That gave her some distance and helped keep the tears from falling.

"So, the violence started when again?" Edwards had his pen poised, waiting to write down her answer. Gabby could see he was building a timeline on the yellow legal pad in front of him.

"Not long after we married." She wondered if those were the exact words she'd used earlier when he'd asked that same question. She knew what the prosecutor was looking for, to see if her answers remained consistent. The third time he asked, her voice cracked, and despite her best efforts, anger welled in her chest. Ruth eased over just a bit and put her hand over Gabby's on the arm of chair.

"Mr. Edwards," she interrupted. "May I ask a question?"

"Certainly."

"Have you given the same grilling to Jeff Jordan?" When Edwards didn't answer as quickly as she thought he should, Ruth leaned toward him and whispered. "Now, you're not just questioning the victim, right? You're going after the bad guy too?"

"Well, he's—"

"You know, funny, I thought that was your job." Ruth stared at him and frowned. "Going after the bad guys, I mean."

Gabby smiled at Ruth. "It's okay. The district attorney can ask me anything he needs to. I don't mind."

"I'm not saying he shouldn't talk to you, but this seems one-sided to me."

"Ma'am, I"—the DA narrowed his eyes—"This would be easier if I had a name to call you. Would you like to give me one?"

"You can call me Georgia," Ruth said. "I always wanted to be a Georgia. This may be my only chance."

Gabby released a nervous laugh, and the DA grinned at Ruth, as if impressed by her pluck. "Well, Georgia, if Gabby brought you along for protection, it looks like she made a good choice."

"Mr. Edwards, you have no idea," Gabby said. Ruth's interruption had eased the tension, and Gabby felt more in control. "But, Georgia, we do need to let the district attorney ask his questions," then, turning to him, "as long as he assures us that this is a serious investigation?"

"Maybe this will help. We will be interviewing Captain Jordan." Gabby flinched when the DA referred to Jeff by his rank. There was a tinge of respect in the prosecutor's voice that troubled her. "But right now, he's conferring with an attorney from the police union. We've agreed that they'll report to my office once they're done to meet with me."

"And Rae Ann? You'll be talking to her?" Gabby pushed. "I'm not Jeff's only victim, you know."

"Yes. Later today, but at an undisclosed location. We're doing our best to work with her. She refused to come to our office."

Gabby looked over at Ruth who appeared pleased. "Okay, fire away. Gabby, tell the man everything."

Forty minutes later, Edwards walked the women back to the lobby. As they approached the door, he stopped. "I appreciate your cooperation, Gabby. Please believe that I am seriously looking into your allegations."

"If you do, you'll understand who Jeff Jordan really is." After a pause, she said, "Mr. Edwards, this has to stop before Jeff makes good on his threats and kills me or someone else."

"I'll do my best to get to the bottom of this. We'll be in touch." And with that, he pushed a button, the door buzzed, and he pulled it open.

Ruth walked through first, Gabby following, but then she stopped. Jeff stood there in his full uniform, tall, imposing, a man in a business suit on one side and the HPD sergeant Gabby had noticed earlier on the other. When Jeff saw her, he rushed toward her.

"Gabby, honey, you're here. Are you all right? I've been so worried."

Leaving no room for misunderstanding, Gabby held out both hands to keep him away. "Jeff, this is over. You'll never hurt me again."

His face flushed scarlet. "Gabby, why are you saying these things? I've never touched you with anything but love. Show me anyone who saw any signs of abuse. Give me a single name. It didn't happen. You're just confused, hurt from the fall."

"What about Rae Ann?" Ruth challenged.

"Who are you?"

"None of your business who she is. And yes, what about Rae Ann?" Gabby prodded. "Did she suffer a concussion, too?"

Gabby heard the familiar ring of condescension in his voice when he said, "Rae Ann has always been unstable. When we were married, I worried about her constantly. I begged her to get help." He paused and turned to the men with him, shaking his head. "Sad, but some people are just troubled."

"Why you—" Ruth started toward him, the look in her eyes telegraphing what she'd like to do to him, but Gabby grabbed her arm.

Holding Ruth tight, Gabby wondered what Edwards was thinking about the sad charade unfolding in front of him. From the blank expression on his face, she had no clue whom he believed. His face expressionless, Jeff kept his eyes on her as Gabby urged Ruth toward the door. "Come on, Georgia. We're leaving."

As they walked away, Gabby wondered if any of it would help, or if she had only made things worse by agreeing to talk to the DA. She had no idea where he stood or if he'd do anything other than bury her charges the way the police had. That seemed even more likely when she heard Jeff say, "You've known me for a long time, Porter. A really long time. You can't seriously think that—"

"Mr. Jordan," the DA interrupted, his voice cold. "This isn't a social visit. It's good that you brought your attorney. You know the way to my office."

Gabby turned back in time to see Jeff's eyes flash with anger, perhaps because instead of "captain," the DA had referred to him as "Mr. Jordan." It was then that she made her decision.

"Wait!" she called out, and the men all looked back to her.

Before she gave the DA what she had tucked in her purse, Gabby considered what she would have asked Jeff if she'd had him in a courtroom, seated on the witness stand. Ruth behind her, Gabby walked closer and peered up at him. "So, what you're saying, Jeff, is that you've never hurt me. Never hit me. Never punched me in the eye or twisted my arm behind my back. Is that right?"

"Never."

"And according to you, every bruise on my body is the result of a fall?"

To everyone else, it probably appeared innocuous, but Jeff's smile showed just the edges of his teeth, and Gabby saw his jaw muscles work as his eyes took on the dark, hard look she'd grown to fear. "Absolutely, Gabby. Unequivocally."

Gabby's reflexes kicked in, and her fears resurfaced. Her instincts warned her to turn and run, to never look back. But she stood her ground and opened her purse. Ruth suddenly understood and let out a soft sigh. "Oh, Gabby. Now is definitely the time."

From her purse, Gabby claimed a black plastic canister. It held the roll of film Ruth had taken of Gabby's eye and arm not long after she'd arrived at the river, including the photos of her arm laid out next to the yardstick.

Gabby placed it in the DA's open palm. "Mr. Edwards, develop this film and look at the bruise on my arm. Compare it to my husband's hand. Then you decide how I got it."

AFTER LEAVING THE courthouse, Gabby and Ruth walked a few blocks, watching to see if they were being followed. They saw one squad car, but it hung back, shadowing them. As they'd planned, Nick waited inside a coffee shop. The two women entered, didn't acknowledge him, and walked straight to the back, where they slipped into the alley through a kitchen door. Ten minutes later, Nick left his empty cup on the table and sauntered out the front door. They reunited blocks away, in a parking lot.

"Maybe you shouldn't have given the DA the film," Nick worried aloud on the drive back to the river. "Maybe you should have had it developed first, given him copies, and kept the negatives."

"There wasn't time. I wanted the district attorney to have it before he made up his mind," Gabby said, lying once more under the blanket on the back-seat floor. "If the DA compares that photo with Jeff's hand, he'll know that Jeff's not telling the truth. And if they catch him lying about one bruise, why would they believe him about anything else?"

"But what if they don't believe you?" Nick worried. "Then what happens?"

AT RUTH'S HOUSE, the television murmured in the background throughout the rest of the day as they hoped for breaking news on the case. But the soap operas and game shows ran without disruption. By five, Gabby feared that Nick was right, and that she shouldn't have trusted the district attorney.

"You can't decide that yet. It's too soon," Ruth argued.

"Maybe, but they should have that film developed by now. They've talked to Jeff, to Rae Ann. It's been hours. Something should be happening."

The evening news aired without any mention of the case, and the ten o'clock news ended without an update. When they turned off the television, Gabby looked over at Ruth in her favorite armchair with her feet up on the ottoman. "You're an incredible woman, and I'm so grateful. You've helped me in more ways than I can explain. I will always remember your generosity and strength. I love you for it."

Ruth eased forward and her eyes narrowed. "Oh no, Gabby. I don't like the sound of that."

"I don't have any other choice, Ruth." Gabby shook her head ever so slightly. "In the morning, I'm leaving. My staying here isn't safe for you or for me. Now that you've been seen with me, it's only a matter of time before Jeff figures out who you are and finds us."

"Oh, Gabby, I'm so sorry. I guess I shouldn't have gone with you. I thought—"

"Ruth, without you, I never would have had the courage to stand up to Jeff. Don't ever be sorry."

"I wish—"

"I do, too, but you know what, Ruth?"

The older woman appeared unsure.

"We gave Jeff one heck of a run for his money, went at him with both barrels blazing, just like you said we should, didn't we?"

Ruth grinned. "That we did."

Gabby walked over and kissed her on the cheek. "I'll pack in the morning. Tonight, I think we both need a good long sleep."

LATER, THE HOUSE was dark, but Gabby lay wide awake in bed. She couldn't keep her mind from spinning. Every time she closed her eyes, she saw Jeff glaring at her, and she remembered how he'd called the DA by his first name, Porter.

She finally drifted off and dozed until tires crackled on the gravel driveway. Too afraid to peek out the window, she rushed into the kitchen, just as Ruth emerged from her bedroom. "Did you hear someone?"

Following behind, Ginger let out a sharp bark, then a long, low growl.

Stiff from lying in bed, Ruth limped toward the window, but Gabby called her back. "Don't! It's Jeff. It has to be. He'll see you." Then she whispered, "Didn't you tell me you have a gun?"

Outside, footsteps approached while inside the house the dog charged the door, snarling and baring her teeth.

Ruth disappeared inside her bedroom, and Gabby heard her rustling through drawers. Moments later, she returned with a small black pistol. Regret washed through Gabby, when she saw Ruth's hands tremble. *I've done this to her*, Gabby thought. *How could I have put her through all this?*

"Take it," Ruth said. "It's loaded."

The twenty-two heavy in her hands, Gabby ignored her churning stomach. "Go in the bathroom and wait."

The aged wood groaned as shoes fell hard on the steps. Ginger backed up a few feet but kept yapping.

"I'm not going anywhere," Ruth whispered. "But we need to take cover."

They hurried to crawl behind the couch, and Gabby craned her neck to see.

The door window framed a shadowy figure. With the porch light shining from behind, she couldn't see a face through the curtain, but she was sure it was a man. It had to be Jeff. Who else would show up at Ruth's in the middle of the night? Even though the house was dark, Gabby wondered if he could see them. The man rustled at the door, Ginger barked louder, and Gabby's heart drummed in her chest. She knew all Jeff had to do was hit the old door with his shoulder and it would fall open.

The man at the door didn't move. He didn't ring the bell or knock.

Gabby raised the gun and took aim. "Jeff, I have a gun pointed at you. Leave now, this minute, or I'll pull the trigger."

Gabby waited. Beside her, Ruth clutched the back of the couch, peeking over the top.

Silence, then someone cried out, "Gabby. It's me. Don't shoot."

A pause while she took a deep breath. "What the—"

"Oh Lord," Ruth shouted. "We could have…"

Gabby jumped up and put the gun on the kitchen table. She grabbed the still barking terrier, tucked it under her arm, and hurried to open the door. "We almost—"

"I know." Nick walked in, looking as stunned as if he'd just seen his life flash before his eyes. "Imagine that. I live through two turns in Nam and end up shot to death on Ruth's stairs." At that, he let loose a nervous laugh.

"How can you think this is funny?" Gabby demanded. "I was ready to shoot you. I thought you were Jeff coming for me."

"I know. I know. I should have called. I'm sorry," he stammered. "I realized when I got here that this was a bad idea. Ginger barking at me. That's why I was trying to decide if I should ring the doorbell or turn around and go home to call you instead."

"Why would you—" Ruth started.

"I wasn't thinking. That's all. I was so excited, that I couldn't wait to tell you."

"Okay. Slow down. Tell us what?" Gabby asked.

Nick looked nervously at them, still appearing shaken by what had almost happened moments earlier. "Well, I couldn't sleep. Keyed up, I guess, about what happened today. So, I stayed up late and watched a movie. That Bush guy broke in with a news report."

"A report?" Ruth sputtered, "What report?"

Inhaling a deep breath to calm himself, Nick put his hands on Gabby's shoulders. "You don't have to worry about Jeff anymore."

"Why? What's happened?"

"They arrested him about an hour ago."

"Arrested him?" Ruth appeared doubtful. "Are you sure?"

Although Ruth had asked the question, Nick kept his eyes on Gabby. "Positive. They had video of him handcuffed doing the perp walk into the jail to get booked."

"No, he…" Gabby started.

Nick's hand over his chest, as if taking an oath, he pledged, "Gabby, it's true. I promise you, it's true."

Feeling lightheaded, Gabby walked away from him and dropped onto a kitchen chair. Turning to Ruth, she asked, "Is it really over?"

# Chapter Forty

**Houston, TX**

**December 1993**

GABBY PRESSED THE buzzer, unlocking the lobby door. Nick had been to her apartment before, but never Ruth. He walked in and gave her a peck on the cheek, and she hugged Ruth.

As Gabby took her coat, Ruth glanced around, and Gabby considered how strange it was to see her away from the river. In the past eight months, those days had begun to feel like a dream. For Gabby the San Bernard had become a magical place, and Ruth the guardian angel she'd found there.

"This is a great condo," Ruth said. "It reminds me a little of my place in New York, although Houston's streets aren't as busy, and mine wasn't on such a high floor."

"I'm so glad you're here," Gabby said, hugging Ruth yet again. She felt like a small mass of bones in her arms, but Gabby understood the strength there, the grit.

"I can never thank you enough, Ruth. Now that it's over…" Gabby started. The bruises had faded long ago, her hair was blond again, but she would never forget those days. She'd prepared a speech, thought about it all week in between working on contracts for a new client. "I'd like to tell you what you've done for me. Without you, I can't imagine what would have happened to me. If you hadn't taken me in,

I don't think I would have survived. I—"

"Please," Ruth interrupted. "Gabby, you've already thanked me. Too many times. None of that. Not today. Today, we celebrate."

Soon they nibbled on cookies and drank hot tea with lemon in Gabby's living room, excitedly recounting Jeff's trial and sentencing—ten years in a Texas prison. Not long enough for what he'd done, they agreed, but enough time for Gabby to reclaim her life.

"For now, I'm safe."

"Have you heard from Rae Ann?" Ruth asked.

"She called me a couple of days ago. She's moving back into her house, trying to get her nursing license back. Her brother's been helping with the painting and some repairs."

"I can't imagine what that was like, to fear every day for so many years that Jeff would find her. To have to be separated from her family," Nick said.

"We talked about what happens when Jeff gets out."

"Are you worried?" he asked.

"We are, but at least now, if anything happens, we'll be believed. Jeff will never be a police officer again, never have a badge to hide behind."

At that Ruth wrinkled her brow. "You know, dear, when you're young, you think you'll be young forever. And when you're old, you look back and realize life passes in a heartbeat. You need to not worry about the future. Right now, today, you need to get busy and live."

"Thanks to you and Nick, I can. And I intend to."

Time passed, and Nick moved over to the couch and rested his arm on Gabby's shoulders. Off and on all summer, the two of them had visited Ruth on the river, spent afternoons and evenings helping her around the house, cooked for her and taken her out to restaurants.

Watching them together, Ruth had wondered if Gabby and Nick had grown to be closer than friends. And now, from the way they looked at each other, the way Nick gently rubbed the back of Gabby's neck, Ruth's suspicions were confirmed.

"Any sightings of our jabiru?" Gabby asked.

Nick shook his head, and Ruth speculated, "He's probably gone home, since he's no longer needed here."

At that, the conversation turned to plans for the holidays, Gabby invited Ruth to join them for Christmas dinner. She accepted, and then something occurred to her. "Gabby, when we were doing all that reminiscing at my house, did I ever tell you about a Gypsy fortune teller I once met in the woods?"

"Yes, you did. But I bet Nick would like to hear about her."

"I would, Ruth," he said.

Ruth leaned forward, excitement in her eyes, and Gabby thought about how her friend relished telling a good story.

"Well, Nick, ever so long ago, I was fourteen or so, and I was sitting under a tree reading a book, when an old woman stumbled upon me. She was carrying a basket, looking for herbs to brew into medicines. She sat next to me and read my palm."

"What did she tell you?" Nick asked.

"About fate, how it would be such an important influence on my life. And it has been," Ruth said with a mysterious smile. "And one of the things I've noticed about fate is that it has the power to bring the people we need into our lives—precisely when we most need them."

**The story behind *Angel Falls***

In a sense, this book has taken more than twenty years to write.

I'm not sure of the year, but a very long time ago, I happened upon a newspaper article that mentioned Ruth Robertson and her trip to Angel Falls. At a used bookstore, I tracked down a copy of the *National Geographic* with her article in it, the November 1949 issue. I read it, and thought about how wonderful it would be to meet her. I should have made arrangements.

Instead, I let life get in the way.

At the time, I wrote freelance articles for magazines, much the way Ruth once had. When I thought about her again, I did an internet search and discovered that she'd died in 1998. She was ninety-two.

Time passed, but I never forgot Ruth.

I continued to write, went from magazines to books, and then one day I realized that, as is the way of the world, I was getting older. I had one of those if-I'm-ever-going-to moments, and I recognized that the projects I'd been putting off couldn't be put off much longer. The *National Geographic* still waited on my desk, and I opened it again.

*Angel Falls* is a hybrid, a blend of fact and fiction.

Take Gabby Jordan for instance. While she's pure fiction, Gabby is loosely based on many women I interviewed as a journalist. For decades, I covered a wide range of topics, including crime cases. All too often, they involved domestic abuse. To write my articles, I interviewed women who were trapped in violent marriages, some of whom had managed to escape. One I talked to, like Rae Ann, had been in hiding for years. The saddest cases were those in which victims lost their lives. For instance, I interviewed the parents of a lawyer who was ultimately murdered by her spouse. They told me how she'd tried to get away and how the police who came to her door in response to her calls talked to her husband, believed him, and walked away.

I hope that's changed over the years, but I know from the experiences of these women that back in the nineties, when this book is set, too often women weren't believed.

I've also fictionalized much of the account of Ruth's life, including parts of her trip to Angel Falls. The jabiru, for instance, is my invention. Yet at their core, the chapters that recount Ruth's history and exploits were inspired by actual events and the life of a remarkable woman.

Ruth Robertson Marietta was born on May 24, 1905, in Taylorville, Illinois, and died on the Gulf Coast of Texas on February 17, 1998.

For the most part, Ruth's history as recounted in the flashback chapters is based on her life. What I had to rely on were multiple sources: her letters, diaries, notebooks, and scrapbooks, many of them described in this book. I also had the benefit of the *National Geographic* article and Ruth's book, *Churún-Merú—The Tallest Angel.* (Whitmore Publishing, October 1977)

Ruth really did grow up in her grandmother's loveless household in Illinois. She was sexually abused by her father. Two horrible experiences.

Yet she didn't let either one stop her.

Ruth broke into the newspaper business with an incredible determination that earned her positions no woman had held before. The first woman photographer to cover a game at Wrigley Field, the only female journalist in Alaska during World War II, she had a torrid affair with a war hero, and ended up in Venezuela where, instead of a man, she fell in love with a waterfall.

Ruth's letters, diaries, and newspaper and magazine articles were available to me because of another extraordinary woman, Patricia Hubbard.

When I decided to forge ahead and write about Ruth, I did what we do in our modern world, I searched on the internet. One site that came up quickly was ruthrobertson.org. When I sent an e-mail through the contact page, Patricia responded.

A fundraising consultant who lives in Maine, Patricia was Ruth's good friend. Back in 1991, she had much the same impulse I did to meet Ruth. She, too, had read about Ruth's achievements, but unlike me, she took the next step. Patricia wrote and called her and eventually visited Ruth in her small house on the San Bernard River.

For the next seven years, Patricia talked to Ruth on the phone, arranged for her to have a gallery showing of her photographs, and accomplished something I will always be grateful for by convincing the University of Texas's Harry Ransom Center to archive Ruth's writings, photographs, and mementos.

In my book, Gabby organizes Ruth's memories. In real life, Patricia Hubbard did that. She spent years searching for a university or history center to take the project on until, finally, she found an ally in Roy Flukinger, the Ransom Center's senior research curator of photography. In all, Patricia turned over to the library thirty-nine boxes filled with Ruth's possessions.

In January 2017, I traveled to the Ransom Center in Austin, where I was able to access the collection. There I found a booklet that held a brief handwritten account of Ruth's early life. I saw her flight record from 1941, when she earned her pilot's license. I paged through her photos from Alaska, her articles and pictures, and her letters.

Holding Ruth's Angel Falls scrapbook in my hand was a thrill, but perhaps my most exciting finds were the notebooks in which she'd recorded her experiences while trudging through the jungle in search of her waterfall.

One of many remarkable things about Ruth was that she not only wrote long letters to friends but made carbon copies and kept them.

Among those letters were Ruth's love letters from Colonel William O. "Eric" Eareckson, who was a well-known officer and influential figure in World War II. An Aleutian Island airbase on the island of Shemya is named for Eareckson, who died at the age of sixty-six in 1966. Many of the excerpts I've included were taken directly from his letters to Ruth. Others I fleshed out or wrote from scratch, adding things I imagined they might have done together, such as attending *Oklahoma!*

Other parts of the book, such as the note the Archibalds left her in chapter 30 and the press release Ruth wrote for Enrique Gomez to transmit on the day they reached Angel Falls, were also taken verbatim from items in the Ransom Center archives. The photographs that appear in the book are included with the Ransom Center's permission.

One caveat: I changed the names of John Hightower and Jim O'Brien. I know their actual identities, but because Ruth gave them fictitious names when she wrote her book, I honored that and did the same. In fact, I used the same names Ruth did, and I had to laugh when I realized how appropriate her pseudonym was for the uppity Hightower.

Unfortunately, another factual aspect of my book is Ruth's battle with dementia. She lived to be ninety-two, but in the end, she recognized little of the world around her. My own mother died of the same disease, so I know the effects well. It's a heartbreaking and unrelenting disease.

One last matter: Is Angel Falls still the tallest waterfall in the world?

Perhaps not. In a 2016 remeasuring, Tugela Falls came in thirteen feet higher, at 3,225 feet. With the elevations so close, a debate has ensued, and at this writing, some are calling for a remeasuring of Angel Falls to put any question to rest.

One record, however, has undeniably stood: Angel Falls is still considered the world's tallest uninterrupted waterfall. Before it is joined by its lower stream, it plunges a stunning 2,648 feet. In contrast, Tugela Falls consists of five shorter tiers.

Today, Angel Falls and the park around it is a UNESCO World Heritage site.

While I worked on this book, I decided that if Ruth could have chosen how she'd died, it probably would have been the way Aleksandrs Laime planned to breathe his last breath.

In 1994, the eighty-two-year-old explorer still lived in the Venezuelan jungles. According to *Wikipedia*, on the evening of May 20—exactly forty-five years to the day after Perry Lowrey called Ruth to tell her that Angel Falls was the tallest waterfall in the world—Laime told a friend that he planned to climb Auyán-tepuí one last time. He'd been having chest pains, and he wanted to meet his end on the great mountain's mesa. Alas, he succumbed to a heart attack in his home that same evening after having a drink at a local lodge.

So that, dear reader, is the story behind *Angel Falls*.

One day on the phone, Patricia Hubbard told me why she had worked so hard to make sure Ruth's artifacts found a home: "I didn't want to see one more woman's story lost to history."

I couldn't agree more. Ruth Robertson deserves to be remembered.

My hope is that this book will preserve Ruth's memory and that her spirit might influence others to pursue their dreams. May her story serve as a reminder that our goals aren't unobtainable simply because they are difficult to achieve.

Kathryn Casey
2023

1) Why does Ruth allow Gabby to stay even though she understands that Jeff presents a great danger? What would you have done? Why?

2) Gabby and Ruth have both been deeply hurt by people they love. What does that do to a person?

3) Why has Gabby kept Jeff's secret and hidden the evidence that he's violent? How does this compare to the reasons Ruth had for not exposing her father?

4) Do you think this cover-up is common in intimate partner violence? Why? What could Gabby have done differently?

5) The societal norms in the book involving Ruth, the attitude that as a woman she couldn't succeed in various ways, date to the first half of the twentieth century. Have they changed? How? How are they the same? What similar experiences have you had in your life?

6) Eric was Ruth's great love, yet in the end, she walked away. If you had an opportunity for a great love, would you take it even though you knew that it would bring heartache? Why?

7) What does the jabiru represent in the book? Is it in any way similar to Ruth?

8) What does Angel Falls represent to Ruth? Why does it become so important to her?

9) Ruth believes in fate. Do you? If so, give an example from your own life.

10) How are the elderly treated in our society? Is there a tendency to
    not think about their pasts? To not take the time to ask them
    about their lives? Why? Have you ever asked an elderly person
    about his/her history? Were you surprised by what they told you?
    What did you learn that you found interesting?

# Acknowledgments

As always, there are many people to thank. First and foremost: Patricia Hubbard. I grew to know Ruth through you, and without you, this book wouldn't exist. Thank you to all the wonderful people at the Harry Ransom Center, especially Roy Flukinger.

I appreciate all the efforts of my agent, Anne-Lise Spitzer at The Spitzer Agency.

Many have read portions or all of this book over the years and given advice. Thank you to my author friends: Julie Cantrell, Caroline Leech, and Judithe Little. Others who offered comments include: Jane Farrell, Judith Kern, Edward Porter, Jan Petrucciani, and Cissie Alexander. To author Kellie Coates Gilbert: I appreciate your patience and your sage advice.

Thank you to Andrea Purdie for the wonderful cover. To Alison Imbriaco for copyediting the manuscript. And to my proofreaders: Bea Armstrong, Terry Bachman, Debbie Blailock, Linda Brown, Sandy Darst, TJ Darst, Jo Ann Engelking, Claire C. Fletcher, Mary McVeigh, Nancy Schultz, Sue Vandegrift, Amanda Widdall, Lorraine Widdall, Jerrilyn Woods, and Mary Zanoni. If you find any typos or such in the book, don't blame them. The mistakes are mine.

Thank you to Lisa Billeiter for my photo on the back cover.

Most of all, I am deeply grateful to my family and friends for their support and love. I'll cherish each of you, forever!

# Other Books by Kathryn Casey

**The Sarah Armstrong Mystery Series**
Singularity
Blood Lines
The Killing Storm
The Buried

**The Clara Jefferies Mystery Series**
The Fallen Girls
Her Final Prayer
The Blessed Bones

**True Crime**
In Plain Sight
Deliver Us
Deadly Little Secrets
Shattered
She Wanted It All
Evil Beside Her
Possessed
Murder, I Write
A Descent into Hell
Die, My Love
A Warrant to Kill

# About the Author

An award-winning journalist and a critically acclaimed bestselling author, Kathryn Casey has written eleven true crime books and is the creator of the Sarah Armstrong and Clara Jefferies mystery series. Her books have been Literary Guild and Mystery Guild selections, and one was made into a movie. In addition, Casey has written more than a hundred articles for national magazines and pieces for *The Washington Post*, the *Boston Globe*, and the *Houston Chronicle*. In 2022, Casey was featured on the Netflix limited documentary series *Crime Scene: The Texas Killing Fields*. She's appeared on dozens of television and radio programs, including: *Good Morning America, 20/20, 48 Hours, Oprah, Investigation Discovery, the Travel Channel, A&E,* and other venues.